FOR PATTIE

IN MEMORY OF GUSSIE

Published 2023
Printed in the United States of America
Print ISBN: 978-1-68463-222-0
E-ISBN: 978-1-68463-223-7
Library of Congress Control Number: 2023907877

Published by SparkPress, a BookSparks imprint,
A division of SparkPoint Studio, LLC
Phoenix, Arizona, USA, 85007
www.gosparkpress.com

Interior design by Stacey Aaronson
Painting opposite Chapter One: "Pentimento" by artist Sally Storch

SparkPress is a division of SparkPoint Studio, LLC.

BEYOND A
THOUSAND
WORDS

A Novel

MICHAEL ROSE

BEYOND A THOUSAND WORDS

PART ONE

CHAPTER ONE

———•·•———

Hanoi 1954

Drawn by rumors of expatriates abandoning the city, a mid-morning crowd gathered in front of the convent. Two elderly French nuns sat in the cab of the truck. Rosary beads dangled from weathered fingers as the women, beseeching safe passage, droned prayers at the windshield.

A fair-haired priest handed them a canteen through the passenger window. As Coty neared the truck, she guessed he was taller than she and about her age—maybe already beyond thirty. He was the first peer she had encountered in the North. The priest gestured a single-handed blessing. With a slight bow, he stepped back, taking his leave of the nuns.

The flatbed was stacked with burlap bags of rice that reached to the roof of the cab. Cigarette smoke clouded the throng and wafted up the cargo. The smell of gasoline led Coty to a kaleidoscopic puddle underneath the vehicle. She thought of her grandfather's warning as she proceeded to the only passage available "under the circumstances," as he often said.

Coty tossed her satchel onto the floor's emptied space, an opening cleared to accommodate her and the priest. Gripping the lanyard in one hand, she shifted the camera draped around her neck and then felt for a hold along the edge of the nearest sack. With the sole of her sandal set on top of the rear tire and a knee bent tight to her body, she pulled with her arm and took one step up.

She now held the advantage of altitude, and, as he rounded the truck, she tracked the priest's bald spot—a patch no larger than the starched white square centered in his black collar. Without glancing at her, he stalled at the lowered tailgate to consider the challenge. In two failed attempts, he displayed far less athleticism than his predecessor. On his third try, he slid a knee atop the flattened tailgate and drew his pant leg through the grime as he wriggled.

The priest stood, brushing himself as he straightened. He might have fared better had the tailgate been raised, she thought. Backing in, he joined the white-haired American in the two-person slot carved out for their escape—standing room only.

"*Je suis* Coty Fine," she said, acknowledging the priest and their shared predicament.

Ignoring her, he searched among those milling in the street. Lush from life in the damp hotbox of Vietnam, tree branches drooped leaves near the cargo. Coty studied his profile as the limbs swayed and their shadows swept across the priest's unblemished skin, which would be exposed to the sun as they rode to the harbor in Haiphong. She shrugged, grabbed her coarse braid, rolled the bundle of premature white curls under her conical leaf hat, and secured the *nón lá*'s chinstrap for the ride.

A harried man shoved the tailgate into position with a *clang*. In slapping sandals, he hustled to the cab, yanked the driver's door open, and scrambled up behind the steering wheel. The vibrating exhaust pipe spewed gray smoke that matched the faded paint of the truck's body. The engine settled into its idle. The driver bullied the gearshift and released the clutch under his sandal, and the truck lurched.

"*Je suis* Père Sabatier," the priest said, without averting his focus.

The driver shifted gears. When the truck accelerated, Coty

grasped at burlap corners. Sabatier gazed out at those who had assembled to gawk or bid farewell. Ever the photographer, she tracked his vision to a young nun, dressed in the white-linen habit of her order.

"*Enchantée*, Père Sabatier. I wanted to stay in Hanoi. It appears that you had more reason than I," she said in fluent French, as she brought the camera to her eye.

The nun's hand stopped waving and dropped, leaden, to her side. The shutter clicked. Sabatier craned his neck until the truck turned at the street corner and the convent disappeared.

The sun, having tunneled through the city's haze, grilled the flatbed. Merciful trees thinned out as they entered the thoroughfare, which bifurcated the business district adjacent to the convent's neighborhood. Ahead, Coty saw a man on a bicycle, ferrying a load of broad grass blades, the raw stock used for caning. He stood on the pedals to power the bike up the rising grade. The rider's hair flopped in cadence with the cane, which hung sideways as wide as the bike was long. Head down, he seemed to be drifting too close to the truck's spinning wheels. Coty held her breath when she lost sight of the bike.

Bang!

She snatched the lanyard to reel in her camera. The truck rolled on, and as she turned back to search its wake, the bicycle reappeared alongside the tailgate. When the man lifted his head, the camera's eye blinked.

The rider tugged on the handlebars and twisted his torso for leverage as he pressed down on the pedals. Cresting the hill, he found the seat of the bike and his facial muscles relaxed. With its pedals at rest, the bicycle coasted down the incline and faded to the rear.

Coty freed the camera to bounce off her flat chest as the truck rattled. She spread her feet farther apart, before reaching to adjust her *nón lá* with both hands. The driver found third gear with a grind. The truck pitched. Off-balance, Coty slammed against the priest's side. Her camera swung on its lanyard, clipping him in the ribs. She grabbed the box with one hand and with the other felt for a handle among the cargo. Her clumsy skid belied her usual grace, an elegance earned over years of studying ballet and modern dance.

"We must brace ourselves, *madame*. The road will be even less smooth in the countryside," he said, as if scolding his mother.

"Madame"? Seriously? she thought, suspecting her white tresses had, once again, led a stranger to the wrong conclusion. Miffed, not embarrassed, Coty shook her shoulders to reset her posture. The adjustment stretched her closer to the height of the priest, who, like she, towered over locals. When he came face-to-face with his traveling companion, his mouth gaped and he recoiled. Coty reveled in Sabatier's befuddlement as he combed her face for clues that refuted the snowy hair of a grande dame.

She followed his gaze to her hand, where freckles on smooth skin gleamed beneath her sweat. The truck slowed, and Sabatier relaxed his grip. She heard grinding at the clutch's release as the driver downshifted into second gear. Exiting the curve, he found third gear again and accelerated. The priest stumbled, crashing against the wall of burlap bags. His knees buckled, and he lunged to embrace the closest bundle.

"*Oui*, Père. I'll try to be careful. *Merci*," she said. *Off to a good start*, Coty mused, regretful of slicing at a stranger with her New Yorker's edge. She smiled, attempting to soften her rebuff of Sabatier's lecture. Voicing a *humph*, he turned away.

Several blocks beyond the business district, industrial buildings grew sparse as city gave way to countryside. A lone paddy, encroached on by urban sprawl, hinted that the holdouts had lost their farming neighbors. Sparkles surrounded the ankles of a beast plodding in the muck—the first water buffalo Coty had seen on the journey.

For weeks, the dirt road had come under siege by traffic and afternoon rain showers. The truck's right front tire splashed into a shallow pothole with an opening as wide as the mouth of a wheelbarrow. When the vehicle tilted to the right, Coty heard the underbody scraping against the puddle's edge. The rig surged up and out, tossing the two standing passengers between the bundles. After slamming into each other, they spun away to clutch separate sacks.

Coty laughed when the cleric turned, and they stood as close as dance partners. He seemed to puzzle over her unwrinkled face. Recalling the nun outside the convent, Coty guessed that Sabatier was a man gnawing at the bindings of his vows.

Few of her intimates would she have described as religious people. Since she had reached adulthood, she had entered synagogues only under duress from her family. A gentile friend's wedding or child's baptism had, on such occasions, drawn her into a Christian church. Coty reserved the cathedrals of Europe for appreciation of art and architecture, as well as for contemplating the crypts of robed perpetrators of unspeakable sins, laid to rest alongside the sainted beneath gilded halls. She had sought out the churches in Hanoi for their stony coolness, elsewhere elusive in the city's oppressive heat.

Sabatier appeared drawn, in need of water. Chivalry had wrought his dehydration soon after he handed the nuns his canteen. Beads of sweat slid onto his forearms from underneath short shirtsleeves of black linen. Without sanctuary from the relentless sun, he tugged on his Roman collar as if he might entice a breeze.

"We'll share, Père," Coty said, as she offered her water.

The lanky priest bowed with gratitude. As he gulped, his Adam's apple bobbed beneath pale skin. Even the backs of his fists were not tanned, much less leathered by constant baking. Coty's deduction was simple: when executing his pastoral duties, the shepherd had enjoyed the luxury of shade.

The burlap bags rocked side to side and bled the rice thresher's dust, which mixed with the swirling air into funnels that danced atop the worn wooden floor. Coty tucked her canteen between two sacks, and the pair rode in silence as the sun raged down.

Sabatier muttered frustration with his handkerchief as he fought to achieve coverage of his exposed fair skin. Under a sun that shifted at each turn of the steering wheel, the jostling ride confounded the priest's attempts. An impossible task, Coty thought, cloaking his sun-scorched ears and neck with that cotton swatch while trying to shield the disk of bare skin at the crest of his skull.

The truck swayed. When they grabbed for handles, his kerchief sailed out above their wake. When she turned to commiserate, the priest's forehead was pinned to the burlap above his grip. Bordered by wafting strands of sandy-blond hair, the exposed skin of his bald spot had been seared crimson.

At the edge of the city, she shouted choppy instructions to the driver in her novice Vietnamese. He pulled the truck over, slowing in front of roadside stands that were set farther apart than had been the stalls packed along the streets of Hanoi. Coty spotted caned baskets hanging in the shade—their still-fresh leaves a moist, dark green. She yelled for him to stop.

An old woman looked up with the expression of a vendor who had not expected the customers she craved. Pausing between her roles of weaver and seller, she fanned herself with the leaves of her craft.

Coty stood. Elbows locked, she leaned over the back of the truck with the heels of her hands pressing down on the top of the tailgate. She called out a price she knew to be high for a sale far from the center of the city. The woman ceased her fanning midstroke and dropped the leaf stock. Beaming, the weaver-turned-saleswoman stepped out from the shade with a fresh hat.

The driver pulled the truck onto the road and stomped on the accelerator. Sabatier accepted the *nón lá* from Coty. He rocked in a clumsy stance while tying the chin strap under his jaw.

"*Merci beaucoup.* Very kind, *mademoiselle.* I offer my simple blessing in exchange."

Coty mimed her proposal to flip a sack down lengthwise, which would provide a bench with less than one-meter clearance between the raised tailgate and the end of the overturned bundle. "If you help me tip this one over, we can sit."

After they had dropped the sack into place, Sabatier hesitated. "*Mademoiselle,* we'll have to sit single file, *non?*"

True to her pattern, she chose not to restrain her tongue. "*Oui.* That's obvious."

The duo agreed to alternate positions whenever muscle cramps overwhelmed the person in the rear. The priest removed his sandals, straddled their improvised seat, and put his back to the cab. He slithered his bare feet down into the seams between the burlap bags.

Compounded by the effects of his sedentary profession, a tightness typical of male musculature must have caused Sabatier immediate discomfort. He was squirming when Coty sat down. She wriggled backward in between his legs and planted her feet flat on the floor.

Slender, tanned arms rose, seeking the centered sun. She wiggled her fingers, her shoulder blades slid, and the muscles of her back relaxed. She had not had time to cycle through her morning stretching routine before she rushed to the convent. As she brought her hands down to rest on her thighs, Sabatier shifted his body. Coty suspected she would spend far more time staring into the back of his paddy hat than he would looking over hers.

Paddies glistened. The sweet rot of vegetation diluted the exhaust fumes from dissipating city traffic. The truck picked up speed, turning their ride on the country road into a hammering jitter. Less than two kilometers later, she felt a hand on her shoulder and heard, "*Je suis désolé, mademoiselle.*"

After swapping places, they rode for more than an hour. Coty shifted her hips, which might have triggered his guilt. Sabatier's hand found her knee, and, with a sheepish twist, he invited her to take his spot. When she slid past him, she wondered if it would be worth the effort.

Minutes into her latest respite, Sabatier pulled his bare feet from the tight slots and stood in a wobble atop their crude bench. He attempted to brace himself by pressing his arms out, hands flat against the cargo.

The truck reeled and bounced. Again, he lost his balance. While clutching for a burlap edge at his side, he fought for solid footing. Coty thought he might pitch over her and crash in the dirt. The teetering priest's safety aside, she did not want to catch a knee in the back of her head.

"Let's change seats, Père. You don't have to stand."

Concrete buildings with stairwells vining up exterior walls gave way to clusters of single-story shacks. Slowing at the first village to avoid hitting livestock in the road, the truck backfired. Chickens stopped pecking and, with eyes stuck open, raised heads that jerked beaks at the truck. The birds ran about, kicking up dust and flapping wings that could not lift them from their terror.

Each successive village seemed smaller than and more distant from the last one. The monotony of traveling through cloned paddies was broken as they slowed to allow agitated chickens their protest. The occasional farmer, hunched over with pants rolled above calves, uncurled a bent spine to take stock of the rare interruption.

Hanoi was gone.

After relieving the priest, Coty rode in the back for another hour. Without intending to change seats, she squirmed to adjust her body. Sabatier, tapping her knee, signaled that he should move to the rear. Coty waved him off.

"I'll stay in back."

"*Non, mademoiselle*, I must take my turns, as brief as these might be," he said, rising. He staggered, squeezed to her side, and wedged one of his feet behind her back, as if to pry her into compliance.

She capitulated, inching toward the tailgate as the truck shook. Coty twisted and glanced up at the man, who was swaying. "I'm limber. Let me sit there."

Without replying, he sent his chin up and his vision out over her head. Irritated by his obstinance, she turned back to the road. The truck bounced. Coty felt her braid slip from beneath her hat and unfurl. She resisted her habit of tucking it back under her *nón lá* so that her inherited trademark would stay hidden from the curious and off the linen blouse that protected her skin.

Mere minutes passed before Sabatier sat. The thick, snowy braid draped down her back, and near him, she grew hot. With a practiced twirl, she poked it under her hat, stinging his chin with the braid's tip.

During previous stints behind her, the priest had immediately started to fidget. This time, he was still. Coty sensed him gawking and craned her neck to one side to catch a glimpse. Though Sabatier's head was bowed as if in prayer, his eyes betrayed him. He was taking in her shape, she was convinced.

The driver found another pothole. The priest jerked when her hips swung, alternating with force, against the insides of his thighs.

"Do you need a break?" she asked.

"*Pardonnez-moi?*"

"I thought you were getting *uncomfortable*."

"*Désolé, mademoiselle.*"

"It's not a contest, Père. We'll unwind our legs in Haiphong as we search for the ship to Saigon."

"I wish that I might do more for you."

"Well, there's one thing: I don't want to call you 'Père.' I'm

Jewish and find it awkward. And, to be literal, you're not anyone's *father*. Are you?"

"*Mademoiselle*, you Americans are most blunt. *Non*, I have no children."

The next question slipped from her lips like a sin. "That you know of?"

Sabatier cleared his throat and said, "Call me Laurent, if you wish."

With a sigh, she sealed their truce and left him to stare over the tailgate with his legs unfurled in the direction of a woman he had not wished to leave behind. Banter at rest, they rode wordless for several kilometers, before the driver pulled the truck to the side of the road. The engine stopped, and steam snuck out from under the hood. Dust swept over the open flatbed as the disturbed road resettled. Coty coughed and waved her hand in front of her face.

Not knowing how long she had slept with her forehead pinned in the valley between Sabatier's shoulders, she had awakened in pain, her paddy hat tilted up and back by the descent into sleep. Her hip joints were strained, and the squeeze of opposing sacks had narrowed the circulation in her feet to a dribble.

Doors swung open; driver and nuns exited the cab. He and the women stepped in opposite directions in search of privacy.

"*Pardonnez-moi*, Laurent," she said, tapping his shoulder. Neither hips nor feet were the source of her most urgent discomfort. "I must follow the nuns."

The truck's open hood angled above the engine. The driver was pouring water into the radiator when Coty returned to the tailgate. Sabatier stood in the shade of a banyan tree that was too far from the road to shelter the vehicle.

The driver slammed the hood down and, with worn canvas straps, secured the metal water canister back onto the sidewall. From behind the steering wheel, he sent out a blast of the horn that flushed birds from their hiding and signaled the priest to return to his contortions.

Coty frowned at Sabatier as he approached. When he neared, she said, "I think I fell asleep on your back."

She raised one foot above her waist, hooked her ankle atop the truck's rear bumper, and stretched with slow pleasure. Exhaling a deliberate breath, she lowered her foot back to the dirt road. As she rotated her body to facilitate unwinding the opposite side, the horn sounded.

"After you, *mademoiselle*."

With a start, she faced him and asked, "Laurent, do you remember my name?"

"*Pardonnez-moi?*"

"Coty," she said, setting her fingers to work on the cargo. A burlap bag offered its rounded corner as purchase. When her feet found the floor of the flatbed, she turned and looked down. Sabatier's eyes were locked on where she had secured her foothold. He seemed to be replaying her ascent, placing his hands where she had gripped. The muscles of his neck grew taut as he pulled himself up.

Sabatier stood upright. He found the white patch at his throat and tugged. "Is Coty your given name?"

"*Non*, Laurent. My name is Rachel."

He motioned that he would assume the cramped position.

"My middle name is Côte. Named for Jules Côte, my grand-father's boyhood friend, born in France, but he lived in New York since he was a baby. Uncle Jules called me his little Coty, and the name stuck."

"Did Monsieur Côte teach you to speak such flawless French?"

She leaned to one side so he could slide behind her. As he passed, she said, "He knew that his surname meant 'coast.' Beyond that, he didn't speak many words that you couldn't find on a menu. Uncle Jules was more of a New Yorker than the mayor."

In less than three kilometers, Sabatier grabbed the bundles to pull himself up. He stood, rocking. Unable to scooch out of reach of the man's knees, she wished he would sit.

Raising his voice, he shouted down at the tip of her paddy hat. "Your lovely French, Mademoiselle Coty. Where did you study?"

"Paris. I lived there before Hanoi."

The truck's right front tire dropped into another pothole. The jostled nuns shrieked in the cab, and a knee found Coty's skull. Before the driver ground the transmission into a lower gear, she heard ringing in her head.

"Laurent, get down!"

Sabatier knelt. He flinched when Coty placed her hand on his shoulder to climb past.

"*Pardonnez-moi*, Coty. One more debt to add to my ledger with you."

The sun was low in the sky when the truck next pulled off the road. They had ridden single file, Coty wedged behind, for almost two hours. Steam rose above the roof of the cabin. The driver was wresting the water canister from the sidewall as Sabatier climbed over the tailgate.

After relieving themselves, Coty and the nuns returned to find Sabatier at the truck. Standing in the dirt road, he pointed to ready shade a few yards away. They walked to a stand of banyan trees, where the two women of the cloth huddled together, clutching their rosary beads. When the priest stepped under a branch of the tree Coty had selected, she took the gesture as an invitation.

"Laurent, tell me something," she said, as she leaned against the tree trunk. "Why did you leave Hanoi?"

"My bishop insisted, *mademoiselle*. Too dangerous, he told me. I had no choice."

"*Non?*"

"Coty, I'm a priest and must subordinate to my superiors."

"You could've relinquished your position, *non*?"

He fidgeted with his collar at the intimation that he might

have considered recanting his vows. Coty wanted to ask about the photogenic nun, a standout beauty among the gathered. Despite the priest's accumulating debts of gratitude, pressing him about the woman seemed aggressive, even by her standards. "Why did your bishop insist?"

Laurent spoke with a full throat. "The North's struggle for independence. It was best for the church."

No need for him to clarify. A scandal had not driven him away; it had been simple politics. Uncertainty about the future of the apostolic nunciature in Hanoi had abounded in prior weeks. Coty understood that with independence, dangers unfolded for Frenchmen left in the North—priests included. "Sorry, Laurent. I, too, wished to remain in Hanoi."

"Coty, you're a freelancer—no bosses. Why didn't you stay?"

Their roles reversed, Coty was glad she had not pressed him about the pretty nun. Not her business, she concluded, now that he was probing hers. "My grandfather asked me to get out of the North."

"Did he not support your coming to Vietnam?"

She blocked her forming scowl and said, "He's my biggest supporter."

"More than your parents?"

"*Oui*, Laurent. Without him, I would've been doomed to a life of drudgery."

The sunstruck priest seemed revived and alert—a trained confessor, curious and ready to listen. "Your grandfather didn't want you to marry and start a family?"

"He never asked me for anything, till the trouble in the North." Coty expounded on her grandfather Sheldon Fine, an indulgent benefactor who had encouraged her pursuit of art. Before she entered kindergarten, Zaydeh, not her preoccupied mother, had escorted Coty to the ballet studio, where, as the tallest child, she towered above tiny dancers. When she was an adolescent, he had given Coty her first camera, a gift that kindled a passion for photography.

"Do you have siblings?"

"I've two older brothers, who work with my father in the family business my grandfather started. As a young man, he was a jeweler. Today, the business is primarily real estate."

"The family business—that's the serious side of the man, *non*?"

Coty wanted to repay his knee to her head. "Zaydeh would tell you that the business is serious, of course, but it's grown simple, straightforward, a steady enterprise. My father and uncles have run it for years."

"He must be very proud of the men in your family."

With a sigh, she continued, "By the end of the war, he had grown irritated with the men in our family. Their bickering over the business disgusted him." The priest looked at her as if she spoke not French. How could she explain that Zaydeh was a frustrated artist who longed to look through a viewfinder? "Zaydeh's an unusual man, Laurent. The business didn't define him. It served him well, but he knew that his sons could keep it going without his daily oversight. After he handed them control, he turned wholeheartedly to amateur photography. I showed interest in his avocation and became his constant weekend companion. Together, we walked about Central Park with box cameras dangling above our navels."

"And now you're a professional photographer." Kindness cloaked his face. She wondered if she had earlier mistaken him for arrogant. "How did you get here, to Vietnam?" he asked.

"I became intrigued by the work of Robert Doisneau."

"Ah, Doisneau. After the Nazis thwarted the French army, he used his skills to forge passports and identification papers for the French Resistance."

By the time Coty had arrived in Paris—years after the war—the German occupation, the Vichy compromise, and the French Resistance hung in the air as remnant scents, dissipated by the breeze of the Allied victory. The upheaval in Vietnam drew her eastward.

She smiled and said, "After the liberation, *Vogue* magazine sought to secure the eye of the genius, but the shots he had taken during the war compelled him to return to street photography. Those same harrowing photos drove me to capture the upheaval here in Vietnam."

The nuns had left their tree and were heading back to the truck. Coty touched her camera. For how long had she told her story?

"Laurent, I've been a bore," she said, as they strolled behind the waddling old women. When they reached the tailgate, he offered a hand, which the limber dancer did not need to step up onto the flatbed. She took it with gratitude.

Dusk faded into darkness. Soon they would stop at a village for the night. She would go with the nuns and he with the driver to separate huts, where they would sleep on floor mats as honored guests.

Their braking tires disturbed the dirt road. Billows of encircling dust ousted the rural smells of beast and vegetation. When the driver turned off the engine, its pings and pops accompanied a chorus of hidden insects.

Stars were out on the moonless night. Amid scant illumination from the twinkling above, Coty strained to see the faint outlines of the huts. The nearest shack seemed to be in motion—a water buffalo, she guessed, from the scent. It snorted, turned, and then lumbered away from the interlopers.

Laurent winced as he unfolded his legs and stood. He reached to retrieve her satchel.

"*Merci beaucoup*," she said.

The bag clipped him when she tugged. He rubbed his arm as he rummaged for his worn leather rucksack, which had slipped between the cargo bags during the jostling ride.

"*Pardonnez-moi*, Laurent," she muttered, wanting to get to her mat, where she could stretch out and dismiss her earlier lapses in judgment when she had droned on about Zaydeh.

"Coty, you wanted to photograph the conflict here," he said. "Why did you let your grandfather dictate your retreat?"

Coty jumped down and waited for him to follow. When they stood face-to-face, she said, "Zaydeh didn't *dictate*, Laurent. He grew afraid. It wasn't a demand, but a request." Grasping the shoulder straps of her camera and satchel, Coty pivoted, drawn by the voices of the French nuns.

"Because he was afraid, you sacrificed your passion?"

"As I told you, he asked; he didn't dictate. Can you say the same of your bishop?"

"I trust that God guides the men who guide me."

Obscured by darkness, the ground felt uneven as they walked. A lantern's glow slipped from the nuns' hut. She responded as they walked into the light. "I sense, Laurent, that you're not as certain as your words."

"Ah, Mademoiselle Coty—the mystery of faith. Not wise to question such a generous gift," he said.

Behind them, she heard the knocking engine quiet as it cooled. Coty realized the priest had no answers beyond divine enigma. "Laurent, I don't have your 'gift.'"

She waited for a reaction. He accommodated with a telltale smirk that seemed to curl from superiority, his smugness portending one of Christianity's seven deadly sins. Any well-trained cleric would cite pride as the first vice to enter a man's heart and the last to leave.

Zaydeh would have told her not to waste any more time debating with a closed mind. She let it drop. When they arrived at the hut where the French women chattered, the priest seemed to relish her newfound reticence, as if he were gloating that she had slipped through the door of doubt, which channeled lost souls into the clutches of proselytizers.

"I'll pray that you, too, will be granted his gift, *mademoiselle*."

CHAPTER TWO

— · —

Worthy? After arriving in Saigon, she had restocked her camera bag with Kodak canisters. The film would go fast. Erected for simple commerce, the Western Union office looked as if it would have collapsed long ago had it not been wedged between two other buildings. Coty studied its facade from across the busy street. No, not worthy, she surmised, although her fingers went to the lens cover and pulled the clasp.

Above the signage, a woman leaned out of an apartment window to test her laundry. Pausing, with a pair of pants in her grip, she twisted to speak to someone indoors. Coty raised her sunglasses, followed by the camera. As she focused, she held her sights on the back of the woman's blouse. Returning to the clothesline, laundress proved faster than photographer. While the woman's forearm was the length of a dagger, she gathered the clothes with the reach and sweep of a scythe. Coty slumped when the window's abandoned sash came into focus. A linen curtain flagged in the opening, which she compared with those that flanked it. Nothing unusual—empty windows, offering scant peeks inside. The woman had been worthy.

The building's architecture did not stop Coty on the way to her rendezvous. Every day she checked. Two days earlier, she had taken from the clerk her grandfather's telegram, an urgent message, cryptic, as telegrams tended to be. She got the point: Zaydeh worried anew. He might have reached his limit. Why else would he fly to Saigon, except to pull in her leash? The shutter blinked.

Concerned she would arrive later than planned, she replaced the lens cover and resumed her walk with one hand on the lanyard. At every turn, the French colonial–Indochine style that permeated the district tested her restraint. When she reached her destination, a lizard raced under the eaves, along vines of purple bougainvillea that adorned the hotel. Her fingers found the clasp on the lens cover. She paused. The light would improve, she told herself as she acknowledged the doorman.

Crossed at the ankles, a man's legs stretched from couch to lobby carpet. In raised hands, he held a newspaper, spread open, its bottom edge at his beltline. The paper masked his head and torso, while the roman lettering of the newsprint betrayed him— a superfluous clue. No Vietnamese man could consume that much space. No Frenchman would wear those shoes, which had been cobbled for walking, with no thought of fashion. She brought her camera up and took a calming breath. Her finger rested on the shutter button as she inhaled to shout.

"Zaydeh!"

The top of the newspaper slid down a few inches, exposing a shock of white hair. She waited for the paper to collapse into his lap. Sheldon Fine gawked over his reading glasses. Beaming, he yelled, "Coty, my darling!" The shutter clicked.

When he stood, she took a second shot, before running to him. The tall Americans hugged under the lobby's raised ceiling as if it had been designed for their reunion. The heads of locals passed by below their shoulders, and for the moment, she forgot about his telegram.

"Zaydeh, I'm sorry I wasn't here sooner. You didn't have to wait in the lobby. I would've called your room."

"Stop that. You're a little early."

"I should've met you at the airport."

"Nonsense, dear. The plane got in after midnight. I was able to get a few hours' sleep. I've already showered and eaten break-fast, or whatever meal that was. Been enjoying the paper—and the daylight."

She took him by the hand and led him back to the sofa. After collecting and folding the pile of crumpled newspapers, she sat too. "Zaydeh, I can't believe you're here. You worried me when I got your telegram. It was a bit brief."

"I didn't mean to frighten you, Coty. Every letter's expensive."

"Speaking of letters, did you get mine?"

"Yes. Sorry I didn't respond. You know I hate writing. And it wouldn't've gotten here much before I did." He paused and searched her eyes. "Didn't your mother write?"

"She sent a telegram shortly after she got mine. I've mailed them a couple of letters since then, but no replies, just your 'ur-gent' telegram. That's what scared me—the word 'urgent' was the first thing I read."

"Listen, darling, your letter had me in a spin. Rushing out of Hanoi on the back of an old truck, then sailing on some rust bucket from Haiphong—if you hadn't mailed it from Saigon, I would've been on sedatives."

"When you saw the postmark, you understood that I was okay, didn't you?"

"I needed to see you—in person."

She tried to deflect, saying, "You missed me so much you flew around the world?"

"That's it in a nutshell, darling."

What had she told Laurent about her grandfather's impact? He had saved her from a life of drudgery. She searched his eyes for a glint of renege on her salvation. "I'm safe here, Zaydeh. Getting out of the North was a bit harrowing, but no need to worry, now that I'm in Saigon. Promise?"

"Sure. Whatever you say, Coty."

Zaydeh twisted his neck, massaging its nape with one hand as he surveyed the lobby. His gaze rose up the striped wallpaper.

He tracked the crown molding into a corner before he lowered his vision.

It had been years since she had received a stern lecture, all such reprimands having come from one of her parents. Whatever Zaydeh was about to say would constitute his first. She had put herself in harm's way and must accept the consequences of her actions—a lesson Zaydeh had imparted in tandem with his insistence that she exercise her own free will, not kowtow to others.

"You wrote a lot about your traveling companion, that French priest. You called him a friend. What's his name, again?"

"Laurent. Laurent Sabatier."

"Have you seen him since you got here?"

"Yes, once a week. I wish I could talk to him away from the rectory."

"Scandalous!" Zaydeh lifted the folded stack of newspapers and then slapped it down between them onto the surface of the couch. "Sorry, Coty, bad joke."

"You'd find many at the rectory who'd agree. We sit in the reception room with at least one wrinkled nun staring at me like I'm Eve shining an apple. Despite everything we went through, Laurent acts like a patronizing cleric, not a friend."

"Hmm. He's safe within his fortress, with guards at the gate, to boot."

"Well put, Zaydeh. Maybe I'll invade his confessional."

"Sounds like something you'd do."

"I was kidding."

He crooked his neck and, eyes racing along the ceiling's trim, said, "Coty, I ran into Elliot the other day." Not the lecture she had expected from Zaydeh. Had he changed his mind about the promising attorney? Didn't he know that Elliot had moved on as well? "He was with his wife—Estelle, I think he said."

"Yes, Estelle, that's her name. When I was in Paris, I got a letter from Elliot; he wrote to tell me he was engaged." The molding seemed to hold a familial fascination. Coty was staring at it as she said, "I hope he's happy. How did they seem to you?"

"As happy as they're going to get."

"Is that some kind of code, Zaydeh?"

"Sort of. You made a good decision."

"Mother's still lamenting that I let 'the one' get away." Her mother would have been delighted with Elliot as a son-in-law. "A lawyer—who could ask for more?" she used to say. Zaydeh had been the only one who defended Coty when she broke off the engagement.

"I shouldn't talk ill of your mother, dear, but she and Estelle share a peapod."

"So, you saw my old beau and his new wife."

Zaydeh coughed, looked straight into her eyes, and said, "You're taken by this Frenchman. Why else would you give a toss about a stranger—a priest, no less? Was it the hazardous journey that drew you in? They say that circumventing danger can create powerful attraction—fleeting, but powerful."

"Who are 'they,' Zaydeh?"

"*Reader's Digest.* You know what I mean!" He let his head fall backward as he closed his eyes.

"Zaydeh, Laurent's kind. Smart, in spite of being confused. I think he's hiding from himself. Hiding in his rectory, hiding in his robes."

Without opening his eyes, Zaydeh said, "Oh, crap, Coty. You found another hummingbird! Like that day in Central Park."

"Apparently."

"Your cat got that one."

"We don't know if Agnes ate it . . . for sure."

He looked at her, smirked, and said, "Your father told the whole office that he found tiny green feathers floating in her water bowl."

They traded grins. He raised his head and shook it side to side. She loved that he seemed not to own a comb. She thought to suggest he get a haircut here, not for the coiffure but for the scalp massage that American barbers eschewed or, if they deemed it necessary, executed with the touch of a new missionary among lepers.

"As we carried that hummingbird home, Zaydeh, I asked you if it would live—if I could save its life. Remember?"

"Yes. I also remember that your mother wasn't thrilled."

"I think she said, 'Get that damn bird out of the apartment.'"

Zaydeh looked up, laughing, and said, "For Christ's sake! What harm could that hummingbird have done?"

"Zaydeh, are you telling me to leave Laurent be, let his fate unfold?"

"Would it matter?"

"No. Maybe I *am* on a mission."

"You like this guy, Coty."

"His name is Laurent. And, yes, I do like him."

"As a friend? A curiosity? A pet priest? Or are you—?"

"I don't know! He's . . . well, he's like no other man I've met." She tried to recall what she had written in her letter that could have so animated Zaydeh.

"Did you take his photo?"

"Several. You taught me to see the unusual in any setting. A tall French priest stood out, so to speak."

"A pun?"

"Well, he did."

Zaydeh searched the lobby. His eyes crawled up the wallpaper. When his vision arrived at the crown molding, he said, "Are you testing his commitment to his calling? Or are you seeing if he's more invested in the nun than in you?"

What had she written about the nun? "No! Laurent's in love with her. I'm just trying to help him—them."

"An altruist? I've yet to meet one. Not even you, Coty."

"What about the hummingbird, Zaydeh?"

"You're my favorite person on Earth, darling, but people

have reasons for the things they do, conscious or not. You wanted to help that bird—and get recognition for saving its life."

"I hate to think he'll go back to France without seeing her."

"I doubt you'll even think about this guy in five years, unless . . ."

"Unless what? I'm in love and pine over him for the rest of my life?"

"I was going to say, unless one of the photos you took of him makes it into your book."

Dreams of her first published book of photographs had accompanied her from New York to Paris to Hanoi and had hopped aboard truck and freighter as she escaped to the South. In her makeshift Saigon darkroom, she had strung selected photos in a proposed layout for the early pages. If Zaydeh pressed her repatriation to the States, it would be a thin collection sent to the printer—less a book than a pamphlet.

Zaydeh leaned back and yawned. Coty tried to read him. "You seem tired, Zaydeh—or irritated. How are you?"

"Both."

She scooped up the folded newspapers in one hand and tossed the stack onto the sofa, on the other side of her grandfather. Scooting over, she snuggled close, which prompted him to melt his arm around her.

"Coty, this isn't about your French hummingbird. It's about you."

"Zaydeh, please don't worry. Trust me. I love that you came all this way, but I'm okay."

When he squeezed her shoulder, Coty lowered her head, which she nestled into his arm as a pillow. She felt safe, closed her eyes, and waited for how he might affect her future, yet again.

"Your father's angry. I want you to move home, not just come for a visit."

"I'm safe here, Zaydeh. You want me to return to New York because he's angry with me?"

"He's not angry with *you*. Well, that's not true, but . . ."

"But what, Zaydeh? Why do *you* want me to move home, if not to appease my father?"

"I had dinner alone with him a couple of nights ago, at my request. It didn't go well. When I get back to New York, I'm gathering the management group: your father and uncles, along with your brothers and cousins. I don't think that'll go much better—probably a lot worse."

He slumped, let his head flop back, and shut his lids. He must be sick. Why else would he bother with the men of the business? Why else would he need her to come home?

"I changed my will, Coty. And you now have power of attorney to conduct business on my behalf."

Shocked into erect posture, she took his arm from her shoulder. Before she said a word, she waited for him to face her. When he shifted to the side, the newspapers crinkled under his weight.

"Zaydeh, you know that the business doesn't interest me. I'm doing exactly what I imagined." Shaking her head back and forth, she frowned at him, folded her arms across her chest, and conveyed without words that his decision might destroy her relationships with the men of the family. When he shrugged, she realized there was little to ruin.

"Your father's stewing. Said it wasn't fair. They've done all the work."

"Zaydeh, they've been running the company for years—thought it was theirs."

They traded stares through identical ice-blue eyes. He winked at his protégée and said, "They've got good jobs. I've paid them more than I would have outsiders. They'll be well off when I die."

"Why are you doing this? Were you worried they might cut me off after you're gone?"

"Once he absorbed the shock, your father said he would've been fair to the grandchildren. First thing out of his mouth."

"You didn't believe him?"

"Your father's not vindictive, Coty. Never has been."

"Why, then, Zaydeh?"

"Because I want you to give most of it away."

"Can't you set up a foundation? You've talked about that for years."

"Did it. You're now the executor of my will, and, once you've signed the papers, you'll have full control of the Sheldon Fine Foundation. You can change the name. I'm not very good with titles; I needed to get the damn paperwork filed."

Was he asking her to give up her dreams to run the foundation—dreams he thought too dangerous? Coty could not believe he would use a clever ploy when her safety was his true motivation. He would tell her. "Have you transferred the business assets to the foundation?"

"No, but I've pulled a lot of what your dad thought was his working capital off the balance sheet to get the foundation going. While I'm alive and while you're capturing whatever interests you on film, the boys'll run the business. Gives them something to do."

Zaydeh had remained steadfast. He had not requested that she abandon her passions. He had found a way to secure them. "Are you saying that the business will fund the family and the foundation?"

"You got it, kid. You won't have to decide who gets what. I set it all down in my will. When the time comes to sell the business, everybody gets their share, and you'll put the rest of the proceeds into the foundation. I assume you'll stay on to run it. Salary's small. It's a charity, and you're the one who chose to be an artist, right?"

He seemed unburdened, ready to levitate off the sofa. The business weight must have been crushing, the load of his sons and grandsons growing heavier as he aged. She wondered if his arduous journey to Saigon had been necessary. "Zaydeh, I'm sorry you traveled so far . . ."

He bolted to his feet. Looming over her, he said, "Coty, I didn't come all this way just to talk." What had she missed? Her reading of him had been wrong, as sometimes happened when she took a passing glimpse at her light meter, anticipating its measurement, rather than searching for the sun's truth. "Be right back. I need to get something from my room," he said, as he turned away.

Zaydeh stepped across the carpet and bounded onto the first step. Papers to sign? The Sheldon Fine Foundation—she liked the sound of it.

As soon as he disappeared up the stairwell, she itched for his return. She picked up the stack and read the beginning of an article on the front page. Coty unfolded the newspaper into a full wingspan. Before she finished the article, she heard, "I'm ready!"

The paper crumpled onto her lap. Gangly legs left the final tread, and her grandfather reentered the lobby dressed in a fashion jumble that she recognized as pure Zaydeh. There, in full regalia, stood the explanation behind his journey.

"Had to grab my camera, bag, hat, vest. You should've seen me getting this stuff on the plane."

Coty felt underdressed, her only accessories a pair of sunglasses, a purse, and her ever-present camera, which lay next to her on the sofa.

As she stood to hug her grandfather, he whispered into her ear, "Can we swing by your place? I'd like to see it."

"Of course. I need to grab my camera bag too; I'm almost out of film."

"I wondered why you didn't have it with you. That French hummingbird has thrown you off your game, darling."

For as long as she could remember, Zaydeh had been her guide. Today would be her chance to reciprocate.

CHAPTER THREE

—•—

The cotton doily, all but lost on her head, capped hair as white as the ad hoc covering, except for random gray streaks. Coty rested in the pew with her head bowed to avoid snickering as she prepared to kneel for the first time in a Catholic confessional. Her grandfather would chuckle at reports of her feigned solemnity, while she was certain the rest of her family would be appalled.

Awaiting her turn, she reflected on Zaydeh's visit and thought of how her father had toiled. Years earlier, after Zaydeh ended what the younger Fine men had called his "meddlesome oversight," they had begun treating the old man as a benign relic. Zaydeh, however, considered respect a matter of reciprocity. *Bread cast*, she thought, as she spied the missal laid open in its cradle on the altar.

Coty crooked her head to gauge the line of sinners. She had not come to partake in their sacrament of reconciliation. Rather, she sought to secure what had been withheld: a private audience with Laurent. The plan was to enter his wooden box and make a donation—a tithe of her perspective, to relieve the man's apparent impoverishment.

Sunlight descended from a circular stained glass window set high behind her in the balcony above the entrance to the nave. The carved wooden crucifix, suspended from the rafters, hovered over the prayer railing in front of an altar awash with color. Casting about the building's interior, she thought the architecture less stark than the parish churches of Hanoi, albeit modest by comparison with Paris's Notre-Dame or St. Patrick's Cathedral in Manhattan.

Coty was tapping her fingers on her camera bag when she flinched, startled by a penitent exiting Laurent's box. In unison, the parishioners stood to move one pew closer to his confessional. She touched the doily as she rose to join the contrite, who ambled in the aisle.

Pad and pencil slipped from her camera bag. Coty liked lists and ran down the one she had written out the night before. *Superfluous*, she thought, chastising herself for documenting the obvious.

Midmorning light, its spectrum liberated by the stained glass, splashed over her as she left the last pew and walked to the back of the church. She took a nervous swallow and stepped through the curtain. Inside, with the drape drawn behind her, Coty paused in the dark to catch her breath and let her eyes adjust.

The confessional smelled stale. The musty scent befitted a venue for whispered sins, she thought. As she knelt, her knees registered the thinness of the pad.

A woman—no doubt a chain smoker—prattled on in raspy French from the other side of the confessional. Bored by the bleak solitude, Coty strained to decipher the sins being confessed. Listening to the melody of the petitioner without hearing the lyrics, she swayed, shifting from one knee to the other.

She heard Laurent's muffled instructions for penance. He cleared his throat and released the sinner with a rote blessing. Curtain rings tinkled as the smoker dragged the drapes across the bar. Coty heard the feet of a metal chair scrape the stone floor.

Laurent settled into his seat, which squeaked under his shifting weight. He drew back the screen's cover to greet his next penitent through the wooden lattice, and said, "Bless you, my child. God wishes to hear your petition."

"Laurent, I hope we can make this brief and choose a more appropriate setting to continue our discussion—one that's outdoors, where we can breathe fresh air."

She dabbed her brow with a kerchief. *No wonder people confess inside this hotbox*, she thought, waiting for her priest to respond. Once more, Coty heard metal rake the floor. The lattice screen blocked a clear view of his face. A dangling bulb shone weak light down atop the priest, whose shadow she tracked as he fidgeted.

"Mademoiselle Fine, I recognize your voice."

"Mademoiselle Fine, is it? Although none of your chaperones is present, we're to be formal today, Monsieur Sabatier?"

Her frustration rose and she felt flush, her skin's fever a match for the stifling temperature inside the sacramental closet. The air was stagnant, unmoving except for puffs powered by her breathing. She reached for her thick hair, lifting it off her shoulders. Twisting a rubber band around the curly bundle, she belted the ponytail's waist. The doily she had pulled from beneath a table lamp in her rented cottage dropped to the floor. Coty snapped it up and shoved it into the pocket of her dress.

"A small accommodation of respect, *mademoiselle*. We're in the house of God."

"Laurent, must we continue the ruse? There are no curious nuns in here. Each time I visited you at the rectory, I addressed you as Père, which I did to protect you, not out of respect for those robes that cause you to chafe."

His throat cleared with a rattle. She heard him rock in his chair as her knees pressed against the thin pad. A little discomfort for the confessor, to offset that which was required of sinners.

"Mademoiselle Fine, your sarcasm has returned to full strength."

"My sarcasm might've rubbed off on you, *monsieur*. I'm Jewish, for Christ's—" She paused and, with a cough to clear her throat, reset herself. "I'm Jewish, Laurent, as you know."

"*S'il vous plait, mademoiselle.* Speak freely. Many people find comfort in telling a priest their troubles. Not everyone who confides is Catholic."

His condescension raced past the screen. Coty shook the irritation from her shoulders and, seeking relief, alternated her balance from knee to knee. "I want to talk about *your* troubles, not mine."

Laurent wriggled, causing his chair to squeak. Finding her position on the kneeling pad an unjustified inconvenience, Coty stood. The low-wattage bulb hanging above Laurent's head showered him in a yellow hue. Looking down at him seated, Coty noticed a pale, circular reflection and supposed the light bounced off his bald spot. He leaned in to listen, arms folded across his chest as if to protect his heart.

"Laurent, you haven't invited my assistance, but I've a photographer's eye. We often observe in people what they don't see in their mirrors." Fighting to hold her loose grip on conciliation, she pulled a manila envelope from her tote bag. "I brought something to show you." She held the photograph inches away from the screen. His shadow crowded the partition, and she imagined him squinting at the glossy black-and-white image of the nun. "Here—I'll slide it under the screen," she said, teasing him with a corner of the photo. As she felt his fingers press down and start to drag the paper, she pulled it back. Laurent's shadow withdrew. His chair protested with a squawk as it caught his full weight.

"I don't understand, *mademoiselle.*"

"I'll explain when we meet again, somewhere other than the rectory—outside, where the air moves." She paused. After receiving no response, she prompted him. "Would you like to have the photograph?"

"*Oui . . . s'il vous plait, mademoiselle,*" he said in a declining voice.

"Tuesday. Meet me at the bistro on Hàn Thuyên. One hour after your late-morning Mass. Don't wear your collar, Laurent."

"*Merci*, Mademoiselle Fine. I know the restaurant."

"And, Laurent, call me Coty. We shouldn't pretend to be strangers anymore."

CHAPTER FOUR

C oty stirred the sheet of paper in the shallow pool with a chopstick. The developing shot revealed the Vietnamese nun, staring into the lens of the camera. The woman's expression—a look of immediate loss coupled with fear of permanent separation—intensified with the photograph's clarity.

Black-and-white images draped from the drying line strung across the co-opted porch, itself devoid of color except for the hue from an amber lightbulb. Coty grabbed a second chopstick. After tip-tapping three pinching, wood-on-wood clicks, proving to herself her proficiency, she dipped the tongs into the solution and snagged the print's white border. Suspended at an angle over the tray, the paper dripped as she waved it back and forth until the time between successive drops increased to allow her a full breath and the solution's ripples shrank to pinpricks.

With a clothespin, she clipped one of the sheet's top corners onto the line. In the heat, despite Saigon's humidity, the duplicate would be parched by the time she returned from her rendezvous with the priest. She had developed this copy for herself to replace the original print, which today she intended to present to Laurent, as promised.

The moisture was gone from the other photographs dangling along the line: candid shots of the priest, the French nuns with their heads bowed in prayer, the flatbed stacked with burlap bags, a man standing on the pedals of his bicycle as it climbed,

huddles of cumulus clouds hovering low above the lush countryside, peasants bent over their paddies, water buffalo with their
tails swatting at persistent flies, huts fronting a fading sunset, an
exhausted freighter at its berth in Haiphong's wharf, and whitecaps that left no doubt about the choppy sea—all reminders of
their journey together. *Why not take these down, crop them, and file
the lot?* she asked herself.

Gliding through the cone of light, Coty felt for the edge of her
crude darkroom's billowy wall, a blackout curtain she had com-
mandeered to block the porch from the interior of the cottage.
Through a slit, she entered a single room that served as kitchen,
bedroom, and living space.

After the tent resettled, she scanned the sunlit room, noticing
the particulars of her temporary home. The mattress she had made
up with fresh linens, which lay hidden under a sky-blue bedspread
with green bamboo stalks and leaves imprinted on its surface.

Unlike her past homes, this one had few books scattered
throughout. Nevertheless, it was recognizable as Coty's nest.
Flower blossoms and loose petals floated in the glass bowls of
water that she had placed about the room—on a petite oval table,
a bookshelf with two tattered volumes, and the windowsill above
the sink. She had compensated for the absence of artwork with
fresh cuttings from the garden, displayed in vases, and lengths of
colorful linen draped as tapestries down the walls in front of
worn paint and cracks in the plaster. She had purchased the bolts
during a visit to the alley where the wares of weavers—lifting,
then falling—wafted in the breeze.

Spying three gardenia blossoms adrift in the dish on the table,
Coty touched her temple and considered a flower for her hair,
which would be her first such adornment since she had left Paris.
She reached out to let her fingers sift through the swimmers. She
rejected each in order: white would be lost in her locks; cham-
pagne, flat against her snowy curls; purple, a grim reminder of his
vows.

Outside, among the dark green leaves in the dripping-wet garden, framed in her vision by the window, a pink gardenia flirted with her. Ridiculous, she thought, to be fussing over the evasive priest.

Coty felt the rumble of a nervous stomach. She dropped to the floor, where she rested supine, eyes taking in the ceiling, nostrils collecting the scents of her private perfumery. Street sounds tapped on the windows, knocked at the doors, front and back, and scratched at the exterior walls of the bungalow. Birds sang, accompanying a gaggle of nearby children in animated play. With the music of Saigon life as her soundtrack, she closed her eyes, forced a yawn, stretched her muscles, and tried to calm her anxious mind.

"Never met an altruist," Zaydeh had chided when challenging her motives for encouraging Laurent to return to Hanoi to find the nun. Her laughter spewed at the ceiling. She scolded herself for procrastinating, sat up, unwound her legs, and stood. Time to get ready.

Few choices available, she picked the dress that seemed coolest for a hot day. The yellow shift draped from her shoulders. Veering back and forth, tiptoeing up and down, she considered herself in a round mirror that was too small to display the full figure of a typical Vietnamese woman. Coty drew a hairbrush through her white tresses. She put the brush down and then brought her freed hand to the nape of her neck to collect her hair. Twirling her wrist, she lifted and coiled the bundle into a French twist, which she secured with a bamboo comb.

She stopped at the oval table. The manila folder that housed the original copy of the nun's picture lay flat where she had deposited it after she had returned from Laurent's confessional. One corner was bent, as if earmarked to separate it from a stack of clones. She pulled out the top half of the photograph. Away from where the image began to coat the page, a slight crease compromised the white border.

Coty reinserted the print into the envelope, which she returned to the table. She left her camera bag and slung over her shoulder the strap of her canvas tote.

The back door closed behind her. Standing at the edge of the garden, she rubbed between thumb and forefinger a leaf that remained moist from the thick morning. Her eyes closed, and she paused to breathe the smell of fresh growth. Her wet fingertips reached for the clasp in her hair.

After releasing the comb, she shook her head side to side, unfurling her white curls, which rippled down her back in a cascade. On the street in front of the cottage, a bus backfired, interrupting her moment in Eden. Coty stepped into a hug of dripping branches and snapped off the pink blossom.

Who dressed the priest? Coty thought as she saw him rounding the corner, head and shoulders above the people in the street, outfitted in loose, pale linen, from the neckline of an open shirt to the tops of his leather sandals. Laurent ignored the chattering vendor trying to entice him to purchase one of her headless birds, stripped of its feathers and hung upside down. He waved off fat flies that circled the plucked chickens and kept his hand raised to acknowledge Coty. The man's gait quickened, as if he needed to cross the piazza before he could take another breath.

"*Bonjour*, Mademoiselle Fine!"

"*Bonjour*, Laurent." Looking up from her seat, she scolded him with a stern smile. "Call me Coty. Remember?"

"Ah, *oui*, Mademoiselle Coty."

"Close enough." Laughing, she said, "You look more comfortable in your civvies."

"*Mademoiselle?*"

"I was commenting on your clothes. Another Americanism. 'Civvies': civilian garb, as opposed to your usual priestly attire."

Today, he seemed far less a cleric, not simply in dress. Maybe

Laurent had dropped his guard when he laid down his Roman collar this morning. Maybe she had abandoned hers as well, when she stepped into the garden.

"*Gardénia, oui?*" he said.

The flower that clung to her temple received her touch.

"The pink accentuates your beautiful hair."

"*Merci beaucoup.* It took me a long time to draw attention to my white hair," she said, recalling how her grandfather, rather than her dark-haired mother, had told her it was not a curse but an endowment, a genetic windfall. Zaydeh had admonished her to wield it with purpose, not pride. Take her pale mane as good fortune, instead of accomplishment—a stunning gift of nature.

Coty stroked the petals of the flower. An index finger twisted a natural curl that required no encouragement. "Beautiful hair," she recalled, and repeated her thanks in private thought: *Merci beaucoup, Monsieur Sabatier.*

About ten years her senior, a waiter—no taller than Coty had been at eleven years old—appeared at the table. The gazes of the two companions tracked up the man's shadow, which had interrupted conversation and sunshine. Upon eye contact, the server nodded at them in a choppy rhythm. With a flourished hand, Laurent motioned to Coty, who made her selection. The priest added his order without considering the menu beneath his elbow. The waiter pivoted. In the draft of his exit, a lull settled between the pair as their eyes lost each other's and found the tabletop.

Coty was staring at the platter in the center of the table when Laurent lifted his water glass.

"*Mademoiselle?*"

His raised voice startled her. Coty brought her attention back to him and said, "*Désolée*, what did you say?"

"I asked you if you enjoyed the fish."

"Ah, *oui*. It was delicious."

A flurry followed her reply. The waiter and his underling, a busboy, swept the table clear. Place settings disappeared, and along with them went the platter, depleted except for the head, bones, and tail. Circling flies followed the sea carrion en route to the heap behind the restaurant, where other insects awaited, prepared to dine.

"Where did you go in your mind, Coty? You seemed to be far away."

"I was a child, standing at the deli counter with my grandfather. We were taking pictures of fish laid out on a bed of crushed ice."

"Very far away, New York, *oui*?"

"*Oui*. He told me they blinked at the same time as my shutter."

"Why did he tell you such a thing? Was he a comedian as well as a jeweler?"

"He has a wonderful wit, but he wasn't being funny at the time."

"Why did he deceive you?"

"To teach me, Laurent. He had told me to keep my eye open whenever I took a shot, any shot. I told him that I always did. He knew I was lying—or at least deceiving myself, as you say."

"He tricked you. Maybe to help you learn, but also a lie, *non*?"

"A white lie, a little white lie. Better than harmless—instructive."

"Was his lie effective?"

"I'm a professional photographer."

"*Touché, mademoiselle*."

The waiter returned tableside with a durian held out for inspection. She had tried the fruit, an adventure in itself, when a street vendor in Hanoi insisted that the pungent smell belied its sweet taste. *Not a harmless white lie*, she thought, recalling her subsequent attempts to purge the nasty odor, which seemed to have infiltrated all things olfactory.

Laurent asked the waiter for the check. When the man withdrew, cradling the durian, the priest said to her, while scrunching his nose, "They learn to love it at a young age. Like foie gras, *non?*"

"I defer to you, Laurent. I've acquired a taste for neither."

Leaving a few coins in the tray for the staff, Laurent paid the bill. As they stood, he pulled her chair away from the table. When Coty picked up her purse, he studied it, as if measuring its capacity. Looking at her with a knowing expression that might have prompted parishioners to seek him out in his confessional, he said, "It's a small bag, Coty."

"You seem puzzled, Laurent."

"Curious. First time I've seen you without your camera."

"A matter of respect for our visit today. I get distracted when I know that anything I see I can capture on film."

"Oh, I thought you might have brought a larger bag, camera or not."

She read his mind but waited for him to expound. *What has gotten into me? The man met me so he'd get the photograph I've withheld like a schoolgirl*, she chastised herself.

"I was hoping to collect the picture today."

"I'm sorry, Laurent. It was ruined, bent by my carelessness. This morning I developed a fresh print for you. It's drying in my darkroom." *Harmless—a little white lie*, she thought.

They ambled across the square, neither speaking as they approached the naked birds dangling upside down amid a cloud of flies. The middle-aged shopkeeper possessed the short memory of a salesperson. She repeated her standard pitch in a shout skyward as Laurent stepped by.

When they turned the corner, the chicken lady yammering at their backs, the sun blazed into their faces. Coty retrieved cat's-eye sunglasses from her purse. After donning her shades, she caught Laurent smirking at her. She pulled the frames down the bridge of her nose.

"Blue eyes, Laurent. I can't take the glare." She pushed the sunglasses back into working position and feigned a coquettish snub with a sharp twist of her head.

"I don't remember you wearing sunglasses on our journey, Coty. Is the glare in Saigon worse than in Hanoi?"

"I forgot them in my rush to catch the truck. We departed in a hurry, *non*?"

He felt for the missing patch at his throat. "You look like an actress, Coty. *Oui*, a famous Hollywood film star."

"Which one? You thought I was an old woman when you climbed onto the back of our truck."

"Impossible!"

In an abrupt counter, she said, "Nothing's impossible." Coty cringed at her own words. She despised using absolutes, a pet peeve inherited from her grandfather.

When she flinched, Laurent drew back. "Lauren Bacall. You remind me of Lauren Bacall, Coty."

"Bacall? I'm flattered." She beamed. "Okay, Laurent, I forgive you for thinking I was an old woman." A man in the business of granting absolution to tortured souls might not appreciate her flippant exoneration. Watching from behind the defense of her sunglasses, Coty expected Laurent's chin to angle upward. Instead, he laughed, accepting her humor as he had her generosity on their journey. "Laurent, your skin's fair, and your eyes, too, are light. Doesn't the sun bother you?"

Squinting, he said, "I've never needed sunglasses."

"Never? Do you often trade in absolutes, *monsieur*?"

"I'm a man of faith," he responded, with an air of victory. His chin lifted with the rebuke.

"So, a man of faith—who squints at bright light. Keep it up, and you'll one day live with blind faith," she said.

After a nervous laugh, she stared down at her toenails, which she had painted red the previous night. Not since meeting Elliot had Coty felt so flirtatious. Drifting away from the priest for her own protection, she let the wedge of humid air between them expand as they strolled.

Along the street, commercial stalls held up stacked apartments. They walked past a string of shops proffering wares for all manner of life: grasses bundled as brooms or woven into baskets, mats, and *nón lá*; flowing dresses and linens of various dyes sewn into genderless clothing; simple children's toys carved of wood; and items such as buckets, boots, and hoses from one vendor who specialized in the commerce of molded plastic and rubber articles. After they turned another corner and passed through a cool shadow, the roof of the building released the sun, which fired down at them. Laurent brought his hand up to interrupt the burning on the crown of his head. Fingernails scratched at the flaky patch of dried-out skin.

After scanning the stalls, Coty made her choice. Her slender fingers slipped between his ribs and arm. She tugged his elbow. The priest ducked his head and followed her into the shade under the vendor's awning.

"Laurent, your attire calls for a proper hat."

"I never wear hats!"

She peeked at him over the rim of the sunglasses, once more drawn down the bridge of her nose. With a playful glower, Coty intimated the paddy hat she had bought for him outside Hanoi and said, "Never?"

"Ah . . ."

The priest halted. The shades rode back up to cover her eyes. She smiled at him, accepting his sheepish expression as his recollection.

"Try this one, Laurent—unless you'd prefer another *nón lá*?"

A man's woven hat, with an orange band encircling the crown above the brim, levitated for his approval. It seemed to have been designed to operate as something between a fashionable fedora and a utilitarian lid. On such days as this, it was the type French businessmen and diplomats wore about in the swelter of Saigon.

Laurent bowed as he received the headpiece, which he brought up to cover his bald spot. "Ah! Much better," he said, without checking his image in the mirror.

"Oh my! You have a large head, *monsieur!*"

Laurent would need a *nón lá*'s chinstrap to keep that undersize top from tipping off his head and falling to the ground. With a slight rise onto the balls of her feet, she plucked the chapeau from its tenuous perch.

Before Coty could speak, the shopkeeper held out an alternative, the largest size in her inventory. Coty traded with the older woman. Tiptoeing, she plopped the replacement onto the head of the priest, who stood with his hands at his side.

"Monsieur Bogart."

"Coty?"

"The mirror. Now you, too, look like a movie star, Laurent."

Titling his head side to side, he considered his reflection and said, "Ah, Bogie." Turning to find her, he crooked his neck and tugged the tip of the brim downward at an exaggerated angle. With a slight bow and a poor disguise of his French accent, he mimicked, in English, one of the actor's famous lines: "Here's looking at you, kid."

The skin of his face flushed. Returning his attention to the mirror, he adjusted the headgear to horizontal, setting it flat atop his head like a cardinal's red galero. Waving off Coty's attempt to pay for it, Laurent handed bills to the shopkeeper.

"Good to hear they let you go to a film from time to time."

"*Oui*, but I didn't tell my bishop in Paris that I enjoy Hollywood as much as French cinema. He's a bit of a snob."

Takes one . . . She caught herself before she spoke. "Maybe he hasn't been introduced to American film. Generational, perhaps? Or life at the rectory? A forceful combination, *non*?"

"Old and cloistered? That would not explain my bishop. In

his case, it's simply France," the priest said with what she took as self-deprecation, the extension of an olive branch. "He's one of many French snobs," he muttered, as they ducked under the awning and merged again with the flow of humans.

"Snobs are a minority by definition, *non*?"

"*Oui*, so it seems." He laughed and shrugged as he gazed into a wavy mirage of rising humidity that blurred the end of the street.

"I met few Parisians that I'd categorize as snobs," she said.

"New Yorkers tend to understand us. What does that say about our home cities, *mademoiselle*?"

"That one doesn't have to be a snob to be curt?" She paused. Repeating her habit, she dragged her sunglasses down the bridge of her nose with the tip of her forefinger. "Should I take your comments as personal critique, Monsieur Sabatier?"

"'Curt'? *Non*, Coty, I don't think you rude."

"Are you saying that I'm a snob but not rude?"

"*Non, non!* Not a snob, not rude! I don't have the words—*pardonnez-moi*."

"During our journey, Laurent, do you remember how you described Americans?"

"Ah, *oui, oui*: blunt! *Oui*, Coty, you are not rude, simply blunt. *Merci beaucoup*."

"You truly know how to compliment a woman, *monsieur*."

"Coty?"

"Laurent, do you know anything about Americans?" she asked, knowing, of course, that he did. "Anything about women—French, American, any women?" she said, wondering if he had experience beyond his own family, nuns, or the ewes of his parish flocks.

His face reddened beneath the shade of his new top. "*Pardonnez-moi*, Coty, I meant no insult."

"You aren't accustomed to casual conversation, are you?"

"*Non*, not with women. I'm seldom at ease except with fellow priests—those who also answered God's calling. They're my family, my friends."

"Since you left for seminary, have you abandoned your family?" She wondered what might have caused such a rift.

"I didn't leave for seminary, Coty."

"Laurent, I'll be 'blunt,' as you say: How did you get to seminary if you didn't leave home?"

"The orphanage—run by the same nuns who served the boys and men of my seminary. I moved from the acolyte's dormitory to the novitiate."

Coty swallowed the bile of embarrassment born of her inference that the man had left a loving family to ascend his maker's hierarchy. "You actually heard a calling?" she asked, reeling from his revelation.

"I wonder. To use one of your 'absolutes,' Coty, I *never* wondered, until . . ." Chin level with the ground, he stopped walking. He turned his head to once again ponder the steamy mirage in the street.

"Until?" she asked.

"Hanoi—when I relocated to Vietnam."

Coty tugged his arm so he would turn to her. When she found his widened eyes, staring as if he was afraid of her next words, she said, "And met the nun?"

"*Oui.* Sister Lan, Bùi Thị Lan."

A tear clung to the inside of his eye, its release suspended. Coty pulled an embroidered kerchief from the pocket of her dress and dabbed the droplet, as Laurent stood motionless.

"Did you kiss her?" Coty probed, while holding at bay the intimate question on her mind.

"*Non!*" Laurent protested, implying the obvious: he was a priest, and Sister Lan was a nun.

Coty walked in silence, watching the surface of the street pass beneath. In and out of view, alternating five at a time, ten red toenails poked from her sandals.

They turned the next corner and drew back, shocked. A rain squall was upon them, flooding their pathway.

Coty faced Laurent, wiped rain off her face, and chortled aloud above the clatter of the downpour. "This is the closest I'll get to baptism."

"Nothing's impossible," the priest repeated.

A pink gardenia floated away in a stream that branched around the soggy soles of their sandals.

CHAPTER FIVE

—.·—

Today, for the fourth week in a row, the two were to meet, as they had each Tuesday since her confession. Coty expected another suffocating bout of midday weather, followed by a cleansing downpour in the late afternoon. Before she left the cottage, she gazed through the window into the garden, where a fourth pink blossom had yet to present itself.

They would not take lunch together, Laurent having reported the prior week that he must attend to important church business during mealtime. With a wink and a coy smile, she had suggested she wait in his cool sanctuary, which would provide relief until the clouds burst. After playful banter, they had reached consensus to meet at a secular stone building—a museum.

Planted months before the museum opened its doors half a century earlier, the banyan tree sheltered Laurent in the shade of its canopy. The woven hat rested to his side on the bench. As he stood to greet her, he snagged the top in one hand and placed it over his bald spot. "No picture today, Coty?"

"*Non*, Laurent. Cameras aren't allowed inside."

"Ah, *oui*. I was asking about the photograph of Sister Lan."

That had been his first mention of it since their initial encounter at the bistro on Hàn Thuyên. The original print remained in its manila envelope, which she had moved from the table to the bookshelf. Each time she left to rendezvous, when she passed the dried copy that hung from the line on the porch, she wondered when he might ask. Their first month of Tuesdays was coming to an end.

"Coty, I talked to the bishop here in Saigon."

"About Sister Lan?"

"*Non*, about me." He pinched the brim of the hat, tugging it back and forth, as if to adjust its alignment. Without looking at her, he returned the hat to where it had been at the start of his fidgeting and then dropped his hand.

"He approved your trip to Hanoi?"

"*Non*, Paris."

"You told Sister Lan you would return, *oui*? That was your vow to her, *non*?"

"*Oui, oui*, Coty. As we discussed, I must find her."

"Paris? I'm confused, Laurent."

"I couldn't tell him I'm traveling back to Hanoi. Too dangerous, too suspicious. I requested a home visit, a sabbatical. He agreed to write my bishop in Paris."

"For permission?"

"*Oui*, and for passage. Saigon's archdiocese won't pay for transport between here and Europe."

"Are you going to Paris? When? After Hanoi?"

"Coty, so many questions! I don't know. First Hanoi, then . . . ?"

"Laurent, you're also one of the sheep they serve. If you tell them, confess your dilemma—"

"Neither bishop would understand. Not Sister Lan, and not you, Coty."

Those people could really weave grass, Coty thought, as she stood in front of an exhibit of artifacts. Laurent seemed distracted. He rolled his hat in one hand, his opposite thumb plucking at the orange wrapper that hugged the crown. Dried sweat powdered the band.

"Laurent, a centime for your thoughts?"

His eyes darted about the room. The band of his hat gaped at the prick of his thumb. He slid a finger between the orange wrapper and the grass wall of the crown. She thought he might tug the band apart, the ends connected by a few simple stitches, over which the sewer had fastened a trim piece of the same material—a sliver of orange.

"A centime's not much of a bribe, is it?" she said.

"*Non*, Coty. I doubt that all the treasure in the Vatican would suffice."

"Sorry, Laurent; everyone needs privacy . . ." she said, her voice trailing off.

"Coty, you're my first friend from outside the church. I wish to tell you what I think, how I feel."

"You're conflicted about Sister Lan, and your vows, *oui*?"

She tugged on his elbow, but he did not turn. His voice drifted as he spoke. "*Je suis prêtre.* A priest was all I wished to be."

"Laurent, how old were you when you moved from the acolytes' dormitory to the novitiate?"

The question broke whatever spell had taken him away. He turned to her and said, "*Quatorze.*"

"Fourteen. When did you take your vows?"

"Many years later. First a deacon, then a priest. I was twenty-six when ordained."

She squeezed her grip. "After you moved to the novitiate, did you consider any other profession?"

"*Non*, Coty."

"All you wished to be?"

"*Oui.* How could I question my calling?"

"You made that decision as a child, Laurent." Coty released her hold and let her hand drop.

"*Non.* As I told you, I was ordained at twenty-six."

"*Oui*, Laurent. However, you never challenged your choice—your calling, as you say. Correct?"

"*Je suis prêtre*," he mumbled at the floor, as his chin dipped and almost met his chest.

Again, she reached to take his arm, which opened to receive hers. They ambled the hallway, skirting exhibits that did not draw them to pause. His muscles relaxed as if his god had granted him the grace to walk guiltless with a woman on his arm.

She stopped. Laurent himself must have instructed his sheep that it is better to give than to receive.

"Walk me home, Laurent. I have a photograph for you."

Three blocks from her rented cottage, the afternoon rain shower surprised them. The deluge descended as if the rooftop water tank, set at the peak of the apartment building beneath which they strolled, had burst, its contents cascading in sheets over the eaves. Laurent attempted to hug the tenement house. Coty giggled when the rampaging water tore the hat from his head.

"Laurent, we're close. Follow me. Run!"

She did not wait for confirmation and, in the deafening splashes, lost the sloshing footsteps from the priest's sandals as he trailed behind. At the front door, she rattled the handle and then slouched in recognition that the key remained inserted into the bolt on the inside. She had locked it out of habit, a practice adopted when she lived in Manhattan as a single woman.

"Around back!" she yelled as he approached, crushing the wet hat to his head.

From first drop to last, they had been exposed to the full force of the cloudburst. Leaves and branches dripped throughout the garden; the sounds of water falling, settling, punctuated the air. Holding his soggy hat, his sandy-brown mop matted against his skull, Laurent arrived with the end of the downpour.

One hand pressed high on the jamb, Coty stood inside the back porch and said, "Oh, Laurent, you're soaked!" When he frowned at her, she said, "I'm going to change my dress. I'll get you a towel. Come inside. Be careful of the chemical trays on the porch. I set up a rudimentary darkroom in here."

As Coty passed the table, her wet clothing splattered the floorboards. She lifted the edge of the blackout curtain and slipped into the main room, assuming Laurent was behind her. She snatched the first dress from her hanger bar and entered a space the size of a broom closet, which she called a bathroom, although it possessed no tub. She bathed under a primitive shower constructed outdoors, in the privacy of the garden.

Next to the toilet, a sink, its basin not much larger than the priest's wet hat, protruded from the bathroom wall. Coty reached a hand behind her waist. Swatting the door closed, she shut off the only interior room of the cottage.

The wet towel fell to the floor. Lifting her damp hair, she pinned it in a swirl atop her head and then stepped into the ivory shift, its linen accented with splashes of vibrant dyes. She reached down for the wet towel to hook it on a nearby nail, which, on her first afternoon in her new home, she had tapped into the wall with the heel of her sandal. Pausing at the threshold, she plucked a fresh towel for the priest from a wooden shelf above the sink.

Laurent was not standing shirtless in the kitchen, dripping on her floor, as she had expected. She drew back the black drape and pulled the string that controlled the lightbulb overhead. The chemical trays were arrayed in a row and reflected the bulb's dimness. She stood alone on the cloaked porch. Had the drenched priest bolted? Curiosity pulled her outside.

"Well, *monsieur*, how long are you going to stand in the garden?"

"Ah, *mademoiselle* . . . I . . ."

"I can offer you this towel, but I can't read your mind," she said, certain that she already had.

"Coty, I don't wish to intrude."

"I invited you in, Laurent."

"*Je suis prêtre.*"

"*Oui, oui* . . . all you wished to be." There was much he had not told either of his bishops, she thought. "Laurent, you're being silly. I'll leave the towel on the table—inside, beyond the curtain. I need to dry my hair."

Coty pivoted in a huff. Did he expect his god to reach through the sky and snag him by the throat at his missing collar? Her simple extension of hospitality was not an apple stolen from the tree of knowledge. She was irritated by the grown boy who long ago had moved, without stretching the limits of his volition, in a mindless trudge from the acolytes' dormitory to the novitiate.

With her last clean towel wrapped around her head, Coty stepped back into the main room. The priest, poised for escape, stood in his soaked civvies with his back to the curtain. Next to his shoulder, the open cupboard shelves displayed the dishware of a loner, a tin that held loose-leaf tea, and a white porcelain sugar bowl with a red mushroom top.

Her smile released him and her own goodwill. "Tea, Laurent?"

"*Oui*, if you, too, are having some."

Coty left him to his towel, which he folded with gravitas, as if it were the blessed pall that covered his chalice. When she turned from filling and firing the kettle, Coty tracked Laurent's vision to a gecko, which had slithered from behind the curtain that transformed back porch into darkroom. The reptile skittered the length of an altar across the wall and halted. In a sprint, it scurried under one of Coty's decorative drapes, reentered her view on the blank wall, and stopped, as if lack of movement would prevent detection.

"Ah, Laurent, the house lizard is awake. I'm afraid my darkroom has confused his nocturnal hunting habits."

"You have a pet, Coty?" he asked, as he stepped into the privacy of the loo.

"*Non*, a housemate." She held out a robe for Laurent. "He's poor company, but I can understand his reticence. I'm the interloper. He was here first."

"Maybe he needs a name to become more responsive. I don't suggest you anthropomorphize a lizard, however . . ." Laurent's voice trailed off as he considered the housecoat in his hand. When he looked up, she chuckled. The garment was what she had to offer. The alternatives were few: wait for his clothes to dry on his skin, hide naked behind the door of the water closet, or sit in a towel wrapped around his waist, which would render any movement a risk.

"Housemate, not a pet," he said, as he leaned into the bathroom and tossed the folded towel onto the sink. The robe floated between his outstretched hands, and he shook his head.

"*Oui*, a free being."

"Free to remain a simple lizard. Free to roam without worry of being bothered by his housemate?"

"As long as he can ignore my soliloquies."

"You talk to a nameless lizard?" He seemed irritated as he squeezed by the basin and reached back to close the door.

"*Non*, Laurent. His name is Elliot."

Through the window above the kitchen sink, she spotted his shirt and trousers flapping in the garden, where she had hung them. His civvies were drying in the air next to the dress she had worn to the museum. Hooked on the scarred nub of a broken banyan branch, his woven hat, powered by a slight breeze, twitched side to side, its brim patting back and forth against the tree's trunk. Four sandals were wedged into the crotches of nearby branches.

The barefoot priest faced her. The lower halves of his arms extended out from loose sleeves. Knobby knees poked in the direction of the two-burner stove top.

"Too small?" she asked with a smile. Laurent lifted a sleeve for inspection. "First time you've worn a woman's housecoat, *monsieur*?" He stared back, intimating that he was not entertained by her humor. "Think of it as a colorful cassock, Laurent."

"I'd rather be wet!"

His petulance drew her to scold him. "A priest in a cassock, a man under a housecoat—you might look silly, but there's no need to feel uncomfortable. Your clothes'll be dry in minutes."

The cottage had been furnished for Sparta when Coty rented it. Laurent collapsed at the oval table, into one of two caned chairs sized to accommodate French children and Vietnamese adults. He shifted and, with obvious frustration, yanked the twisted tail of the housecoat trapped beneath his buttocks. The chair creaked under his weight.

Long legs spread apart in a V that was wider than his seat. One hand chopped the center of the robe, which tightened around his thighs, mimicking short trousers. His kneecaps, their skin stretched taut by bent joints, had turned to bloodless beige and bulged out, duplicating his bug-eyed glower at Coty.

She sensed she had gone too far with the wounded orphan and said, "*Pardonnez-moi, monsieur.*"

Laurent patted his exposed knees. Lifting his arms, he glanced from sleeve to drooping sleeve. As he considered himself in the housecoat, he grinned and said, "If my bishop in Paris could see me . . ."

Coty stepped to the window. One of her sandals had escaped its wedge in the crotch of the tree and fallen out of sight. Their garments, the original hues of the fabrics restored, shifted in the breeze.

"Looks like the clothing is almost dry, although our sandals will be soppy," she said.

Laurent stood. He flattened the front of the housecoat against his chest. Gathering material below the cloth belt into a fistful, he tugged it downward, as if to protect his chastity.

"Before you change back into your civvies, shall I take a photo for Sister Lan?"

"*Non . . . s'il vous plait, non!*"

Wind picked up, and a burst of air swept in from the porch, causing the blackout curtain to drift into the room. As the drape wafted, she saw the drying line that drooped with hanging photographs. Knowing he had passed by the images, she wondered if he had paused before each or sought only the face of the nun.

Holding the curtain, Coty faced him. "Laurent, you said you never kissed her." His eyes grew wide, and his head shook side to side. "Do you wish you had?"

Laurent took the tip of her chin in his thumb and forefinger. With pressure that would have lifted little more than a feather, he tilted her face upward. The last of the clean towels unraveled and dropped to the floor.

On the wall behind Laurent's head, a lizard darted across one of the linen drapes. The gecko halted its sprint in the middle of the swathe and clung there. The sheer flagged under the weight of the reptile, which rode up and down like a dinghy lolling on the waves of a calm sea. Clutching the tapestry, the lizard stared at Coty, who closed her eyes and tried not to think of Elliot.

CHAPTER SIX

———•◦•———

Haze hung over Saigon. Sick to her stomach, Coty sat alone outside the bistro in a sliver of shade. Bubbles popped on the tip of her nose as the tumbler of mineral water came to her lips. She sipped, hoping her nausea would subside before the priest showed up.

Camera at the ready by her elbow, Coty had arrived early to get situated. She had chosen the seat after estimating his path. With the midmorning sun at her back, she opened her light meter. By local standards, the reading was satisfactory, although the humidity muted all she saw. The fabric of her dress fell limp, as the breeze that had been wafting around the table died.

Common climate for Saigon: the motionless air felt hot and moist. Passersby bustled about at speeds she had not observed in either Paris or New York on such rare oppressive days. Scanning the plaza, she remained pleased with her choice of vantage. Laurent would approach, as before, from the corner by the poultry shop. She focused her lens on one of the plucked chickens that hung upside down beneath the tattered awning.

Yesterday marked the close of their second month of Tuesdays after her confession. Over the course of that month, time spent with the Frenchman had opened wide her aperture on life: bicycling old men; children splashing in a puddle; and—as found in her sights at the moment—a few yards out onto the square, not far from the hawking chicken lady, a dog sniffing for morsels inside crevices of the piazza's stone floor.

Every image in front of her seemed worthy of the precious film. While awaiting the priest, paced by the unconscious rhythm of the artist, she shot two rolls.

The third and final roll slid into the camera's open cradle. Practiced fingers locked the leader into the winding mechanism. Coty closed the door and twisted the spindle. Restraint—she must reserve her remaining film for the man who would leave Saigon today. Maybe she would return tomorrow, she thought, as she tightened the spindle. That might take her mind off his journey and unspoken questions about his return.

Laurent cornered the building and ignored the vendor's plea for a sale. Coty raised her camera off the manila envelope, which she had taped shut. Inside, the photographs were protected, insulated by stiff cardboard. Only one had he requested.

Bracing an elbow on the tabletop, Coty steadied the camera. Unlike on that first Tuesday, when they had met here two months earlier, today his gait was labored as he tromped, not glided, across the square. The priest was dressed in black and wore his Roman collar. She focused on the starched white cotton square at its center. The tip of her index finger depressed the shutter button, and his approach was sealed forever.

What seemed a forced smile floated toward her obscured face. With an unfamiliar rigidity to his long-legged stride, the man she now knew so well appeared agitated.

Twice more the shutter clicked; then the camera dropped away, exposing her face. With an embroidered handkerchief, Coty wiped a line of sweat from her cheekbone, before patting the cotton against a tear forming in her viewing eye.

Laurent leaned over as if he intended to plant a kiss on her cheek. His hand went to his throat, and he drew back.

"You were wise to wear the collar, *monsieur*," she said, rallying her New York sarcasm to pierce their shared anxiety. Days before, Coty had warned of the dangers for a tall European man heading north. Albeit a common disguise, appearance as a cleric improved the odds for safe passage. The cloth was not armor, but it might discourage confrontation. If suspicious authorities were to hassle him, the garb would match his credentials. Despite their time together, Laurent remained a priest to the rest of the world.

He stood stiff, waiting for some signal to sit. Coty accommodated with a nod while moving the camera and manila envelope to open the table to him. After the leather satchel came off his shoulder, he dropped it onto the tabletop and, scraping metal against stone, pulled out the wrought-iron chair. Side by side they sat, glancing about the piazza, avoiding each other's moist eyes.

Coty's shoulders rose and fell as she anguished over how to break the lull. She stared at him. When Laurent turned, her eyes started to well. Fighting the flush of tears, she picked at a corner of the manila envelope.

"*Merci*. Thank you for bringing the photograph, Coty."

The envelope slid across the table. "*Oui*, as promised. It might help you find her if the convent has been closed."

One of her hands rested on the housing of the idle camera, while with a trained eye she scanned her subject, who sat fidgeting. He slid his forefinger inside the starched collar and tugged. Then he looked away. People rushed by, offering convenient distraction to the priest, who combed the crowd.

Coty took his hands in hers. She rubbed the pads of her thumbs across his knuckles and asked, "What are you thinking, Laurent?"

"I hid behind my vows until you chased me into my confessional. Now, I'm confused. About her . . . and about you." He pulled his hands away to raise and fold them behind his head. He leaned back in the chair. Within the hour, his ship would depart to the North.

"You would've wondered for the rest of your life, Laurent. In a matter of days, you'll know."

Squirming in the chair, he blushed and tugged on his collar again. Then he reached to take her hands, which had returned to clutching the camera. They looked at each other without speaking. She tried to gauge him, wondering if he knew he had not been manipulated; he had been loved.

Standing, he grasped the strap of his satchel and, with a sharp tug, returned it to his shoulder. He took a deep breath and eked out, "*Merci beaucoup*, Mademoiselle Fine."

The screech of her chair ripped their moment when she, too, stood. With the heel of his hand, he mashed a tear into the flesh of his cheek.

The man—not the priest—touched his throat, claiming the Roman collar as earned disguise. Not a spy, but neither was Laurent the unfettered man of God that his garb presented. A convenient prop for his journey north, the collar might soon be discarded in the wake of vows no longer held nor holding.

Reaching back to the tabletop, Coty shifted her camera and took up the manila envelope. "Open it after you set sail, Laurent. The photograph of Sister Lan might help you find her. The others might help you find yourself."

Laurent took the envelope. He leaned forward, bowed, and reached for her hand. He did not raise his eyes; rather, he shut them. The kiss on her hand radiated through her body as she stared down at his bald spot. The round patch of tanned skin reminded her of their journey, his futile attempts with a kerchief to cloak himself, and the paddy hat she had offered as a truce.

He pledged, "I'll telegraph you from Hanoi."

"*Merci*," she said, as she started to cry again. After patting the corners of her eyes with her damp handkerchief, Coty raised her arm to find the dial on her wrist. "The freighter won't wait, *monsieur*."

Before slipping his fingertip inside the stiff collar, he wiped away another tear. With a tug, he swallowed, then let his hand fall leaden to his side.

"*Adieu*, Coty."

The resting nausea stirred when she picked up her camera to

snap his departure. Given her experience over the past week, Coty knew her upset stomach would not abate by noon. While she lived in France, a pregnant friend, who experienced "morning sickness" that lasted the day, had dubbed the term a cruel misnomer.

The shutter clicked. The camera and her troubles were too heavy. She found her chair, set the box on the table, and watched through a blur not caused by mirage. Past a hanger lined with naked fowl, Laurent disappeared around the corner.

CHAPTER SEVEN

———·———

Each day last week, she had visited Western Union without collecting the telegram that Laurent had promised. Yesterday, when she arrived home, wedged into the crack of her front door had been a notice indicating that a package was at the post for pickup.

From the opposite side of the street, she studied the empty window above the entrance to the Western Union building. The linen curtain hung lifeless in the still, moist air. Coty walked onward without crossing the street to check for his wire.

Inside the post office, her pulse raced as she slid the ticket across the counter. Carried between the hands of the clerk, returning from the storage room in back, was a square box cloaked in brown paper, with string encircling all sides. She wondered what Laurent might have sent and why he had gone to such lengths, rather than transmitting a telegram. Had he shipped some token of appreciation for her encouragement to find the nun? Had looking into Sister Lan's eyes sealed his fate and Coty's, too? What could it be? The box was too small for a paddy hat, which was the first possibility that pricked her imagination.

Swirling her signature, she signed for the package without inspecting its labels. She kept her chin up, thinking of Laurent as she exited.

With no blade to cut the twine, she refused to stop outside the post to attempt to tear it open. She would get back to the cottage and deal with the contents in private. Its heft was light; only her worries would weigh her down on the way home. As she walked, Coty plucked the hemp cords with her thumbs.

Steamed rice might calm her stomach. The package stared at her from the table as she stood at the stove. What would he have sent had he known of her pregnancy? Would he have left Saigon if, at the bistro, she had told him her suspicion?

Water boiled, and the grains of rice rumbled in the pot, which she covered before lowering the burner to a simmer. Maybe, through some psychic extension of sisterhood, the nun knew Laurent was to be a father in more than title bestowed by the church. Had Sister Lan led her priest to the market and selected an item for Coty's baby? Might the victor have insisted that her lover author a thoughtful letter, rather than sending a cryptic telegram? Had Lan suggested he place a handwritten note on top of the wrapped present—not a bribe but a peace offering? *Send your other lover an explanation of why you cannot return. Send her closure.*

Minutes passed without her opening the package. She grabbed chopsticks on her way to the stove. The rice was plump and sticky. She scooped steaming relief into a bowl and leaned against the sink.

The wrapper won't tear itself from the package, she thought, as she took a second mouthful of rice. With a sigh, she walked her bowl to the table.

A month prior, a shipment from New York would have caused her mood to soar. The US postmark corroborated the name on the return label: Sheldon Fine. Zaydeh's intuition was what she should have trusted, not some mystic—a woman she had not met, a woman who loved the same man as she.

Coty recalled the last gift from her grandfather—one she had received while living in France. After she had noted their rarity in a letter to Zaydeh, he had sent several pairs of stockings to Paris. Not more nylons, she assumed, wondering why anyone would wear them in Vietnam. She lifted it off the table and shook the wrapped package side to side. The contents shifted, slamming against interior walls of cardboard and knocking on the heels of her hands.

Maybe he had loaded it with some deli treat that would not decompose in transit: her favorite rock candy, or perhaps a beef salami. Racing through the alternatives caused her stomach to churn anew. She brought another clump of rice to her mouth.

Setting the chopsticks across the rim, she pushed the bowl away. After she had pulled the present to her, she closed her eyes and let her brow fall against the wrapper, crinkling it.

Her head rose. She resolved to go again to Western Union in the morning. Laurent had said he would send word. Staring over the package in her hands, she smiled, thinking how he might enjoy that his faithless friend had become a believer; she trusted him to send the telegram.

A blade snapped the twine. She tore at the paper. When the box revealed its contents, she said to the room, "Oh, Zaydeh, if only this could bring him back."

As Coty held up the item for inspection, light from the window glittered on the glass in her hand. The cylinder sparkled at her. With the gentleness of a mother-to-be, she placed the fragile chamber back inside its cardboard cradle.

The sheet of paper she held was not a message from Zaydeh, nor could she decipher it through teary eyes, except for one word written in capital letters at the top of the page: "CONGRATULATIONS!"

After wiping her eyes, she read the instructions for assembly and then a recipe for filling the enclosed hummingbird feeder.

It was Saturday; a week had passed since Zaydeh's gift had arrived. Coty had collected one territorial hummingbird, but no telegrams. Empty-handed, she left the Western Union office and retraced her steps through the city to the Catholic church where, months earlier, she had hunted down her former traveling companion.

Today, she sat in a pew on the periphery for the sacrament of reconciliation. There she would sit until the confessor closed shop. Father Buchon, Laurent's friend from Hanoi and confidant in Saigon, had refused to receive her at the rectory. She dismissed the temptation to invade another confessional. Instead, she resolved to block the priest's exit and demand an audience.

Coty contemplated the trudging parishioners as they rose to advance pews, and wondered how many were repeat offenders, sinners who took the sacrament each week, incorrigibles without hope of cure. She planned to approach the priest after he left his confessional, when the last of the petitioners would be kneeling in bliss, heads bowed, praying penance before one of the icons scattered about the church.

The final sinner pulled the curtain open and scurried in the direction of the altar, selecting an empty pew to kneel again, this time to drone the prayers assigned by Father Buchon. Metallic chair feet scraped the stone floor, and the priest's wooden door shut in a whisper. She heard tinny rattles as he searched for the key.

Father Buchon bristled as Coty rose to address him. He must have recognized her from their past encounter at the harbor. As then, the short Frenchman seemed intimidated by her stature. "*Mademoiselle, s'il vous plait.* How may I help you?"

He feigned surprise, as if he were oblivious to having met her on the wharf, much less to her recent visits to the rectory. Assuming his cowardice would persist, she decided not to poke at him about his rebuff and instead committed to enticing the man's assistance. He seemed more sheep than shepherd—a stern look alone might prompt him to run to the vestibule, gripping the hem of his cassock.

"*Bonjour*, Père Buchon. We met months ago, at the harbor. *Je suis* Coty Fine, a friend of Père Sabatier."

"Ah, *oui, oui* . . . Mademoiselle Fine. The ship from Haiphong."

"Père, have you heard from him?"

Buchon recoiled, as if he were hiding Laurent in the rectory's attic. He averted his gaze in the direction of the altar and, through slits in his cassock, sent his hands into what she assumed were the pockets of his trousers.

"*Pardonnez-moi*, Père Buchon. I'm worried for his safety. Père Sabatier told me he would send a wire when he arrived . . . in Paris."

"Ah, *oui* . . . Paris." The priest held his focus forward. In a niche behind the altar, the door of a carved wooden tabernacle hung open.

Coty followed his eyes to a copper ciborium. "Have you received word from him?"

"*Non, mademoiselle*, no word . . . yet."

"When did you talk to him last?"

"Before he left to board the ship, Mademoiselle Fine."

"On his way to the bistro?" The cleric shifted his line of sight from the altar to the safety of the vestibule. Coty thought he was about to bend over for the edge of his cassock. "What did you mean by 'ship'? The airplane to Paris?"

Father Buchon brought his hand to his throat and slipped an index finger inside his collar. It must be a nervous habit of priests everywhere, she thought. Over the past week, she had taken a single picture: a shot of one of her hummingbirds, the one who needed wings to fly away. It was time to track the other, who left a trail at the water's edge.

"Accompany me to the harbor, Père Buchon. *Merci beaucoup*."

———◆◆——

The taxi driver grunted his acknowledgment of the destination and tapped the turn signal. Coty shifted her attention to the man next to her in the back of the cab. The priest whom she had conscripted shrank into the cracked upholstery of the bench seat, with the look of a man who had overheard words of deception—a temptation—not the straightforward, unadorned imperative she had voiced in rudimentary Vietnamese: her address. With raised eyebrows, she inquired about his consternation.

"Mademoiselle Fine, I thought we were going to the harbor . . . *non*?"

"*Oui*, Père. I must retrieve some things from my home." His bewildered expression twisted into one of fear. Reading his mind, while wondering how much detail Laurent had confessed, she tossed a lifeline to the cleric. "A couple of photographs. Will you wait with the taxi, so he doesn't leave us?"

"Of course, *mademoiselle*," Father Buchon said, collapsing in palpable relief.

When she stepped onto the back porch, the drying line held no moist images. The captures of Laurent en route with her from Hanoi were gone, replaced by shots of the man in his civvies, taken during their second month of Tuesdays. She sighed as she drew back the blackout curtain and entered the main room of the cottage.

A stack of prints waited on the table. At the top of the pile rested one with a slight bend in the upper right corner of its border. Coty fingered past the photograph of Sister Lan. Digging through the stack, she found the first of two images she sought.

In hopes of triggering recollections among strangers harborside, she selected a photograph of Laurent in his Roman collar. His mien was somber. Rifling her way to the bottom of the stack, she plucked the sole shot she had of their tired freighter. She opened a fresh manila envelope, slipped the photos inside, and slid the envelope into her canvas tote.

A new housemate, a glimmering gecko smaller than any she remembered in residence, raced across the floor. It froze at the feet of the bookshelf. Was it a baby? Male? Female? What did it matter? She resolved to treat it with the same respect as those slippery homesteaders who had occupied the cottage before she arrived. As her fingers found the blackout curtain, she looked down at the youngster and said, "*Au revoir*, Elliot."

Alongside the taxi, Father Buchon stood poised to bolt. Coty paid the cabbie and turned to the anxious priest.

"Père Buchon, we should try the pilothouse. Over there."

With an open hand, he motioned for her to proceed—less a gentleman than an acolyte resigned to follow her lead.

The clerk must have noticed her towering above the others who stood in line ahead of them, she thought. Coty and the French priest approached the counter. The administrator drew his glasses down his nose. As he gawked at her, she assumed that he, too, had become lost in the contradiction of a youthful face adorned by white curls.

"*Monsieur, parlez-vous français?* Do you speak French?"

His eyes shot to the priest. Buchon looked down, exposing the authority in their duo. The clerk turned back to Coty and said, "*Oui, un petit peu*—a little bit."

Coty explained their mission to discover the fate of a friend who had sailed to Haiphong. The photograph of a stone-faced Sabatier slid across the countertop to the clerk. After taking in the image, he murmured recognition and said, "*Oui. Très grand*—very tall—*non?*"

"*Oui, monsieur, très grand.*"

"I remember him pacing about the dock. He seemed reluctant to embark."

"*Merci beaucoup, monsieur.* The vessel?"

"*Mademoiselle* . . . so many ships."

The clerk implied, by shuffling a stack of papers, that finding one name among myriad manifests was impossible. He shrugged, turned, and—intimating that he could not assist them further—drew his hand through the air to display the binders that lined the credenza behind him. The man held his back to them, as if he were content to wait for the foreigners to slink away in disappointment before he faced the next person in line.

Coty slipped her hand inside the manila envelope. She extracted the second photograph and slapped it on the countertop, drawing the clerk's attention. "*Monsieur, s'il vous plait.* Do you recognize the ship?"

The man, who had flitted about his tight domain, halted above the image. "Impossible. Not a passenger ship." Fixated on the photograph, the clerk shook his head side to side and clicked concern with rapid pops of his tongue. Without taking his eyes off the image of the vessel, he asked Coty, "Why this ship, *mademoiselle*?"

"Three months ago, the tall priest and I sailed from Haiphong on that freighter. He said he had booked passage on the same ship—its regular return voyage."

"What day did he sail?"

"Wednesday, two weeks ago."

The clerk turned again to his credenza and consulted the row of frayed binders. He selected one, whirled around, and plunked it down onto the countertop with a *whomp*. The volume cracked open. Pages fanned the air until he arrived at his destination, which Coty assumed held entries from the Wednesday on which Laurent had sailed. The fingers of his anchored hands tapped on the counter as he studied the list. "What was the man's name?"

"Sabatier. Laurent Sabatier."

With a fingertip nailed to the page, he spun the binder on the countertop and pointed to an entry. Under the ship's title,

Laurent's printed name and scribbled signature were displayed on the final row in the registry. "*Oui, mademoiselle*, your friend was on the vessel. *Je suis désolé.*"

"You found him! Why apologize?"

Without glancing up, shaking his head side to side, the clerk mumbled at the page.

Coty pressed him to speak up. "*Pardonnez-moi, monsieur.* What did you say?"

"*Je suis désolé, mademoiselle.* The ship sank. There weren't supposed to be any mines in Haiphong harbor. No survivors."

PART TWO

CHAPTER EIGHT

—•—

Lagos 1990

The other gravely ill children for whom cardiac surgeries had been scheduled would wait in their beds until after the emergency operation. The surgical team was well rested except for the two members who had traveled overnight with the fragile child.

Dr. Odette Walsh sipped hot tea, summoning its caffeine to battle her exhaustion. As her crew prepped the patient she and her lead surgical nurse had escorted from Gabon, she telephoned her husband, Brady, back home in San Francisco—their only contact in more than four days. She had been in Africa for three weeks, volunteering for the first time with Médecins Sans Frontières, the international humanitarian organization known in the States as Doctors Without Borders.

Since they had completed their internships, the married surgeons' habit, whether away or at home, was to each recount their most difficult procedure of the day. Jette, as her family called her, listened to her husband's tired voice crackle over the transatlantic line.

"His wife knew it was a long shot, too, but their kids wanted to give it a try," Brady said.

Eyes closed, thumb and forefinger squeezing the isthmus between her sockets, Jette yawned. She drank the tea as he told of his patient, a man in his late forties who, while being poked and prodded in pre-op, had shrugged at Brady when the neurosurgeon let slip staid words of encouragement that neither believed.

"I need some solid rest, Jette," Brady said. "No surgeries in the morning—maybe I can sleep in."

"Mother'll get Evelyn when she wakes up." She knew that her mother or Magdalena, the nanny who had helped raise Jette and her twin sister, Noémie, would be leaning over Evelyn's crib before Brady heard the toddler's voice. "Did you tell her to let you sleep?"

"The surgery went way over. I didn't call Coty when I came out. It's past midnight—too late now."

"Well, leave a note on our door. You'll probably sleep through Evelyn's morning call to action anyway."

"Not sure about that, Jette. It's like reveille around here. What a set of lungs on that kid. After I get a little sleep, I'll spend some time with Evelyn before my afternoon rounds."

He rambled on about taking their "little bug" to the playground—and maybe, later, an ice cream to placate the active toddler. Jette suspected that the treat might also soothe a failed, albeit guiltless, neurosurgeon. Worried by his babbling, she said, "Be careful, Brady—you're tired. I wish you'd take a taxi."

Scalpels and trailing instruments were arrayed in the metal trays as the surgeon preferred. Jette shook herself to stave off fatigue, before exchanging nods with the anesthesiologist at the boy's head. She took up a scalpel, placed her left hand as guide upon his exposed torso, and began the day's initial procedure.

Blood ran as she razored down the orange scrub line. Beneath his dark-brown skin, pink flesh retreated from the incision. Slit open, the boy's chest released puffs of steam, which rose past her mask into the bank of lights above the operating table.

To concentrate, she rolled her shoulders and exhaled with force. The echoes of Brady's drowsy rant intruded again as she fought to keep her mind on the here and now. The best on the West Coast would bounce back tomorrow. He always had.

Jette's three-year-old patient was tall, although she had yet to see him stand. Spreading his rib cage, she found evidence of waning life at her fingertips. As the operation began, the boy's compromised heart pumped blood through his narrow body and bewilderment into her mind. How had he survived the trip to the hospital? How had his heart been beating when they lifted him onto the table? *Focus*, she commanded herself.

Skilled fingers cramped. The operation had lasted an hour longer than she had anticipated. The team shifted in place to alleviate strain upon feet and backs—discomfort rebuked by the priority of the child, slipping away.

Operating rooms were supposed to be cold, but Jette felt a foreign pressure in the theater. The air conditioner's fan seemed far too weak to explain the encroaching breeze—a cool gush that tightened as it wrapped its way up her body. She stiffened. The frigid constriction felt akin to a recurring omen. When certain patients had passed at her hands, she had sensed an outbound escape brushing her, as if the child's soul were sailing up from the table.

Relief permeated the operating room as the sides of the child's chest were drawn together. Stepping back, Jette hovered over the shoulder of the closer, an intern made nervous by her presence.

"Slower, as we did with the ventricle sutures," Jette coached as he sewed. "Everything about this little one is delicate."

The anesthesiologist held his attention on the patient's vital signs as the intern found a natural cadence with the needle. When he neared the end of his stitching, the novice looked up to collect her approval. She smiled behind her mask as she nodded at him.

The worn-out team settled into their final push, readying

the boy for transfer to Intensive Care. The odd, sourceless chill returned, intercepting Jette as she drifted away from the edge of the table. Worried that she would faint, she stepped back to brace herself against the wall and looked for one of the wheeled stools set about the room.

Arms crossed, rubbing hands on sleeves to warm herself, she marveled that none of her crew appeared bothered by the cold airstream's intrusion. Rather than dissipating at her touch, the sensation intensified like a beast challenged. The iciness snaked up and down her body as if teasing with mere threats of its full strength.

Distanced from her patient, she rested on the roller stool and watched the team. Unable to stand, she called out, "Is he okay?"

Without looking in her direction, the anesthesiologist responded with assurance, "All signs are stable, Dr. Walsh. Remarkable—he's ready to head to the ICU."

Accepting a plastic bottle of water from the lead surgical nurse, Jette nodded. She would obey the implicit instruction to sit there and drink until she was rehydrated. As the crew exited the operating room with the boy, the draft from their departure seemed to coax the cold beast, which, in a slither, chased the rolling gurney out into the hallway.

The doors folded back, leaving her alone, sitting, staring, rubbing the arm that held the water bottle. She sipped. She couldn't wait to get back to San Francisco, hug her baby girl, and, in spite of their difficulties of late, maybe snuggle with Brady until they fell asleep in front of the television.

The operating room was dark except for the glow of instrument panels and, over the metal table, a bright funnel that shone like a beam from heaven, waiting for one less fortunate than the rescued boy. The last of the bottle reached her lips as she stared at the cone of light, thinking, *Not today. Not this little bug.*

In a start, she turned to the closed double doors. The chill slunk back inside along the floor and encircled her legs. The draft wound up her body in a swirl. When she felt a cold threat on the bare skin of her throat, Jette dropped the empty water bottle, which pinged against the tile floor and then rolled to a stop beneath the operating table.

An overpowering maternal alarm lifted her to her feet. She stood teetering. Hugging herself, eyes closed, she longed to feel the frame of her vulnerable daughter. Something at home was wrong. She reopened her eyes and strained. On wobbly legs, she left the chair behind and stumbled toward the double doors. A phone. Wake Brady. Or Mother. Or Magdalena. Something was wrong.

Flung open by the shove of a frantic mother, the double doors winged apart. Under the lintel, she fell to her knees, face in hands. *Lost. Lost forever.* The double doors swung back, smacking her shoulders.

The absence was palpable. Somehow she knew that her baby was safe, yet she felt torn asunder at her core. Then, as if startled by a thunderclap, she knew who had been taken. The *always* of a twin had been reneged. Noémie was gone, not Evelyn. Jette's soulmate, Coty's "wild child," had left the womb before her sister and, now, abandoned her to life.

A phone, she thought. *Reach Brady; call Mother. Mother'll have the words.* None she desired, but words of truth nevertheless.

CHAPTER NINE

San Francisco

The yellow blink from the lighthouse lamp tapped the wall near Coty's head as she lay staring at her bedroom ceiling. The foghorn's drone rolled into her room with the light, conjoined sentries of separate talents, together warning those who, hampered by the fog, sailed near the shores of the San Francisco Bay.

When it came to sleep, Coty felt lucky. Whether she was at home or away, slumber arrived soon after her shuttering eyelids settled. She often told her twin daughters that if she could fall asleep on a rattling flatbed in the backcountry of Vietnam, she could doze at will in the comfort of her own home. Tonight, she tossed in bed for more than an hour, before rising to stretch out her body in hopes that might relax her mind as much as her muscles, which were tight from the current stress of her family in flux.

Returning to bed, she rolled onto her side, shut her eyes, and, with a two-handed tuck, brought her pillow under her ear. The horn's mantra, a throaty *om*, coaxed her to look outside through the French doors and beyond the railing of her balcony. A spray of light speckled the hills of Marin. The glitter from seaside homes set above the village centers of Sausalito and Tiburon, suggested to Coty that others, too, had yet to slumber.

Why the sudden worry? Jette was in Nigeria for her final week of the monthlong stint. Given the time, she might already have called Brady to check on him and Evelyn, Coty's sole grandchild. Jette's fears would be assuaged when Brady reported how Evelyn was enjoying the extra attention from Aunt Noémie, who had graced San Francisco unannounced, as usual, for a rare visit.

Coty's eyes registered the beam, causing her head to tilt. When the fog light turned, she settled back to center, creasing a valley into the middle of the pillow. She blinked twice and looked up. No answers dropped from the ceiling. She slowed her breathing, but the protracted cycle did not soothe her agitation.

I must learn to meditate, she mused, unable to blame her petering menopause. Having exited the daily cycle of intense hot flashes, she found that its hormonal grip had grown weak, the remnants generating less heat than the warmth of fresh toast.

This is ridiculous, she scolded herself. Legs that demanded a king mattress slipped from underneath the sheets, and her feet found the floor. She would check the baby before brewing a cup of herbal tea. The parlor's somnolence awaited.

The telltale snoring brought reassurance as Coty walked by the adjacent bedroom: Magdalena's. The woman, sixteen years her junior, had Coty's gift for sleep, and the noisy proof seeped into the hallway. Stopping next at Noémie's door, Coty's bare feet ground divots into the carpet's pile as she leaned sideways to listen. Silence.

Half suspecting a coarse scolding, Coty teased the door open. Stiff vertical arms rose through the shadows—Noémie's unoccupied poster bed. Magdalena had swaddled the mattress in the morning with fresh linens and a plumped-up duvet. Noémie had not so much as sat on the edge of the bed since her childhood nanny exited.

Where's my wild child? Coty wondered, as she closed the door.

Years earlier, after severing ties with formal education, Noémie had slung her camera over her shoulder to begin an endless cycle of adventure and homecoming. *Better when I don't know if she's home or not, wherever home might be at the moment for my sweet vagabond.*

The bedroom, shared by Jette and Brady, Coty passed without stopping to check for inhabitants. Her daughter in Nigeria and Brady at the hospital, he had called to ask if Noémie was around to feed Evelyn and put her to bed. Coty told him she had not seen Noémie since the morning but that two experienced women stood at the ready to fill in for him tonight. She laughed at the implication of freeing Daddy from his least favorite duty when Brady asked if those two skilled caregivers might consider pulling up tomorrow's scheduled bath night by twenty-four hours.

Coty imagined that she could feel the heartbeat of budding life pulsing into her fingers as she held the nursery's doorknob. The door swung inward, and she stepped into the glimmer emanating from a terror-blocking night light. The dwarf bulb, ample for the space and task, illuminated the playful wallpaper, the crib, and the long-bodied sleeping beauty. A fish tank, the size of two stacked shoeboxes, supplemented the peaceful ambience with anemic rays and a bubbling pump.

Cooing as she hovered over the crib, Coty brushed a curl off Evelyn's brow. The baby spun, reassured herself that the stuffed rabbit remained nestled at its post, reached for the warmth of her comforter, and pulled it to her torso with an inward twist. Knees snuggled to her chest as she compacted her fetal pose. A wet thumb returned to her mouth. Moist slurps formed a duet with her grandmother's coos.

The door to Evelyn's room kissed the jamb and sealed the child in her safety. Coty stepped along the runner that descended the staircase and terminated where the carpet's edge met the hardwood floor of the parlor.

The grandfather clock, a decades-old housewarming gift from Zaydeh, promised serenity for those afflicted with insomnolence: *ticktock, ticktock* . . . She pressed past the dining-room table and entered the kitchen through the double swinging doors. She turned on the under-cabinet light fixture and walked through the faint glow to the stove, where she reached for the teakettle.

The steaming teacup clinked on the saucer in her hands as Coty reentered the parlor. She walked about in the dark, hoping the interlude would quiet, not exacerbate, her sleeplessness.

Whomp! When her hip bumped the corner of an antique side table, a picture frame slapped the surface like a gavel deployed in anger. The interruption quickened her pulse. She twisted the light switch as the room recaptured its calm.

Ticktock, ticktock . . .

In one hand, she picked up the wooden frame. She stroked the glass as if she might feel the moist skin that gleamed on Laurent's face the moment she had taken the photograph. Four grandparents. One Evelyn would never meet: the grandfather who had never held her; the father who had never held her mother or her mother's twin.

When she righted the frame, a possible culprit for tonight's sleeplessness hit Coty: Janice Walsh, Evelyn's paternal grandmother, whose views on family values and "traditional" roles had calcified years before she married Robert Walsh. Janice found her son's living arrangement heretical; two practicing surgeons should own their own home, not reside with a parent, she had posited to any available ear.

Soon after starting their internships at the University of California, San Francisco Medical Center, Brady and Jette had wed. At the northern tip of the peninsula, atop a hilly street in Pacific Heights, Coty's was the only home the married couple had

known. Jette had confided that they were content to remain in
her childhood home, a predilection that Coty embraced as good
fortune. The family of three could stay with her as long as they
wished, which would, of course, be only as long as the marriage
lasted. Of late, it had seemed a union not destined to see Evelyn
enter preschool.

The empty teacup had grown cold. Thirty minutes had passed in
the parlor. With much to do before Jette's return next week, Coty
started a mental list—an exercise that might help her disgorge
subconscious sources of her angst. Blaming Janice Walsh had not
proven efficacious, nor would scapegoating the woman's son.

After Jette left for Africa, Brady had not fulfilled his commitment to extra "daddy time" during her absence. Tonight was
the third night this week he had not been home to tuck Evelyn
into bed. Brady was not the most attentive husband, but his wife
had not been naive; Jette had not expected the man to change.
Coty wondered why she herself still did.

She set down her cup and saucer and rose to address the
piano's open keyboard cover. Whenever Noémie came home,
she regaled them with music from Mozart to Monk and solicited
Coty as mentor in the basement darkroom. They had long
planned a mother-daughter publication of photographs. In
spite of Coty's cajoling her to collaborate on the project, during
each home visit, the book fell below the immediate on
Noémie's list of priorities. After her daughter had littered the
drying line with exposures and escaped to her next adventure,
Coty would clear the string of dried prints and archive each
photograph.

Coty lowered the lid, hoping it would rise again for another
of Noémie's impromptu performances before the day was out.
Sighing, she ran her hand flat across the lacquered top.

The foghorn's lament coaxed her to the parlor floor. She

stretched herself atop the Persian carpet, toes pointing toward the foyer and hands in the opposite direction. As her fingers tickled Steinway's foot, her back muscles unwound and she willed her legs to soften. Letting go of the piano, she let her body sink into the carpet's pile.

The parlor rug proved no more conducive to slumber than had her mattress. Coty yawned as she walked up the stairs and down the hallway to her bedroom. She slid back under the covers and rolled away from the twinkling lights on the bay.

Within minutes, Coty surrendered to the pointless rumination and opened her eyes. The fog light tapped the wall in a steady rhythm. A trick of the mind, an optical illusion—the room seemed to undulate.

Coty was punchy. She cringed, thinking of how often she had chastised her friend Madeleine when the groggy woman mentioned her recurring insomnia. *Do your crossword puzzles, dear, till you get drowsy. You really must learn to relax.*

On the next revolution of the lighthouse beam, it stroked a photograph that Coty had taken in France, en route from Saigon, before she returned to New York with a noticeable bulge in the front of her dress. She thought of her grandfather whenever she studied that shot: a street scene with a behatted old man, tall and thin like Zaydeh, standing in a threadbare trench coat, leaning on a cane, staring at the carcass of a bombed-out church.

Had Zaydeh endured such sleepless nights? How would he have reacted to Coty's last phone conversation with Jette from Nigeria? Her daughter had voiced her conclusion with a clarity that belied the crackling transatlantic line: "I've heard my calling, Mother. This is what I'm meant to do. At least a couple trips a year—maybe three or four. Brady and I'll work it out. Might help save our marriage."

As she recounted Jette's words, the gerund "calling" sent

chills through Coty's body. It seemed a haunt gifted by a French ghost—the same word Jette's father had used in Vietnam. She tugged the duvet to a stop beneath her chin.

Hours earlier, Jette must have risen from her cot at Holy Name Hospital. She might have already finished her first surgery of the day. Since sleep remained elusive, Coty decided to try to reach her daughter. Maybe she could catch her in between addressing broken hearts. They had not talked in days. Jette's voice might prove to be the sedative Coty needed.

Twisting upright to sit on the edge of her bed yet again, she reached for the phone on the writing desk. As if the handset leaked electricity, her fingers snapped back when the device's peal shattered the quiet. Coty swept the receiver up to her ear. Despite crinkles on the line, the panic in Jette's voice was clear.

"Mother, what happened to Noémie? And where the hell's Brady?"

CHAPTER TEN

—•—

Ticktock, ticktock . . .

Coty turned on the front-porch lights, before returning to the parlor. The beveled glass of the side windows and the overhead transom let in sparkles reminiscent of the pinpoints across the bay. She had mulled over the twinkling in the distance as her frantic daughter, over a crackling phone line, fought to explain how her fears were not apprehension, not premonition, but rather an inexplicable sensation of finality, the destruction palpable to Jette when she called from an operating theater a world away from San Francisco.

Ticktock, ticktock . . .

Spilling down the staircase, the light from the landing's table lamp sloshed onto the Persian carpet. Coty could not make out the images in the picture frames scattered about the parlor. Brady was not home. Noémie had not called. The San Francisco Police Department had tried to calm her: "Nothing reported— yet. Happens all the time. Usually, they just come home."

Ticktock, ticktock . . .

The highway patrol car's light bar sent a shimmering invasion through the windows. In a start, she rose to reach the foyer before the doorbell rang and woke the baby and her nanny.

"Ms. Fine?"

Deep-brown eyes; not forty years old, she guessed. Hat in hand, the officer revealed the spikes of a military-style flattop, while his clean-shaven face gleamed under the porch light. He must have done this before.

"Yes, I'm Coty Fine."

"Officer Frank Rivas, ma'am. There's been a traffic accident in Marin, Ms. Fine. Two fatalities." He waited. Without moving her lips, her eyes tearing, she compelled him to continue. "I'm sorry to report . . . we believe the two victims lived here, at this address. Brady and Odette Walsh."

Impossible. She shook her head side to side when the officer presented her with Brady's California driver's license. "Yes, they live here. Brady's my son-in-law. His wife, my daughter, is out of the country."

Officer Rivas seemed puzzled.

Coty asked, "Do you have the woman's ID?"

"No, ma'am. I found a shoulder bag tossed onto a child's car seat in the back. No wallet, no ID."

"Why do you think Odette was with him?"

"The motel owner. She said they'd been coming there for years."

"Did she see the woman . . . this time?"

"The man checked in, mentioned that his wife was sleeping in the car."

"Can you describe her—the other victim?"

Rivas considered her with a dubious expression, as if she suspected that her son-in-law was a womanizer. Coty willed the officer to describe a short tart with straight, mousy brown hair. Led by the motel owner's assumption, he had jumped to a conclusion. Coty fought not to do the same.

"Did she have short hair?" she asked.

"No, ma'am. Quite long, actually—long, curly white hair."

The description vaporized any hope. "Yes, that's my daughter." Then Coty blurted out an imperative she wanted nothing to do with. "Someone needs to call Brady's family. His parents live in Sacramento."

Rivas stalled and, swiveling his hips, turned to find the street. He twirled the stiff-brimmed hat in his hands and glanced back at his patrol car. When he returned his attention to her, he seemed unable to mask his incredulity. "First, we need to get positive IDs; then you can call them, Ms. Fine."

"I understand. Let me change. I'll be down in a minute."

The former dancer, her balance compromised, clung to the banister as she rose to the next floor. The doorknob turned with her knock, but the snoring roared on when she entered. Magdalena Castro had been with them since the New Yorker had moved to San Francisco as a single mother. Coty sat on the edge of the mattress, rubbed Magdalena's arm until her snoring stopped, hushed away her discombobulation, then told her that Brady was dead and the police believed that Noémie had died with him.

The wide-eyed woman's breath chopped short for a second time when Coty reported that she would follow the officer back to the morgue to identify the bodies. When she asked the devout Mexican to pray, Magdalena's breathing halted once more and she blessed herself.

Inside her bedroom's walk-in closet, Coty dropped her robe to the floor in a heap. As was her practice each day, after she and Magdalena had shared breakfast, she reached for the denim smock that heralded time outside in her gardens, watching the shifting weather over the bay—nature's constant tug-of-war between threat and promise.

Slipping into the garment, she thought of the parlor. Was Officer Rivas sitting in the dark? Had she turned on a lamp? Offered him a glass of water? She could not remember anything after confirming that his description of the victim, Brady's passenger, resembled Noémie, the twin who had not sheared her locks. Coty snatched the hairbrush from her dresser as she passed.

———◆◆◆———

The light bar on Rivas's patrol car flickered out. In the middle of the parking lot, Coty pulled her sedan to a stop next to him. The chain-link gate was sliding to a close in her rearview mirror when the slam of his cruiser's door startled her.

Rivas bowed as he approached the driver's side window. Her door swung open. She accepted his unnecessary hand, climbed out of the driver's seat, and shut the door. Side by side, in one neat row, five automobiles, headlights staring out, watched as they walked by.

Rivas addressed the entry to the building, drew his ID badge, and placed it flat against the electronic reader. The officer pulled the door open, exposing a tiled corridor lit by a series of four-foot rectangular ceiling fixtures, each containing flickering neon tubes. At the end of the hallway, the door to the coroner's office was ajar.

"Dr. Fallsmead, this is Ms. Fine. She's here to ID the victims."

"Ms. Fine," he said, as he rose from his creaking desk chair. "I'm sorry for your loss. I understand that you're willing to identify both. Is that correct?"

"Yes, Doctor." She turned to Rivas. "Thank you, Officer. I'll be okay. You should go home."

"I'm willing to stay, if you prefer."

"You've been very kind. I'm okay."

She followed Fallsmead to the morgue and stalled in the doorway, unable to see beyond the splash of hallway light that bathed the first few tiles of the floor. The tail of the coroner's white lab coat slipped beneath the blackness as he disappeared into the room.

The air was frigid. She rubbed her hands together as she stood blinking into the darkness. When the coroner summoned the ceiling lights, Coty squeezed her eyes shut. She brought a hand to her brow to dampen the glare as she reopened her eyes.

The room came into view: Fallsmead, facing her, hands crossed behind his lab coat, standing with his gaze averted.

Spotless metal cabinets lined two walls. She cast her vision in a circle to locate the sources of the pings that ricocheted off the hard, reflective surfaces. Four prep tables—empty except for the folded sheets placed at the ends where the feet of the next unfortunates would rest—stood in the middle of the room. Drain plates in the floor drew her attention.

The faithless woman spun through another round of false hope before she faced the doctor. Without words, the coroner escorted Coty to a wall of cabinets. The *swoosh* of her garden smock marked her strides in concert with the tapping of the man's shoes against the floor. They stopped at a wall of burnished doors whose handles suggested the necessity of a living grip.

The coroner held his hands behind his lab coat, looked into her eyes, and said, "Are you ready, Ms. Fine?"

"Ready?" she asked. "Please, go ahead."

"The woman first?"

"Yes, please."

Fallsmead reached for his chosen hatch, gripped the handle, and turned it forty-five degrees. The door, rotating on greased hinges, swung out in a hush. Reaching inside, the coroner probed for the horizontal steel bar. His posture straightened. As he yanked on the end of her daughter's gurney, Coty reared back at the resultant *clang*.

The reverberation slowed to a whimper. When the room returned to its stillness, she heard the crush of rollers as he pulled the body from the drawer's lightless cavity. They stood there for a moment, the two of them, in what Coty thought must have been an established routine wherein the coroner allowed a merciful lull to steady a novice identifier of the dead.

"I'm going to open the cover now," Fallsmead said. Shifting his stance, he reached for the victim's masked head. Then the retracting zipper severed their silence.

The coroner reentered the room and said, "Ms. Fine, are you ready?"

"For Brady?"

"Yes, Ms. Fine."

"May I come back to her?"

She glanced at Noémie's hair, which she had brushed over and over, removing every piece of broken glass she could find. A small mound of bloodied honeycomb chips was piled at Noémie's feet, as if the glass bits were too important to discard but not allowed near her girl's face. Coiled strands of white rippled from her crown, over her shoulders, and down past her elbows. Next to her daughter's hip, Coty placed the hairbrush on the gurney, not wanting to set it down on top of her baby's breathless abdomen.

"Yes, of course." Fallsmead hesitated. "Thank you, Ms. Fine; that would help. I could finish the paperwork. Sorry—I don't mean to rush you."

After patting Noémie's cold hand, Coty raised her gaze to find the coroner. "I'm ready," she said.

Fallsmead asked her to shift positions so she would stand on the corpse's right-hand side. She did not challenge him; what did it matter? The cabinet door swung into the room. Another loud *clang*, and then her son-in-law's gurney rolled out under the light. The coroner retracted a second zipper.

What confronted her she had not contemplated on the Golden Gate Bridge as she followed Rivas's light bar, awake and patriotic, casting about its red, white, and blue rays. She now realized why she had been redirected to the opposite side of the gurney. Noémie seemed as if she might blink open her eyes and tell her mother that everything would be okay. But inside the second bag was a dead body.

Brady's head was turned. An ear was missing, his torn temple matted with bloody hair, his cheek dented into a fist-size crater. The collision had met her son-in-law full force. The left side of his skull was caved in from eye socket through mandible. The coroner had turned him to offer a less repugnant viewing angle. The intimated instructions for identification: ignore the earless, eyeless mash and study the man's less compromised right side.

Whenever Coty, as a grandparent, looked at either of her daughters or stared into the framed black-and-white portrait of Laurent Sabatier, she saw Evelyn. As she examined Brady's profile, the resemblance was certain and the future presented itself. She wanted to get back to Noémie.

"Yes, Doctor, that's Brady. Brady Walsh."

The early morning fog sailed in fast from the Pacific as Coty approached the Golden Gate Bridge. Once, when her twins were argumentative teens, the three Fines were driving north across the bridge to meet a family friend for breakfast in Mill Valley. The scene had been eerie with sunlight fighting to pierce the spooky mist. Noémie had commented on the spectral warning as the sweeping fog sideswiped their car. Riding in the back seat, Jette, ever the resident fact checker, rolled down her window and, extending her bare hand toward the sea, had announced, "No ghosts. Just water vapors."

With the tip of her right index finger, Coty depressed a button above the windshield. The moonroof engaged. When its seal broke, a gush of refrigerated ocean air filled the cabin. After the moonroof's glass had retracted, she ordered the car's heater to blast hot air into her flat chest and curl around her legs and feet. Her haphazard French twist exposed her nape while insulating her scalp from all but a few polar pinpricks.

Staring down her unoccupied lane, Coty squeezed the steering wheel and murmured aloud, "Just water vapors." She repeated her mantra—over and over—until the moist air triggered a mother's imagination about her daughter's final moments: the incomprehensibility of fast-approaching headlights, the realization that Brady's halted car had exited the motel's gravel driveway and straddled the asphalt road, a frantic grasp for the steering wheel to take matters into her own hands—all followed by the deafening impact. Into the cold, Coty shrieked aloud at the thought that her broken child had gurgled red over bright white teeth as Noémie spat out blood in a violent attempt to suck in her dying breath.

The operator inside the bridge's toll booth reached out as Coty drove up, dollar bills extended. She blinked her eyes and nodded, unable to muster a smile, knowing full well that each future trip, back and forth across the Golden Gate, would rip at her heart.

She turned into the Presidio to wend her way through the former military housing and the ill-considered plantings of now choked-out cypress and eucalyptus. Nascent morning light mixed with the fog, filtering down through the trees and shifting as the sedan swerved around each bend.

By the time she arrived home, Evelyn would be awake, sitting in her highchair in the kitchen, spoon in hand, further mashing whatever mush lay before her in the food tray. Magdalena's weary face would meet Coty. Together, they would turn to the cheerful, jabbering toddler.

Leaving Magdalena and Evelyn, the frazzled matriarch would trudge upstairs to the privacy of her bedroom. She would sit at her writing desk, elbows pinned to its wooden surface, head drooping, phone receiver at her ear. First, she would reach out to Janice and Robert Walsh. Soon thereafter, she would call her daughter at Holy Name Hospital in Lagos.

Jette's reticence persisted as Coty listened to static fill the vacuum on the line. She had talked to the point of babbling and could not countenance another repetition of the gruesome facts.

"Mother, I need to see Evelyn, and you, and Magdalena."

"We're here for you, darling."

"Do the Desais know?" Jette asked of her and Brady's best friends, fellow doctors at UCSF.

"No, only Father Thom and the Walshes—and Magdalena, of course." Coty pressed her palm over the handset to muffle her own crying. As she heaved, she listened for Jette to react.

"The last thing I want is to go into our room and deal with Brady's void—much less what he did. What Noémie did."

"First things first, dear. Come home. You'll get through it, but it's going to take time."

The sound of electronic crickets flitting over the transatlantic cable accompanied doleful croaks in the voice of her daughter—words that Coty could not decipher. Palm muffling the phone again, she grieved for her two lost children.

"What did Janice say when you called?"

"Robert answered. They're devastated, of course."

An omission of detail; a merciful white lie—Janice had ripped the handset from Robert, insisted that Coty repeat the tragic story of the accident, and demanded a recap of her trip to the morgue. When Janice heard Coty describe the ordeal of identifying Brady's body, his mother wailed for her only child. She harped for several minutes on the premature death of a great man. Not once had Janice Walsh expressed condolences for another woman's dead offspring.

"She's predictable, Mother. You know she'll blame this on me. She didn't want him to marry a doctor. Told him he needed a wife at home, not a colleague."

"She's been the same since you met Brady."

"Janice will never let up. If she has her way, Evelyn will think I was selfish and didn't want to take care of her or her father. Janice will get inside her head. Brady—perfect *Prince Brady*. He'll be remembered as my victim, and I'll live on as his villain."

Again, crickets; Coty waited. She picked up the photograph

that had adorned her writing desk for more than two decades: a black-and-white shot of her girls—age seven—baking cookies with Magdalena. In the photo, Jette focused on depositing the next dollop of dough onto a precise location atop the cookie sheet. Her sister was covered in white powder. Before Coty snapped it, Noémie had raised a snow-coated arm, attempting to wipe her face, removing less flour in the process than she applied. The grieving mother slipped back through time and smiled. Then, a crinkle of harsh words from Nigeria broke her pleasant spell.

"Janice is a total—"

"Odette, please!"

They were seldom short with each other, but during the past several hours, each had absorbed her limit. Coty slowed her breathing. Her hand found the edge of the writing desk. She pulled on the beveled wood and swung her legs out to face the bay. Framed by the French doors, boats moored off Sausalito lolled in calm waters. Somewhere over there, Noémie and Brady were filed away in separate silver cabinets. She was in the queue for the crematorium, while he awaited his parents' arrival from Sacramento.

CHAPTER ELEVEN

———•———

O ne look at Jette when she appeared at the baggage claim, and Coty knew: her daughter was still in shock and, now that she was back in California, disoriented. They stood there, hugged, and wept. When Coty pushed back from their embrace, Jette's eyes were racing.

"Where's Noémie?"

"Jette?" Coty waited for her daughter to catch up with their new reality.

"I mean, where's Evelyn?" Jette scanned the sparse crowd, before turning back to find her mother's eyes. She was only part-way home. "I hoped you'd bring Evelyn to the airport, Mother."

"She's sleeping, dear. It's after midnight."

"Midnight? She should be asleep, then, right?"

"Darling, the flight was delayed; you're exhausted. How many bags did you check?"

"Um, not sure."

"You must've collected them in Houston to get through customs and then rechecked them for this flight. Didn't you?"

Jette glanced at the sole piece of luggage by her side. She seemed baffled. With one hand on the roller bag and the other cupping Jette's elbow, Coty led her grown child to a row of hard-backed seats.

Bang!

The carousel engaged, and Coty jumped. As the fanning

panels began their sideways shift, Coty stared down onto the oval track at worn plates that had rubbed their neighbors for countless revolutions.

One at a time, the bags peaked at the top of the underground ramp, splashed down into the trough, and churned past her shins. Within minutes, all the delivered luggage had been collected.

The spinning conveyor belt stopped, and the track's sliding plates froze. Coty realized that Jette already had her luggage: the roller bag and a canvas backpack. Sitting erect, Jette was pressured forward, away from the seat back—she had not removed her rucksack.

"Are you ready, Mother? Can we go see Evelyn, please?"

"Of course, darling. I think we've got everything."

Coty pulled the roller bag toward the escalator. Jette walked in a trance, with her thumbs inserted between her ribs and the shoulder straps of the backpack. Her low-volume moaning agonized her mother.

"How're you feeling, dear?"

"Tired, Mother. Really tired."

"You need some rest."

"Yes. A long nap when we get home—after I see Evelyn. Tonight, I'll get a good night's sleep. Tomorrow, I'll take her to the park. She likes the park."

"Tomorrow, Jette? Noémie's service is tomorrow. Reception at the house afterward. Do you remember?"

"I must've gotten the days confused. I just want to hold my baby, Mother. I'm not sure I can deal with anything else."

Brady's services were set for the weekend in Sacramento. Whether tomorrow or in a few days, Jette would soon have to face her in-laws.

———•••———

Madeleine reached over the back of the pew, brought her hand to a gentle landing on Coty's shoulder, and said, "Can I get you anything? Water, maybe?"

Coty shifted her hips and turned to find Madeleine. "No, dear. Thanks. Thanks for everything. Sit here with me, please, until everyone arrives."

The two deaths had been announced in separate obituaries. Noémie's was succinct and requested that the wishes of the family be honored: a private service and, in lieu of flowers, donations sent to a favored charity in her name. Brady's obit had to be trimmed before the staff at the newspaper in Sacramento would place it. On Friday, his services would start. The planned events would cover most of the weekend.

When it came time to contact people about today's service, Madeleine, with the aid of Parvani Desai, took the bulk of the load. They placed their calls after splitting up the list Coty provided. Parvani handled Brady and Jette's UCSF colleagues and their casual friends, as well as those who had drifted apart after med school or whatever had brought them together in the first place. Madeleine addressed Coty's contemporaries and Noémie's local friends—those who had stayed in the city after the wanderer left to explore a broader world.

Others who knew Noémie and would want to be informed, want to grieve, had not made the list. Coty wondered about those strangers in the stories Noémie had told whenever she returned from an escapade. How would word get to those people, who, even though Coty had never met them, cared for her girl? How would they discover her passing? Would they believe that the itinerant was out there somewhere, loving them in her present and thinking good thoughts about them? Would they stop themselves in a few years and wonder why the free spirit had never again come their way, as she had promised? Would they speculate about what had happened to the tall, charismatic woman with long, curly white hair who had bonded with them in such a short time? Would they be ambitious enough to try to find her? Or, as Coty suspected, would they leave it all to chance? That was how Noémie had found them in the first place. Coty envied them, Noémie's unreachable strangers.

"Are the in-laws coming?" Madeleine asked.

"I doubt they'll make this service, but Janice indicated they'd come to the reception at the house for a bit, to 'do the right thing,' she said."

Yesterday, Coty had been ambushed by the call from Brady's mother. Janice sounded miffed. She mentioned how inconvenient it would be to drive to San Francisco. She had much to do for her boy's farewell and had met the "other woman" only a few times. After snide remarks about how Coty's two daughters had destroyed her life, she said that she and Robert would put in an appearance at the house. Janice finished the call by stating that she expected her son's widow and child to attend Brady's services, and that, of course, Coty should come, too, if she thought Jette might need her support to "avoid making a scene."

Wishing to switch subjects, Coty fought to stave off resentment of the woman she was bound to by shared progeny for the rest of their lives. "Everyone'll be arriving soon, darling. Thank you again for making those calls."

Coty turned her back to Madeleine, who she knew would take no offense. The two women settled into the moment, silent in their separate pews inside the nonsectarian building—not church, not synagogue, not mosque, but a gathering place for mourners with nowhere else to assemble, grieve, and say goodbye.

Rows of removable wooden pews faced a portable stage bookended by matching three-step aluminum staircases. A stained-glass window, devoid of religious icons, was framed behind and above the raised landing. On the left side of the platform stood an easel with a photograph of Noémie, beaming at her mother, the photographer. Centered in the stage was a rectangular box covered in pink satin. A matte-finished bronze urn stood alone on the pedestal. A posse of vases spouting long-stemmed white roses encircled Noémie's remains.

Coty paused. The light was off. She had photographed countless churches and cathedrals and assumed the builders had given prayerful consideration to the year-round patterns of the sun. The architect of this secular mortuary must have been transactional, an atheist, she guessed. Why labor over angles to encourage divine inspiration when none was expected?

Coty twisted in her seat. Madeleine looked up as her friend spoke.

"They must have crosses and Stars of David in storage, don't you think?"

"Maybe, but why wouldn't they use their own buildings?"

"You're probably right, dear. I guess this must be reserved for the fallen and the faithless, huh?"

"I'm worried about you, Coty."

"I know, darling. I can't imagine what my poor Odette's going through. I have to be strong for her."

"No one expects you to be yourself. I'm amazed you're able to do any of this."

"It's been a bit much. Losing Noémie, losing a child—well, that's more than any mother can handle." Coty watched Madeleine cross her legs and shove her purse away from her hip and spotted the corner of a folded newspaper protruding from the leather bag. She asked, "Crossword puzzle?"

"What else?" Madeleine quipped, with a subdued smile.

"Not the *New York Times*?"

"Yes, from yesterday's paper."

"Yesterday's *Times*? You do the puzzle first thing in the morning with your coffee. Did you do today's?"

"Not yet."

The double doors behind them opened, unleashing sunlight that raced down the carpet to mix with filtered rays descending from above the stage. Voices hushed at the threshold; then Coty heard the rustle of clothing as the guests walked down the center aisle.

She stood to face the trudging mourners and whispered, "Madeleine, will you step out to tell Magdalena, please? She'll bring Jette and the baby."

"Where are they, Coty?"

She pointed to the wall beyond the left side of the raised platform, where two long slits in the wood paneling intersected at ninety degrees. "They're behind that door, waiting with Thomas."

After suffering, for almost two hours, innuendos that sailed about her parlor, Coty shuddered, realizing that she could not summon Noémie's scent. They had brought in from the gardens too many flowers, which filled the air and blocked her memory. Women mourners lent their perfume to the baffling atmosphere, while the rare man donated his cologne or aftershave.

Coty wanted to excuse herself, climb the staircase, and run to Noémie's room, where the scrambled suitcase promised a bouquet reminiscent of her lost child, whose essence would waft up from the abandoned, wrinkled clothing. Instead, with two bodyguards—Magdalena Castro and Dr. Parvani Desai—at her elbows, Coty stared as Janice Walsh continued spewing a diatribe at the three women standing before her in a semicircle.

"You must've known that he'd been trying—really trying—Coty."

Lips sealed, Coty ordered her jaw muscles to relax as she employed an old trick of berated photographers. Rather than look into scowling eyes, she foraged for another focal point on her subject's face. High on the sidewall of Janice's nose bridge, she located the mole that had sprouted years ago. Coty had shot countless portrait sessions. Captivated by the challenge, she considered the light and wondered if she could get one good shot.

"Coty, you drifted off," Janice scolded.

"Forgive me, Janice. Brady tried to do what, exactly?"

"Save the marriage, of course. You had to know it was strained of late."

"Oh, yes . . . I suppose that was apparent. Difficult, I imagine—two doctors with a young child, that is."

"Well, Coty, you had a *different* family life than most of us."

Coty felt Magdalena heating up. "Yes, Janice, it's true that I never married, but with Magdalena as part of our family, my girls and I were never alone."

Batting her eyes and crinkling her nose, Janice appeared dismissive of Magdalena. Just as well, Coty thought, before her assumption was shattered when Janice said, "Well, that could have ended rather abruptly, right?"

On her first visit to the house, years earlier, Janice had recoiled during her introduction to the nanny. Later, she asked for a "word in private" with Coty. At the time, Brady and Jette had been engaged less than a month and announced their intention to move in with Coty after they wed. When Brady had rebuffed his mother's protests, Janice had made her case in private to Coty, glomming on to the threat from the hidden Mexican. Brady had big plans that should not be jeopardized by living with a family that was "harboring an illegal alien."

"Anyway, Coty, despite having had some hired help, you were virtually independent. I doubt Jette ever thought to ask you about being a wife. I tried to interject, but evidently it wasn't my place."

Evelyn chortled from the far end of the parlor, where she squirmed on her mother's lap. Drawn in the direction of the toddler's giggles, Coty traded sympathetic looks with her daughter, before turning back to answer the mother-in-law Jette reviled. "I'm sure she appreciates your support, Janice."

Magdalena turned her wide hips and, muttering in Spanish something about Sacramento, huffed away in the direction of the kitchen. Coty's grasp of the language was sufficient to catch Magdalena's implication: the one thing about Janice Walsh that

Jette appreciated was that she lived in the state's capital, which was a two-hour drive from the Pacific coastline.

"Not from what Brady told *me*, his own mother. He said that Jette had asked him to tell me to 'butt out.' I thought that was rude. I was trying to help her, as a role model. Who else could she turn to for advice on being a mother and a wife?"

Parvani—wife and mother—squeezed Coty's hand. Before the doctor spoke, Coty felt the woman's thumb stroking back and forth across her skin.

"I'm going to check on them. Looks like Jette could use some help," Parvani said, as she released her caress and stepped away.

Jette and Parvani had met on their first day as residents at UCSF. Along with their husbands, Brady and Karun, they soon became a social crew. Four expanded to six when they added two baby girls—Evelyn and Neeta—as wee passengers on their shared voyage.

Parvani approached the wingback chair with her arms spread wide. Evelyn's face glowed, and she reached out to be gathered up by the short, familiar woman with dark hair and deep-brown skin.

The two grandmothers stood alone, face to face, arms hanging straight toward the parlor's carpet, fingers wiggling as if flexed by itchy duelists. One woman towered over the other, who glared up as if wanting to shout that, in their case, altitude offered no advantage.

Robert Walsh had granted his son slender height. Janice, on the other hand, seemed to have been built for battle. Low center of gravity. Thick. Thick at the waist, wrists, ankles, and neck. Not fat, thick. Hands as strong as those of a milkmaid who could manage a lactating herd on her own—as dense a musculature in a woman as Coty had ever witnessed, much less photographed.

Unsettled by her opponent's glower, again, Coty glanced around the room. At each stop, eyes met hers and then looked away. Some people might have averted their gazes out of respect because such a moment between grieving mothers seemed welcome, even necessary, while others—those who knew of the women's mutual animus—seemed to have read Coty's mind.

Evelyn's grandmothers watched as Parvani slid the fidgeting toddler back onto her friend's lap. After leaning over to kiss Evelyn, she took the empty glass from the side table, tapped its outside wall below the brim, and said something to Jette. She smiled and turned to walk to the kitchen.

"Look at them, Coty. Evelyn keeps calling 'Mommy,' but Jette just hugs her and stares out into space."

"It's a difficult time for all of us, Janice. You lost your son, I lost my daughter, and Jette lost them both."

Janice shifted her feet. Coty looked down at the woman's black pumps, grinding into the pile of the Persian carpet. She wondered if her nemesis had grown uncomfortable, standing in one spot for too long, or if she was rebalancing herself, readying for another charge.

"Coty, I'm sorry to tell you this, but Robert and I aren't supportive of our granddaughter's current situation."

Built for battle, Coty recalled.

Janice shifted her weight again. "Jette is hardly the right role model for Evelyn."

"She's the girl's mother—what are you talking about?"

"Brady was going to leave Jette. There, I said it!"

"Janice, this isn't the place."

"Coty, Robert and I must follow Brady's wishes—what our son intended for his little girl."

Identical while different—a fact that she had celebrated and nurtured since, as toddlers, her daughters had first deviated from each other, much to her delight. Now, her wild child was dead and that girl's overachieving, hyper-responsible sister was being indicted as an inadequate mother. Remembering Janice's not-so-veiled threat to expose Magdalena, Coty swallowed the bile that Evelyn's "other grandmother" raised in her.

"Coty, Jette's unfit. We're going to petition for custody."

———————

"It's a beautiful letter, dear," Coty said.

In it, Jette defended Brady and her sister and asked for everyone's support and understanding. She closed with her decision to resign from UCSF and requested the good wishes of her colleagues as she took her child and moved forward with their lives.

Coty continued, "Darling, I'm sorry to tell you this, but I don't think you should resign just yet."

"What? Why, Mother? It's been two weeks since Brady's funeral. I must resign or go back to the hospital. You know I can't go in there."

Coty reached out to touch her daughter's forearm. "Janice has made me very nervous."

"Me, too. She has that effect on lots of people."

"She intimated that Magdalena could be deported with a phone call."

"Mother, she wouldn't!"

"It's not where she wants her victory, but Janice isn't playing around. I wouldn't put anything past that woman—anything that she thinks will help achieve her goals."

"What goals?"

"I called an attorney. A woman in New York."

"Why?"

"We need to protect ourselves."

"What did you tell the lawyer?"

"Everything. She said the conversation was confidential—attorney-client privilege. Do you understand?"

"Yes, but why on earth—"

"She recommended that you not move ahead with your sabbatical. She was firm about delaying your relocation to New York, at least for the foreseeable future. Her advice was to stay at UCSF, given the lawsuit. She also suggested backing off on your volunteer plans. Maybe go overseas once or twice a year—that's all."

The lawyer had told Coty that each state could be tricky and that they should bring in a local attorney. She also said that, as the child's mother, Jette would probably have no problem with custody if she stayed in California full-time. Probably.

"Lawsuit?" Jette asked.

PART THREE

CHAPTER TWELVE

———•———

San Francisco

All week long, the morning fog had faded by noon. Forecasting imminent glare, Coty donned her sunglasses in the foyer before commencing her walk to the Victorian that, six decades earlier, she and Zaydeh had purchased to house the San Francisco offices of the Sheldon Fine Foundation.

A premature move, she realized, as she strained through self-inflicted darkness to locate the doorknob. Coty chuckled at her decision not to fumble in her bag outdoors. Madeleine would have suggested that she first open the door and then put on her sunglasses in the cloak of the entryway. She missed her deceased friend, who had solved such minor puzzles with ease and good humor. When Coty pulled the tortoiseshell frames down the bridge of her nose, the doorknob mocked her within easy reach.

The transplanted New Yorker, sunglasses back in working position, closed behind her the entry door to her family home. A sweater's empty sleeves draped over her shoulders and crossed the front of her flowered ivory dress in a pink X flat against her chest. *Always wise to bring an extra layer*, she mused, recalling advice from Madeleine, the first native San Franciscan who had befriended her. With one hand on the canvas strap of her tote and the other on the banister, she stepped from under the cover of her front porch.

Zaydeh had accompanied the new mother to California to

find not only a West Coast office for his foundation but also a home for her and the twins. He rebuffed her plans to rent a small place. Sheldon Fine had made his money in real estate and believed that Coty, as sole provider to her daughters, should own a home. She worried aloud that a significant investment would deepen the rift with her father. The twins would share a room, and she needed little else, other than space for a darkroom.

He had not argued when she had waxed on about making her own way as a photographer. Zaydeh encouraged her, citing also that he wanted to assist. She countered that his granting her power of attorney over his estate and the role of foundation CEO had already caused a widening divide within the family, not to mention her pregnancy, which had been received with disdain and embarrassment.

Zaydeh told her that, despite those two roles, she would not garner a greater share of his estate and reminded her that his new foundation would absorb most of his wealth—most, not all. He wanted each of his progeny to be secure but not kept. As he had done for his own kids, he granted each grandchild his largesse on two fronts: education and housing. He stipulated consistent allowances for both. If anyone did not take advantage of the education allowance, the money would go to the foundation. He was adamant that the real estate allowances be spent in full and that the acquisitions not be sold unless they were rolled over into other residential properties that were equal to or greater in market value—a stipulation that he knew could not be enforced but that communicated his intention to protect all family members and provide some security for their futures. In addition, upon his death, each would receive a small bequeathment, while those who had worked in the business would enjoy more significant inheritances. The "boys," as he called them, had shown rare unanimity when they had voiced their opposition to Zaydeh's decision that the majority of his net worth was destined for the foundation bearing his name.

On their San Francisco house-hunting trip, Coty steered him toward several small dwellings for sale in bohemian enclaves where other artists had collected. Ever the opportunist, Zaydeh discovered a rare offering in the neighborhood of Pacific Heights. Without inspecting the property, Coty considered the area too fancy for her tastes. Then, together, they visited the location.

The wooden structure—modest among the grand old homes and mansions in the neighborhood—predated the earthquake and fires of 1906. The shake-covered building was set high on a natural berm and, from the sidewalk below, appeared more reminiscent of a seaside home near Seattle or on Cape Cod than a house facing the San Francisco Bay. It had high ceilings, leaded-glass windows, an ample kitchen, an outsize dining room, a palatial parlor, and a wide staircase that rose to the bedroom floor. The half basement—unusual for the city—was a bonus. The site's elevation lent clear views of the bay, including the Golden Gate Bridge and Alcatraz Island. Coty told Zaydeh that it was far more than she needed—or wanted—and then, as she cast about, murmured that the light was a photographer's dream.

When she realized that the price of the house was below his allowance, Coty capitulated and accepted his benevolence. Zaydeh reminded her that he intended to be consistent across the family. She smiled and said he had been more than generous, thinking that the less expensive property might engender goodwill with her father. While they sat at the title office to sign the paperwork, she realized the purchase agreement included a second property—the adjacent uphill lot, which was vacant except for a crumbling foundation that outlined where once an imposing building had stood.

Soon after the war, the mansion had been destroyed in a blaze. The owners had fought the city for years over redevelopment options, until Sheldon Fine made an aggressive offer for the encumbered property. Rather than continue to battle city hall in hopes of slapping down an apartment building, the owners swept up Zaydeh's offer, much to the delight of Coty's soon-to-be new neighbors. Her grandfather encouraged her to keep the space open—raze the site and plant gardens for her and the twins. He winked when he told her that she would need several hummingbird feeders to service the park outside her windows.

Pac Heights gave her daughters a safe neighborhood, which insulated her first real-estate investment. Her minor salary at the foundation, along with any money she made with her camera, would be hers, of course. The property would be bought outright and secured with a trust sufficient to maintain her new home, taxes and all—just like everyone else in the Fine family orbit.

Today, the terraced arms of her gardens spread open and stretched skyward, as if giving thanks for the blessed rays that fueled the miracle of photosynthesis. The extra lot next door allowed the house to breathe among its grandiose neighbors. Looking back, she pressed the sunhat against her nape and thanked Zaydeh for both his generosity and his prescience.

As she descended toward the office, sunshine chased away the remnant fog, which threatened to return by sunset. The skin on her face radiated warmth, heralding a bright afternoon for fertile patches across the city. The fog's retreat took with it any remaining doubts about her latest plan.

Several blocks from the Victorian, she rolled up the pink sweater and shoved it inside her handbag. Despite the pleasant temperature outside, the office would be cool, the furnace dormant on a weekend day when she expected only one other.

There it was—a painted lady with heather-gray clapboard siding. Gingerbread gables fronted the attic. Window shutters and porch spindles were coated a deep green as dark as fresh oak leaves, while the balusters, railings, and double doors were the hue of ripe plums.

Coty opened the door and stepped into the empty foyer. Darkness and cool air surrounded her. The stark contrast caused her to remove her sunglasses in a swoop. The soles of her walking shoes made soft contact with the carpeted runner that cushioned the hardwood floor of the hallway, which led to the desk she had occupied for more than half a century.

The meeting was about to start in a high-ceilinged conference room decorated with photographs. Coty took a quick inventory. Each framed image hung where she had placed it over the years. Next to the old slate blackboard was a favorite shot of Zaydeh, beaming, that she had taken of him on the day they wandered about Saigon with their cameras. One hand rubbed his paunch, while he pointed with the other to the bulbous tummy of a giant bronze Buddha. Zaydeh's grin had not lived long after her shutter closed. Next to him in the shot, she had captured an encroaching monkey, reaching into the camera bag slung over his shoulder.

Across the conference room table from the chairwoman of the foundation sat the institution's new CEO, who slid a manila folder over the uncluttered surface and said, "Nana, I've been scrambling to get out of here. Was that a test?"

Coty took the file she had requested at breakfast and, feigning shock, said, "Oh, my, that's right—you're leaving tomorrow! Have you checked in? Printed your ticket?"

Her only grandchild held up a smartphone, its screen displaying a QR code. "Checked in before you got here; e-ticket. Vietnam, here I come."

Coty flipped open the worn folder and asked, "Evelyn, why did you think my request for this child's file was a test?"

"When I came in this morning, I couldn't find it; I had to go fishing around the office. It took me more than half an hour. Speaking of tests, Nana, you want to guess where it was?"

"It wasn't in the filing cabinet?" Coty braced herself, thinking

Evelyn was going to complain, again, about the old-fashioned paper trail. Now that she was running things, the legacy files, dating back decades, would soon be digitized. Coty looked at the ashen blackboard and sighed at its empty chalk tray. The time had come for the foundation to be dragged into modernity, she concluded, while thinking how proud Zaydeh would be of his progeny.

"Not inside, Nana—on top. The last place I looked. It'd been pulled already, earmarked for Father Thom."

"Oh. Sharon must've taken it out yesterday. I might've mentioned that I needed it for my talk with Thomas tonight."

Evelyn furrowed her brow, as if not buying either of her grandmother's memory lapses.

Coty smiled and said, "He grew to become a Catholic priest, Evelyn. Father Matheo Aubert. Did you read his file?"

"Right before you got here. Is that why Father Thom's been involved?"

"More or less. Did you see the letter that he wrote as a teenager?"

"Yeah. The kid refused help from the foundation. Asked that you send money to the orphanage but wanted nothing for himself. Was he wearing a hair shirt?"

"He didn't need anything; he had recently started seminary when he wrote that letter."

Evelyn pointed to the folder spread open in Coty's hands. "Nana, your handwritten notes about his personal life were a frightening read."

"Sad story," Coty said, flipping through the pages. "He lost his whole family in a raid. Insurgents destroyed their village."

"My grandfather—he, too, was an orphan and went on to become a priest. Is that why this patient's special?"

"Partly."

Evelyn sent a wry look across the table. "He's also a native French speaker. Once a Francophile, always a Francophile—*oui, madame*? You've shown a real weakness for French-speaking priests, Nana."

"True. However, in his case, that's interesting but irrelevant."

"Then what else makes him so special?"

"You tell me, darling. Did you read the entire file? Or were you too busy 'scrambling to get out of here'?"

"I knew it was a test! You're getting me ready to find the nun, aren't you?" Evelyn stalled. She tapped the fingernails of her left hand atop the table and said, "He didn't refuse everything, did he, Nana?"

"Well done, Evelyn. I thought you might have missed the clue."

"Hard to miss the receipt for a one-way airplane ticket from Libreville, through Frankfurt, to San Francisco."

"Yes. It was the only gift he accepted from the foundation." Coty flattened the file and sent an approving grin across the table. "You'd make a fine detective, darling. You'll do well on your search for Sister Lan."

"The date was smudged. Looked like it was almost two years ago."

Coty nodded, tightened her lip seal, and wondered why her granddaughter bothered to pause, again. Evelyn's reticence crumbled within a breath.

"He's still right here in San Francisco, isn't he, Nana?"

"So far, so good. You've passed the first test, dear."

"First?"

"Yes. Care to continue?" She assumed her granddaughter would take the bait. Those familiar with the family joked that Coty had her own twin in Evelyn. Seldom did either refuse a challenge.

"Does Jette know?"

Coty cringed. When Janice Walsh died of cancer, then fifteen-year-old Evelyn was in high school. Within days of Janice's funeral, Jette resigned from UCSF, citing her intention to work at the family foundation. She spent little time in the converted Victorian; instead she volunteered for mission after mission with Médecins Sans Frontières. By the time her only child entered university, Jette was overseas with MSF more than she was home in California.

While Evelyn was a student at Berkeley, she stopped calling her mother "Mom." During the college student's junior year, Coty took her to Sri Lanka to see firsthand her mother's work with MSF. On the flight back to the States, Evelyn commented that "Jette" had found her true passion, which Coty took as a euphemism for children other than her own.

"No. I haven't told your mother that he's been living in the city for the past couple of years."

Evelyn looked to the window and resumed tapping her fingernails. Staring through the panes, she said, "You kept his presence here secret from Jette for some reason. That's the second test?"

Clicking drew Coty's gaze to the tabletop. The nail polish, the color of arctic ice, suited Evelyn, who splashed gray-streaked white curls onto the table. The ringlets undulated as she bobbed her head side to side and tapped away in thought.

"Hmm. His file is odd, Nana. No photographs—not like the rest of Jette's patients."

"What a sleuth. Keep going, dear."

"How often have you seen him since he came here?"

"On occasion." Coty paused. Such were their games of cat and mouse. "I've seen him, but we haven't actually met."

"No way. Are you stalking him?"

"I've spotted him walking by our house, several times. We wave to each other, but he doesn't know who I am. One morning, I went to his parish to hear him say Mass."

Evelyn scratched back the folder. Thumbing the pages, she said, "Lagos . . . Jette's first trip with MSF . . ." The tapping fingernails halted. "Nana, was she operating on him the night my dad and Aunt Noémie died?"

A shadow passed over the leaded-glass window and swept

across the conference room table. Coty kept her attention on the glass, sighed, and, without finding Evelyn's eyes, murmured, "Actually, darling, it was well after midnight here. Daytime in Nigeria."

"Nana, why are you sharing this with me now?"

Coty turned and said, "Things have gotten complicated."

"Jette's going to find out about your priest, isn't she?"

"Yes. I wanted you to know before you came home from Vietnam. Your mother should be here by the time you get back."

Evelyn frowned; it wouldn't be the first time Jette had missed an estimated time of arrival. "Why do you have to tell Jette that he's been here for two years?"

Coty sighed again and said, "I want to invite him to live with us."

"Nana, you've got to be kidding. He's a priest," Evelyn said, shaking her head.

"He needs a sabbatical."

"Who thinks so? You?"

"When I went to his Mass, I could tell that Matheo was struggling. Couldn't have been six people in the pews. He gave a homily on the Good Samaritan that broke my heart."

"'Matheo'? Although you haven't met him, you refer to him by his first name?"

Coty felt injured. To Evelyn, it must have seemed obvious.

"I'm sorry. Struggling with what, Nana?"

"With life. With his calling."

"And why are *you* intervening?"

"Whether he returns to Africa or stays here for sabbatical, he won't be allowed to live in either rectory. He'll have to take a room somewhere and support himself."

"That's cold. How's he going to 'support himself,' as you say?"

"During seminary, he trained as a carpenter's apprentice. The bishop in Gabon said that they'd help him find work. He could take a room as a boarder and do carpentry while he sorts out his confusion."

"Sounds like a plan."

"He's a carpenter, and we're about to start a major remodel at home. Living with us would be far better than being in a boardinghouse, here or in Gabon."

"Why get involved, Nana? Let him go home. That would prevent another dustup with Jette."

"I can't." Coty choked back her tears, and the room grew silent.

"Okay, Nana, I get it. You want to take in another stray. I love that about you."

Coty hummed near-silent thanks as she waited for Evelyn to continue.

"Assuming Father Thom approves, when do you meet your priest? You're not planning to invade another confessional, are you?"

Coty giggled at the thought of a recalcitrant Laurent Sabatier. "Funny you mention that, darling. I shouldn't have pulled Thomas's leg, told him I wanted to surprise the young man, like I did your grandfather."

"That's hysterical. What did Father Thom say?"

"He wasn't amused; he scowled at me as if I'd actually chase Matheo down inside that dreadful box. Sometimes I wonder what Thomas thinks."

Evelyn tapped the bottom edge of the manila folder on the table, then laid the file flat and said, "Everybody loves that story about how you tracked down my grandfather. When you last told it at a dinner party, Esben laughed out loud. First time in months."

Coty seized on the comment and asked about the famous Silicon Valley entrepreneur. "How is Mr. Ueland? Still struggling?"

"I think he's getting worse. Must be something in the water around here that affects foreign men."

"Doubt it's the water. Once the company went public, he became a rich man."

"On paper, Nana."

"True, and he's getting richer on paper every day. Success often confuses people, darling."

"Well, it's been hard to watch. Esben's lost his footing of late."

"Maybe he should talk to someone. What does Neeta think?" Evelyn's best friend and former college roommate, Neeta Desai, had started working at Zemi soon after its inception.

"She doesn't know; she keeps saying that a founder's life is a lonely existence." Evelyn returned to the window that had recaptured her nana's fascination. "Maybe I'll tell him about your priest. A fellow expatriate might be who the suffering entrepreneur needs."

"I wouldn't. It might add to Matheo's dilemma. Although he's a grown man, he's an innocent adult."

Ticktock, ticktock . . .

Bishop Thomas Brennan plucked a beefy thumb across glass bevels. One finger of scotch, poured neat, was the drink that he often stretched over an hour of their verbal fencing. He raised the tumbler to his nose for inspection, lids closed. When he reopened his eyes, before he took his first sip, he said, "Thank you, Coty. May we please get down to business?"

"Thomas, are you in a rush?"

He brought the drink to his mouth, took a sip, and said, "I've an exorcism in an hour."

"Funny. May I observe?"

"Funnier." Another sip. "Now, about the matter at hand . . ." Thomas closed the manila folder and handed it back to his hostess. "Coty, I'm afraid Father Aubert's not in good shape. Father Ralph told me yesterday that the man wants to know when he can go home."

She sensed that her old friend was going to lobby to end the

African's secondment to America, which she had convinced him
to secure two years earlier. "I wish he'd let us help more. Monsieur
Aubert's been the least receptive of Jette's patients."

"*Father* Aubert, Ms. Fine. And I'd suggest that he's probably
been the least greedy."

They faced each other in the parlor from seats they had occupied countless times. The bishop reclined into the supple leather
of the familiar wingback chair. At his elbow was a convenient side
table, where, upon a coaster, he set the tumbler of amber liquid.

Ticktock, ticktock . . .

Poised forward of surrounding throw pillows, Coty occupied
her preferred seat at the sofa's edge, with her knees together and
angled away from the coffee table that separated her from the
priest. Her chest was aimed at the foyer, affording her a sentry's
view. Over decades of visiting Coty's home, one time alone had
Thomas sat next to her on the couch—early in the morning after
her daughter and son-in-law were killed. There, on that sofa,
with a guardian's arm around his friend, he hugged and rocked
her as she wept.

Little in the parlor had changed. Photographs remained
where they had been sown as seeds of promise—seeds that, after
one fateful night, would never germinate. On the side table at
Thomas's elbow was a framed image: the photo that a new
grandmother had captured of a baby girl on that same sofa,
propped up in between a glowing couple dressed in hospital
scrubs.

Ticktock, ticktock . . .

The photograph had been set there long before Evelyn could
reach it. As the child grew, she would often pull the frame from
its perch, inspect the scene with a precision expected from the
offspring of surgeons, and ask if they—we—were as happy as it
seemed.

Watching Thomas avoid eye contact, Coty grew worried. For
her scheme to work, she had to convince him to allow Matheo to

remain in California. "Thomas, do you think that living in America affected his faith?"

"He was in a funk before we offered to bring him over. That said, it does seem he's become more confused by his two years here. Ralph thinks that the young man needs to go home so he can sort things out."

"If he returns to Gabon, he'll be trapped for sure."

Thomas snapped his retort. "Father Aubert should take time off; a sabbatical's in order. Cardinal Omu agrees, as does Bishop Myboto in Gabon. All three of us have witnessed what happens when a priest feels trapped."

"How long will the church support his confusion, Thomas?"

"The church won't abandon him."

"You said he couldn't stay at the rectory during his sabbatical. Where's he going to live—a boardinghouse?"

The bishop raised a muscled arm that stretched the woolen sleeve of his black suit coat. A physical force, albeit in his seventies, the former wrestler drew fingernails as wide as nickels through thinning gray hair to scratch his scalp. "He needs time, Coty. A rented room might be best."

"How will he pay his bills? He's a priest."

"Stop it. We both know he worked as a carpenter while in seminary. Cardinal Omu assured me they'd help him find work."

"I have work for him right here."

Thomas looked confused. In a flash, his face relaxed. "Oh, of course—your renovation project."

"Honestly, Thomas, I worry about your memory."

"It might be fading. Haven't we been down this road before, Coty?"

"Can't remember?"

"Coty, please. You win. I ask, in all sincerity, that you notch your victory belt and we move on."

"Fine. I won't pray for you, but I'll do a little reading about your symptoms."

"*Coty!*"

His face flushed red, and the last of the scotch disappeared in an abrupt swallow. The miffed bishop sighed, then brought the glass to a gentle landing on the coaster. Coty waited. The last time he drank, rather than sipped, he had been going to an exorcism. That day, rather than ruddy-faced from irritation, the seasoned cleric had looked to be as white as the ghost he feared he might confront.

Ticktock, ticktock . . .

Thomas seldom granted himself more than one drink. He studied his empty tumbler and asked, "May I please have another modest pour?"

"Certainly, Thomas."

Coty rose and smiled without a smirk. Returning with the bottle, she tilted its neck over his glass. A pencil-thin stream of whiskey slipped through the bottle's mouth and splashed into the bottom of the crystal.

Ticktock, ticktock . . .

She signaled him with the *whomp* of the cork's return to its bottle, which she followed with a somber expression. Thomas took up his glass and said, "Even if you have work for him here, Coty, he'll still be far from home."

The scotch that Coty hoped would numb his irritation, rose to his lips.

Ticktock, ticktock . . .

"Coty, wasn't it your grandfather who counseled you not to let anyone become too dependent?"

"'Teach a man to fish'—from the *Tao Te Ching.*"

Thomas took another sip while scanning the parlor, which had been a separate sanctuary for him, a mortal laden with the preternatural expectations placed upon a Catholic bishop. Her home was a retreat from pastures filled with needy sheep, as well as the barracks he had shared with their shepherds. "Very impressive. Sheldon was a renaissance man, huh?"

"Zaydeh wasn't a scholar of Chinese philosophy; he was simply a pragmatist with a subscription to *Reader's Digest*."

Thomas laughed as if he never tired of the self-deprecating grandfather who had been her personal savior. "Coty, if he were alive, I bet Sheldon would argue that since Father Aubert knows how to pound nails, he'll be able to eat."

"You have a glass of scotch in your hand, Thomas."

The last of his shallow pour hovered in the air. The bishop considered the cut glass, turning it in the light, mixing its sparkles with those from the chandelier. Then he drained the tumbler and, as he brought the empty vessel in for another soft landing, said, "Before I meet with Father Aubert, I'll call Cardinal Omu. And, Coty, he and Bishop Myboto will decide. Understand?"

"Yes. Don't forget to mention that Matheo would be a great help to our visitor—if Evelyn returns with Sister Lan."

"That's a stretch, Coty. You and Evelyn are fluent in French. Jette too. He'd be superfluous on that front."

"We're far from being among the faithful. Sister Lan might find comfort in a French-speaking priest."

He rose from the leather wingback chair. "Speaking of Jette, have you discussed this with her?"

"You'd think me unwise if I talked to her before you agreed to inviting Matheo to live here."

"I'm stunned. The Coty Fine I know would be rendered tongueless from chomping while trying to keep quiet. What did your girls used to call you?"

"The Great Manipulator, which I took as a mother who gave a—"

"Coty."

"A toss. I was going to say, Thomas, a mother who gave a toss."

CHAPTER THIRTEEN

—•—

The ivory-colored shade remained open, where it had been rolled to the top of the window frame after yesterday's sunrise. Every evening since his arrival from Gabon, Father Matheo Aubert had slept with his toes aware of the far edge of the mattress. The undersize bed had not prevented him from falling asleep each night in America—each night until the last.

Chamber music pulsed at low volume inside the rectory bedroom. With his elbows dug into the twin mattress, the African transplant knelt aside the desk. He had received faith as a boy—a gift that later disappeared without warning or consent. Could it be stolen back or, as he prayed, might it be returned in the night without question or accusation?

The radio's static scratched at the music and his hollow prayers. Frustration pressed his lips together. He stood, abandoned the unfinished rosary to the surface of his desk, and shuffled to the bathroom.

Showering hinted of baptism as he straddled the drain plate, water cascading down his body from a coiled crown. Years after graduating from seminary, whenever he stood beneath the raining luxury of hot water, Father Aubert gave thanks for spiritual cleansing and renewed his vows to God. During his time in the United States, the prayerful pleasure had become for him an early-morning ritual that, by reliving salvation and ordination, girded the priest for the day's pastoral duties. Today, his jumbled head drooped in the warm stream. He could not speak the words, recollection less an issue than conviction.

Standing underneath the spray, the blinking priest inspected his nut-brown skin. He soaped his torso, pausing to slide fingertips atop the ridge of the scalpel's incision. As he rubbed the scar that ran down his chest, he retraced the journey to America that began his temporary assignment to a distant continent: visiting priest—a secondment that would bring him perspective as he worked through his struggles.

Body cleansed, he cranked the faucet closed, drew open the shower curtain, and reached to the hook for yesterday's towel. As on any other Saturday, he planned to hear confessions. Today, however, a private breakfast with Bishop Brennan had been set as a prerequisite to the sacrament.

Pinned alone onto the wall above the desk, a crucifix held his attention. Vigil before that cross had not prevented the loss. How can one get back something that has vanished without trail? Not hidden or misplaced, his faith seemed a gift rescinded, vaporized in a blaze of divine disappointment. Sitting naked on the edge of the bed, next to the damp towel, he stared at the floor and wondered how the bishop might alter the weekend's routine.

Matheo trudged down the back stairs and then entered the rectory's kitchen to the familiar face of Father Ralph Warren, who greeted him with a sleepy grin. Born and raised in Orange County, before strip malls and tract houses claimed the rural suburbs near Los Angeles, Ralph joked that they had both arrived in San Francisco from foreign lands. Not a morning person, per se, Ralph must have pressed himself to rise in time to intercept his younger colleague before he met with Bishop Brennan.

Rolled into a pudgy ball, Ralph outweighed the lean African, who stood at least one foot taller. The American appeared drowsy, standing in a wobble before the coffee machine. He yawned as he lifted the pot from its cradle. "He's here, Matheo." Ralph's pale, bald head motioned at the dining room door. "In there, reading the paper, waiting for you," he said, suspending the pot in his hand.

"What's his mood, Father? You know him; I don't." Matheo reached for a coffee cup. Surprised that his hand was steady, he held the mug out as Ralph tipped the pot over the rim.

"He's in good spirits, as usual," said Ralph, who scanned Matheo's face as if he were looking for clues.

Matheo read his colleague's concern. "I'm fine, Ralph. Please don't worry." Patting Ralph's shoulder, he said, "You're a wonderful friend. *Merci*. I prayed, as you suggested."

"Bishop Brennan's a servant of the Lord, Matheo. Be honest with him." Ralph returned his attention to the dining room door. "You're not the first man he's met for breakfast."

"*Toi?* You?" Matheo looked at him, wondering if this spiritual rock had weathered such a crisis when he, too, was a young priest.

"Yes, many years ago." Ralph looked away as he said, "That morning, I was prepared to renounce my vows before I buttered the toast." He faced Matheo, smiled, and said, "Our bishop's kind. He'll guide you to seek God's will."

"*Merci*, Ralph. Confession at ten o'clock; I'll see you in the vestibule." He stopped at the door to the dining room and, hesitating, turned to Ralph.

"Bless you, Matheo. Pray after your breakfast. Come back here to the kitchen at fifteen before the hour. We'll walk to church together."

Although the bishop stood not much taller than Ralph, he was an imposing force Matheo had not anticipated. While his housemate was wide from the compounding effects of an American diet, their bishop warned of brawn beneath familiar black garb. The man's firm, dry handshake corroborated Matheo's suspicion of physical power.

"Pleased to meet you, Father Aubert."

"*Enchanté*, Bishop Brennan. Sorry—nice to meet you."

The bishop, sweeping his freed hand over the dining room table, offered the young priest a seat before reclaiming his own. Brennan reached for the bowl of cut fruit, which he deposited in front of Matheo's place setting, and said, "Father, please."

Seeking less temporal sustenance, Matheo stared at him.

Bishop Brennan blinked and said, "I hear from Father Ralph that your English is quite good. I'm sorry that we cannot speak French or your native dialect."

The ironed cloth napkin relinquished its silverware. Matheo draped the cotton swath across his lap and paused, looking down at his empty plate. Without making eye contact, he lifted the water glass for a drink that lasted longer than needed to dampen his dry tongue. After landing the tumbler, he found the bishop's eyes and said, "*Merci*, Bishop Brennan, I'll do my best."

"Again, my apologies. Take as much time as you need to form your thoughts. I want to make certain that I understand what's on your mind, my son."

Before Matheo had abandoned the cup of coffee in the kitchen, he had drunk a third of the contents, which now sloshed with the water in his otherwise empty gut. Nature drove him to the toast. The slices had been wrapped in a matching white napkin and placed inside a wire basket. As he lifted the cover, no steam escaped.

"Matheo, you're aware of why I'm here today, aren't you?"

"*Oui*—my confusion." Holding the toast's rounded edges, he bit off one square corner. The water glass rose. He sipped to rinse down the bread. The bishop waited. Resigned to his fate, Matheo said, "Bishop Brennan, I'll do as you instruct."

The bishop shook his head. With a look of irritation, he reached for the wire basket, selected a slice without inspection, and said, "Matheo, you're aware that Father Ralph and I have known each other many years?"

"Ah, *oui*, Bishop Brennan—during your days together in his first parish."

"Matheo, you and I, too, are brothers in Christ. Please call me Thom."

"*Merci*, Father Thom."

The bishop slathered butter on the cold toast, rested his knife across the face of the plate, and reclined without taking a bite. He looked at Matheo and waited.

"I'm ready to go home, Bishop Brennan, if that's your decision."

The bishop sighed as he lifted the slice. "Do you think Libreville's the best place for you, Matheo?"

"*Oui*. I pray that when I move back to the rectory in Gabon, God will bless me again."

Brennan bit off a squared corner, matching his subordinate. He reached for the glass as he chewed. Assisted by a sip of water, he swallowed the toast. "Matheo, I've talked with Cardinal Omu. He's discussed your situation with Bishop Myboto. They—we—have reached consensus that a sabbatical might help you. Have you considered a sabbatical?"

"*Sabbatique—oui*. Father Ralph told me about this option. He agrees too?"

"Yes, Ralph agrees."

"*Merci*. When I return home, I'll obey."

The bishop closed his eyes and shook his head. "Matheo, if you return to Libreville, Bishop Myboto has stipulated that you may not move back into the rectory until you've completed your sabbatical and renewed your commitment to the priesthood."

The room spun. Where would he live, if not among the shepherds? No village, much less family, survived to take him in. He looked at the missing corner of his toast.

"Bishop Myboto and his staff will help you locate temporary accommodations, take a room somewhere. He said they'll assist with finding work; you were a carpenter while in seminary, weren't you?"

"*Oui*, I was apprentice to Father Henri LeDoux, a master carpenter."

The old Gabonese priest, as patient as a grandparent, had taught him more than carpentry with such pragmatic axioms as "measure twice"—a wise practice, whether before applying the saw or judging others.

"Matheo, there's another option: you could remain in California."

Father Henri was long dead. If Matheo returned to Gabon, he faced living in a boardinghouse and working for strangers. The thought of residing with Ralph was as irresistible as cool water on a parched tongue. The glass rose again.

"You know about the Sheldon Fine Foundation, of course, given that they sponsored your trip here as a visiting priest."

"*Oui*, they've been most generous; they send money each year to the orphanage and also to the clinic where I visited the sick." He recalled the story of why the foundation had sought him out. "The surgeon who saved my life is affiliated: her great-grandfather was this man Fine, *non*?"

"Yes. I've known Dr. Walsh since she was a little girl. Her mother, Coty Fine, is one of my closest friends."

"Do you often visit her in New York?"

The bishop took another sip, then lifted his napkin and dabbed the corners of his mouth. He returned the linen to his lap and peered across the table. "She lives here in San Francisco, Matheo. I had dinner with Ms. Fine last night."

"I thought the foundation was in New York."

"They kept the original office, which remains the formal address; most of the staff are here, in San Francisco. Ms. Fine moved here more than fifty years ago with her two children: Dr. Walsh and her sister."

Matheo wondered why he had not learned that the woman lived here. One more puzzle to add to his list on America.

"She lives in nearby Pacific Heights. You walk there often, don't you?"

"*Oui*, beautiful homes and views of the bay."

"Ms. Fine told me that you two wave to each other whenever she's tending her flowers as you walk past. Her house is yellow, with wooden shakes. It's smaller than those nearby but stands out; it sits on a double lot at the top of one of the hills."

"Ah, *oui, oui*. Madame Bonjour!"

"What?"

"The gardener! Very friendly. She waved to me and shouted '*bonjour*,' which reminded me of home. Now, I look for her. I call out and wave if she's in her gardens."

"Has she ever waved you toward the house?"

"*Non*, Bishop Brennan. She smiles, waves, and turns back to her flowers. A most pleasant person." Madame Bonjour seemed not repulsed by his dark skin, but she had never waved him forward. Of all he felt about his adoptive country, the sting of difference pricked him the most. Even the brown-skinned Americans studied him. The needles were sharpest whenever he was among the wealthy pale people he encountered, whether as a priest in his pasture or as a Black man walking the dramatic hills of San Francisco.

"Matheo, Ms. Fine expects a visitor from Vietnam. She hopes you might agree to help."

"The option to stay in San Francisco?"

"Yes. Her guest is an elderly woman, a nun, who, Ms. Fine suspects, speaks no English. You'd be her interpreter."

"Ah, *français* . . . Vietnam . . . But of course, the woman speaks French."

"Ms. Fine hopes that, with your help, her guest might consider moving to San Francisco."

Ralph would greet him each morning, as before. And, despite a sabbatical from his pastoral duties, he could kneel in the familiar sanctuary and plead for the return of his faith. He could be helpful, not simply lost. Matheo straightened in his chair.

Brennan perked up as well and said, "You seem interested, yes?"

"*Oui.* You discussed this with Cardinal Omu?"

"Yes. He and Bishop Myboto are supportive. Your decision, of course, Matheo."

Ashamed of his weak faith, he accepted the invitation as divine intervention—a gift of fate. "*Merci,* Bishop Brennan. When will you tell Madame Fine?"

"Before you decide, meet with her; talk to Father Ralph."

"You believe that helping her is best for me, *oui*?"

"I can't say, Matheo. Go meet Ms. Fine, then make your decision."

Brennan slid his black suit-coat sleeve, exposing a wristwatch. He frowned at the time, rose, and, with practiced civility, brought their session to a close. After the bishop departed, Matheo returned to the kitchen, where he would wait for Father Ralph until it was time to hear the confessions of the faithful. He refused his friend's counsel to retreat to his room after breakfast to beseech his Maker. The bishop's instructions had stopped him from ascending the staircase.

"Matheo, you're made in His image, and you must be the creator of your future. You have control, my son—as He wishes. Love Him with all your heart and soul, and with full the power of your mind."

Matheo contemplated the wall clock. The ratcheted sweep of the second hand seemed to track his heartbeat. As he sat alone at the communal table, the porcelain coffee mug grew cold in his hands.

Far more persistent than the morning fog, the bishop's spell held. At half past the hour, behind Matheo's back, the dining room door creaked. Upon entry, Father Ralph sucked in a breath, apparently startled that his friend was already sitting at the kitchen table. Through the window above the sink, Matheo was staring into a dissipating haze. Without turning, he felt the older priest approach. Ralph stopped next to the table and stood by Matheo's shoulder.

Twisting in his chair, Matheo angled his face at the stout priest and received the grace that had never failed to comfort him.

"What's left of that fog should burn off in short order. We'll walk back from confession in sunshine," Ralph predicted, as he rubbed the top of his ear.

"I hope you're correct, Ralph. I miss the warmth of the sun." The fog and his dank mood might lift if its rays broke through.

"Bishop Brennan's a wise shepherd, Matheo. I've known him for decades." Ralph paused, found the African's eyes, and then said, "Frustrating, isn't it, not to be given the answers?"

Matheo stared at the clock above the sink and, shaking his head, said, "Ralph, I can't quiet my mind. When I close my eyes to pray, I see a wall in front of me. No doors or windows—just a solid wall."

"That wall might be the Lord's gift. Sit with your back against it, Matheo; look to your past; pray and wait; listen."

The duo exited the kitchen. A refreshing mist, a remnant of the fog, sprayed their faces as they walked the breezeway to the staff entrance to the vestibule.

The door closed with a somber baritone *thump*. Sealed inside the church, behind the main altar, Matheo looked around the anteroom—a familiar, peaceful space. Against the dark wood paneling, paired cassocks and surplices hung in anticipation of priests, choir members, and fidgety young altar servers. Two years ago, a fresh black-and-white set—the longest—had been draped from a higher hook.

"Do you think I'm a good priest?" The pain was so intense, he was ready to accept his mentor's conclusion as his own.

"Father Aubert, you're a good man. Good men make good priests."

Matheo's feet shifted in place as he stood before the clothes hook. He hung up his nylon jacket: a royal-blue Golden State Warriors windbreaker, a gift Ralph had granted after the African arrived with no outer gear to stave off the cool ocean winds that whistled through the city. As he reached for the cassock, Matheo said, "I pray that today I'm a good priest. They deserve a confessor who's able."

The two men dressed in silence. The cassock, followed by the surplice, slid over Matheo's tight hair. He kissed the stole and, bowing, strung it around his neck. Dripping down his chest, the purple trim reminded him of the blood of Christ, symbolism set long ago.

When they finished donning their uniforms for the sacrament, Ralph laughed out loud. Casting a shrewd expression, he said, "Do you think gambling's a sin?"

"It depends," Matheo replied, guessing that his friend wished to lighten the moment with a wager.

"What if the winner donates the prize to the poor?"

"Difficult to know the heart of a gambler."

"All right. I'll bet you that Mrs. Flaherty is on my side of the church, sitting in the last pew, waiting to be first to receive the sacrament."

"She's always there, Ralph. I don't think it's much of a bet if I stand no reasonable chance to win."

"I agree that the odds are in my favor, Father Aubert. Okay, let's make it five-to-one. You bet one dollar to my five."

"Father Warren, while I'm sitting against my wall, praying, should I implore God's grace for your gambling problem?"

The elder priest grinned and said, "They'll have an able confessor, today, Father Aubert." Ralph brought a chubby arm behind Matheo and patted him on the back. "Let's go administer the sacrament to the needy, shall we?"

—•••—

With the rope's downward pull, the bell rang throughout the sanctuary. Matheo's spirits improved when he saw parishioners in two single-file lines that ran partway down the nave's main aisle. Mrs. Flaherty sat queued as the first penitent in the longer line—Father Ralph's.

The pair of priests held somber expressions as they stepped out from the vestibule and rounded a marble pillar. Ralph's shoulder brushed Matheo's elbow. They stopped at the center of the prayer railing, genuflected before the tabernacle, and, in a synchronized upward gaze, took in the hanging image of Christ crucified.

Mrs. Flaherty's dull green eyes were fixed forward as the priests approached her pew. Upon arrival at the confessionals, Ralph whispered, "Matheo?"

"*Oui?*"

"One dollar, Father Aubert—for the poor, of course."

CHAPTER FOURTEEN

———•———

Matheo arrived early. Out of politeness, he strolled past Madame Bonjour's house and stepped uphill to the adjacent lot, which was bathed in sunlight and chockablock with plant life. Coty Fine was not kneeling in the gardens, as he often spotted her. At the top edge of her property, rather than escaping down the other side of the hill, he paused in the middle of the sidewalk and contemplated the gardener's giant white calla lilies, which reminded him of Easter. He took a deep breath before he headed back downhill, toward the bishop's planned encounter. A silver sedan drove through a cutout in the sidewalk and pulled into the driveway. When he arrived at the cutout, his eyes followed the car to a stop in the middle of the drive, where three of its doors winged open.

"*Bonjour, monsieur!*"

He did not turn to her; rather, he stared down the hill that he had climbed many times over the last two years.

"Matheo Aubert, *bonjour!*"

After she called him by name, his eyes found hers and she waved him up the driveway. When he reached the side of the automobile, he bowed to Coty and her company. "*Enchanté*, Madame Fine."

"*Enchantée, monsieur.*"

"*Pardonnez-moi, madame.* I'll wait in front until you're ready for me. *Merci beaucoup.*" In a defensive reflex, Matheo's right hand went to his heart, where he found the Warriors team logo sewn on the front of Ralph's gift. His fingers rose from the embroidered patch to the Roman collar at his throat. Matheo turned in the direction of the street. He would wait on the sidewalk in front of the house unless she invited him to rest on her porch. He did not want to intrude or presume hospitality—Madame Bonjour had never before waved him forward.

"*Non, non, monsieur.* You must meet our friends—family, really." Coty removed her garden gloves. She stroked fingertips over a sunspot on her left hand and said, "Ah, youth. *C'est la vie.*"

A petite woman standing by the car closed the rear passenger door. Matheo guessed that she was in her late twenties, or maybe, like he was, a bit beyond thirty. Her facial features were as sharp as those of northern Europeans, although her skin coloring approached his own chestnut hue. She sported natural eyelashes, the length of which suggested cosmetic trickery. Exposed by her smile, brilliant white teeth were bookended by golden hoop earrings. Lush dark hair cloaked her shoulders. The woman stepped to greet him, one hand extended.

"Nice to meet you, Father. My name is Neeta Desai."

The driver, a man, late in middle age, walked up to take the priest's hand. He exhibited the long eyelashes of his irrefutable daughter. "Karun Desai. My pleasure, sir."

Matheo clenched the man's hand and said, "*Enchanté*, Monsieur Desai."

Karun opened his trunk, leaned into the cavity, and wrestled with an apparatus wedged inside. The vehicle bobbed as he freed his catch. Unfolding the wheeled walker, he faced Matheo and, head cocked, gestured at the front passenger door, where an older man with severe curvature of the spine was laboring to exit the vehicle.

"Father Aubert, this is Videsh Joshi, my father-in-law."

Trembling, Joshi pressed the walker into duty as Neeta and Karun hovered near the man's sides. Everyone's attention narrowed to the contraption, which rattled and shifted. Joshi fixed his left grip, steadying himself to shake hands with the priest. Bent over, he tugged his tremulous right fist from the handlebar. The quivering hand rose above his temple and hovered there. Matheo, reacting as would any good shepherd, arrived in time to clasp the gnarled paw before the walker and its pilot tipped over.

When the priest took his hand, Joshi's face brightened and he said, "Pleased to meet you, young man. Call me Videsh." At Matheo shot a gleaming grin with a fraction of the teeth any first-world dentist would have expected.

Neeta cupped her grandfather's elbow. She stuck a shoe in between the pavers of the driveway and one of the walker's rubber tires. Joshi ignored her hypervigilance and held his focus on Matheo.

"*Enchanté*, Monsieur Joshi."

"You must call me Videsh," he said, with a ferocity dismissive of his tremors.

Charcoal-tinted half-moons draped from Videsh's sockets to his cheekbones. Staring into bloodshot eyes, Matheo slid his hand over calluses born of labor. Conscious of an octogenarian's delicate bones, he was gentle. To seal the moment, Matheo placed his left palm atop their embrace.

"I understand from my friend Coty that we'll be working together. She promised me an apprentice. I'm glad you're tall too!"

Blood flushed hot under skin that could keep a secret. Matheo suspected that Madame Fine had in mind more than Bishop Brennan had unveiled.

"Monsieur Aubert, I'm delighted that you arrived in time to meet everyone," Coty said. "Neeta's my granddaughter's best friend. They were constant childhood companions and then roommates at Berkeley. Karun and his wife, Parvani, have been colleagues of my daughter since they interned together. Even before Neeta and Evelyn were born, the Desais were part of our extended family."

An encore of the walker's rattling drew everyone's attention back to Joshi. "I'm fine. You two can go now." Videsh faced down his skeptical family. "I'm fine, really! I need to talk to my apprentice in private. Go!" Wobbling at his walker, Videsh brandished a dismissive hand, which, once again, caused him to compromise his tenuous balance. "Coty and I have everything under control. Don't we, Coty?"

"Of course we do, Videsh." Coty spun to release his escorts. "You're free to leave. And, Karun, Neeta can come back alone. We'll help her with the walker, won't we, Matheo?" She looked at the priest, who, in silence, added to his list of questions. He nodded in subordination, doing nothing in the moment to challenge her.

"*Oui, madame*—as you wish.*"

"Ah, *français*. Don't you love his accent?"

"Yes, Coty. He's as charming as you predicted," Neeta said, liberating her grandfather's elbow. "I'll come back in ninety minutes, NaaNaa Joshi."

"Two hours! Not ninety minutes. I've much to discuss with Matheo and Coty."

"Okay, NaaNaa Joshi. I might be a little early; I don't want to get stuck in traffic. I'll wait in the kitchen with Magdalena."

The hostess looked at the woman's father and said, "Neeta hasn't changed since she was a little girl. Ever the diplomat, don't you think?" Karun chuckled his agreement as he pulled open the driver's side door. "Karun, go back to the hospital, and don't worry."

Videsh laughed while shouting at his son-in-law, "You heard her. Go!"

Coty waved goodbye to the dubious father-daughter duo. As she lowered her hand, she slipped it inside the crook of the priest's elbow. Matheo twisted when she cranked on his bent arm.

At the speed of Videsh's walker, the trio traveled to the back end of the driveway. The old man stopped in front of a two-door garage and said, "Our shop, young man! You won't believe your eyes." Matheo could not believe his ears. "Where's that little remote you gave me, Coty?" Risking a tip-over, Videsh released his right hand and patted his pants pocket. "Oh, here it is."

While he struggled to brace himself inside the frame of the walker, Videsh extended the fob in a tremble and squeezed the button.

Snap!

One of the doors began its upward roll. Videsh's face opened, and he said, "Come look, young man. As fine a shop as I've ever seen—and it's ours."

With the arm-in-arm duo close on his wheels, he rolled into the open bay. Coty tightened her hold on the priest's elbow, tugged him closer, and leaned in to whisper about how Videsh had worked his way up India's slippery economic ladder to secure his daughter's education. The man's only child, Parvani, married Karun Desai, whom she had met at Grant Medical College, when its city had been called Bombay. After Parvani's mother died, Videsh succumbed to the curls and shakes of age and abandoned carpentry, the work that had broken his family out of their station. In a hushed voice, Coty told Matheo that, weeks earlier, when Parvani had flown back to Mumbai to retrieve her father, she had carried an impassioned plea to help Coty Fine.

Videsh paused and, beaming his broken smile, took in the marvel that the priest understood had infused a will to live back into the disused carpenter. Matheo contemplated the space with a slow, respectful scan.

"Monsieur Joshi, your shop—*magnifique.* I've not seen such tools since Gabon. How did you know?"

"Know that you were a carpenter's apprentice while in seminary?" Videsh motioned in the direction of his source, standing nearby, with garden soil mashed into the knees of her blue denim skirt. "She told me."

The men looked at Coty, who, after acknowledging her contemporary with a broad grin, turned to send, in flawless French, a crisp request to the priest. "*S'il vous plait*, Monsieur Aubert, take inventory with my friend. He grows tired with that walker; if you sit at the workbench, he'll follow. *Merci beaucoup!*" For Videsh's benefit, she switched back to English and said, "I must get back to the garden. Let's meet again before Neeta returns. Videsh, in one hour, please bring Matheo inside. We'll talk and have some tea." Coty reached into her skirt to retrieve a tattered spiral notepad. She flipped through the pages, consulting the script. Closing the cover, she shook her head and said, "Make a list if there's anything lacking. I work best when I've a list. We'll find whatever you need."

It was in Matheo's fiber to remain reticent in front of elders, but he was confused and had grown wary. He broke a guest's decorum and questioned her, "Need for what, *madame*?"

"Whatever's required to complete the renovations."

"Renovations?"

"Yes, we've a lot of work to do to prepare for our guests."

"Guests?" He wondered who else would be invited to live there besides the Vietnamese nun. "*Madame*, there must be a misunderstanding."

Coty shot curt, albeit chirpy-sounding, French at Matheo: "Monsieur Aubert, my friend has difficulty performing certain tasks these days. He'll guide you to do what he cannot. We'll talk about your sabbatical after his granddaughter returns to collect him for the evening."

"My sabbatical?" Matheo asked.

"Bishop Brennan assured me—ah, *oui*, as you said, there must be some misunderstanding. I'm certain the bishop will clarify everything. For now, please don't embarrass my friend. He's excited to work with you." Switching back to English, she commanded her new crew, "Come for tea within the hour, or I'll be very cross."

———•••———

Ticktock, ticktock . . .

After helping Neeta load her grandfather's walker into the trunk, Matheo had tried in vain to escape. Alone in the parlor with Coty, he sat before tepid china. Abandoned on the tea tray, the master carpenter's empty porcelain cup drew the attention of his dumbfounded apprentice. The grandfather clock meted out the seconds from a corner of the room.

"He's a remarkable man—more than a gifted carpenter. Don't you agree, Matheo?"

Ticktock, ticktock . . .

He swallowed a muted cough. Having failed to clear his throat, he croaked, "*Oui, madame.*" Then came another, more robust cough—a loud, clumsy hack. "Very knowledgeable. Monsieur Joshi rivals the master I served in Gabon," he said, with an admiration for the elderly that he had learned, early on as an expatriate, was not common in America.

"Oh, what a relief! I'm delighted this is working out for everyone."

"*Pardonnez-moi, madame.* I have many questions."

"Take your time, Matheo. Whatever you need to be ready to start tomorrow morning."

"*Impossible, madame.*"

"I thought—" Coty paused. Shrugging, she asked, "Shall we call the bishop?"

"*Non, madame.* I don't wish to cause him trouble."

"He talked to you about a sabbatical, *non*?"

"*Oui.*" His gaze escaped Coty's hold. Bishop Brennan expected an answer—soon. As Matheo contemplated, he picked at an intransigent splinter that had lodged itself in his right palm.

"You're right-handed, *non*?"

"*Oui.*"

Coty stood and said, "Excuse me. I'll be back in a minute."

He watched her ascend the staircase with grace. Drawn by the grandfather clock that whispered in the background, he scanned the parlor. Despite the opulence he often witnessed on his walks through Pac Heights, hers felt like a warm home. In the corner opposite the grandfather clock, a baby-grand piano awaited learned fingers. He had seldom played since he had come to California.

Ticktock, ticktock . . .

He raised the pierced palm and, with his tongue, felt for the wood's heel. Once he located it, he gnawed at the stubborn splinter, unable to pinch it in his teeth. Mesmerized by the shimmering black lacquer coat of the piano, he sucked in vain at the sliver plunged into his flesh.

Ticktock, ticktock . . .

He heard her chuckle. The mistress had descended the staircase and reentered the room undetected. With his lips pressed against his palm, he watched her through spread fingers as she crossed the carpet.

"May I?" she asked, extending her hand to take his. "I had twin girls when I was your age. Identical twins. One of my daughters died in a traffic accident. She, too, was about your age when . . ."

The priest, his open hand cupped in hers, felt first the warm, soft caress, then the delicate touch of her fingertip as she hunted for the end of the splinter.

"My condolences . . . the loss of a child . . . there is nothing that . . ."

"My other daughter went to medical school. She became a pediatric cardiologist—a surgeon." Coty snagged the jagged tip with her tweezers. After pulling the wood out, she deposited it in a swipe onto his palm.

"*Merci beaucoup, madame.*" Pinching the irritant between the thumb and forefinger of his left hand, he rubbed it in minute circles as he might a bead on his rosary.

Coty shook herself and, posture reset, exhaled a full breath before she spoke. "Matheo, I understand that Bishop Brennan told you that my daughter was your surgeon." She paused, looked about the parlor, then turned back to him, and said, "When I heard about your family . . ."

Her tone was benevolent, he thought. She knew of the raid on their village—the slaughter of his parents and sisters. He could not recall his mother kissing him goodbye, nor the treacherous journey to the hospital. The piercing chest pains, he did remember—repetitive, throbbing pangs that caused him to cringe at the very cadence of life as his repaired heart beat out the minutes, the hours, the days until his release from the ICU.

The facility in Nigeria, where his life had been saved, was as foggy a memory as his bus ride, two years ago, across the Golden Gate Bridge. For months after his release, he dreamed about tiled walls everywhere. He remembered the bleached odors of medical hygiene; the singsong voice and warm, fleshy embrace of his plump nurse; the clear, clean water; and the abundant supply of food to which he had been unaccustomed—food that he could not taste, although it filled his stomach each day.

He looked at Coty and said, "Do you know why I was sent to the United States?"

"*Oui*, Matheo." Her vision went behind him. Lifting her hand, she stuck out a forefinger to direct his attention. He twisted to find a framed photograph and, even from that distance, recognized the setting with the Golden Gate Bridge in the background. A white-haired young woman, her curly tresses floating in the breeze, stood on the shore of the bay near Crissy Field, where he often walked. "She was my artist—Noémie. I miss her so."

Ticktock, ticktock . . .

Madame seemed to have left their shared space. He had experience with sorrow's hold and sensed she needed to be called home. Beseeching her return, he coaxed her with unforced tenderness. "*Madame?*"

"*Oui*, Matheo?"

He glanced at the Steinway and asked, "Do you play?"

"Chopsticks! Noémie played. And, now, my granddaughter, Evelyn, on occasion." Coty pointed to the piano and said, "I know that *you* play, young man. Would you mind?"

"Your pleasure, *madame*?"

"You take requests?" She giggled, which tossed him a hint he had not anticipated. And then she sent a second clue. "How about Bach—a selection from the Goldberg Variations, perhaps?"

Ticktock, ticktock . . .

He lifted the keyboard cover with the reverence he had displayed at the altar of his church. After cracking long fingers well suited to such an instrument, he paused. Hovering over the keys before he struck the first note, Matheo thought that his instructor at the orphanage, Sister Grace Noel, might be listening from on high. The grandfather clock set his toe tapping before he rolled into a piece that had once, long ago, presented its own steep hill to climb.

Ticktock, ticktock . . .

When he finished, his face flushed, again, as in the driveway when Videsh had disclosed the news of an apprenticeship. He turned to find his hostess. Moist eyes on the pianist, Coty stood in the center of the Persian carpet. She was weaving as only a dancer could, clutching to her chest the framed photograph of her daughter, the artist.

Although he felt rusty throughout the piece, Matheo wondered if Sister Grace Noel had derived pleasure from her earthbound student's brief recital. As he lowered the keyboard cover, he grew anxious to address his concerns before bidding Madame Fine adieu. He could not bear to leave her with the misconception that he could fulfill the apprenticeship Monsieur Joshi expected. It was an unfortunate misunderstanding that he was certain the bishop would correct when she next talked to her old friend.

"*Madame*, Bishop Brennan mentioned a nun—a French speaker from Vietnam. I'm here to talk to you about assisting her, *oui*?"

Coty reared back into the throw pillows and flung open her arms. "I don't even know if she's alive, Matheo. We never met. I saw her once, when I took that shot." On a nearby bookshelf, another framed photograph was masked by a shadow. She rose to retrieve it. As it slipped into his outstretched hand, she said, "We'll know soon if my granddaughter has located her."

Matheo studied the face in the crowd. *Madame* had captured what he saw of late in the mirror. He set the frame on the coffee table and bowed his head as he reached for his teacup in desperation. How had he arrived here, in this country, at this home? "My bishop wishes me to help Monsieur Joshi?" Bishop Brennan must have sought to fill the days of sabbatical with practical occupation. Matheo wondered if Ralph had suggested this to draw him away from hours seated with his back to the dreaded wall.

"*Oui*. Ask him."

The fingers of his left hand stroked the palm where she had removed the splinter. He had placed a plain sawn board at the mouth of the planer, as the master carpenter had requested. It was an obvious test to see if the apprentice remembered how to set the device at the proper gap, to preserve the thickness of the stock and smooth the wood's surface to a condition suitable for sanding.

Rather than being pinned against his wall of doubt, he could build real walls with the jovial carpenter. The prospect promised days of tiring labor, at the end of which he could report to Ralph and their brothers at the rectory's communal table.

Matheo blurted out his agreement. "I'll help you, *madame*. Bishop Brennan has rescued other men—priests like me. I must trust those whom God guides to guide me."

"*Magnifique!* Now, Matheo, you should return to the rectory to pack your things. I'll send a car for you in the morning at seven thirty. You must be ready to start at eight o'clock sharp!"

"My things? What 'things' do you mean, *madame*?"

"Whatever personal items you have in your room, *monsieur*—your clothing and such. Videsh will need you here when he arrives in the mornings."

"*Madame*, I prefer to remain at the rectory. I commit to rise each day in time to walk to the workshop before he arrives."

She seemed flustered and looked away. "Oh, my. It appears we have another unfortunate misunderstanding. Best for you to discuss the living arrangements with Father Ralph or Thomas— Bishop Brennan, I should say." A sympathetic look cast his way. "Would you like a car in the morning, or do you prefer to walk to meet Videsh?"

"I'll walk. *Merci.*"

Coty rose and approached him. When he stood in response, she grasped his limp arms above the elbows. After a slight rise onto her tiptoes, she kissed the man on his cheek. His brown eyes widened as she pulled back from her peck and rubbed his arms, moving her hands up until she held his shoulders. Accepting her crisp nod, he let her lead him from the parlor to the front door.

"Arrive early for breakfast, if you like. Magdalena's a glorious cook. Whether you eat with us or at the rectory, don't dawdle, young man."

CHAPTER FIFTEEN

M ornings at the rectory, after rolling from bed, Matheo had knelt to pray before washing his face. Today, at first dawn in his temporary home, he stood perplexed, looking down at his body's impression in the middle of the longest mattress that the tall African had ever lain upon. How could he not have slept well in such comfort? How many more restless nights awaited him in Coty Fine's home?

Prayer. He retrieved his beads and, rather than kneeling, lay supine. As Matheo sank into the billowy duvet, the pleasure of saying the rosary seemed assured.

The tempo of his rote recitation raced. Hope-filled words rushed from his mouth. On he droned; however, the fervor he had known as a youngster refused his summons. The repetitious prayers faded as his body levitated and his mind drifted.

Needles of conspiracy pricked him. Had he encountered betrayal by Father Ralph or the benevolence of a friend concerned? Had coincidence precipitated his collision with an eccentric old lady? Did Bishop Brennan work for God or for Coty Fine?

With the ceiling in focus, he held the rosary's crucifix, rolling it over from side to side as if readying a coin to flip for resolution. He released the cross, piled the beads in a heap on his chest, and brought his hand to join its mate behind his head.

The smell of coffee brewing slipped upstairs; he was not alone. As yesterday, Videsh Joshi would arrive on time and be ready to get to work at eight o'clock sharp.

Vexation lifted Matheo to his feet. The rosary snaked down his stomach and slithered to the floor. As he reached over for hurried collection of the venerable beads, the hum of a car engine drifted up from the driveway below his window.

Matheo grabbed a cup of coffee on his way through the kitchen to the back porch stairs. When he approached the rear of the vehicle, a frustrated Neeta released her two-handed hold on the walker and stepped back from the lip of the trunk. She turned and let her arms go limp when he said, "*Mademoiselle, merci.* Allow me."

The walker was wedged inside, under the curved hinges of the trunk door. He pressed the frame down and, with a smooth tug, pulled it from the cavity.

"NaaNaa Joshi, I'll come back for you at five o'clock, like yesterday. Okay?"

Not turning back to locate his granddaughter, the old man squeezed the handles of his walker and pressed forward in the direction of the garages. He was bent over his contraption, shuffling his feet, when he shouted, "Yes, yes, of course. Seventeen hundred hours. Go now, Neeta!"

Matheo looked at Neeta, who shrugged her shoulders. "Thanks for getting that thing out of there. He's all yours until five."

"*Oui, mademoiselle.* Five o'clock sharp, *non*?"

Neeta laughed as she dipped into the driver's seat. Before restarting the car, she smiled at her grandfather racing like a determined turtle up the driveway.

Her horn tooted out a goodbye to the apprentice, who was chasing his master toward their tools. Without breaking his crawl, Videsh cast a sideways grin up and over his stooped shoulders. Matheo suspected that Monsieur Joshi had perceived in the priest a greater interest in the carpenter's granddaughter than in Videsh himself or his workshop.

The walker stopped. Videsh looked at the steaming mug in Matheo's hand and said, "I trust you got a good night's sleep, young man. We were slow yesterday. Today, we must pick up the pace."

"*Oui*, Monsieur Joshi. *Madame* must see that we're making progress each day," Matheo said with feigned enthusiasm, straining to insulate the master from the private turmoil of his apprentice.

The day before, as they labored, Matheo's worries had dissipated with the return of the physical pleasures of the craft he had acquired as a seminarian. Rooster tails of sawdust had blanketed his forearms as he fed roughhewn planks into the mouth of the planer. The touch of warm wood, smoothed and heated by the spinning blades of the cutter head, had restored tactile connection to a happier time. He sensed it had done the same for the master carpenter whom he now served.

Coty called out and waved. When she neared the bottom of the brick staircase, she shouted, "A cup of coffee, young man? Have you had any breakfast?"

"*Madame*, Monsieur Joshi wants to get to the shop. We have much to do, *non*?"

The mistress huffed, cleared her throat, and turned her attention to Videsh as she arrived in front of his advancing wheels. She placed outstretched hands on the walker's frame and braced herself with ample leverage to halt his progress. With their stalemate set, Coty spoke to her octogenarian peer. "Videsh, you'll drive your apprentice into the ground. He must eat a hardy breakfast before you begin work each day."

Videsh stopped, bullied his posture into a less acute slope, and craned his neck to face her. "He should've eaten before I arrived. It's already 8:03!" he proclaimed, without consulting his wristwatch.

"Men! Seriously! I refuse to mother you, Videsh. You're incorrigible."

Coty cast her gaze over Videsh's curved back and aimed her

voice at Matheo. "Monsieur Aubert, yesterday you devoured Magdalena's sandwiches as soon as she brought them to the shop. If you don't eat a good breakfast, your master will, once again, drain your energy before noon."

"*Madame*, I can't eat unless Monsieur Joshi eats as well, *non*?"

"*Non*. I said he was incorrigible. Even on an empty stomach, that man has an inhuman capacity for work. Without a proper diet, you won't keep up."

Videsh unveiled his aerated grin. Shuffling ahead, he shrugged his bowed shoulders. Coty stepped aside, allowing the wheels of the walker to roll in escape. Matheo laughed.

With a faint cough, Coty insisted that he return his attention to her lecture. "Monsieur Aubert, don't encourage him to contest me. Come into the kitchen and eat, or you'll have master and mistress at each other's throat."

The hunched-over carpenter winked at Matheo and said, "All right, have a little breakfast. But tomorrow, young man, eat *before* I arrive. We'll start work promptly at oh eight hundred hours."

"*Oui*, Monsieur Joshi. Eight o'clock—sharp!"

Matheo smiled into the beaming eyes of their patroness, who had lavished commands, insisting without belittling. As maddening as she was, Matheo found her adamant voice a soothing paradox, reminiscent of the city noises that had grated against the sides of the rectory and, at first, delayed his sleep in America. After his inaugural weeks in California had passed, those same sounds persuaded him to close his eyes at night.

With three long-legged strides, she overtook Videsh again and placed her hand on his stooped shoulder. Matheo sensed her concern. His admiration grew as her words kissed the ear of the master carpenter.

"Videsh, please, come inside with us."

"Coty, I must get to work. It takes me time to get back there."

"I want to show you something on my computer. Come to the kitchen and have a tea, and we'll discuss the project."

"I can't see drawings on a computer. Neeta tried to show me. Didn't she tell you? I asked her to tell you."

"She did. I'm having the large-format blueprints made, as you requested. I want to show you something else: a few three-dimensional renderings. No schematics. The blueprints will be ready in a couple of days. Matheo and I will roll them out on the shop table before you start work the next day."

"Oh eight hundred?"

"Yes, Videsh. Eight o'clock sharp! Now, bring your apprentice in for breakfast and have that cup of tea."

"Can you believe it, Nana? We found her."

"Darling, that's wonderful news. You thought it was a long shot, but I had a good feeling."

Coty sat back on her ankles as she knelt before the flowerbed. Her granddaughter's clear voice rushed from Hanoi, the sound so crisp that it seemed Evelyn was kneeling next to her, wielding the spade she had used since childhood to assist her gardening grandmother.

"Nana, it was simple. She's still a nun. Or, better said, she's a nun again."

"What? She reenlisted, or whatever they call it?"

"You crack me up, Nana. She was right there, where you last saw her: at the convent."

From the time Evelyn was a little girl, Coty had told her the tale of the grandfather she had never met. Evelyn knew about the French priest and the beautiful nun—a bedtime story she had begged her nana to tell over and over, night after night.

"Oh, Evelyn, I'm so happy. Hold on; I've got to write this down." She pulled her tattered spiral notepad from the denim pocket and freed her pen. "All right. I should've done this years ago. Tell me, what's Sister Lan's surname?"

For decades, she had tried in vain to claw back the

woman's full name, which Laurent had spoken aloud at least once.

"Bùi Thị Lan," Evelyn said.

"Can you spell it, dear?"

"The lettering's strange. Give me a second; I'll text it to you."

A flight of the city's famous green parrots, known for their domicile on Telegraph Hill, swept overhead, yakking. She watched them trail away as she waited for Evelyn's message.

"Okay, Nana; is it there yet?"

"No, dear. It's been driving me crazy for—"

Her phone vibrated, cutting off her commentary: *Bùi Thị Lan*. Coty adjusted the phone's screen in the daylight. Her pen clicked. She transcribed the nun's name into her book, as if only on paper could she trust what she read. After clicking her pen closed, she stroked the handwritten name.

When she stood to stretch, she heard cracks in one knee. A sharp bolt shot from her hip. The dancer's legs were still limber but each day shouted painful reminders of their mileage. "Tell me, Evelyn, what did she say when you found her?"

"She remembered you. Her vision's bad—severe cataracts; she couldn't really see your photo. 'The pretty American with the camera,' she said. I had to laugh when she told me you were taller than any Vietnamese man she'd ever seen."

Down into turned soil, Coty flung her spade. There it stuck, handle up, parked on an angle like a hatchet sunk into a chopping block. She brushed the dirt off her freed right hand and transferred the phone to her other ear.

After finishing her account of the hunt for Sister Lan, Evelyn took a long breath. When she paused, Coty asked about the priest. "Did she mention Laurent?"

"I showed her the shot of him on the back of the truck. She squinted, and even though she couldn't see it clearly, she stroked the picture with her fingertips. She cried, Nana, and said what you already knew: he never returned to Hanoi."

CHAPTER SIXTEEN

———•———

D ays later, after breakfast, with Matheo and Videsh at work in
the shop, Dr. Odette Walsh arrived from the airport. Jette set
her luggage down on the back porch, slipped into the kitchen,
and called to her childhood nanny, who stood busy at the sink
over running water. Magdalena splashed in shock and, blessing
herself with wet fingers, turned to the porch door. "Oh, Jette!
How did you get inside without me hearing you, *querida*?"

Arms spread wide, Jette stepped to embrace the woman who,
in her early seventies, stood reaching over the edge of a basin
higher than her pillowed waistline. Magdalena pressed the dish
towel into the small of Jette's back, brought her other hand to
close around the twin, let her temple find the doctor's chest, and
squeezed a loving welcome. Jette returned the hug and addressed
her with the Spanish moniker Noémie had given their nanny:
little mother.

"I heard *you*, *madrecita*. Half singing, half humming—why
are you so happy?"

"Evelyn found Sister Lan! And the nun is coming home with
her."

"Ah, wonderful news," said Jette, without disclosing that,
after landing less than an hour earlier, she and Coty had traded
updates when she'd called her mother from the tarmac.

"*Si, si.* Coty's so excited."

"Mother wasn't out in the gardens. Is she home?"

Minutes ago, Coty had not answered her daughter's shout from the driveway. Jette suspected that her mother was in a pout and had instigated, not for the first time, a game of hide-and-seek as payback for another overextended absence.

"Sí, querida—up in her room. Do you want me to call her?"

"No, Magdalena. I'll go surprise her, too."

Bags in hand, stuffed canvas rucksack slung over her back, Jette lumbered to the bottom of the staircase, dropped the suitcases at her feet, and aimed her voice at the second floor: "Mother?"

Nothing.

"*Mother!*"

No response. With one hand on the banister and the other on her hip, she stared over the carpeted landing into the stained-glass window. With a *humph*, she dipped to grab the luggage and resumed the climb.

Stepping into the second-floor hallway, she kept her momentum until she reached her bedroom. She abandoned the bags outside her door. Shaking her head in frustration, she walked down the corridor to her mother's room. Tired and jet lagged, Jette did not possess the energy to stomp her disgust.

Three knocks on the closed door yielded no response. With one hand on the knob, she paused. Clenching her eyes and lowering her head, she cracked the door, then held her breath and listened. Silence.

Jette's annoyance grew fresh shoots. "*Mother!* I know you can hear me. I'm coming in." The bed floated in the space between the entry and two matching doors at the far end; one led to the walk-in closet, while the other secured the bathroom's privacy. "Mother, please. Are you on the toilet? Call out from your throne, Queen Mum!"

The duvet had been pulled halfway off the mattress—unusual for the woman whose custom was to make her bed each morning before descending to the kitchen. Next, Jette saw the exposed bare feet. Coty's long, lean body lay still; her chest did not heave but seemed to rise and fall on the margin.

Questions rushed at the physician as Jette knelt by her mother's head. If she had had a stroke, time was of the essence; a heart attack, the same. When had it happened? How long had her mother been on the floor?

Thrust in the direction of Jette's face, the gap between her mother's forefinger and thumb indicated a slight tolerance. A fist formed, collapsing the digital calipers. Appearing frustrated, as well as melodramatic, Coty brought her arm down to her side with a dull thud onto the carpet.

"Argh! Odette, I was this close!"

Hmm, she only calls me Odette when she's really ticked off—or extremely happy, Jette thought. She let it go. "Mother, do you have to scare me *every* time I come home?"

"Dear, I wasn't trying to scare anyone. I was meditating."

"On the floor, next to your bed, with your covers pulled halfway across your body? Seriously, do you take me for a complete fool?"

"I wouldn't say a *complete* fool. That's an absolute. You know how I feel about absolutes. 'Always,' 'never,' and 'ever' *only* lead to problems. No, darling, you're not a *complete* fool."

"Nice to see you, too, Mother. Why are you, uh, *meditating* down here on the floor? We just talked on the phone! You knew I'd get home about now. It seems like you wanted to freak me out —*again*. But please help me understand. I know how you hate it when I jump to conclusions."

Coty reached her arms into the air and embraced her daughter, pulling Jette's head tight against her modest bosom. She rocked back and forth while tousling the doctor's short hair. Jette, eyes closed and mouth curled into a wide grin, cooed in the safety of her mother's hug.

"Dear, your tone. Hmm, sounds very conclusive, if you ask me."

"You frightened me." Unraveling Coty's embrace, Jette pushed herself up and sat back on her heels. She grabbed her mother's hands, which she brought in a fold to her lips. After an exaggerated kiss, she released them. "Meditation? New hobby, Mother?"

"Parvani and Neeta have been training me."

Raising her right hand into view, thumb and forefinger separated by less than an inch, Jette squinted, mocking her mother's figurative pinchers. "You were this close . . . to what?"

"Oh, darn, I can't remember the Hindi word for it—one of their higher levels of sublimity. Sounds divine—and without an implicit godhead messing with you."

"Ahem. Why now?"

"I was tired in the gardens this morning, which *never* happens. After you called, I came in to lie down." Coty beamed a truce at her daughter. "Really, darling. I tried to take a little nap. Lying there, wide awake, I decided that I might as well practice my mediation. I slid off the bed for a harder surface."

"I don't believe you. Anyway, when does Evelyn get here?"

"She lands the day after tomorrow."

"Where'd she find the nun?"

"Where I last saw her: at the convent in Hanoi."

When her plane had departed for San Francisco, Jette had been in Frankfurt, on Central European Time, nine hours ahead of California. Home in the childhood room that she had shared with Noémie, she awoke in the dark, disoriented. Unable to fall back asleep, she sat, curled under a blanket in the window seat, and read for hours.

Artificial light from below tapped on the glass when her mother illuminated the kitchen to assist the nascent dawn. Jette imagined Magdalena's singsong greeting as the two older women shared the commencement of a morning that, after breakfast, would fork into separate daily routines.

Jette stopped behind the dining-room doors. She heard the two women chortling. With a broad grin, she entered the kitchen. When she waved hello, Coty stepped next to Magdalena and wrapped her arm around the stout woman's waist. The mismatched duo—one tall and lean, the other short and round—angled their heads toward each other and raised their voices to belt out the theme song to Magdalena's favorite telenovela. Shaking her groggy head at how her mother's New York accent butchered the Spanish lyrics, Jette played along by acting as their choir leader. With an invisible baton, she scratched out time in the air.

The housekeeper's cell phone chimed, and Magdalena stopped her performance. Answering the call in excited Spanish, she laughed into the device as she shuffled through the dining-room doors with the phone at her ear. For Jette's exclusive benefit, Coty continued solo.

With her feet fixed on the floor, her legs on a slant from tailbone to the soles of her shoes, Jette sipped coffee. She leaned back against the countertop as Coty milled about in song, trailed by her timeless snowy braid. From behind, the matriarch resembled Evelyn, leaving Jette wondering what to anticipate when her daughter returned with the Vietnamese nun in tow.

"Mother, I love to hear your voice. It makes the coffee smell better."

"Darling, that's sweet, although ridiculous, and understandable, coming from you. Hmm, 'understandably ridiculous'—I like that, don't you? I've got to jot it down." From the front pocket of her denim garden smock, Coty pulled the tattered spiral notepad. She scribbled in it while humming the chorus of the interrupted tune. The click of her ballpoint pen telegraphed a task completed. "Now, my dear, tell me what time you got up."

"A bit after three. It'll take a couple of days. Right now, it seems like I should be thinking about dinner."

"Yes, of course. Well, by this time tomorrow, you'll think it's only afternoon teatime. How do you feel?"

"A little nauseous; a world without caffeine would be brutal." Jette combed her ringless fingers through her cropped white hair. While interning as a new surgeon, before her first tour with MSF, she had cut the trademark family locks out of convenience. She had never grown her hair back out.

"Maybe this time you should stay home longer. You seem like you could use a solid rest. When do you leave for Seattle, dear?"

"I fly up on the first." She could see her mother's wheels turning, calculating the days before her side trip to Seattle Children's Hospital.

"How long can you stay in San Francisco—I mean, after you finish training in Seattle?"

"As long as possible, Mother, as you asked."

"Good. I want to throw an old-fashioned party while you're home, after Sister Lan has had her surgeries."

"What does she need surgery for?"

"Evelyn said the woman's cataracts are bad; for all intents and purposes, she's blind."

For weeks, Jette had known about the intended party, which she had assumed would take place before she flew to Seattle. She had not anticipated the delay resulting from the nun's condition. She felt compelled to repeat what her mother knew all too well. "Mother, you realize that when I go, it'll be with little notice, right?"

"Yes, as usual. Forgive me, but . . ." Coty reached into her skirt to retrieve her notebook. The pen was clipped between the worn cover and the page of her last entry. With theater that Jette had come to expect, Coty replaced her reading glasses in a flourish. She lifted the pad before her eyes and said, "I do find the method of your disappearances 'understandably ridiculous.'"

"Mother?"

"Yes, dear?"

"I prefer your voice when you're singing."

———•••———

Evelyn would arrive soon from Hanoi, escorting Bùi Thị Lan, the near-blind nun. Coty's prediction of clangs when her daughter and granddaughter crossed swords caused Jette to acknowledge to herself the lost affection she had enjoyed when Evelyn was a young girl—a time when Jette had been present and attentive.

She opened an upper cabinet door, pulled down a coffee cup for her mother, and presented, without words, a communal invitation. Coty nodded. As she sauntered to her seat, she burst into an encore of the throaty chorus that she and Magdalena had staged. Jette poured coffee into the cup, refilled her own, and joined her mother at the table, kissing elbows on purpose as she deposited the steaming mugs.

Buoyed by the physical touch, Coty glowed. After taking a sip, she asked, "Have you given any more thought to my request? You know how much I'd like to publish that photo."

"I have, Mother. I thought about it during the flight over. I'm sorry, but I haven't changed my mind."

"I'm disappointed to hear that, darling. I won't pull out the age card—"

"You just did." Jette raised her cup. As the coffee touched her lips, she stared over the mug's edge and gave her mother a winkless look of *gotcha*, before she herself resurrected a bit of family theater, which Coty was certain to detect. Jette sipped, then deployed the audible sigh that her rebellious twin sister had used as a teenager to lodge dissent. "*Hmm.*"

"Well, that's reminiscent, darling. I accept your objection, but I do think I'll play that age card."

"You already did, Mother."

"Well, technically, maybe, but since it was subconscious—"

"Some would say passive-aggressive, not subconscious."

"That's most unhelpful."

"British understatement, Mother?"

"Indeed. At least admit that my use of the age card was an incomplete play, ham-handed at best. Please grant your mother a do-over, dear."

"Even though I asked you the last time I was home not to play the age card about the photograph?" Jette chided, drawing bent fingers through her hair.

Coty sent her an injured look.

Exhausted, with few other tools to deploy, Jette repeated Noémie's wordless protest. "*Hmm.*"

"Odette, is that the best you can do?"

Smirking at the use of her given name, Jette lowered her coffee mug and, knowing she had caused but a minor delay, braced herself.

"Why are you being stubborn?"

"Mother, don't stoop so low. I hate it when you use that word."

"Yes, I remember how indignant it made you as a child. Much like how those groans bothered poor Magdalena."

Jette resisted the ploy of invoking their beloved nanny and waited for her mother to continue.

Coty cleared her throat and said, "Darling, I'm simply asking you to reconsider letting me publish the photograph."

"I will."

"I'm asking you to do it before Evelyn gets back. Our book is otherwise ready to go."

"*Our* book?" The agitation escalated, and her tongue tasted more of riposte than of coffee bean. Jette raised her cup again, as a barrier between them.

"The publisher has given up hope that I'll release it to production. My agent won't even talk to me."

"Sounds like the timing is clearly your decision, Mother."

"It'll sit there until you grant me permission to include that shot. I've never captured anything that telling, that wrenching."

"Exactly! You didn't capture it, remember?"

"Yes. At the time, I was driving home from the morgue where I left Noémie."

"Harsh, Mother."

"Jette, I know it's not my shot, but *please* let me incorporate it into this final book."

"Publish your own photographs—they're brilliant! Why can't you let this one go?"

"Closure."

"Evelyn doesn't need to see that shot. She knows the truth. Why rub her nose in it?"

"Closure."

"My relationship with her is too strained. It could make things even worse."

"Maybe it would help your relationship."

"That's not my impression."

"Odette, please. This is important to me. It's one of the most poignant pictures I've seen in my professional career."

Odette—the repeated use of her given name caused Jette to quiet.

The lull must have been too much for the matriarch, who said, "The Great Manipulator, huh? I can't even get you to grant one small accommodation. If your mother-in-law were alive—"

"It's not a small accommodation, and all rants must end when Janice comes up."

"Odette, please don't deflect."

"Mother, stop. I'll take it under further consideration."

"A spot of your own British understatement?"

"Indeed, Queen Mum."

"Well, how cultured of you, darling."

"*Hmm.*"

"*Bonjour*, Madame Coty!"

As had become their early-morning custom, Matheo entered

the kitchen and greeted Coty in French. He spotted the stranger with short white hair, resting in a tired stance against the counter. Jette knew that her mother had prepared him to meet his surgeon; however, in the moment, he appeared the embarrassed interloper.

"*Pardonnez-moi*, Madame Coty. Sorry for the interruption."

"You live here, *monsieur*. Remember?" Coty said, with a playful scowl.

"*Oui, madame.*" The nervous priest bowed, before he turned to stare at Jette. Yesterday, after she had arrived, they had not met, since she had gone to sleep before he'd finished in the workshop with Videsh.

Coty paused and, sweeping her arm out into the room with theatrical flair, pointed to the yawning woman, who was smiling at their exchange. "Matheo, let me introduce you to your surgeon—my daughter, Jette."

"*Enchanté*, Docteur Walsh."

"*Enchantée.* Please, call me Jette."

"*Enchanté*, Madame Jette." He patted his open right hand against his chest and bowed once more. "Père Aubert . . . uh, Matheo." The priest looked at Coty as if he had committed a grave error.

Coty laughed and, in French, said, "The coffee's fresh, *monsieur*. Join us?"

"French, Mother?" Jette asked, arching her eyebrows.

"Darling, we're trying to sharpen up our French around here, since Sister Lan will arrive soon." Returning to French, Coty faced the priest and said, "Matheo, my daughter's fluent."

Jette decided that, after refusing permission to publish the photograph, she would grant her mother a minute accommodation. She nodded at Coty, turned to Matheo, and let her French flow as advertised. "*Monsieur*, how would you prefer me to address you?"

"Matheo is fine. And, please, Madame Jette, speak English. I must improve."

"Dear, he's being modest. He studied English in Gabon, while at seminary. And Matheo's been listening to the sins of our neighbors for over two years. His English is quite strong."

"You're most generous, Madame Coty." Matheo looked from mother to daughter and waited for Jette to respond.

"I'm a bit jet lagged, Matheo; I might be speaking Frenglish for the next few days."

His eyes welled as he struggled to find his voice, before he blurted out, "Docteur Walsh, I must thank you for saving my life. I don't know—"

"*Merci*, Matheo. I remember you well, and I'm pleased that you grew tall and strong. We'll have time to talk of such things when I'm truly awake."

Rather than exacerbate his discomfort, Jette looked away from the flustered priest. It would take her days to adjust to the Pacific Time Zone, as well as to the presence of the vibrant man whom she remembered as a fragile boy.

Her mother's voice punctured the awkward reunion. "Jette, would you please take your coffees and show Matheo the dark-room? When he moved in, I gave him a quick tour, but we didn't descend into the catacombs."

"Mother, 'catacombs' is an apt description. The darkroom's an empty tomb. You haven't used it since you went digital years ago."

"Darling, Videsh will be here soon. I spread some blueprints out on the table down there. Would you please bring those up-stairs for me, dear?"

"Mother, the darkroom?"

"Please, Jette, my hip is acting up again."

Mother's hip was "acting up" in concert with the rest of her. Jet lag had drawn down Jette's patience, although she stopped short of indicting her mother in front of the priest. She settled for shooting a coded daughter-mother stare, then turned and said, "Matheo, care to see the basement?"

"*Oui*, Madame Jette. I admire your mother's photography very much. I'd like to visit her darkroom."

"It's a dusty relic. For more than a decade, she's *manipulated* the images on her computer. Prints out copies right in her office."

Coty cleared her throat, drawing her daughter's attention. Once they made eye contact, she brought the coffee cup to her lips and executed a sigh in private rejoinder to her daughter's embedded sarcasm.

Touché, thought Jette. Maybe it was the co-opted sigh. Maybe it was the gloating expression on her mother's face. Jet lagged, irritated, and no longer wishing to insulate the priest from the family dynamic, Jette poked at the matriarch by saying, "Mother, why did you put the blueprints downstairs?"

Her mother's feigned shock put Jette on high alert. She had grown wary and assumed that the basement ploy was payback for continued obstinance over the controversial photo. The priest had become the spectator of a perennial match between longtime contestants. She thought him oblivious, a man who might not detect their verbal fencing, much less when a staggering, nuanced blow had landed.

"I thought your hip was acting up, Mother. Why'd you decide to hide the blueprints in the basement? When was the last time you used the darkroom, anyway?"

"Every day for several weeks. I've been working on our retrospective project, my dear."

Jette shook her head as she waited for her mother to proceed down the forbidden path.

Coty accommodated with dramatic flair. "That's why my hip's been troubling me. Up and down those stairs! I've made progress, though. Please take a look and tell me what you think, darling."

The door to the basement creaked open. The steps groaned under their rhythmic sways as the two descended. Every footfall suggested the next timeworn tread might snap, causing one of them to stumble and slam a shoulder against the wall.

The basement was musty, as Jette remembered from childhood excursions with Noémie into the underbelly of the old house, back when, for abandoned and forgotten treasure, the cellar had been challenged only by the attic that capped their home. Today, there would be no happening upon lost riches, hibernating until discovery by prepubescent explorers. As they stepped out onto the cement floor, Jette anticipated that she and the priest would encounter a trap.

The cool air felt clammy against her skin as they approached the darkroom door. Foreshadowing the once-hazardous chamber, a padlock hung open.

Jette felt for the string to turn on the hanging lightbulb, shrouded by a conical bonnet that Coty called a metal *nón lá*. As it flashed over the table, it illuminated the dusty trays, dry of chemicals, stacked to one side.

Mother had planted her bait—Videsh's blueprints—in the open, atop the table, as promised. Unsuspecting prey, drawn to the tabletop, would wander head down into the center of the trap's jaws. Bowing over the plans, Matheo stood aside Jette at the table's edge.

Hung from the old drying lines, the glossy prints surrounded the table from above; each photograph had been taken at one of the hospitals Jette frequented as a visiting surgeon with MSF. She cringed as she searched for the contraband—the photograph of her, dressed in scrubs, with a stethoscope draped around her neck, sitting on the edge of the bed next to Matheo, who lay propped up in the ICU, staring, through a fog of drugs, into the camera's lens.

With an audible *swoosh*, Matheo turned the top, blue-dusted page, which rustled in the air close to the suspended photographs. There it was, inches above the back of his head. Claiming a technicality, Coty would insist that she had not compromised their agreement, since she had blurred the two faces. Jette noticed that the rest of the image was clear, except for their hands, which were also blurred—an odd treatment of the original shot.

The forbidden photograph hung alongside other pictures of Jette with her patients—molars set in the trap's jaws to bite down hard and grind through a daughter's resistance. She ripped the outlawed print from the line without Matheo noticing.

"Oh, Madame Jette—pictures of you," he said, looking up after he had reassembled the stack. Mesmerized by the dangling images, he rolled up the blueprints as he advanced down the line of photos, studying each individual shot. "Madame Jette, was our picture taken, too?"

She swallowed her anger and said, "*Oui, monsieur.*"

"Is it here?"

"Matheo?"

"I have no snapshots of myself as a young boy. Only a group picture, taken years later at the orphanage, when I was in second grade."

"Our photo's not hanging there," she said, squashing the paper into a white lie. "The quality was poor—too blurry. Maybe we can ask Mother to take one of us while I'm home. Would you like that?"

"*Oui, madame.* Very much."

He returned to the photos of the doctor and the other children she had saved. His fingers touched the front of his shirt. She knew that he was reading, as if it were written in Braille, the tale of her scalpel. He looked at her, and his eyes filled as he croaked his thanks: "For my life . . . *merci,* Docteur Walsh."

When Jette patted his shoulder, the crumpled photograph crinkled against his shirt. Pressing his back, she turned him to face the door before she jammed the picture into the rear pocket of her pants.

Matheo stepped out onto the open cellar floor. Flummoxed, he tapped on the end of the rolled-up blueprints as he waited for his escort—his earthly savior. Before following him out into the dim light of the basement, Jette reached to pull the string. With her downward tug, the darkroom reclaimed its moniker.

The engine's rumble announced the arrival of the master carpenter. Passing by the basement window above their heads, the vehicle cast a shadow, which drew Jette's gaze. As she rethreaded the padlock by feel, she watched black tires roll to a stop.

With a hushed *whomp*, the driver's door was resealed. Coty's voice joined Neeta's in salutation. After a pause in their chattering, they were laughing at what seemed to be failure at a joint task.

"What're they doing out there?" Jette asked, abandoning the door's padlock.

Matheo perked up as he looked through the window and said, "They're removing Monsieur Joshi's walker from the boot. He'll be on a fast track to the workshop."

"Fast track?"

The priest laughed. Then, frowning, he said, "We promised to have the blueprints and a cup of hot tea ready for him when he arrived at his workbench this morning."

"You might have enough time to get that roll to the shop before him. I'll make his tea and meet you there in a couple of minutes."

Magdalena's elbows darted above the sink. Without turning to face them, the housekeeper noted that after they had descended into the basement, Coty had returned to her gardens. Jette thought it convenient that her mother had escaped, after insisting she and the priest visit the darkroom.

"Videsh and Neeta are outside. Did you hear the car?" Jette asked her nanny.

"No, *querida*, the water's been running. Is your mother out there, too?" Magdalena asked, as she closed the tap. She rose on her tiptoes, peered through the glass, and cocked an ear to listen to the world outside.

"*Si, madrecita*. We heard her come down to the driveway to greet them." Magdalena reached for a dish towel. Next to the coffee machine, a cell phone rattled the marble countertop. "*Ay!* Your mother forgot her phone—again," she lamented, looking down at the wriggling device as it clattered in an aimless jitter.

"*Again?*" Jette asked.

Drying her hands with the dishtowel, Magdalena said, "Leave the phone there, *querida*. Let me talk to her about it; lately, she's embarrassed about her memory."

Neeta and Coty exchanged goodbye hugs as the old man inched his way toward his beloved sawdust. To intercept Videsh en route, Matheo, with the rolled-up blueprints in hand, hopped outside.

Jette marched across the kitchen to the walk-in pantry. She ducked inside and, without flipping the light switch, dropped the blurred duplicate of the original photograph behind forgotten cans on the top shelf. She exited the pantry, mumbling, "I can't believe her."

Dish towel in hand, Magdalena reacted to the words, which Jette had intended as a self-indulgent grouse. "*Querida*, don't be angry with her."

"Who's angry?"

"Jette, I've lived with you and your mother since you were a little girl. You two can't hide your thoughts from each other—or *me!*"

"It's nothing—jet lag. I just need more sleep and lots of your wonderful cooking."

The towel snapped. Magdalena folded it while, in silence, she cast a doubtful expression that triggered Jette to continue.

"When Evelyn gets back, we'll be fine," Jette said.

The two women stood side by side over the sink, facing the window. Outdoors, female voices laughed. The sedan's driver's side door thudded shut, and Neeta drove away.

Jette wondered why her mother had not sent Neeta inside to

say hello. Of late, she felt it easier to talk to Neeta than to her own daughter. She shrugged. Better to see Neeta in the afternoon when she came back for Videsh, who might view their reunion as less important than the delivery of his morning tea.

The kettle whistled. Through the window, Jette watched Coty plod up the brick stairway to the upper gardens. Her mother's head hung over her knees and her steps appeared more labored than Jette remembered from her last trip home.

Jette was filling a porcelain mug for Videsh when the priest banged against the door. Matheo yanked it open and leaned into the kitchen from the porch. He was panting and appeared frantic.

"He's fallen! Monsieur Joshi doesn't answer me!"

"Is he breathing?"

As she listened for his response, Jette grabbed her mother's phone from the countertop and dialed 911. Matheo held the door until she reached it; then he pivoted, leaped down the steps, and sprinted toward the workshop.

Magdalena followed Jette outside, where they met Coty, negotiating her way down the brick stairs. All four streamed ant-like over the driveway to find their fallen craftsman. A distant siren cracked the morning as Coty, the last to arrive, entered the garage bay. Atop a layer of sawdust, Videsh was splayed on the concrete floor in an awkward position, one leg twisted at an angle in the direction of a shiny new bandsaw. The walker lay toppled less than two feet away. Jette knelt at his side.

Wood chips stuck to his clothing, while sawdust frosted his shoulders and speckled his thin white hair. Videsh aimed his words at Coty. "I'm fine. My apprentice overreacted, Coty. It's slippery in here. He must sweep up better." He scrunched his face into a warped grin, a clear attempt to dissuade mass worry. "I was meditating, Coty. Like you."

Jette placed her hand on his wrist and took his pulse. When his eyes sought hers, she said, "Videsh, can you slow down a bit?"

The fallen man beamed at the woman he had not seen in years. "Jette, good to see you! Tell them I'm fine. They'll believe you—you're a doctor," he said as she and Matheo helped him sit up.

Although she suspected he had not had a stroke, she stepped Videsh through the simple FAST test. His closed-lip smile was even—neither side drooped more than the other. He raised a trembling arm, as instructed. He spoke without confusion. The siren's volume rose, indicating the ambulance was close. Jette rubbed his arm and, relieved, slumped back onto her heels.

"I think you're okay, but the ambulance crew will want to make sure themselves. This won't take long, Videsh. Stay calm and breathe slowly."

The EMTs arrived at his side and captured the old man's attention. One of the attendants repeated the FAST protocol, which Videsh passed a second time. The other wrapped his arm with a blood-pressure cuff and squeezed the pump. They talked in calm voices, apparently having ascertained, too, that the man was not in any immediate danger.

"You're going to be fine, sir."

Videsh sent a passionate appeal to his benefactress. "Please, Coty, don't tell Parvani or Neeta. Not even Karun. They worry too much."

"Videsh, are you concerned that they won't let you work here?" Coty asked, with a touch on his shoulder that was not lost on her daughter.

"I can't sit around their house. I'm not an old man." When the younger of the two EMTs failed to mask his grin, Videsh refined his statement. "I'm not that old, anyway."

"You're a free man, Videsh. Working here is your choice," Coty said.

Videsh's shoulders drooped farther, and, averting his eyes, he drew a shaky, wrinkled finger in an oval through the sawdust on the floor. "I knew a man—a boyhood friend. He was wobbly like I am. One day, he called me from a place his family took him—

without asking. Assisted living, he called it. Sounded like nice words, but it was a trick—a mean trick, I tell you."

"Do you think your family is mean, Videsh?"

"No, Coty, that's not the point. People—younger people—are told to do such things. They buy peace of mind for themselves, not for old people like me or my friend."

"Why ever would they ship you off to such a place, Videsh?" Coty asked in a tender murmur, as she stroked the top of his shoulder.

"They want me to use a wheelchair, Coty," he muttered. The oval track in the sawdust widened as his finger lapped. "First, the wheelchair; then off you go, like my friend."

Crouched down to talk to him, Coty shifted her weight and adjusted her pose with a groan.

Mother's hip again, Jette thought.

The matriarch cleared her throat. "Videsh, I've many friends who use wheelchairs. It doesn't mean you have to go to a nursing home, does it?" she asked, rubbing his curled back as he trembled.

"I don't want to burden my daughter. She's busy and can't take care of an old man who can't walk. And Neeta! She hasn't married. She can't be trapped like this. They're going to send me away if I can't walk. I'm the one who's trapped."

The EMTs shifted in their squats. Their uniforms were faded; gray hair lined the temples of the more fit of the duo. His stout counterpart was not a youngster, either, and seemed to struggle for balance as he adjusted his pose. The two men glanced at each other. Jette guessed it was not the first time either had heard such angst voiced aloud as they attended a fallen senior.

"Nonsense. I won't let you go to a place like that," Coty stated, with what Jette knew to be the overarching confidence that her great-grandfather had seeded in her mother's fertile mind as a child. "You can stay right here, Videsh. Study the blueprints—the ramps, the elevator. When you've completed the renovations, this'll be the perfect home for you."

"What?" He shivered from sitting on the cold concrete. Averting his eyes again, he deployed weathered hands. The artisan's wrinkled fingers scrolled symmetrical patterns in the sawdust aside his hips.

Coty stared at him with intensity that Jette understood was meant to transfer strength. "You're assisting *me*, Videsh. You need to have Matheo build those ramps. How can you help me if you can't get around here?"

Videsh capitulated. "I'll need a wheelchair," he muttered.

"Of course. We'll have two delivered straight away—hopefully today, before Neeta returns. Now, let's give your daughter a call. She'll be relieved. You know how Parvani worries."

"Why two?" Videsh snapped.

"Well, one is to fold up and take in the car, like that walker."

"And the second?"

"You'll need to be motorized to move around this place with speed. We'll get you an alpine edition—a beautiful machine."

"A what?"

The EMTs unwrapped the blood-pressure cuff. Coty held her response. Videsh seemed agitated by the pawing strangers who had interrupted his good fortune.

When they moved to raise him from the cement floor, he yanked his arms away and repeated the question to unfurl her suspended answer. "What 'beautiful machine'?"

"An alpine edition. It's a ruggedized version of an electric wheelchair. Big, knobby tires. Lots of power. Outdoorsy types use them to go hiking on trails. A friend of mine showed me. His son's a paraplegic. Climbing accident. Indomitable spirit, that lad. Much like you, Videsh. Yes, that's what you'll need to get around this place." She turned from him and found Matheo staring. "I trust you, too, have done enough 'meditating' for one day?" she said to the priest.

"*Oui, madame*," Matheo said, voicing relief.

"All right, Videsh, have your apprentice sweep up this messy sawdust, and we'll let these men go take care of somebody who really needs their help."

Magdalena had returned to the kitchen. Alone on their walk back to the house, Coty wrapped her arm around Jette's waist. When they arrived at the back porch steps, she released her grip and said, "Well, that might've helped your jet lag a bit. Nothing like a little excitement to clear the fog."

"Mother, I thought you handled Videsh very well. Impressive bedside manner."

"I put a daughter through medical school. Something must've rubbed off."

"Apparently."

"That bedside manner can be applied in many situations. Wouldn't you agree?"

Jette recoiled, read her mother's expression, and suspected a transition back to the verboten photograph. She raised her shield. "Mother, stop! I'm tired. I'm going to take a nap."

"That's a good idea, darling. Get some rest. Evelyn will be home soon."

CHAPTER SEVENTEEN

———•——

The arduous expedition to America had left her drained. Drowsy, the nun doubted herself and wondered if they were still on the jet. Could she be asleep en route, over the ocean? Or had she collapsed on a hotel bed and fallen into slumber? Maybe Lan was simply dreaming that she and Evelyn were shuffling behind the others. Since no bodies crowded her from the sides, she was certain that it was a line. The front of the procession was not visible, nor, behind her, its terminus.

The broad-backed person ahead, whose hair smelled of herbal shampoo, she thought a man, because of his baritone whispers. Had she dreamed of her dead father in recent years? How might his apparition have appeared? Would she have detected his familiar scents? Could she remember dreaming of any odor—ever?

A flapping sound; mere inches from her face, she felt an air-conditioned breeze as something swept in front of her. The man covered his back in fresh leather that hung below the faint waft of his shampoo. As the line tromped forward, huddled in the draft of the stranger's jacket, she followed the scent of the tannery.

Blurred by her cataracts, the blue-uniformed agents stood melting. The officers were separated as handlers often set themselves, occupying far-flung positions in open space. From the sides, she heard their confident voices in speech that was authoritative—sharp, instructive, and insistent. The language they spoke was their language.

Slicing through the smell of leather, a female agent appeared in front of her—a crisp talker in their strange language of domination. The uniformed woman stepped up to Lan and leaned in, close to her nose, inserting herself where breath, good or bad, made unambiguous the intrusion of personal space.

The woman's breath was minty, and Lan thought of her father again. A sudden epiphany: the air she breathed was too clean. The absence of the repulsive odor—expected, while missing— hinted that she was in truth held in a dream. The telltale scent had not been present on the intruding agent's breath, which Lan thought odd for such an authority. How could she be awake? It must be a dream. No one was smoking.

Evelyn stared down at the intruder's badge: US Immigration and Customs Enforcement Agency. Before she spoke, the female ICE agent cut her off, "She's fine, Ms."

"But she can't see you—cataracts. May I please come in with her?" Evelyn was anxious about separating from her charge. The fragile nun spoke no English and, because of her weak vision, struggled to navigate the simplest of paths.

"No, Ms. You can sit over there until she comes out. We need to search her."

The ICE agent was thick waisted. A tight hair bun exposed narrow, bent-over shoulders, which slumped above the crown of the diminutive nun. Evelyn eclipsed the two women, her broad shoulders set for confrontation and defense. Her gray-streaked white mane draped near the shorter pair. "She doesn't speak English. Do you know any French?"

"Not required for our process, Ms. This'll take only a few minutes. Have a seat, please."

"Is this really necessary?"

"Ms., please, don't tell me how to do my job. Sit, or show your passport at the counter and proceed through customs."

The ICE agent turned to guide Sister Lan through the doorway into a private room. She caressed the old woman's sleeve and, with a light touch from behind, placed her other hand on Lan's shoulder. Guiding the nun forward, the officer cooed into her ear. Evelyn knew that Sister Lan could not have understood the English words. The nun nodded and shuffled ahead, as peaceful as a willing martyr.

During their layover in Japan, Evelyn had called home. She insisted that no one come to the airport and make a fuss. The nun was blind. A crowd of unseeable strangers, cackling and pressing close, could toss aside the trust Evelyn had worked hard to establish. Coty had been reluctant but agreed to scrap the planned entourage. Evelyn told Jette that she would text her when they were in the car, and then she could wake Nana and Magdalena.

Rising from her bed, Jette showered and went downstairs to the kitchen. Coty had crafted a bold, colorful, hand-painted collage of Vietnamese and French salutations, which she had hung high across the kitchen wall. They would enter from the back porch. Through her cataracts, Sister Lan would not be able to read the banner. With the coffee machine rumbling, Jette stepped onto the back porch and turned on the outside lights for the travelers' imminent arrival.

To her side, the cell phone lay flat atop the kitchen table, where she sat. Jette nestled her forehead down on top of her folded arms, which brought back childhood memories of her and Noémie, sitting side by side at their desks in a grammar-school classroom. Whenever their overexcited class had been told to "rest" for a few minutes, the twins had exercised what they believed was an exclusive gift. Foreheads pressed into the crotches of bent elbows, sensing each other across the aisle, they stared into private chambers from which they transmitted cloaked communications. Safe in the belief that no others could intercept their thoughts, the girls giggled, while fast breathing fogged their desktops.

Jette whimpered, recalling how their telepathic bond frayed as they moved from elementary school, with teacher-imposed naptime, to upper-grade levels and independent study—independent of each other. In high school, Jette, the senior-class president, plotted to become a physician and mother. Noémie, the artist, was often on probation. Rather than expel the notorious free spirit for bouts of truancy, the high school principal allowed Noémie to walk at graduation. The administration demonstrated pragmatism. Her class-president sister was also the school's valedictorian.

The plane from Tokyo's Narita Airport would land on time. Within minutes, Evelyn and Sister Lan would be in a car, heading north. Jette snuggled in her arms' cradle and listened through jet lag's trance for her sister. Seldom had she felt lonely when she thought of Noémie; often, she felt alone. Jette released a groggy giggle into the privacy of her tabletop tent and, for a brief moment, felt neither.

The phone came alive with her mother's ringtone, and Jette's head jerked up. Across the device's screen was a current photograph of Coty, smiling under her sunhat, kneeling before the backdrop of one of her flower gardens in full bloom.

"Have they landed? Why on earth didn't you wake me?"

Jette touched the screen and, after seeing Evelyn's text, said, "Mother, I'm so sorry. Yes, they're in the car."

"I'll wake Magdalena, then shower. Please, Odette, be welcoming if I'm not down there when they arrive."

The phone clicked to silent. Overhead, two showers went on in quick succession. The older women were up and on the move. They would race to get downstairs, but Jette knew that neither Mother nor Magdalena would arrive in tatters for their guest, who, regardless of their preparation, would not be able to see their faces.

A car door slammed shut. Jette heard words exchanged, then a trunk lid close. She batted her eyes, which went to the welcome banner.

Evelyn pushed on the back-porch door and, with a broad smile, greeted her mother, who was rising from the table. The nun appeared to Jette as if she were her daughter's shadow: a faint impression pinned against the door's frame. Evelyn whispered into Sister Lan's ear, then left the nun at the threshold and rushed into the kitchen to embrace her mother.

No tears, no laughter. Standing there in each other's arms, they embraced as when Evelyn was a child, less aware of time lost, happy to see her mommy, hug her, and receive her love in the now. Jette heaved, sensing Noémie's elusive presence. Hands fell away, their embrace collapsed, and two pairs of slender arms slid toward the kitchen floor.

Jette looked past Evelyn's shoulder at the porch doorway. Dainty fingers wrapped the inside edge of the jamb. The nun, dressed in rumpled white linen, steadied herself at the threshold and presented a peaceful, patient demeanor.

"Sister Lan, let me help you," Evelyn said in French, as she walked across the kitchen to sweep her nana's guest into their home. When Evelyn touched Lan's sleeve, the nun released her grip on the doorjamb and took the arm of her escort. "Sister Lan, this is my mother, Dr. Odette Walsh. Everyone calls her Jette."

Not wanting to startle her, Jette stood in place and also addressed Sister Lan in French: "*Enchantée, madame.* You must be very tired from your journey. Sit for a moment. Tea?"

Sister Lan bowed at the second voice and answered, "*Enchantée.* If you are having tea, *oui*, I will join you." As the duo shuffled in the direction of the table, Sister Lan asked, "Evelyn, may I first visit the toilet?"

As Evelyn cupped the nun's elbow, Sister Lan took the detour from table to powder room. Jette watched her daughter shepherd their guest. Evelyn glanced back with a gleam in her eye.

The door enclosed Sister Lan inside the powder room. Evelyn spun into the open space of the kitchen as Jette looked up at the ceiling and said, "Your grandmother's angry with me. I just woke her up."

"Missed my text, didn't you?"

"Uh-huh. I fell asleep in the chair. Had the phone right here, but—"

"Whoa. You're in big trouble, aren't you?"

"She's been acting tired. Stressed out, I guess. I'm glad we let her sleep."

"Well, that's why it made sense to text *you* when we landed," Evelyn said, sending a look of accusation, which Jette did not need elucidated: *If you had spent more than a few weeks in San Francisco over the past couple of years, you would have witnessed your mother's steady decline.* "As impossible as it seems, Jette, Nana's getting old."

The floor above their heads was pounded, startling all three women huddled in the kitchen. Sister Lan's coated eyes shot up to the ceiling. At the rumble on the staircase, Jette looked at Evelyn, expecting Magdalena to burst in at any second.

With her unbraided hair pulled back into a bushy ponytail, Coty entered first. The erstwhile dancer, known for floating down the staircase, had descended with thumping footfalls reminiscent of their beloved nanny. Ignoring her daughter and granddaughter, she cast her energies to the nun.

In teary French, the women offered each other sips of their histories. Then, in a move that beguiled Jette, who did not remember her mother speaking any Vietnamese, Coty pulled the notebook from her pocket and began reciting a prepared script.

The rehearsed welcome grew lyrical when she reeled off an excerpt from a poem that must have been well known to Sister Lan. The sweet tension broke when Coty misspoke, saying something odd in Vietnamese that brought the nun to laughter. In French, Sister Lan explained that she had been welcomed into a "chamber pot." Evelyn translated for a puzzled Magdalena, who, relieved, joined their giggling.

Mentioning the vibrant banner on the kitchen wall, Coty invited Lan to imagine what she herself would see after her cataract operations. "I made you a welcome sign, Sister Lan. I'm not going to read it to you. You'll do that yourself soon enough."

Opaque disks turned back to face the gleaming hostess. Lan stretched to stroke Coty's cheek. Speech, touch, and smell invited intimacy, while the missing gift of sight delayed its full promise. Jette sensed that the women yearned to stare into eyes that had known those of her father: Laurent Sabatier.

Upstairs, Sister Lan slept. Coty had gone to kneel at the edge of her most remote flower garden—beyond the gazebo that she had had built in the adjacent lot. Matheo milled about the workshop, while, jet lagged, Evelyn sat with Jette on the front porch, awaiting the arrival of the master carpenter and his granddaughter. No words had been spoken for several minutes. Evelyn felt nauseous and stared out across the street, her vision unmoved by any passing vehicle.

"They're here," Jette announced as she stood, waving. Neeta smiled through the windshield and pointed up the driveway. Turning to Evelyn, Jette said, "Neeta wants to meet us out back, near the workshop. Videsh is using a wheelchair; she likes to get him as close as possible."

"Wheelchair? When?"

"It's brand new."

"How did Parvani get him into a wheelchair?"

"She didn't. Your nana did." Stepping off the porch stairs, they saw Neeta, brandishing a polished hickory branch.

"I don't need that silly stick, Neeta," Videsh said.

"NaaNaa Joshi, lean on the cane until he brings the wheel-chair."

Videsh fought to steady himself in the gap between the car's roof and the passenger-side door. Arms suspended, he stood crooked, staring at the closed garage bay, waiting for Matheo to appear. With a forlorn look, Videsh said, "He doesn't know we're here, Neeta. Beep the horn!"

Neeta pulled the back-door handle, tossed the cane onto the rear seat, and, bending down inside the cabin, retrieved an article of dark-blue clothing. She closed the door, reopened her own, and leaned inside to launch two quick blasts of the horn.

"Thank you, Neeta. He'll come now."

Evelyn called out, "Miss me?"

With Videsh's navy-blue hooded sweatshirt draped over Neeta's shoulder, the former roommates hugged each other, swaying back and forth at exaggerated angles. As they swung side to side, a swath of Evelyn's white curls danced atop raven hair.

Off to the side, Jette stood watching. Neeta spotted her and raised one arm, inviting Jette into the middle of the hug fest.

Videsh, struggling, cast a look of the abandoned. With his head slumped at an angle, the master carpenter cried out, "Isn't my other granddaughter going to give *me* a hug, too?"

"NaaNaa Joshi, I missed you!" Evelyn left the mini-cluster and, arms spread, hustled in choppy steps to the old man. He reached out when she arrived at his side. "Oh, no, NaaNaa Joshi, hold on to the car. I'm losing my balance."

A shaky hand reached back for the roof of the sedan. "Where's my apprentice? Neeta, beep that horn, again, please."

A *clang*, followed by a mechanical din, drew the attention of everyone in the driveway. The garage door whined as it retracted. First, the sawdusted cement floor was exposed. Then, the chair's foot platforms came into view, with the fawn-colored tips of Matheo's steel-toed work boots pointed at the curious. Replete with tea and toast, the service that Magdalena had prepared straddled his long-legged lap. He steadied the tray with one hand while the other steered the wheelchair out onto the driveway.

The beaming gardener descended the brick stairs. In mock ceremony, Coty pranced behind the rolling priest. Evelyn marveled. Matheo seemed more animated than when, earlier in the kitchen, she had met him for the first time. Maybe he had needed a cup of coffee. Maybe she herself had been so groggy as to put him off. As he drove the chair up to the car, she noticed that his eyes were locked on the driver's side, where Neeta stood, returning his broad smile.

Her grandmother's voice broke Evelyn's spell. "Matheo, you seem to be enjoying your ride. Should we order another captain's chair?"

"*Non*, Madame Coty. Only one captain in our ranks." He stood, holding the tea service flat in the air at chest level. "Monsieur Joshi expects his tea first thing."

Coty reached out to take the tray. "Here, give me that; you help Videsh settle into his chair."

Evelyn walked with her nana at the rear of the procession. The whir of the wheelchair's motor reverberated within the workshop as Videsh rolled inside. Then he spun around to disband the troop and said, "Matheo and I must get to work."

"NaaNaa Joshi, I'll be back by noon to pick you up."

"Noon? That's when Magdalena makes us lunch. You come back at the end of the day, like always."

"NaaNaa Joshi, you heard Mommy this morning. Your tests start at one thirty."

"I don't want any silly tests. You tell Parvani to take care of sick people and leave me alone. Come back this afternoon, Neeta."

"I'll be here at noon. We'll eat with Mommy at the hospital."

Videsh scoffed as he drove his machine over to the new bandsaw. Pouting, he tilted a trembling oilcan, lubricating movable parts of the unused saw. Matheo's expression signaled to the women that it might be wise to let the master compose himself without an audience. With unspoken consensus, they did what many of their predecessors had done over millennia: walk away and let an embarrassed man make his solo trek back to self-possession.

Grandmother and granddaughter again in the rear, the four women stepped out from under the raised garage door. At her grandmother's tug, Evelyn drew closer. Their heads touched, tilting the brim of Coty's garden hat up on a slight angle.

"It's good to see Neeta and Jette together. Like old times, isn't it?" Evelyn knew a Nana rhetorical when she heard one and waited for her to continue. "I did talk to her, dear. I hope you two will have that conversation I mentioned before your trip. It's long overdue."

"Whenever Jette's ready, Nana."

The pair stepped forward in silence, coordinating their foot-steps. Ahead, Neeta and Jette laughed, not in a whisper.

"I'm not working right now, Jette. Maybe I could tag along on one of your trips?"

Evelyn felt her grandmother's arm muscles constrict. Neeta stopped. Jette turned to face her and said, "I'd welcome that someday, Neeta."

Coty burst into the kitchen through the dining-room doors, her face as expressive as the welcome banner taped high above her head. "Is Evelyn still sleeping?"

After feeding the last bowl into the mouth of the dishwasher, Jette turned from the sink and asked, "Is Sister Lan alone on the porch?"

"No, darling. After Videsh and Neeta left, Matheo came out

front from the workshop. He's keeping her company." Coty seemed agitated and repeated herself: "Is Evelyn still sleeping?"

Leaning back against the counter, Jette wiped her hands with a tired dish towel. She took a moment to adjust to her mother's frenetic animation on the heels of Evelyn's listless exit. "Got up a little while ago. When she saw that you two were having a private talk on the porch, she went back upstairs to take a shower." Jette glanced up at the banner and asked, "Is Sister Lan doing okay?"

"Seems so. Matheo's such a gift. I'll bring them both some tea." Coty stepped to the back porch to hang her garden hat. "Magdalena already took off to get the groceries. We've collected a lot of tea drinkers lately; I hope she remembers to get more." Clutching her wiry braid, she paused and seemed uncertain.

"Mother, I'll get the tea. Wash up; then sit at the table and keep me company."

"Thank you, dear. I can't believe how exhausted I feel. Must be all the excitement."

Jette set the water to boil while, at the sink, Coty scrubbed garden soil from under her fingernails, prattling about how she had failed to keep her gloves on; she had wanted to feel the dirt in her hands today, for some reason.

"Mother, you seem nervous. Are you concerned about Sister Lan?"

"No, she seems content, and I'm not worried in the least about her operations." Coty looked up at the banner and cleared her throat. "Maybe I want to monopolize her time."

"You're wise to let her settle in with Matheo. For his sake too. As you said, he's also a long way from home. And he's been going through a lot, adjusting to his sabbatical." Jette shoved off from the countertop and, as she headed to the dining room, said, "Sit! I'll be right back with the tea tray."

On her way out, she stepped into the pantry and reached behind dust-covered cans on the upper shelf. Once inside the dining room, she flattened the scrunched-up photograph against her thigh, and then placed it on top of the empty teacups before lifting the tray from the rolling teacart.

The tray settled on the kitchen table. Jette hovered, waiting for Coty to notice.

"Oh—I thought you might do something dramatic."

"Mother, your stunt in the darkroom . . ." Jette paused to receive the feigned remorse she expected.

Instead, Coty's throat cleared, and she said, "My, my, dear. You're upset over a little nudge?"

They stared at each other.

"Mother, this is about Evelyn, not the priest. He'd still be in Gabon, and maybe less tormented, if you hadn't gotten involved in his life."

"Impossible to know, but Thomas also thought that Matheo needed our help, so here we are."

"We?" Fuming, Jette waited for her mother to break their silence.

Coty complied with more than a nudge. "The longer you wait, Odette, the harder it'll be."

"Mother, I'm sorry, but—"

"But what, dear? Let her see what the accident did to *you*."

"Why would I want my daughter to see me like that?"

"You've let misconceptions about her family history fester in her imagination. Show her *your* truth!"

"Mother, can't you see that it might cement Janice's indoctrination?"

"To hell with Janice Walsh!"

"If there is a god, Janice might already be there."

A lull settled over the kitchen. The only interruption came from tinkling china. After filling the porcelain teapot, Jette returned the kettle to the stovetop and walked in silence back to the table. She lifted the tray into the air and, elbows at ninety degrees, extended the service.

"Mother, your tea's ready to deliver."

CHAPTER EIGHTEEN

———

B uilt with a prodigious family in mind, back when clusters of siblings shared bedrooms, the utilitarian building predated the neighborhood mansions that surrounded it. The house featured a working kitchen with a narrow, winding staircase to the bedrooms above and the only access from inside the building to the basement below. For more than a century, the ample dining room had accommodated extended gatherings of relatives and friends. Albeit modest by nearby standards, the parlor was considered the signature room in the home, with its tall, leaded-glass windows, solid hardwood paneling and built-in bookcases, and an outsize firebox under the marble mantelpiece. The original layout of the upstairs level comprised six separate sleeping rooms and three baths. One bathroom was accessible only from the hallway; a second had two doors: one to that same corridor and another that could be opened from inside one of the spacious bedrooms. A third full bath was private, set within the master suite—Coty's boudoir.

Over the initial weeks at work on the renovations, the two-man crew had framed walls that split two cavernous bedrooms into four private nests. The blueprints called for each of those four to enjoy an en suite bath. Jette slept in the bedroom that she and Noémie had shared as kids. Matheo occupied the other room being bifurcated.

Upon completion of the renovations, Coty could house eight,

including herself, in separate bedrooms. Magdalena would remain in the room next to Coty's. Both Sister Lan and Videsh, Matheo thought, seemed disposed to accepting her invitation. Although Evelyn insisted that her recent return to her childhood home was temporary, if Coty reserved separate rooms for both her and Jette, the number available for additional guests would expand from one to two whenever he concluded his sabbatical and vacated his room, which was also temporary, having been offered as provisional domicile to the project's apprentice.

A temporary room in her house, not a permanent place in their home; those with a room and a place he heard laughing downstairs. As on prior Saturday mornings, he planned to seek his confessor, Father Ralph Warren. They would meet at the rectory, as usual. Matheo had been thankful, when, after he moved to Pacific Heights, Ralph told him to stop by his former residence for confession before the sacrament was offered to parishioners in the sanctuary. The younger priest thought that his friend was being magnanimous. The blunt truth croaked over the phone when Ralph, after fumbling a bit, found his voice and replied to Matheo's offer to wait in the pews like everyone else. A priest was not like everyone else.

Bishop Brennan had agreed that Matheo should be welcomed at the rectory; after all, he was a brother in Christ. However, the congregation had been told that Father Aubert was busy with important diocesan business; the implication of the news was that he had been sent away. Having Matheo present in the sanctuary, in street clothes, might portend undue worry and confuse the sheep.

There was another, smaller Catholic church within walking distance of Coty's. If, for the past weeks, he had not escorted Sister Lan to services at the neighboring parish, the erstwhile priest would have knelt in church alone, among total strangers. Lan had replaced Father Ralph as Matheo's thin tether to his frayed faith.

Lying in bed, dawn no longer a threat, Matheo stared at the blank wall and ruminated over what he had intended for the empty space. Nearby lay a human form with limbs stretched, hands and feet nailed to a wooden cross—a replica of an abandoned Son, searching for His silent Father. The crucifix remained flat upon the desk, where Matheo had set it the first day he occupied the enormous bedroom. With no other task at hand today, maybe the apprentice would tap the single nail necessary to rehang the icon of his anguished Savior—a chore of less than one minute, yet to be completed after weeks of residency.

Since they had started the renovations, Videsh had grown weaker and, at Parvani's insistence, cut back his work hours. Still, the master carpenter implored Neeta to drive him over to Pacific Heights by noon each Saturday to "help Matheo."

Yesterday, Friday, Videsh had said he would not be able to come today. Parvani had stood firm, demanding that her father return to the hospital for what he called "more silly tests." He had been emphatic when Matheo suggested he could manage alone on weekends. "Next Saturday, half day, we start at twelve o'clock—sharp," the anxious craftsman stipulated.

Before Matheo began his descent to the rectory, he rued the empty workshop and longed for Monday. A fresh workweek promised the distraction of labor alongside the jovial master carpenter, and with it, the physical exhaustion that invited the escape of sleep.

No master to serve today save the One unseen, Whose voice remained quiet. Pushing down the indictment with the heels of his palms, Matheo forced his body up off the edge of the mattress to start a day that he already wanted to end.

Gripping the bedroom doorknob, Matheo stopped when he heard Coty and Magdalena chirping in the hallway. A private getaway to the rectory would allow him to slip out with his despair unnoticed. He waited until the shutting of their bedroom doors cut off their fading voices, and then he stepped into the corridor.

A crown of short white curls crested into view when he spotted Jette ascending the staircase. His dark brown hand clenched the railing as he stood frozen on the carpeted runner. She stopped on the landing and paused at the table below the stained-glass window. With a look of silent encouragement, she waited for him to climb down to her.

"*Bonjour*, Madame Jette."

"*Bonjour*, Matheo. Forgot my sunglasses. You off to church?"

"To the rectory. I make my confession this morning."

She knew of his status—persona non grata—in the sanctuary that had, not long before, been the pasture where he tended his flock. "Getting any easier?"

"*Non, madame.*" His eyes grew moist as he spoke. "I look forward to seeing Father Ralph. My weekly visits with him help a bit."

"Sister Lan's sitting on the front porch. Mother and Magdalena should be back downstairs soon. I'm sure Lan would enjoy your company till it's time to go."

"Go?"

"Yesterday, Sister Lan's doctor told her that she's ready to enjoy the daylight without restriction, other than wearing sunglasses while outside. Mother asked her if she'd like to 'see the sights,' so to speak. I volunteered to drive."

"Where will you take her?"

"We're going to cross the bridge and drive up to the Headlands. Look back over the Golden Gate to see the city from on high. Postcard views, as I'm sure you know."

"*Magnifique.* Sister Lan must be thrilled," he said, without revealing that he had never visited the famous overlook.

"Not sure how long she can hold up, but we're also hoping to stop at Muir Woods. Lan wants to see the redwoods. On the flight over from Vietnam, Evelyn described the tallest trees in the world."

Matheo had lived in California for more than two years and during that time had seldom ventured far from the parish.

Jette, who knew that Videsh was not coming today, said, "There's five of us, but we can make room, Matheo. I'm sure Mother would jump at the chance to have you join us."

"*Non, madame—merci*. I've confession this morning. And . . . I must see that the workshop is ready before Monsieur Joshi returns," he said, looking away and skirting Jette's scrutiny.

"Well, maybe you can visit with Sister Lan on the porch for a while, before walking down to see Father Ralph. Do you have a few minutes?"

Without checking the time, he consented, "*Oui, madame.* You're leaving soon, *non*?"

"I'll bring the car to the front. Less than ten minutes."

The aroma of coffee teased him as he left the final step. He retrieved a hot cup from the kitchen, before searching for Lan on the front porch.

"*Bonjour*, Sister Lan. You're off on an adventure today, *non*?"

"*Oui*, Père. Much to see."

"The redwoods—very exciting."

"How often do you go?"

Without answering her question, he watched the passing traffic. Lan was staring at him when he turned to find her now limpid eyes. "Matheo, God acts in strange ways, *non*?"

Since his calling had faded from whisper to silence, Matheo mourned his lost faith. He let his head flop backward and stared up at the covered porch's ceiling. "Why would His gift be taken back, Sister?" he muttered, as he searched her crystalline eyes. *What does she see, now that she can?*

———•••———

Two seconds—the time required for the human brain to override its instantaneous decision on a primal choice: fight or flight. Two seconds for two sub-Saharan Africans, not of the same tribe, who came face-to-face in their first encounter, their differences sensed in the brief seam of time between footsteps on the open grassland or the ticks of a clock hanging on the wall of a rectory kitchen in San Francisco.

"Ah, you must be the man in our prayers," chortled the round priest, who stood at least a full foot shorter than the towering visitor. "Father Aubert, yes?" said the man, whose second dark chin lapped over the stiff edge of his Roman collar. As he reached down to take the man's extended hand, Matheo thought that he was much younger—a new priest.

"*Oui.* Yes, I'm Matheo Aubert. And you, Father?"

"Emmanuel Tinubu. Nigerian, from Port Harcourt. Nice to meet you, Father Aubert. You're Gabonese, correct?"

Matheo felt like a tired hunter who had returned to his village to find another man in his hut. "Yes, from Libreville." Out of character, he struggled to apply the Golden Rule and bit down on his words. "A pleasure to meet you, Father. Have you seen Father Ralph this morning?"

"He just finished breakfast. Went upstairs to brush his teeth and change for confession. Mentioned that you'd be visiting this morning. He'll be back down shortly."

Ralph's cheerful whistle heralded his return. The dining room door opened, and the American's bright smile greeted his Gabonese friend.

"Matheo! You're a bit late, aren't you?"

"My apologies, Ralph. Should I come back later?"

"No, no, of course not. It shouldn't take long. You couldn't have racked up that many sins in the past week. And if you have, we better address those before I invite Mrs. Flaherty to start today's procession for the sacrament."

For two years, parishioners had commented that the chubby,

middle-aged American priest and his lean African understudy made an odd pair. Matheo scrutinized the new clerical team: a well-fed yin-yang; a balanced black-and-white duo, matched in height and girth.

Tinubu looked at the elder priest and said, "Father Ralph, twenty minutes, correct? I'll meet you here; we can walk to the sanctuary together, as you suggested."

Pale skin flushed to red. Matheo stiffened at Ralph's embarrassment. When had the rotund youngster slipped inside the hut?

"Yes, Emmanuel. Twenty minutes. If I'm not in here waiting, come to the sitting room. I'll hear Matheo's confession in there."

"Oh, I won't want to interrupt."

"We'll be well beyond the sacrament and just catching up. Come when you're ready, but no longer than twenty minutes. Any later, and Mrs. Flaherty's pew might start to rattle."

The Nigerian laughed, bowed his head, and, out of habit that must have traveled with him to America, turned his body at a slight, unnecessary angle to squeeze through the ample doorway. Matheo smiled. Whenever the previous African in residence had moved about the rectory, he had watched his head; the new man, his hips.

After his confession, Matheo trudged back up the hill, having fled before Tinubu returned and reattached himself to Ralph. Since he had entered the workshop, he had not cut a single piece of wood. He first oiled the well-lubricated machines. Then, piece by piece, he inspected and, in a far corner, restacked the latest delivery: crown molding that would one day visit the miter saw before being coped with hard-fought precision by the skilled, albeit shaky, hand of Videsh Joshi.

Outside, a vehicle advanced up the driveway. *Clang!* The idling engine died, and the garage door began to rise. Videsh's surprise arrival elbowed away Matheo's plan to wander the hills of the city for the rest of the day. Hard work would better diffuse his nervous energy, which the unsolicited prayers on his behalf by a novice Nigerian priest had exacerbated.

As the garage door rose, first, the car's tires were exposed, followed by its familiar chrome grille. Then the windshield came into view: one driver, no passengers. The sting of enduring the day alone repeated with a slap.

Neeta exited the sedan with the sheepish expression of one who had dashed another's hopes. "Hey, Matheo." She pushed her sunglasses up and over her forehead. "You look disappointed."

"When I heard your car, I was excited to see your grandfather."

"Sorry, I left him at the hospital with my mom."

"Yesterday, he said he couldn't come to work today because of 'some more silly tests.' I didn't understand. He wouldn't discuss it with me."

"They also keep me in the dark. I was told the tests were a precaution. Mom's not only a careful doctor but an overprotective daughter, too." Neeta flinched as if she remembered a pressing duty. With one hand on the roof, she turned to reach inside the car. She retrieved a folded piece of paper and, offering it to Matheo, said, "NaaNaa Joshi asked me to give you this."

Inspecting the writing, he slumped. He refolded the paper and shoved it into the pocket of his shirt. "Neeta, please tell him that I finished this work already."

"Matheo, why the sad look? Free day—that's good, isn't it?"

"Ah, *oui*."

"I didn't see Coty outside. Where's everybody?"

"They took Sister Lan on a tour across the bridge."

"Why didn't you go with them? Already seen the sights too many times?"

Looking about, he said, "I had confession."

"When was the last time you drove across the bridge?"

"Two years ago, after I arrived in San Francisco; I took a bus to Sausalito. The fog was thick, but I saw glimpses of the orange cables inside the mist."

"Matheo, I'm going to drive you over the Golden Gate Bridge," Neeta said, dipping her head as if she intended to sling the lanky giant across her shoulders and carry him to the car were he to refuse her invitation. "It's a gorgeous day. I'll open the moonroof; you can watch the massive cables rise and fall."

"I don't want to impose. I'll just walk down to Crissy Field."

"I insist. We'll cross the bridge and slip up to the Headlands."

"Jette said that would be their first stop. After that, Muir Woods, to see the high trees. It's close, *non?*"

"I'll call Evelyn. Maybe we can meet them if they stop for lunch."

He spun once more, scanning the shop for answers that could be found only outside its walls.

"Mom asked me to pick up NaaNaa Joshi after his tests. Do you want to come with me? A small detour; then we'll drive you back here."

"If it's not too much trouble. When I saw that you were alone, I realized how much I missed him."

"He'd like that very much, Matheo. You're like a son to him. He told me so."

Light traffic spread out across the lanes. The bridge was clear, save a trickle of vehicles flowing in each direction. The priest's troubles flew from the car, cleared vermillion girders, and splashed below into the unforgiving current that had swept away the bodies and cares of those who had tossed themselves over the railings of the most popular suicide site in North America.

Neeta raised her voice to carry her words above the music and the rustle of the wind. "Different without the fog, Father?"

As well as glare, Neeta's sunglasses blocked pinpricks from her swirling hair. Embarrassed by staring at the driver, Matheo peered up through the open moonroof. Mammoth cables rose from the bridge's center to the peak of the north tower, before descending in a swoop to meet the pilings on the Marin side, where their car slid from the trestle.

Once they had parked the car and hiked to the overlook, Matheo recognized the viewpoint. To their right was the Pacific Ocean. To the left, at the northern shore of the peninsula, stood a collection of buildings that had gathered over two centuries. Staring down at a tanker slicing its way through the whitecaps, he considered what he had learned about the bridge's price. Built between two World Wars, the monument to peacetime engineering had cost eleven lives during its construction. In 1937, the first traffic drove across the steel expanse that would offer 1,500 jumpers permanent embrace in the cold, wet arms of a deceptive savior.

For decades, such crystalline days had fed artists, such as Coty Fine, sparkling views of San Francisco, which stretched to the southeast beyond the bridge. He recalled a framed photograph perched amid leather-bound volumes on one of the bookshelves in her parlor. In the foreground were two grammar-school children. Long, curly strands of unruly hair floated timeless, lifted by a strong Pacific breeze. Squinting identical faces pressed cheek to cheek for the lens. Four slithering arms intertwined, the twins squeezing themselves into one being. In the background, the bridge drew its line behind the lean youngsters.

"The photograph on Madame Coty's bookshelf, *oui*?"

The priest had broken their silence. Neeta seemed blissful, taking in the view. An upstart ocean breeze pulled her dark tresses beyond her shoulders. She nodded without turning to find him.

"Few pictures remember me," he said, shocked at exposing himself. He hesitated, knowing his English phrasing had been wrong.

She turned and disarmed him with a smile. Her family, as individuals and as a collective, seemed able, without effort, to coax him to relax—healers of people and houses.

"Sorry, Neeta. The words hide from me sometimes. I'm getting lazy. We speak much French at Madame Coty's."

Neeta's right hand swooped into her purse as they walked down the asphalt road to her parked car. A drape of hair flagged about her face as she stood, tapping out a text message with thumbs not much larger than Sister Lan's. When they ducked into their seats, a chime alerted her to an incoming text. The doors slammed, one after the other.

In the quiet, staring at her phone, Neeta giggled. She brought her head up and, turning to him, looked amused as she said, "I knew it! NaaNaa Joshi won't be ready for at least another ninety minutes. He's happy, watching the computer in Mom's office—Indian soap operas, streaming in high def. I'll call Evelyn to see where they are."

The phone went back into Neeta's purse. She started the engine and turned to speak before putting the car into gear. "Let's get some lunch. Evelyn said that they're about to leave Muir Woods and are heading back home."

"Sister Lan grew tired? Are her eyes troubled?"

"Not Sister Lan—Coty. Halfway through the flat walk, she sat down on a bench. She used to lead us up the steepest trails so we'd learn to be 'strong women.' NaaNaa Joshi and Evelyn's nana; hard to believe two such indomitable people—"

"Neeta, lunch isn't necessary."

"We've got plenty of time to shoot down to the old Fort Baker, right on the water, near the north tower of the bridge. It's now a spa and conference center called Cavallo Point Lodge. Inside the barroom, they've got a café that's perfect for a quick bite."

The former military compound reminded him of the Presidio, where he often walked. Eucalyptus trees provided shade for the buildings, whose landscapes consisted of fragrant deposits of discarded bark and fronds. White, wood-clad structures were arranged in an arc around the northern tip of a lawn that sloped downhill to the bay. Atop a prominent flagpole, America's colors kited in the breeze of the open parade grounds, where boys in uniform had marched in anticipation of an imminent Japanese attack.

Neeta pointed and said, "That far building's the hotel. This one's got the main restaurant and the bar I mentioned."

Stepping up the wooden staircase, Matheo looked over at the hotel's porch. Most of the rocking chairs lining it were empty. The few patrons who swayed were heads down over minuscule screens and appeared oblivious to nature's tranquility, a mere glance away.

Orders taken, the waiter sprinted to the kitchen and their quiet returned, until Neeta said, "She doesn't hate Jette. You know that, right?"

"*Oui,*" the curious orphan said.

The waiter raced by to greet fresh patrons. Matheo sipped water as he waited for her to continue. Amid the silence, he held his half-filled glass up to the light of the window, marveling at the liquid's clarity. Cold, clear tap water never ceased to register with the African. He drained the glass. Neeta's reticence prompted him to tilt his head at the returning waiter and present his empty tumbler for a refill.

Two matching salads were deposited before them, and they reached for silverware. Freed from eye contact by the pursuit of cutlery, Matheo fiddled with his fork and waited.

"NaaNaa Joshi said that Father Thom suggested you take a sabbatical."

He lowered his head and dipped his fork into his salad.

"Matheo, do you have anyone you can talk to?"

"*Oui*, Neeta: your grandfather, Madame Coty, and Sister Lan. I see my friend Father Ralph each Saturday—"

"I mean, someone your own age. I don't know what I'd do without Evelyn." She paused. Matheo sensed that his face betrayed him, she must have seen his expression as a cry for rescue. "Matheo, maybe I can help. Another perspective, perhaps?"

"Neeta, my thoughts are confused," he said, and turned to the window.

"Well, then, try telling me about those thoughts of yours— whatever's on your mind."

Leaving window for salad, he put his fork to work. One failed stab—the tines grazed his target and propelled the cherry tomato over the lip of his plate.

"Ignore it; happens to me all the time," Neeta said.

He parked the fork on an angle against the porcelain plate and, beneath the table, hid his hands on his lap.

"Sorry, Matheo, I didn't mean to pry."

Without looking at her, he blurted out, "I wish to ask how women think."

She laughed. He recoiled and stared at her.

"Okay, I think you'll need to narrow the topic a bit, or we'll be late picking up NaaNaa Joshi." Her napkin rose. Neeta patted her lips while her eyes twinkled. With a coy expression, she said, "All right—curious about how women think. You've heard con- fessions from both men and women, right?"

Flashing a closed-lip smile, he said, "Men aren't surprising, Neeta."

"You mean, their sins? That wouldn't surprise me, either," she said, with a chuckle. Then, narrowing her gaze, she asked, "Do you *want* to be a priest?"

"How can I doubt God's calling?" he stammered, chasing away unwanted revelations.

What he had told those who entered his confessional hungry and wanting, he had been told. The Savior had paid the price in full. All would be made whole who accepted faith—a ready gift for the taking.

"Don't we all doubt?" Neeta asked. He froze, and she appeared flustered. "I'm sorry, Matheo. Who am I to say?"

"Seek and you will find Him—in all people, all things," he answered, trailing off, unsure of the same words he had intoned with conviction, over and over, since seminary.

"Matheo, I want to ask you something that I hope isn't too personal." She waited until he nodded. "I know you've talked to NaaNaa Joshi about your village being attacked while you were in hospital. Are you afraid that your god might block you for eternity from your family?"

The fork descended. Stainless-steel tines pierced the red skin and slid into the belly of his second cherry tomato. Turning the fork over and over, he considered the impaled fruit and her query. Then she asked another.

"If you were guaranteed a reunion with your family, would you stay a priest?"

"It's fear," he said, being clear without answering her last question.

Neeta led him along the sidewalk, past their parked car, to the body of water that cut them off from the northern shore of San Francisco. Overpowered by the Golden Gate Bridge, which loomed high above them to the west, Matheo lost focus on their path and tripped over a raised crack in the concrete.

"Watch your step, Father Aubert!"

He righted himself and stopped to stare. "Neeta, I've never seen anything like that," he said, gawking up through the abdomen of the steel colossus.

"Pretty impressive driving on top of it, but from the water you really get a sense of the scale."

"You're an engineer. You must notice things that I don't."

"Not that kind of engineer. They were civil engineers. I envy them at times. Anyone can see what they've accomplished."

"Your grandfather speaks as if you were the secret to the company's success."

"He loves me. I had a minor role: UX engineer."

"Computer science, *non*?"

"Not computer science, but related. I studied human factors engineering. It's all about how people *use* technology. We want customers to find our services intuitive, simple, easy to use. UX engineers focus on the user experience; the 'u' stands for 'user,' and the 'x' means 'experience.'"

She had been looking down at the pavement as she spoke. He prompted her to elaborate by saying, "Videsh said that he wanted you to become a doctor, but you knew better."

"My whole family hoped I'd be a physician. NaaNaa Joshi was especially upset when I decided not to continue pre-med."

"Free will, like Madame Coty, *non*?"

Neeta's head lifted. She beamed as she took in the view of the city across the bay. "Yes, and I owe a lot to Coty—and, frankly, to Jette. They supported me when I was trying to figure out how to tell my parents that I didn't want to be a doctor."

"Was it as you wished, human factors engineering?"

"For the most part. I loved being on a creative team that was transforming health care. Zemi provided a bit of redemption for me at home."

"When I arrived, Zemi was in the news a lot."

"Of course. Even before the IPO, we dominated the press in Silicon Valley."

"You were there from the beginning, *non*?"

"I was hired soon after the founder got his initial seed funding."

"The Swede? I remember him on TV. Tall, like me, *non*?"

She pulled up, heaved a sigh, and said, "Uh-huh. Esben Ueland, from Sweden. And yes, he's almost as tall as you."

———•••———

Behind them, as they walked uphill, he heard the bay's edge, lapping against the pier. When they reached Neeta's parked car, in unison, they looked up at the hotel. Sprinkled along its porch, a flock of guests rocked in primal rhythm through a gentle breeze.

"Matheo, I've a weakness for rocking chairs. Do you mind?"

"Do we have time?"

"At least ten minutes. Twenty might be cutting it tight."

Neeta rocked in a steady tempo. Matheo slowed his chair, gauged her speed, waited, and then, tugging the armrests, leaned over to match her cadence. After acknowledging their synchronicity with a smile, she closed her eyes and angled her face into the sun's warmth.

"Neeta, are you on sabbatical as well? Your grandfather told me that you're 'unemployed.'"

"Hmm . . . I definitely prefer 'sabbatical.' If NaaNaa Joshi doesn't see a person go to work every day, he thinks they're either unemployed or retired."

"A sabbatical implies that you'll return to your former job," the priest said, channeling his own faded hopes. She bristled, and her chair accelerated. "Will you return after your sabbatical?" He wondered if hers, too, had been forced.

"Not Zemi. It's complicated." Her rocking chair stopped. Standing, she stretched her arms skyward and said, "Time to fetch the master carpenter, Matheo."

Alone in the lobby of the hospital, Matheo stared at the burnished elevator that Neeta had entered fifteen minutes earlier. The doors slid open, releasing strangers and breaking the spell. His vision flitted along the fabric panels affixed to the lobby walls. He wondered if the interior of Parvani's office had such treatments, or if, throughout the floors above, where the sterilized business of medicine was conducted, there were only glossy, easy-to-clean surfaces like those he remembered at the Libreville clinic. Over and over, against those white tiles, the pubescent boy had heard the echo of what he thought was a divine voice calling him.

With another mechanical *swoosh*, the elevator doors spread open. He discovered the exiting crowd in his peripheral vision and turned to catch Neeta's eye. She was alone and sauntered over to his chair.

"Mom had to pull NaaNaa Joshi away from the computer for his final test. She'll bring him down to us; she wants to give you a hug."

"Parvani's so thoughtful. How long?"

"Twenty minutes at most, Mom said."

"Would you like a hot cup?" he asked, knowing that Neeta shared her grandfather's penchant for afternoon tea.

"That sounds perfect, Matheo."

"Sit in the cafeteria?"

"Let's take out. I want to be where they can see us when they exit the elevator."

Extending her paper cup, Neeta motioned to a cluster of open seats in view of the elevator. When she settled into the chair, Matheo noticed that her feet—crossed at the ankles—swung back and forth above the carpet. She was even shorter than Emmanuel Tinubu, the novice priest, who might have been, at that very moment, back in the rectory on his knees, intervening on behalf of his Gabonese brother.

"Ah, that's what I needed," she said, after taking a sip.

They sat in silence, their vision shifting from the elevator doors to the outside entrance. Mixed into the flow among those who worked there, patients and loved ones streamed in and out. Many crossing the lobby seemed numb, others delighted. Did

Neeta see the same things? Were the sad-faced passersby fearful of the next step on a journey that they had just commenced or one they had been on for years? Were the looks of gloom proxies for hopes abandoned? Which of the happier faces hinted at the cure of their loved one's malady or the healthy baby that awaited their glee in the maternity ward? What did the daughter of doctors see?

"Matheo, the day's almost over. I owe you an apology." Neeta's mood seemed somber. Why would she, who had saved him from a miserable day alone, need to apologize? "You told me during lunch that you're curious about 'how women think.' I took us off track, remember?"

"*Oui*," he said, wishing that she had forgotten.

"You knew women in Gabon, right?"

"Nuns, of course," he said. Neeta reared back as if she were ready to laugh. He rushed to add, "There were girls from our sister orphanage. We were children. I went to seminary before—"

"Before you discovered that you liked girls?"

From a molten source beneath the skin, his face grew hot.

"What about now, Matheo? For instance, did you notice, when you first met Evelyn, that she was a beautiful woman?"

Cheeks on fire, he looked away and willed the elevator doors to crack open. How could anyone not see Evelyn's beauty? Or Neeta's?

"Sorry, I didn't mean to embarrass you. I'll be less specific, okay?"

"*Merci*," he said, fighting the urge to follow a passing nurse in escape.

"All right. When you encounter an attractive woman, how do you react?"

The priest felt for the missing white patch at his throat. "Pretty women . . . I become . . . uncomfortable."

"How about handsome men?"

"Sorry?"

"That answered my question." She chuckled and said, "I guess I could've asked if you were gay or straight."

"That would've saved time, Neeta," he said, as he welcomed his own laughter and slumped in relief.

"Okay, Matheo. The orphanage: all boys; no girls. Correct?"

"*Oui*. Boys only."

"From the time you entered the orphanage, you haven't been close to any girls or women your own age, have you?"

"*Non*. You're the first woman that I've talked to about such things." *Is this how women think—answering questions with their own?*

"Well, that's an honor I'm happy to accept. I'd like to think we're friends. Add Evelyn, and that's two women your own age. *Voilà!*"

"*Merci*, Neeta." He puzzled over the immediacy of Americans, who could shake hands, exchange names, and declare friendship. He had not spoken often to her former roommate, who had been in New York more than San Francisco since he had moved into her family home. "I really don't know Evelyn. You're the only one that I feel I can ask."

"Are you wondering what women think about sex?"

"*Oui*," he said. He felt his face glowing anew and blurted out, "I did read one counseling guide."

"A primer on female sexuality?"

"*Oui*."

"I hope nuns weren't the source."

"*Non*, a secular university in Paris. It was a book for psychologists, not priests."

"That's comforting." Neeta cast a curious look and asked, "What do you remember?"

"The research indicated that often men worry about performance, while women fret about betrayal—about being abandoned." He thought of the confessional: baritone tales of proud conquest reported as sins for absolution, along with what he suspected were unvoiced hopes of recidivism.

Her feet stopped swinging. After a long exhale through pursed lips, she muttered, "What's good for the goose, as the saying goes."

"Neeta, the guide—it claimed that men compete for virgins. They want a *prize* they don't have to share, *non?*"

"A lot of men fear being compared. That said, women are concerned about the past, too. Anyone can be a hypocrite when it comes to sex."

"Neeta, are many men hypocrites?"

The elevator doors separated. When he spotted his apprentice, Videsh's face lit up, exposing his compromised grin. Parvani waved, trailing her father's wheelchair.

Neeta stood. Before she stepped forward, without looking at the curious priest, in a firm voice, she answered, "Many, if not most. Ask Evelyn."

CHAPTER NINETEEN

Magdalena understood. She tugged two tissues from the box on the counter and offered them to Jette. With a loving frown, she encouraged her to wipe her eyes, exit the kitchen, and join the others in the dining room.

Returning home after months in the field, the surgeon had prepared herself, somewhat, to encounter her former patient, but had no way of anticipating his playing. No matter where she was in the house whenever Matheo addressed the Steinway, she wept.

Reminiscent of Noémie's jaunty manner, what their mother had called the "wild style of my wild child," the notes were struck with a liberty that belied what she knew of his history and current dilemma. It seemed to Jette that her twin's ten fingers, not Matheo's, marauded the keyboard.

When Jette asked her mother if she had had a role in his learning to play, Coty admitted that, after his release from the hospital, she had asked the foundation to deliver a piano to the orphanage, accompanied by duplicates of Noémie's favorite sheet music. By his sixth birthday, his music teacher—Sister Grace Noel—had sent a letter, asking how Ms. Fine had known that he was a prodigy.

"*Merci*, Matheo. That was lovely. Please, come sit," Coty called out, then turned to find Evelyn. "Darling, would you please put on some nice dinner music?"

Jette did not look at him as he took his place next to Sister Lan. She wished that her mother had warned her before she had flown home. Mother must have felt Noémie's presence, too, whenever his music filled their home.

"Please . . . everyone . . . please," Coty appealed, accompanying herself with a tinkling tap of spoon to crystal. She stood at the head of the table, extending a wineglass above her place setting. "Let's toast Sister Lan and the success of her operations."

Coty's long and graceful fingers rolled to rest on the shoulder of the diminutive nun, seated to her left. The matriarch paused, waiting to meet Lan's shy upward glance.

Bowing in her chair, with one hand cupped over her mouth, Lan blushed as the towering hostess, whose eyes were tearing, pulled the nun inward with an affectionate tug. Wineglass at her lips, Coty took a sip as she caressed Lan's shoulder with her free hand. The audience murmured approval as they, too, drank. Jette watched, convinced that her mother would milk the moment.

With protracted theater, Coty made eye contact with each guest. Having completed her lap, she sat. "Where's Father Thom, Nana?"

The table quieted. Evelyn's question had preempted Jette, who wondered if the bishop had been called away on church business or was conducting it, by keeping his distance during Matheo's sabbatical.

"It isn't the same without Thomas," Coty said. "He sent his apologies and assured me that he'll be here for the next party; he doesn't want to miss our first big bash in a long time."

Feathery jazz music floated about the room as Magdalena came in from the kitchen with a pitcher of ice water. The drummer's metal brushes dragged across the snare's skin as Karun raised his wineglass for another toast. Evelyn mimicked her grandmother with a delicate tap on her water glass. After acknowledging her with a modest bow, Karun turned to their hostess, presented his glass, and released his query to flutter the full length of the table.

"May I?"

"The floor is yours, dear," Coty said.

"A toast to Coty: You dazzle us with your hospitality and the bounties from your gardens. From these beautiful flowers to the lush salad in front of us, you delight." Lifting his glass and voice higher, he said, "To our inimitable hostess, the divine Ms. Fine."

Raised goblets greeted their crystalline tablemates with tinkling kisses. Karun basked for a moment in the room's energy and then continued, "And you, Sister Lan. We're grateful for your presence and the success of your surgeries. It's a joy to look into your eyes and see through to your gentle spirit."

Matheo leaned over to whisper the French translation into Lan's ear. She beamed and, in her burgeoning English, from behind a cupped hand, said, "Thank you, Karun!"

A blissful lull descended. Aiming her moist, sparkling eyes in another sweep, Coty lapped the table and shot affection into each guest. With outstretched arms, she invited everyone to eat. "Please, start. We'll enjoy dinner, then move to the parlor to talk about the renovation, which I know is on everyone's mind."

The liveliness that had graced their intimate dinner table continued as they moved to the parlor. Magdalena and Jette served coffee and tea. Evelyn, acknowledging the resolute look from her grandmother, snagged Magdalena's arm and pulled her down onto the love seat.

"Thank you all, again, for coming tonight," Coty said. "And special thanks, as always, to Magdalena for a fabulous dinner."

The housekeeper, squirming next to Evelyn, did not acknowledge the compliment; rather, she pined in the direction of the kitchen. Dragging a leather wingback chair across the Persian rug, Jette brought her seat alongside the lone wheelchair.

"Well, now, on to our not-so-little project: transforming this home." Coty paused. "Yes, I've changed my mind. I want to focus on the main house for the time being. I'll get my cottage eventually."

Jette had agreed with Evelyn, who wanted to create a stable, safe environment for her nana; the cottage had been the solution for preserving Coty's independence. Without debate, the matriarch had put those plans on hold.

Jette completed her own lap of the assemblage. Mother seemed out of character, nervous amid her extended family. Each guest held a look of encouragement, tempered by concern about Coty's abrupt change. The long-planned cottage was to be her private retreat, all on one level, in the middle of Zaydeh's secondary lot. After a site had been cleared in the gardens, the building of the cottage had been postponed. That project could have lumbered along, with Coty residing inside the main house during construction. Jette considered the recent switch a hazard—too much, too late—for the woman who, over her long life, had accomplished more than most would ever attempt.

"All right, first things first: I love my home. Magdalena and I have been here for decades. We raised our two girls here, before welcoming our sweet Evelyn."

Coty's face took on a baffling glow—placid yet troubling. Jette was haunted by their abbreviated day trip to Marin: the scene of her mother panting on the bench beneath ancient redwoods. The once unbounded domain of Coty Fine had shrunk.

"Extensive travel has been a passion to which I must bid adieu," Coty said.

Magdalena fidgeted again, and Evelyn squeezed her tight.

"Given that my most precious memories are of shared experiences," Coty continued, "I want to share this home with people who'll build new memories with me, people who'll respect the special gift it's been, people who'll ensure it remains a vibrant home for years to come. Their home."

"Nana, you're not planning on turning this into a nursing home, are you?"

Evelyn's voice had pricked the collective tension, and palpable relief swept through the parlor. Jette marveled at her daughter's technique. The Sheldon Fine Foundation would be in good hands, she thought. Days earlier, the three women, sitting together on the front porch, had put to rest the nursing home question. Evelyn was ensuring that everyone in the parlor heard it straight from the mouth of Ms. Fine herself.

"Oh, my, no! I want to give our home new life, not make it a business." Again, she paused. The audience edged forward on their seats in unconscious unison. Lifting her chin, Coty cleared her throat and shook her shoulders. Jette thought, *Here comes the performer who raised me.* "That said, I've no intention of entering my nineties *well behaved.*"

As derrières slid back from brinks, Jette asked, "Mother, besides Sister Lan and Videsh, who do you hope will come live here?"

"Darling, I haven't invited anyone else—yet."

Videsh toggled the joystick in opposing directions, grinding his wheelchair's tires inside carpeted ditches. "I haven't made up my mind," he shouted, with the voice of a man who wished to remain in charge of his life.

"Mother, what happens if—when—one of your guests requires additional care?"

Videsh stiffened. The wheelchair jittered. Before the response came, Jette realized that her hand was resting on his forearm.

"Parvani and Karun have agreed to act as house doctors. They'll guide us when we need to seek help outside our walls for anyone living here, including me."

As Sister Lan received the translation from Matheo, Jette noticed that her mother's line of sight shot over the heads of her guests. Rather than collecting their tepid confirmations, she was taking in familiar items that she herself had scattered throughout the room. The surgeon scanned the faces in the parlor. Everyone seemed to clutch her same worries, even Lan. Jette moved to bring her mother back into the present.

"I've another question, Mother. Would you please explain what you mean by 'pleasure versus comfort'? After comparing notes, I'm not the only one who's baffled."

Coty took a deep breath while contemplating the parlor ceiling. Hands on thighs, her fingers rippled as if she were playing scales on the nearby piano. Then the finger rolls came to an abrupt stop. An inaudible weakness slipped from her lips.

"Mother, what did you say? We couldn't hear you," Jette said, scanning the group for verification that she was not alone in having missed the comment.

"I said, 'I've lost many friends.' Dear, dear friends." The grandfather clock ticked. Coty lifted her hands and patted her thighs. "As I was saying, I've lost many friends in the last years. Beautiful people. Confident, loving, smart people." She sighed. "Everyone dies. But I didn't like how most of them lived at the end."

"Weren't they given good care by their doctors?" Karun asked. Jette searched the face of the man who she knew had witnessed the pattern repeated, year after year, patient after patient. His wife rubbed his sleeve as she whispered to him in the soothing language of their youth. With an ear next to Parvani's lips, he held his eyes on Coty.

"Karun, their doctors weren't the problem. Most of us want to live long lives, but I watched as many of my friends were deposited and then lingered. Some were deposited by loved ones. Some deposited themselves out of a sense of duty, not wanting to burden their families." In their comfortable seats, they squirmed in the familiar parlor, where Coty had staged decades of entertainment. "Remember my friend Madeleine?"

Sister Lan and Matheo appeared perplexed. Addressing them, Jette explained, "Madeleine was her dear friend who died last year after she moved to Walcott Towers."

Neeta joined in, announcing to the uninitiated, "You should've seen the two of them; Coty and Madeleine were the life of the party."

Jette recalled how the enthusiastic duo would pull the resistant—from little kids to the oldest dinner guests—out onto the cleared parlor floor, where a persuasive social brook would flood into irresistible rapids that swept up and carried reluctant revelers in a rush.

With a croak in her voice, her mother said, "Remember how she'd . . ." The words drifted into a whimper.

Diving in to rescue her, Jette said, "Mother, Walcott Towers is the finest assisted-living facility in Northern California. Was Madeleine unhappy there?"

"She was stoic. Never complained. The last time I saw her alive, I was fighting back the urge to bawl my head off. She patted my hand and told me she was the luckiest person she'd ever known. It wasn't like Madeleine to complain. Instead, she praised the staff, said that they were making her 'comfortable.'"

Parvani wriggled in her seat and shifted forward. In reciprocity, Karun placed a healer's hand on his wife's shoulder. Parvani wiped her eyes as she addressed their hostess: "Coty, are you saying that Madeleine simply let go? That, in a way, she died before she expired?"

"Parvani, you're my angel. I'm not talking about when my friends passed. I'm talking about when they gave up. When they stopped hoping for anything other than relief."

Evelyn perked up. "Nana, are you saying that, comfort aside, Madeleine had to sacrifice many of her pleasures? Like how she loved doing the *New York Times* crossword puzzle?"

"She finished it the day she died. And I have to agree with Madeleine: she *was* lucky. Near the end, most of our friends gave up everything that had brought them joy."

Blanketed with gloom, the parlor grew silent, except for the ticks of the grandfather clock and jazz music that pulsed at low volume throughout the first floor. Jette considered what Madeleine and the others had sacrificed—joys that could not have been delivered to Walcott Towers. The surgeon's own joie de vivre hinged on mobility and independence. Lost for words of rescue, she knew that someone else would have to break the parlor's woe.

"I want to hit my thumb with a hammer!"

All eyes turned to the ventilated grin. Videsh was beaming. Matheo whispered the French translation into the ear of Lan, whose face brightened as she cupped her hand over her mouth and shifted in her chair.

Laughter filled the room with a chorus of relief. Personal accounts of pleasures that transcended simple comfort poured forth. After minutes of frenzy, a breath-catching respite settled. Lan waited until Matheo completed the translations before she raised a petite hand. He leaned to her and murmured a question in French. She nodded.

"Sister Lan would like to share an example," he announced.

"*Magnifique.* How wonderful," their hostess said.

In deference to the Desais and Magdalena, Sister Lan whispered in French to Matheo. Captivated, they all listened to the priest, whose face grew somber as he translated.

Lan's father, a vigorous, hardworking man, died a pauper. For years, he had hauled bundles for a caning factory—everything from chairs to baskets to *nón lá*. On a bicycle. Strong for so small a man. And fast on his bike. High stacks. He could balance as much as any rider.

One day, while he was coasting downhill with a full load of cane, his bicycle was struck by a swerving taxi. The bike toppled, and her father's hip shattered. As he lay in the hospital, the factory owner gave the bent bicycle to a younger man who said he would repair it overnight and be at the factory door in the morning.

No one knew the streets of Hanoi better than her father. With a hip that had healed in a twist, he would never ride again. When they saw the encroaching mist in his eyes, no one would hire him. No angel named Evelyn came in search of him. No trip of mercy would clear his sight.

A proud man, he would not beg. Instead, he strung beads all day. Along with a hip that had fused into permanent misalignment, arthritis had conquered his spine and colonized every joint from the tips of his fingers to ends of his toes. When he could no longer walk, he dragged himself around their tight two-room apartment. No motorized wheelchair like Videsh's replaced the factory man's bicycle. Lan's father would not beg. He strung beads all day.

Near the end, he groaned whenever she rubbed his sore hands and feet. One day, collapsed in a chair, he winced when she reached to take his hand. Since her massaging had not given him comfort, she cradled the limb and poured warm, herb-laced water over the tortured extremity. He cooed as she splashed the soft stream to soothe his tired, achy fingers.

After she placed his second hand on its mate in his lap, Lan knelt to take up a foot. When she began to pour the mild palliative, he jerked. Agitated, he shook his head. With coated eyes, he faced her and implored his daughter to rub his feet. He cried for her to press against his arthritic toes and deep into the cramped arches of his soles. At one point, with a sharp flinch, he grimaced, and she pulled back. Angry, blind commands slapped at her in desperation.

"Push harder, daughter." He had moaned with pleasure. "I feel the pedals of my bicycle."

CHAPTER TWENTY

———•———

Coty Fine's tribe had given Matheo a communal buffer against violent withdrawal from the rectory's dual opiates of haven and camaraderie. Since the intimate dinner party, he had enjoyed an extended period of longed-for peace, as well as fresh trepidation; Videsh had exhibited his characteristic jocularity while growing feebler.

Pupil asked master about moving into Coty's house after the renovations were completed. The frail carpenter made a weak joke. He said he was waiting to see if his apprentice completed his work with requisite quality. When Matheo stared with worried eyes, Videsh grew somber and confided that he would decide later, when he had more energy.

The old Indian's waning pluck was obvious when Neeta arrived Friday afternoon on the heels of the remodelers' productive week. After a precarious transfer from his wheelchair, Videsh crumpled into the passenger seat. In his daily custom of farewell, Matheo tapped on the glass. When Neeta gestured her thanks for loading a failing grandfather into the car, he thought she looked preoccupied—a bit lost.

Another Saturday morning. Matheo rose for his walk to the rectory to make his confession. Since his move to Coty's months earlier, Matheo had not returned to the wooden chamber to kneel before his confessor, much less sit inside himself, listening to the gradients of sin that ranged from minor transgressions through mortal tickets to hell.

Today, he looked forward to seeing his friend Ralph and also, in a way, the enthusiastic Nigerian. Matheo stood on Coty's front porch, taking in the elegant homes across the street. He descended the stairs and, when he arrived at the sidewalk, turned back. How had he come to such a place? Should he thank God for working in strange ways? As he walked downhill, Matheo wondered if he would ever return to his confessional or, once again, find a place to lie in the hut.

Motors revved and car horns honked. Gone was the morning fog that, after breakfast, had cooled his descent to the rectory. A few blocks away, bathed in sunshine, Coty's house stood out, perched on its berm near the top of the hill. He held it in his vision as he hiked closer to home—a word that, since his expulsion from the rectory, he had not spoken aloud.

A spotless, midnight-blue Tesla Model S was parked on the street in front of the house. Talking to a tall man on the porch, Evelyn remained inside with one hand on the entry door, which was cracked for little more than guarded conversation. Dressed in a suit on a Saturday, the man stood before her. Through the narrow space, she handed him something compact, which he took in one hand.

As Matheo approached, he heard an abrupt *thwack*—the slap of wood on wood. The man's head jerked up from staring at his cupped palm. A door-to-door salesman, accepting the odds of his profession, would have expected rejection. The man in the suit seemed startled that Evelyn had shut the entry door without further ceremony.

The tall stranger stood motionless, facing the closed door long enough for a couple of deep breaths before he trudged away.

The tailored facade could not disguise his disappointment as he plodded down the stairs. At the curb, he seemed surprised by Matheo, who was nearing the automobile.

The man gathered himself and, without salutation to the priest, opened the passenger-side door. He tossed a jewelry box onto the seat of the Tesla, removed his coat, and, after cloaking the container in worsted wool, closed the car door with a defeated shove. He stepped back onto the sidewalk and, facing downhill, took one long-legged step with his open right hand extended.

Matheo recognized the man's face from television and online articles about Silicon Valley. Above the priest loomed the lauded genius behind the company that Neeta had joined early in its start-up phase. Matheo's eyes shot to the back of the Tesla, where he found the personalized license plate: ZEMI.

"Father, my name's Esben Ueland."

No Roman collar or black linen clothing betrayed the priest; yet, the man knew. Bewildered, Matheo took his hand.

"*Enchanté.* My name's Father Aubert—uh, I should say, Matheo Aubert. Please call me Matheo."

"Nice to meet you, Matheo." Ueland paused and stared. "Father—I mean, Matheo—are you no longer a priest?"

"I'm a priest on sabbatical."

Ueland turned and looked back at the house. He seemed to pull away, resisting as if its mass held him against his will. "I was *summoned* here to retrieve something."

Matheo swallowed. Then, he, too, took in the sight of his current residence. "*Monsieur*, you're familiar with the family, *non*? With Madame Fine?"

Ueland's face creased into a scowl. "Yes, Matheo. I know Coty well—and her family. I've spent many hours inside that place."

"You knew I was a priest. Did Coty tell you about me?"

"She did. I learned of you shortly after I met her. She was very happy to see you come to San Francisco." Ueland faced the passenger side of his sedan. His voice cracked as he continued,

"I was summoned here, as I said. Summoned to take back a diamond ring—an engagement ring."

"*Oui.* Most difficult, my son—uh, I mean, Monsieur Ueland."
Matheo wondered who had broken their engagement, this crest-
fallen man or Evelyn.

"I'm sorry, Father. I can't talk about this right now. I've got to
go," he said, while stalling in place, as if sentenced to squirm
until released by his confessor.

Matheo said, "I'm living here for the time being. Please,
come sit on the porch. I'll bring you a glass of water. We can talk.
If you wish, I'll ask Evelyn to join us."

"No—too late for that. She was terse. Wanted only to give me
back my 'property,' as she put it."

A single lost sheep, the erstwhile priest reminded himself.
"Let me talk to her. Maybe . . ."

Shaking his head, Ueland said, "I didn't want the ring, but I
was *summoned*, as I told you."

"You're in great pain," Matheo said. Unable to abandon the
man for want of a collar, he suggested, "Please, come sit with me."

"No, thank you, Father. You're a caring priest." He looked up
at the house and said, "The women who live there . . ."

Ueland shuffled his feet. Matheo noticed that the man's
shoes appeared to be new—spit-shined, unscuffed, and not
broken-in. One stiff leather sole scraped a pebble across the
cement. With a brisk drag on the concrete, he pulled his foot
back, sending the stone flying off the sidewalk and bounding
out into the street. Matheo twisted to watch it dribble to a stop
on the asphalt. When the priest returned his gaze, Ueland's
eyes had narrowed.

"Be careful, Father."

CHAPTER TWENTY-ONE

———

*W*ho was at the door?

Grinning at her phone, Evelyn wondered how many octogenarians texted their grandchildren at all, much less when in the same building.

u no

While she waited for her nana to type a response, Evelyn went back to her messages on the foundation's email site. She was lost in thought when Coty's response triggered the tone that signaled a new text had been delivered.

Your education is being diluted to mush by modernity. Please, come upstairs and help me pick an outfit for next week's dinner party.

cff r t?

May I buy a vowel?

?

Tea, please.

"He was insufferable, as expected."

"Who, dear?"

"Nana, really—at the end of this charade, I'd like to probe the efficacy of your feigning ignorance."

"I wish you'd text like you talk. I was worried that you'd regressed to early language development."

"Don't change the subject. Let's get back to *your* text, please."

"*My* text?"

"Nana! The text you sent a few minutes ago. When you asked who was at the door, remember?"

"Yes, of course, dear. You sent a confusing jumble in reply. Young people employ secret hieroglyphics, don't they?"

"No secret, and you do know who was here, don't you?"

"If I were to hazard a guess, Esben Ueland was at the door. Correct?"

"How *do* you keep a straight face?"

"I see that you're quite agitated. What happened?"

"I opened the door and handed him the ring. He looked down at it, and I closed the door. Anyway, Nana, let's look in your closet. I don't want to talk about him, please."

"It isn't wise to keep such strong emotions bottled up."

Evelyn rolled her eyes and said, "Finished?"

"I think I'll wear my black dress."

"Which one?"

They glided into Coty's walk-in closet. One hanger had been pulled from the rail and hooked sideways, draping the garment over the shoulders of its neighbors.

"Oh, Nana, I remember this dress—sleek and chic. I hope I can wear something like that when I'm—"

"We're lucky women, naturally slender. Runs in the family." After another micro-pause, Coty touched her head and said, "Sorry about the hair."

"I love my hair." Evelyn recoiled at her nana's frown. She thought of junior-high school, her hair laid across an ironing board, under a towel, and Neeta's failed attempts at flattening the inherited curls. "Nana, take off your gardening getup and slip this on. I want to see it on you."

Coty stepped out of the denim smock, but when she reached to snag it on the hook, she slumped. Shaking her head, she said, "I can't keep up with it all. Magdalena suggested we hire a part-time gardener."

Evelyn had wedged her trip to Vietnam into an already crammed calendar. She missed kneeling at the flowerbeds beside Nana and worried that she herself had not been present enough to appreciate the full extent of her grandmother's waning vitality. "Isn't Matheo helping? He's sort of your handyman, right?"

"Yes. Fortunately, he does like to keep busy."

Evelyn turned the black dress around and unzipped it. After removing the hanger, she offered the garment and asked, "So he doesn't have to decide about being a priest? That's what Neeta thinks."

"Well, Neeta's been spending a lot of time with him." Evelyn noticed another slump as Coty took a deep breath and said, "Thank goodness for her and Lan."

The nun and Evelyn's best friend had absconded with her nana's French-speaking priest. All for the better, since she seemed no longer to possess the requisite energy for each of her side projects.

"According to Neeta," Evelyn said, "he's still trying to figure out our country, as well as his 'calling.'"

Coty stepped into the dress. As she tugged the spaghetti straps over her shoulders, she said, "True. I see how he looks at people, takes everything in." She perked up. Addressing the mirror, she cleared her throat and said, "For instance, I see the way he looks at *you*."

Evelyn rolled her eyes again and said, "You've got to be kidding me. He seems fixated on Neeta when we're all together."

"Neeta's his friend. He's comfortable around her, not wobbly."

"Wobbly, Nana?"

"Well, dear, from what I see, Matheo seems to fumble and stutter only when he's around you."

"I've barely talked to him. I've been traveling a lot since Lan and I got here; I've been in New York more than California."

"I'm simply pointing out—"

"Nana, stop! You're not credible here."

"Well, dear, I, too, have spent a great deal of time with Monsieur Aubert."

"Has he asked you about women?"

"He's shy. Seems to be wary of certain topics."

"Neeta says he's very inquisitive, especially about American culture."

"That's nice. I'm sure it's a generational thing." Coty stepped out of the dress and handed it to Evelyn, as if to suggest the topic had ended.

"You talk to him every day, Nana. How much longer does he think his sabbatical will last?"

"That's the rub. He thought that by now, it would've brought the return of two rescinded gifts: faith and his calling to the priesthood."

"Not to be cynical, but he could tell Father Thom what he wants to hear, right?"

"Evelyn, I wonder if Matheo has the capacity to lie."

"Do you think he feels lied to?"

"No one in the church lied *to him*. They passed on whatever they'd been told themselves."

"And, in your opinion, he hasn't decided one way or the other?"

"It's not simple, or he would've looked at a woman like you or Neeta and known." When Evelyn gave her a skeptical look, Coty added, "Darling, you rolled your eyes again, by the way."

"Nana!"

"He's a man. You're put off by men right now. Fair to say?"

"What's your point?"

"Matheo doesn't seem like a man destined to return to the rectory."

"What'll he do if he doesn't go back—work here for you?"

"Well, that would be a start, but it seems that he needs to *be something* to be someone. It's a male thing that more men suffer from than you might suspect."

"That virus infected a lot of women, too." Employing her nana's idiosyncratic pause, Evelyn stroked the black dress. While replacing the garment on the hanger bar, she said, "By the way, you, Ms. Fine, were a carrier."

"Clever, dear." Coty coughed, and then continued. "Well, Matheo's options aren't limited to carpentry. That said, I can't see him playing piano in some seedy lounge. The man's a natural caregiver. If not a doctor like your mother, maybe a nurse. Yes, I could see him becoming a nurse."

"Nana, I trust you're committed to his free will being exercised."

"Of course. You'd think me a hypocrite, otherwise."

Evelyn sent a wry smile and went back to the closet's inventory. Humming from Magdalena's songbook, she promenaded in front of the hanger bar. Picking her way through her grandmother's wardrobe, she envisioned herself in a department store. She giggled. It had been a favorite childhood game that Nana had let her and Neeta play in there. Hanger by hanger, Evelyn pulled each garment along the bar for inspection. Pleasant memories flooded the closet. Stopping in the middle of the rack, she addressed her grandmother with a look of consternation and asked, "Has to be black?"

"Well, it makes one look slender . . ."

"Good genes, remember? Let's pick something fun—an outfit that'll drive the mood of the party."

Her nana pulled out a slim pink shift. "Hmm, how about this one?"

"Getting closer!" Lost in her role as department-store salesclerk, Evelyn rifled through the section where springtime hung. She pulled out a sleek yellow dress, the one her nana had purchased for a roof-popping graduation party she'd thrown for Evelyn and Neeta. "Do you remember this one, Nana?"

"Yes. Oh, my, that's a youthful number. You can pull off that one, Evelyn."

"You loved this dress! And *you* can still 'pull it off,' as you say." Evelyn pressed her face into the fabric. Long ago, her nana's scent had faded, displaced by a pungent odor that repelled moths and humans alike.

"Well, I suppose someone—you or Jette—could wear it."

"Jette'll probably want to wear her dress scrubs."

"Evelyn! Please, give your mother a break."

"Think she'll get back from Seattle in time for the party?"

"That's the plan. She observed surgeries last week. This week she's assisting; she's very excited about the new technique. Told me last night how helpful the trip's been."

Soon after Jette had agreed to come home for an extended visit at Nana's request, she had scheduled a side trip to Seattle Children's Hospital. Whenever her mother was in San Francisco, she seemed to find ways to escape. Evelyn held out the yellow dress and, while inspecting the fabric, said, "Nana, I'll get it freshened up for you to wear at the party."

"I bought that when you graduated from Berkeley. That was such a fun day."

"Day? Your 'afternoon' party lasted way past midnight. You danced with my friends until the neighbors complained."

"Old fuddy-duddies. I told them three weeks in advance that we were going to have a big party. I even invited them to come over and dance."

"Nana, no one called till two in the morning."

"Well, that's true, but you only graduate once, dear."

Spiraling the garment, Evelyn offered it to be modeled. Coty slipped into the dress and tugged it up over her narrow hips. They faced the floor-length mirror. She seemed pleased. Yes, Evelyn could see that the selection gave her grandmother "pleasure."

"Nana, I like this one. Better for dancing."

———◆◆◆———

Evelyn thought the music sounded glum as she exited her nana's bedroom. She had yet to grow accustomed to Matheo's impromptu playing. Whenever her grandmother requested that the man regale them, Evelyn felt a tinge of displacement. She had been the resident pianist, although her ears made her aware that his casual musicality transcended her best performances. Maybe she had eschewed Jette's encouragement to execute a duet with the priest because she was competitive and knew that with him, there would be no contest.

She paused at the bottom of the stairs, watching and listening, wondering about her aunt Noémie. Evelyn had been too young to remember her aunt's whimsy. Nana, Magdalena, and Jette all said that, when at the piano, Matheo seemed to channel the lost twin. At her nana's recent dinner party, his music had sounded breezy. Today, he seemed despondent.

He did not notice her approach and continued to seek solace at the keyboard. When she stopped at the bench, his eyes were closed and his lips pressed together as if to block a lament. She slid next to him. He recoiled, and the last struck note hung abandoned. She looked down at the keys and nodded for him to carry on as she lifted her own hands. His eyes closed again, and he continued with a succession of woeful notes until she segued toward the lighthearted.

Matheo followed her lead. A smile broke across his face while he riffed to her melody like they had been partners for years. *How does he do that?* she puzzled, as her pace accelerated. If she got ahead of herself or struck too hard, he stroked the keys to slow her. After she recovered, he pushed her forward, encouraging Evelyn while never outrunning her.

When her improvisation tapped out, she signaled Matheo to take the lead. She watched his long, coffee-colored fingers roam the fullness of the instrument. His pace picked up, and he closed his eyes once more. Captive to musicianship she could simply admire, not emulate, Evelyn thought of her mother and her mother's twin. She lifted her hands from the keyboard, and stilled fingers found her lap. Had Jette felt comparable ineptitude at the Steinway while sitting aside Aunt Noémie on this same bench?

Matheo found himself playing solo once again. When he opened his eyes and turned to find her, she averted her gaze. He downshifted the speed of his ad-libbing to beckon her back. She looked at him and returned his fresh smile, before raising her hands. Next, he insisted that she resume the lead with a waggish run along the keyboard, followed by raised eyebrows as he alternated scales, treading water until she jumped back in.

She never lost him and began to tease her accompanist by testing the boundaries of her own proficiency. When she pushed herself to her limit, he was there. He never ran into or around her, much less fell away. When she withdrew, he made ample room for her retreat. He was in complete control, playing only in service to her.

She struck a definitive conclusion to their duet. Matheo's hands hovered. Another note would have been intrusive. His frisky manner had routed her qualms, and her familial displacement vanished.

"*Magnifique*, Evelyn. You play with such delight."

"*Merci*, Matheo. I had hoped to cheer you up. The music sounded so sad when I came downstairs. Are you okay?"

"*Oui*. Much better now."

When they stood, he seemed embarrassed, a bit wobbly.

CHAPTER TWENTY-TWO

——•·•——

Seattle Children's Hospital—her mother might as well have been in Sri Lanka, or Lagos, or some other place a world away. Tomorrow was Nana's big bash, and tonight Jette was supposed to fly back to San Francisco. Evelyn herself had just landed, returning from the foundation's office in Manhattan.

She wondered if Jette would, as promised, make it home in time for the party. She had been scheduled to arrive before Evelyn but had, yet again, found an excuse to change her itinerary. Evelyn texted Coty from SFO to let her know that she was on her way home.

The driveway was crusted with dirt, another layer added since she had left. Unable to fathom why Matheo had not swept it, she balked at the back-porch route. Before the party, he would have to attack it with a broom and then hose down the pavers. She dragged her suitcase up the flower-lined brick walkway and over the threshold, where she confronted the pre-bash bivouac that occupied the ground floor. Rented tables and folding chairs were stacked in the foyer. The invisible evidence of another invasion drifted into her nostrils. After navigating her way to the parlor, she saw the source of the aromas. All the ready blossoms in her nana's gardens seemed to have crept inside en masse. Awaiting ultimate placement, the bundles drank from water buckets on the floor.

When she traipsed into the kitchen, her nana looked up

from the table, where she sat with a depleted water glass. Coty, hand to hip, winced as she rose to embrace the weary traveler.

"You must be in a fog, darling," she said, as she unwound Evelyn's grip on the handle of her roller bag. Her grandmother kissed her cheek and gifted the hug Evelyn expected.

"Great—you can tell? I must look a mess."

"Well, you've got those telltale bags under your eyes, but . . ."

"But what? That's my NaaNaa Joshi look."

"But, I was going to say, you pulled your roller into the kitchen. Want to drag it upstairs the hard way?" Coty said, aiming her smirk at the tight kitchen stairwell.

Evelyn stared down at the luggage and laughed. Yawning, she said, "Off my game, Nana. I usually come up the driveway, but it's really a mess. That said, I'm hauling this thing up the back stairs, just to prove I can!"

"Well, it's for the best, dear—you couldn't have rolled your bag around all the buckets on the back porch."

"Got enough flowers, Nana? Don't tell me you ordered more from the flower market."

"They're supposed to deliver a dozen giant calla lilies before ten o'clock tomorrow morning. Anyway, thanks for the text from the airport. You made good time, didn't you?"

"I guess. Frankly, I think I was asleep for the ride in. What time is it, anyway?" she asked.

"Almost six o'clock. Go take a nap, darling."

"Doesn't Jette get in soon?"

"She called to say she had to take a later flight; she's on standby."

Evelyn yawned again, fighting the urge to dis her mother. "I should try to stay up. Looks like there's a lot left to do."

"I'm exhausted. Done for the day, dear."

"Me, too, but I've been sitting all day. It's only nine o'clock in New York. How can I be wiped out?"

"In my humble opinion . . ."

Those words had never failed; in a moment of weakness, before her nana could finish her statement, Evelyn grinned and rolled her eyes.

"Are you laughing at me, Evelyn?"

"No, Nana." She melted at the playful scowl. "Okay, yeah, a little."

"*Ahem.* As I was saying—on your behalf, by the way—the physical and mental effects of a coast-to-coast whipsaw can be worse than an around-the-world tour."

"You don't believe that, Nana."

"Suit yourself. Go take a nap. I'll call you for dinner in ninety minutes."

Maybe Nana was correct about the toll on a person of bi-coastal ping-pong. She had committed to wake her in less than two hours. Evelyn doubted that her mother would make it home before dinner. She wanted to stay up on the off chance that Jette grabbed one of the earlier flights, but she was too tired for guilt.

Pastel eyelids announced a nascent sun creeping over the hills of the East Bay. Evelyn blinked. The slats on the inside shutters of her windows were opened on a slant, causing striped shadows that raked across her bed. Nana had let her sleep through dinner and the presumed arrival of her mother from Seattle. Stretching her arms in the air, she gave thanks—better to see Jette after a solid night's sleep.

Standing in a daze, she stared at the carpet and shook her head; she needed a cup of coffee. After floating up to the ground-floor ceiling, the scents of her nana's harvest had flitted into the bedroom corridor. Light-headed and a bit unsteady, Evelyn trudged down the formal staircase.

She paused on the landing, where she took in the site of the impending party. From her current elevation, she gazed through the foyer to the front door and could see much of the parlor. Underneath the sparkling chandelier, the rented tables and chairs had been unfolded for dinner guests who could not be accommodated in the dining room.

White tablecloths draped over round edges. Centerpieces of arranged flowers marked each bull's-eye. Candles and place settings were positioned as her nana preferred. Name tags had not yet been propped before the fine china, although, during such events, Coty ate in the parlor so that no guest seated there would feel slighted.

The Persian carpets had been rolled up against the wall opposite the Steinway. Matheo would have to grab one of the caterer's crew and move those rugs. When dinner ended, the rental items would be refolded and stacked outside before the parlor could be transformed from overflow-dining room into dance floor.

Ticktock, ticktock . . .

Amid her discombobulation, the hardwood floor's exposed herringbone pattern appeared. It was good to be home for a while. She acknowledged that she had to back off her fierce travel schedule, while wondering if she had more in common with Jette than she had ever thought possible.

Ticktock, ticktock . . .

She sauntered into the dining room. The table had been extended to its full length and set for sixteen. Hand-drawn place cards sat in neat rows for the hostess to determine ultimate placement. The handwriting betrayed common genes and schooling: ornate cursive strokes, distinctive in the family manner. It was Jette's script, not Nana's, although Evelyn had to look twice to make certain.

Moving about the parlor in a glide, she scanned her mother's handiwork. Jette had lifted much of the burden from Coty's shoulders while the hostess slept. Replete with gardenias floating in glass bowls, and rose petals sprinkled about, the tables required little else. Decide the seating, light the candles, and pour the wine.

Evelyn turned to the kitchen and its promise of coffee. She wondered if Nana had been awake when Jette came home. Jette could not have moved the furniture by herself, much less the carpets. Evelyn looked from the cylinders of Persian wool to the Steinway, where she located her mother's accomplice. Heads down on the closed keyboard cover, Matheo dozed atop folded arms.

"*Ahem.*"

He snapped up. As if he had no idea of what had woken him, or from which direction it had come, he stared ahead into the sheet music spread open before him.

"Cup of coffee, *monsieur?*"

"Evelyn . . ." He glanced about, flummoxed.

"Did you and Jette work while the house slept?"

"*Oui, mademoiselle.*"

"Why are you sleeping on the piano? Did she abandon you in the middle of everything?"

"*Non*, Evelyn. The airport—she left an hour ago."

Coty's granddaughter stared in disbelief at the man who, according to her nana, was the resident expert on abandonment.

"She asked me to wait up for Madame Coty. I thought—"

"What? You thought what, Matheo? That it was okay to let Jette leave without seeing her?"

"She said that 'under the circumstances'—"

"Never mind." Evelyn turned in a huff. After she had taken two steps in the direction of the kitchen, she stopped, looked back, and said, "I'm going to make coffee. Would you like a cup, or will that disrupt your sleep?"

He stared down at the shiny keyboard cover. The priest's ignominy reflected her disrespect, and she felt more deserving than he of the shame he exhibited. Jette's latest escape was no excuse for being rude to her grandmother's charge, whether houseguest or hired man.

"I'm sorry, Matheo. I'll bring you a cup," she said, while

telling herself that her gruffness had been inadvertent. As she
crossed the parlor, she spotted an envelope leaning against the
mirror above the mantelpiece. Its placement was conspicuous;
Nana would see it as she came downstairs. Across its front was a
single word written in Jette's flamboyant hand: "Mother."

PART FOUR

CHAPTER TWENTY-THREE

—•—

Five Months Later

During their brief phone conversation yesterday, Bishop Brennan had persuaded Matheo to rendezvous at the rectory. Noting Matheo's preference for walking, the bishop argued that he should not have to take the bus to the fringe of San Francisco, where Brennan shared a residence with retired men of the order. Matheo accepted, responding that he welcomed the chance to visit his old home. He did not mention that he had been there Saturday, two days prior, to meet his confessor, Ralph Warren.

Tinubu had grown fatter, Matheo thought, as he reached down to take the priest's hand; the fleshy crease encircling the Nigerian's wrist might have hidden a rubber band or a thin bracelet. Belying Matheo's recollection of their first encounter, the affable novice seemed happier.

"Father Tinubu, good to see you."

"You, too, Matheo. May I call you Matheo?"

"*Oui*, but of course."

"Please, Matheo, call me Emmanuel. We are brothers in Christ, no matter your decision about your calling."

Matheo nodded. There were no secrets in the rectory, as he remembered from when he lived among them. The Nigerian must have known that the bishop would be arriving soon.

Bishop Brennan and Father Ralph entered the kitchen, suspending the Africans' shared awkwardness. Ralph embraced Matheo and, pushing back in a start, sneezed. Brennan turned to Matheo and said, "Shall we sit in the sanctuary?"

Ralph, with a kerchief pressed against the sides of his nose between prayerful hands, signaled Tinubu with a sideways jerk of the head. He folded the handkerchief and slid it into the back pocket of his pants. The pair of priests, in unison, bowed and stepped into the dining room as if they were offering a bereaved family time alone with their dead.

Matheo replied, "Bishop Brennan, might I cause a disruption?"

"We're beyond that concern, my son."

The church was vacant except for the two men at the back, sitting side by side in one of the pews near the confessionals. Matheo's gaze passed over the wooden icons that marked the Stations of the Cross, the carvings he had cherished since the first time he walked the side aisles—his silent lips moving in prayer while rosary beads slipped through his fingers as he neared the gaping entrance to the tomb of the Arimathean.

"Your first time inside since . . ."

"*Oui*, Bishop Brennan. Many months."

"Matheo, call me Thom." The pew squeaked under the African's shifting weight. "Now that I'm retiring, I can admit that I never liked the title; it made me feel distant, isolated. And, Matheo, we must be candid with each other, yes?"

"*Oui*, Bishop—uh, Father Thom." He paused, searching above the altar where for two years he had lifted the body of Christ. His eyes found the hanging crucifix before he eked out in a whisper, "Candid, *oui*."

Brennan raised a brawny arm, turned to face him, and brought his bent elbow to rest on the top edge of the pew's seat back. He looked deep into Matheo's eyes as he asked, "How've you been, my son?"

"Since we last saw each other, at Madame Coty's party?"

"Yes, yes, since Coty's party. You've been well?"

"*Oui*, Father Thom."

"Good." The bishop narrowed his eyes and said, "Matheo, I'm wrapping up the last of my official duties. I want to make this as simple as possible. It won't be easy, but I think it can be made a bit simpler."

"Simpler? Simpler than—"

"Than what it's been so far."

"Father Thom, my English—*sabbatique?* I mean, my sabbatical?"

"Yes, exactly, Matheo. It's time to bring your sabbatical to a conclusion. Do you agree?"

"*Oui*, Father Thom."

The bishop sighed and said, "I've been talking with Coty. She sounds quite tired. Thankfully, Evelyn has taken over the last of her grandmother's duties at the foundation."

The burden of friendship seemed to press the bishop into the pew. Matheo wondered if his superior had requested that they meet here to grant himself an excuse to check in on Madame Coty while he was on this side of the city.

"She's worried about Videsh—and *you*," said Brennan, who held forward to the front of the church. Without turning to make eye contact, he said, "Matheo, I worry about *her*."

Matheo's vision followed Brennan's to the veiled ciborium set atop the altar. Shoulder to shoulder, they sat as men often do: staring out at a flowing stream or crackling campfire, sharing the front seat of a pickup truck while driving on a country road, or enjoying a sporting event from stadium bleachers, looking anywhere but face to face—the primal stance of confrontation between men, the inviting pose of empathy between women. Sunlight cracked through the stained-glass window, splashing opaline rivulets over the edge of the altar and flooding the dull stone floor of the nave.

"Shall I propose postponing the renovations?"

"No! The remodel has given her a great cause. I don't want to pull you away from her; however . . ." After letting his elbow slide off the seat back and fumbling with empty hands, Brennan looked at him. When their eyes met, he said, "I don't know if you understand how important you've been to her, for many years. Do you, Matheo?"

"*Oui*, Father Thom. It helped her to help me, *non?*"

"Very much so." Brennan offered a tight-lipped smile and said, "Well, then, as she would say, first things first."

"Which things, Father Thom?"

"Have you decided about the priesthood?"

"*Non.* I'm confused about many things, many people."

"Evelyn?"

No secrets in the rectory, no secrets within Coty's intimate circle. "*Oui*, Father Thom. Evelyn causes me confusion."

"What else troubles you, Matheo? America? San Francisco?"

Evasion might also be made "simple." Matheo could tell him how difficult it had been to leave his cocoon in Gabon. How he had been flailing in his attempts to assimilate in the United States, with all its self-absorption and self-promotion. He could put the onus on the country itself, but his curiosity had snagged on his American hostess.

"Father Thom, I lived in San Francisco for two years before I met the mother of my surgeon. She waved to me whenever I walked past her home, but we did not meet until you suggested my sabbatical."

"You know that you're not like Jette's other patients, don't you?"

"*Oui*, Father Thom. I know the story of the accident. Madame Jette was operating on my heart."

"When you were sent here as a visiting priest, Coty insisted on anonymity. She didn't want you—or her family—to be caught up in tragic memories." The bishop fidgeted again. The wooden pew squawked as he returned his elbow to the edge of the seat back.

Unable to speak, Matheo stared at Brennan. If the pain caused by his presence repelled her, as well as Jette, why had Madame Coty not left him alone in Gabon?

"Once she heard that you wouldn't be allowed to go back to the rectory in Libreville, she was happy; she thought you'd stay in San Francisco, near her, while you worked through your dilemma. I told her that you couldn't reside at the rectory with Father Ralph, either. That's when she asked if she could invite you to live with her during your sabbatical. It was an unselfish request; she knew that she'd have to identify herself, which would exacerbate a difficult situation between her and Jette."

"Father Thom, have I offended Madame Coty, or—?"

"No, Matheo. Not Coty, not Jette. Neither of them would lay any blame at your feet, my son."

Brennan once again rattled the pew, and then Matheo asked a painful question: "Does Madame Coty wish me to leave her?"

"No, but I asked her to think about what's best for you. She admitted that it might be difficult, if not impossible, for you to decide while you're so far from home."

Matheo chewed on the word "home," remembering that he had been granted only a temporary room in her house.

The bishop said, "Would you like to return to Gabon, Matheo?"

What interloper, with a longing soul, would not wish to retreat to his cradle? He thought of his friends in Libreville, food he had not tasted in years, a womb's warmth in the humid air. "What do you advise, Father Thom?"

"You haven't been home for almost three years; you've been on sabbatical for months without resolution. You might benefit from going back."

Matheo stared up at the carved icon, suspended in the nave. The Crucified raised His eyes to heaven in a vain search for His Father. Considering the Forsaken and the bishop's counsel, Matheo asked, "I'd remain in Gabon?"

"Matheo, you're fortunate to have Coty Fine. I doubt you'd have trouble coming back to the States, if that's your wish—priest or not."

As trained, he deferred to authority. He would miss his family on the hill. His friend Ralph. The Desais and Master Joshi. He would miss Evelyn far more than the clear tap water from Hetch Hetchy. "As you suggest. I'll go back to Libreville. *Merci*, Father Thom."

Madame Coty was growing feeble, like Videsh. What of Magdalena and Sister Lan? Many of those he loved were quite old. Would he see them again? Would Madame Jette visit the clinic in Libreville, or could he fly to her in Lagos? How would he remember Evelyn when he sat against his wall in Africa? Would her absence make his repaired heart grow fonder, or would it fuel the torment from what had become an unshakable conundrum: his imagination about her past?

"Mother, I meant what I said: show her the photograph."

Jette would leave Sri Lanka in the morning. She was exhausted from a week of operations and waited for Coty to internalize the surrender.

"Thank you, Odette. It's what I've wished for years."

Odette? Jette took a breath to calm down. Evelyn and Matheo were scheduled to fly to Lagos in a few days, after Jette herself returned to Holy Name Hospital. Maybe it was the impending end of Matheo's sabbatical that had prompted her to invite him and her daughter to Nigeria before he repatriated to his native Gabon. Maybe it was the memory of her mother's age card, staring up from the kitchen table. Maybe it was the return of the Ice Age with Evelyn. Since Jette had slipped away on the eve of the big bash, they had seldom talked.

"And you're sure I can release the image for publication? I won't be able to pull it back from the printer."

"Yes, Mother. I'm sorry it took me so long to get to this point."

"Please, dear. I know what a big deal this is for you. Will you look at the photograph yourself before you see Evelyn?"

"I'm afraid I'd better." A white lie. Jette closed the manila file folder and slid it back inside the desk drawer. She crossed her arms, shut her eyes, and dropped her forehead to one of two creased elbows.

"I think that's wise under the circumstances, darling." Coty paused and then asked, "What about Matheo?"

First, Evelyn's gaze landed on the pained face of the boy who would grow to be the man she loved, even though she had yet to kiss him. The features were his, no doubt. He was half-naked, chest exposed, with patches of gauze, hiding a vertical track of stitches that seeped with moisture. Was it blood breaking the sewn line of defense or trace fluids that marked the natural process of healing? She followed the path beyond the crawling bandages, up the patient's neck, to his head, which tilted at his surgeon.

Evelyn often bristled when she heard about stricken patients "fighting" cancer or another cruel malady. What was involved in the battle? Could the afflicted conscripts halt their mind-numbing agony? Would that boy in the photograph have released his grip on the gunwale of life and sunk into oblivion if he could have unwound hands curled by instinct?

His facial muscles seemed taut, constricted as if the camera had captured a repetitive flinch, registering a beat-by-beat endurance of the sharp pounding in his chest. She studied the exhausted dark eyes, reflecting sadness that accompanied his physical anguish, windows through which, in a blur, he scanned for relief, teased by a deceptive, primal drive to survive—not a promise, not a hope, not a simple matter of faith.

Next, curly white hooks snagged her attention and tugged

her to look away from his side of the glossy print. The doctor—
about Evelyn's current age—in her operating scrubs, with a
stethoscope draped around her neck, stared through the camera
and out to a distant daughter.

The photograph portrayed two broken hearts, one repaired
and resealed by the woman whose wiry ringlets had been sheared,
not coiffed, into a pixie. Unlike her patient's, the doctor's heart
had been left wrenched open, its impairment permanent. Evelyn
recognized them all in the image of her mother: shocked widow;
Aunt Noémie's grieving twin; Nana's overachieving, empathetic
little girl, Odette; the tireless visiting angel, Dr. Walsh; and, as
Evelyn stared, coming back into focus after years of her own re-
fusal to strain for clarity, Mom.

Elbows pinned to the surface of her nana's writing desk, head in
hands, Evelyn stared down at the photographic evidence that
loosened her rusted preconceptions about her mother. She could
sense the presence of her grandmother, who stood a few feet
away by the French doors, peering at the bay.

"Darling, you haven't said a word."

Grabbing the edge of the desk, Evelyn twisted at the waist.
Inside the glare, Coty was framed by the casement of one French
door. Blue-green rays bounced off the water, backlighting her
presence as if she were surrounded by an aura acquired throughout prior lives.

"All these years, Nana, I thought that Jette was being dramatic—overblown victimhood. Now I don't know what to say."

"A first?" Coty's smile came into focus as she left the window.
When she reached the writing table, she waltzed her open hand
across Evelyn's back.

"Fair enough, Nana. Why didn't she show me years ago?"

Coty sat on the edge of the mattress. She swung her legs up
and leaned back, letting her head settle into a splurge of pillows.

She opened an arm, offering a clear invitation to join her in repose. Evelyn left the photograph on the desktop and scurried to snuggle with her nana. She pulled the matriarch's wrist up and ducked her head under the raised arm, wrapping herself in safety. Together, they stared at the ceiling.

"Frankly, darling, I'm amazed that you've seen it. I'm not sure what it means for any of us, now that it's exposed."

"Well, sort of."

"What do you mean, Evelyn?"

"It's odd that she won't let Matheo see it. Will he have to buy your book?"

The Great Manipulator stiffened. Evelyn caressed her nana's hand until it relaxed. As she rubbed her thumb over loose skin, the rest of the dancer's body unwound. Hypnotized, Coty kept her eyes closed and said, "She wants to show him herself."

"Why? She didn't show me—you did. Why can't you, or I, for that matter, show the man a photograph of himself as a child?"

"It might be best for your mother to tell you, dear."

Evelyn's body temperature spiked, and she tossed off the embrace like an unwanted blanket. "I'm sick of you two keeping secrets!" She pushed herself off the mattress and spun to find her grandmother. "Why can't you tell me? She's being a control freak, right? Or are *you*?"

"I think that under the circumstances—"

"Foul! I cry foul! She didn't ask you not to tell me, did she? Exercise your free will, Nana."

"I am, dear. And judgment. Better for you to talk to your mother about it. She's adamant that she show him in person. I respect her decision. I suspect you will, too, when she explains."

Why the distrust? Coty had long been Jette's apologist but seldom withheld information from Evelyn over the years—years when she and her nana had labored side by side in the gardens and at the foundation; years during which Jette had inhabited their lives at a distance.

"Well, help me respect her decision, Nana. Of course I wouldn't show him without her permission, but I've seen the photo and I don't understand why he has to wait."

With a wince and clutching her hip, Coty left the bed. She hobbled to the writing desk, took up the photograph, and, without examination, folded the manila file. She handed it to her granddaughter and said, "She worries it'll trigger suppressed memories that he's ill-equipped to handle on his own."

"Nana, you're sidestepping on purpose, aren't you?"

"Evelyn, she's a physician who's seen things we can't imagine. Talk to her. Listen to her. Please."

"Why can't she just talk to him over the phone?"

"Her experience with other patients. She says he should have someone with him—someone who was there when it happened."

Evelyn cleared her throat and said, "I can't imagine what she's worried he'll recall."

Coty swiped fingertips across the skin on her wrist. She sighed and looked through the French doors. Facing Marin, she said, "Dying."

Alone in her room, Evelyn sat on the bed with the manila folder closed. Coty had told her that she didn't know how long it had taken Jette and her surgical team to bring him back. After a deep breath, Evelyn opened the folder. Again and again, her eyes trailed across the page, examining their faces. Scanning down, she noticed Matheo's hand on Jette's, as if patient were comforting physician.

With a start, Evelyn shut the photograph inside the folder and rose from her bed. Squeezing the file in her hand, she raced down the hallway to the private sanctuary of the self-described "convicted agnostic." Evelyn ran to confirm her nana's hope, if not belief. What Coty might have long wished the surviving twin would see if Jette, too, combed the images she had shunned for decades. Might Noémie have been there, in the room with them, when the shutter flickered, horrified at their pain and placing a warm hand on her sister's—the familiar, loving caress of her soul mate?

———•———

CHAPTER TWENTY-FOUR

M adame Coty had insisted that he not only borrow her largest suitcase, but that he, himself, return it to her in San Francisco—someday. Relieved that the jumbo luggage had wheels, Matheo gripped its handle and tugged. The width of the piece caused him to pause at the open door to his bedroom and think of Emmanuel Tinubu's expanding hips.

He tossed it atop his mattress. He would slip his own small bag inside and surround it with the gifts he had purchased for friends in Libreville. As he opened the lid, it exposed a deep cavity, which was empty except for a surprise Coty had left: a handwritten note paper-clipped to a thick fold of faded blueprints. She had requested that he study the plans and make a list of his suggestions.

The paper clip slipped off in his fingers. He unfolded the blueprints and read the title, printed in bold capital letters across the top page: "GARDEN COTTAGE."

Matheo finished packing in less than ten minutes, swaddling in a shirt the only personal possession, other than clothing and a worn Bible, that he had carried from Gabon to the parish house in San Francisco. Not for want of nail or hammer, he had never hung the crucifix on the wall of his temporary bedroom.

Scanning the private sanctuary, he contemplated how his surgeon's mother had kept a faraway eye on him for years. One woman had saved his life, and the other confounded it. *What does it matter?* he thought, before he registered a flash across the window. Maybe it was a bird, or a falling branch that should be picked up before Neeta arrived.

He stepped across the carpet to look down into the driveway below his room. The bronze window pull felt rich in his fingers. Had he ever seen such sturdy hardware back in Gabon? The blueprints for the main house stipulated additional windows, and he wondered how they would find matches for the antique pulls. Then he realized that was no longer his puzzle to solve.

He pushed open the window and leaned outside. One of the garage doors rose. Crashing off the back-porch ramp, the motorized chariot entered Matheo's field of vision. Over dirt-encrusted pavers, Videsh aimed his wheelchair at the rising bay door. He must have assumed no witnesses to protest his cavalier driving and pushed his machine to top speed. On a roll, the hunched-over pilot disappeared inside the workshop.

What's Videsh doing in there? wondered the African, who, in a few hours, would leave America and the master carpenter to his business. Was there a final task that Matheo could accomplish? A burden he might lift from bent shoulders?

In his peripheral vision, Matheo saw the grille of a sedan. As the car advanced up the dirty driveway in a quiet crawl, debris crinkled under its radial tires. The telltale thrum of a car's engine had not announced Neeta's arrival; still, she was behind the wheel.

A loaner? Was the car in the shop for repairs? Neeta waved at the open bay. Although Matheo knew little about automobiles, he recognized the make; its midnight-blue coat reminded him of one he had seen parked on the street in front of the house.

The wheelchair flew out from the workshop. Videsh exited with several rolls of the project's blueprints held akimbo across his lap. Neeta stepped out from the driver's side and rushed to save her grandfather, who was losing his grip on the blueprints. Videsh dropped one roll, then another. He stopped the wheelchair and then cranked it around in a spin. Matheo heard his master's voice shouting, "I've got them, Neeta."

"NaaNaa Joshi, let me help," she said, as she leaned down in front of the Tesla with her hand on its dark, shiny hood. In a quick sweep, she retrieved an errant roll before it disappeared below the car's undercarriage. As she rose, a retreating drape of her hair unveiled the license plate: ZEMI.

CHAPTER TWENTY-FIVE

—·—

Coty settled in the chair, as instructed, and Magdalena began their late-night ritual with a gentle tug of the brush. *Still no humming*, Coty thought.

"He'll return, dear. Don't tell Thomas, but I *believe* Matheo will come back."

"To visit? Or—"

"Well, yes. At the very least, he'll visit. That said, I'm hopeful that he'll come back to live here with us. We're his family now. That's what he told Sister Lan, isn't it?"

"*Si, si.*" Magdalena sighed as the boar bristles raked the wavy tresses from Coty's scalp to the pooch of her friend's tummy.

"Videsh is in denial," Coty said, as her head swayed with the strokes. "Matheo was almost in tears when he came in from the driveway."

"He's not coming back, Coty. Why else would he cry?"

"He's worried about Videsh. The poor man is slipping, dear. Anyone can see that. Matheo's probably concerned that when he does return, his master might not be here."

"What does Evelyn think?"

"I guess she's being agnostic about *her* priest."

"You taught her, *si*?"

"Maybe." Coty laughed. "I did think her grandfather was going to run away with Sister Lan, take her back to Paris and raise a bunch of little straight-haired baguettes."

As Magdalena pulled, the matriarch thought of her family—Laurent's shared progeny. She turned to locate the photograph that Magdalena had taken last year. On the sofa, with crossed ankles, Coty sat in front of the parlor's fireplace. Jette stood behind, with a hand on her mother's shoulder. On the other side, Evelyn leaned over, touching her nana's cheek with her own. All three sported colorless curls and unforced smiles.

"Ouch!" Coty said.

"Don't move your head!" Magdalena's cadence settled back into predictable strokes.

Coty pondered her granddaughter's impending arrival in Africa with the confused priest. Soon, Evelyn would be with Jette and bidding Matheo adieu for the foreseeable future. She worried for her granddaughter, who would be voicing a sad goodbye to the priest and an awkward hello to her mother. "I'll try to reach Evelyn after breakfast. They'll be landing in Frankfurt about that time."

Magdalena yawned.

Coty reached for her friend's wrist. "You worry too much, my dear. You're tired. Go to bed; get a good night's sleep."

Magdalena entered the walk-in closet to place the brush in its berth on the bureau, while Coty settled in at her desk. Magdalena was humming when she exited the closet. "Don't turn out the light, *querida*?"

Coty addressed her notepad and said, "Please leave it on, darling. I've been teased by ideas all day. Didn't have time to jot everything down. I need to write a new list before I forget."

Her friend closed the door. Through the dense wood, Coty could hear her humming. *She's going to be okay*, she thought. *We're all going to be okay.* As Coty picked up her pen, Magdalena's wordless song faded down the hallway.

Once her cataracts had been cleared, each day Sister Lan merged into the predictable pattern of the household's early-morning traffic, streaming out of bedrooms, flowing along the carpeted runner that covered the second-floor hallway, and cascading down the staircase. First, Coty would tap on Magdalena's door and chirp her morning greeting in tolerable Spanish. Next, she would step down the runway, repeating the salutation at Lan's room, albeit in a mixture of pitch-perfect French and clumsy Vietnamese.

Throughout the night, Lan's sleep had been deep and undisturbed. Fresh air from a cracked-open window swept her face. Complementing the warmth beneath her blanket, the breeze was cool and dry. With her head nestled on the pillow, she recalled the thickness of her home country.

The sun rose and a calm slipped over her, waking her, stroking the hair on her head as if she were a child in want of reassurance for the day ahead. Lying on one side, at peace with what she felt, Lan batted her eyes open. Folded hands pressed flat beneath her cheek. With her knees tucked up, she thought of her father for the first time in days.

She had been awake for several minutes when Magdalena's frantic knuckle found her door. The nun lifted her covers and rose into the cool air. Unlike on prior mornings, Lan had expected their Mexican sister, not Coty.

Sister Lan twisted the knob and pulled the door into her room. She smiled to soothe the stout housekeeper, who was wringing her hands and shifting her body side to side.

Wide-eyed, Magdalena pleaded, "Did Coty knock?"

All the French speakers were gone. Piecing together English morsels, Lan said, "Coty goodbye me head." To explain that Coty had bidden her a sweet farewell, Lan brought her two hands together as if to pray. She pressed them against one side of her face, tilted her head, and closed her eyes to mimic a person asleep. When she reopened her eyes, the housekeeper's puzzled expression twisted into alarm.

Magdalena croaked out her panic—stuttering in English, before plummeting into excited Spanish. Lan did not comprehend the words but read the unequivocal terror in the woman's brown eyes. The nun smiled as she repeated her imitation of a sleeper. She kept her eyes closed, but this time she lifted one hand, placing its open palm against her other temple. She did not raise her voice when she spoke: "Coty no sad—Coty goodbye me head."

Magdalena clutched Sister Lan's wrist and led her out into the hallway. As they waddled to Coty's room, Lan repeated assurances in crippled English: "Coty no sad, Magdalena. Coty happy. Coty goodbye me head."

With a tug, Magdalena implored Lan to stand next to her. Frozen in the hallway, the nanny appeared unable to open Coty's bedroom door. The nun rubbed Magdalena's arm, up and down, as Coty would have done. Then she turned the knob and sent the solid wood door into the bedroom.

The lights had been turned off, including the desk lamp. The French doors' linen sheers filtered the early sunlight off the San Francisco Bay. Coty lay supine in her bed with her eyes shut. A pleasant expression had settled over her face. Rivulets of white curls ran down the duvet, petering out before reaching Coty's waist.

"No, Coty, no!" Magdalena shrieked, as she crushed one knee into the edge of the mattress and threw herself across Coty's body.

Sister Lan stood over them, smiling. She did not have the words for Magdalena. They would telephone Jette in Africa and try to reach Evelyn and Matheo in Germany, during their layover. The French speakers, too, would reel at the news, but they would understand and could tell Magdalena in English. Tell her in words that Lan did not possess.

Rubbing her weightless hand across Magdalena's heaving back, in a murmur, Lan repeated, over and over, "Coty no sad. . . . Coty happy. . . . Coty goodbye me head."

CHAPTER TWENTY-SIX

On the first flight of their journey, after spent meals were cleared and sated passengers settled in, Evelyn was reading. Reclining his seat, Matheo let his crown fall against the headrest and closed his eyes. Visions of Coty's world accompanied him over the North American heartland en route to Frankfurt. Pleasant memories elbowed out his persistent cycle of doubt. He would have hours aplenty to sit in privacy against his wall in Gabon.

He kept his eyes shut when he heard Evelyn fiddling with the seat-back pocket in front of her. A plastic tap let him know she had closed the window shade. Her arm rubbed against his as she pressed the knob to match his slope. By the time the jetliner escaped the continent's northeast coast, they were asleep, sailing high above the Atlantic.

Hours later, after they entered German airspace, the plane hopped and luggage shifted, causing rattles in the overhead compartment. Matheo awoke in a start. As he blinked through the retreating fog of slumber, he witnessed an endless row of parked Teslas, headlights aimed at him, with a recurring script affixed to each car's grille: ZEMI.

The pilot's voice broke through the din. Evelyn wriggled in her sleep. The flight attendants were stepping down the aisle for the last time. One stopped at their row and reached across Matheo to tap the shoulder of his traveling companion.

"Fräulein, may I see your seat belt?"

Dazed, Evelyn batted her eyes open and, without looking at the attendant, let robotic obedience lift her blanket to expose the buckled restraint.

"Danke."

Evelyn raised the back of her seat. Upright, she blinked, staring straight in front of her. Matheo waited. Rather than jostle her mind with vapid comments, he looked past her grogginess at the sunny blue sky above a field of steely clouds that portended midday gloom below. As the jet pierced the murk, their sharp descent caused Matheo to lean into his seat belt. Rain drummed the aluminum hull; plump drops splattered the window.

Ground appeared. They were flying low over an industrial district of the city. With its nose upturned, the plane slanted for the runway. Through the droplets on the clear plastic window, he witnessed earth's breath—smoke and vapor, rising through the falling rain. The gray buildings reminded him of postwar scenes in the photographs from Coty's early career. The runway greeted their tires with a wet welcome.

The soaked tarmac popped as raindrops splashed into shallow puddles. Evelyn reached into her handbag, produced her mobile phone, and said, "I should check to see if Nana or Jette called." After a quick glance, she shoved the phone back inside her bag. Her irritation was apparent. She closed her eyes, leaned back against the headrest, and said, "Five texts from Neeta, followed by two from Parvani. Now she's got her mother lobbying on her behalf."

"You didn't read them?"

"I don't have to; I know what they're about. It can wait till we're in Lagos and I've had a shower, maybe even a good night's sleep."

"You're angry with each other, *oui*?"

"Neeta's not angry. That said, I'm furious with her—with him."

"Who, Evelyn?"

"Someone you've met."

He waited, haunted by the recurring moniker on a dreamy row of electric cars.

"You look puzzled, Matheo. You talked to him in front of the house. Tall guy in a suit. Remember him now?"

The uninvited topic—a feared stowaway—had slipped from the hold and slunk down the aisle. Evelyn's history with the famous entrepreneur had plagued Matheo since the day he had watched her return the man's ring. "Monsieur Ueland?"

"Yes, the famous entrepreneur, the brain behind Zemi."

Matheo remembered Esben staring at the box cupped in his hand when she slammed the front door. He wondered what the man had said to his erstwhile lover—and what she had said to him.

"Yesterday, Neeta drove his car to pick up Videsh. Is that why you're angry with her?"

"Yeah. I found out after she said goodbye to you and took NaaNaa Joshi home. She came to my office at the foundation, wanting to see me before we left. We got off to a bad start when she made a joke about you and me."

"Us?"

"She said that her two best friends had ostracized her and that she felt like she was in eighth grade, excluded from the tall kids' clique."

"She told me that joke, too, Evelyn. I think she wanted to come with us but couldn't because of Videsh."

"It would've been funny—maybe—if I hadn't seen her with his car."

"You're angry because he let her use his car?"

"Actually, she was doing him a favor. I couldn't believe she'd even talk to him again, much less do anything for that man." She scowled at him with the look of an interrogator and said, "Matheo, Esben told Neeta that he ran into you in front of our house. What did he say?"

They had faced each other—man to man—on the street, not in a dank confessional with a wooden lattice screen that masked their countenances. As a confessor, the priest had guarded revelations from those who knelt before him. Although confidentiality with Esben Ueland had not been requested or guaranteed by sacrament, he applied caution. "He knew I was a priest—Coty had explained my background to him. Mentioned he'd spent many hours inside your house. Told me that he'd been summoned to retrieve the ring."

"That's it?"

"He looked back at the front porch, at where you'd been standing in the doorway," Matheo said, without disclosing the man's haunting caution about the family on the hill: *"Be careful, Father."*

"He didn't mention that my grandmother saved his venture, did he? After he had spent his initial seed money, the VCs balked." Her face contorted with fresh anger. "The Sheldon Fine Foundation owns more of Zemi than he does!"

Evelyn turned to the window and raked the inside with her fingers, tracing Germanic tears that streamed down the plastic.

After a jittery landing in Lagos, Evelyn reached again into her handbag for her phone. "Wow, strong reception," she said, after the device had awakened.

Africa was making progress, Matheo thought, as they coasted along the tarmac. He looked through the window for expected haze and familiar trees.

Evelyn gasped. Frantic, she opened her contacts and tapped one name. As the call streaked out of Nigeria, she said, "Something's wrong, Matheo."

With her heels raised and the balls of her feet pressed into the carpeted floor of the plane, Evelyn's knees jumped up and down. Listening, she held her gaze on the seat back in front of her. She slapped the phone against her leg and said, "Father Thom's voice mail—damn it!"

Rather than leave a message, she ended the call and then showed Matheo the list of new texts on her screen. Eight messages had been added to those she had ignored when they landed in Frankfurt: three more from Neeta, three from Parvani, and two from the source marked "Father Thom." The last pair of texts drew Matheo's fears to the surface. Bishop Brennan's first message was terse: *call me.* Sent less than an hour later, the second dispatch read, *Evelyn call asap—urgent.*

When Matheo's head bobbed in recognition, she touched another contact and waited with the device at her ear. Despite the low volume, Matheo recognized the lilting sound of Parvani's voice mail introduction. Evelyn squeezed her eyes shut as she pressed the phone against her forehead.

CHAPTER TWENTY-SEVEN

——•——

No carousel dominated the baggage claim area. A metallic *clang* stopped foot traffic. Heads turned as a corrugated door to the outside rolled up, exposing a laden cart and the flat, late-afternoon light of Lagos.

One by one, the plane's bags were tossed through the opening onto an iron ramp. Pieces of checked luggage slid across the dulled floor, each one spinning to a stop at their feet.

Lean arms hung out of his shirt's short sleeves. Matheo had collected their luggage and waited for Evelyn to finish a tearful conversation with Parvani.

A blessing, he thought. If, during their layover in Frankfurt, she had answered the pleas of the two Desai women, Evelyn might have headed back to San Francisco and left him to his homecoming. He wanted to be with her, to support her and, soon, Jette. For himself, he needed to be with people who also loved Coty Fine.

Evelyn slipped the phone inside her purse, then nodded at him and collected her suitcase. As they rolled their luggage up to the counter, she retrieved her passport from her handbag. Matheo wondered what the man thought when he held it up to compare her laminated photograph with today's sad, drawn face. The agent returned her passport, and Matheo presented his.

"Purpose for visiting Nigeria? Personal or business?"

"Personal."

"How many days in country?"

"Two."

"Are you flying back to the United States or home?"

Home? he questioned himself. Without glancing at Evelyn, he said, "Gabon."

Father Thom had arranged transportation. Cardinal Omu, an old friend of the bishop, had stipulated that his car and driver be at Evelyn's disposal while she was in Lagos. Whenever Jette was working in Nigeria, she slept each night at Holy Name. Evelyn and Matheo would be put up at the house of the cardinal's sister—another insistence of the reigning cleric.

Omu's driver, a broad-chested man, who, although much shorter, dwarfed Matheo with his muscular bulk, stood beyond the exit with a hand-printed sign: MS. EVELYN WALSH. The sign rose higher for the approaching white woman. The man nodded and, without further recognition, lowered his hand.

Evelyn half-smiled as she relinquished the handle of her suitcase to Omu's driver. Turning to address Matheo, she said, "Jette warned me about spotty coverage on the drive to the hospital. I'd better call Magdalena, too, before we leave the airport. Parvani's heading over to the house right now."

"Does Jette know?"

"Yes. Parvani talked to her hours ago. She explained to Jette that we wouldn't get word till we landed."

The cabin was still hot when they pulled out into traffic. Evelyn depressed a button to lower the tinted glass at her side. Dust snuck in through the rear passenger window and clouded the back of the cabin. She coughed as she lunged to raise the window, and then reached into her bag for her handkerchief. Flying her white flag, she waved airborne soot away from her blinking eyes. The two wiped-out travelers, heads bobbing, dozed in and out, jostled by the car's assault on potholes that dotted the road to Holy Name.

They stood in a shared trance, staring at the hospital's main entrance. Matheo had cautioned Evelyn about the heat, but it seemed to her that he, too, had trouble adjusting from San Francisco's temperate climate. Inside the building's reception area, the chill of air-conditioning brought relief to the exhausted couple. She heard him mutter a rote prayer of thanks.

When the trip had been conceived, Coty and Jette had planned a surprise for the pediatric heart patient's return to Holy Name Hospital for the first time since his successful surgery, decades earlier. Evelyn had been their willing accomplice, but, given the news of her nana's death, she had forgotten their plot. Double doors popped open, and a short, rotund nurse burst into the hallway, shouting, "My baby! My baby! My first little one, Matheo Aubert."

A match for Magdalena in height and girth, the nurse beamed as she threw flapping brown arms around her stunned former patient. Matheo's head protruded above her uniform's starched white hat, which scraped his chin as she swung him side to side. Evelyn stepped back for fear of being bruised in the reunion.

"It's me, Nurse Lolo!"

"*Enchanté, madame.*"

"*Madame?* You don't remember me? I'm Lolo. I rocked you like a baby." Pushing him away, she held him in a tight grip at arm's length. "Let me look at you, my baby. You're so tall! A beautiful man, Matheo Aubert. You're a miracle. Thank the Virgin Mary."

"Ah, yes, excuse me, Nurse Lolo—but of course I remember you," Matheo said, after cooled air had rushed into his lungs and fueled his gratitude, if not his recollection. "Nurse Lolo, this is Evelyn Walsh, Dr. Walsh's daughter."

Lolo did not seek permission to hug the surgeon's daughter. She crushed into Evelyn as she had greeted her former patient. "You look like your mother with long hair! Ah, come with me, child. I've pictures to show you. Of your mother and her patients. You must be very proud."

Evelyn pinched the bridge of her nose and squeezed her eyes shut. "Is she here?" she asked.

"No, she left before dawn."

"Left to go where?"

The ebullient nurse grabbed Matheo, again. He gasped for air, his ribs bent by another hearty hug as Lolo answered Evelyn. "Took a plane out of the country. An emergency."

"Emergency?" Evelyn asked.

"Went to escort a patient back here for surgery. Tomorrow, I'll have my new baby."

The house of Omu's sister was modest, albeit luxurious by local standards. The smell of coffee reminded Evelyn of home—her nana and Magdalena. While the reminiscent aroma wafted into her room, an impossible promise of their morning ritual mocked her as she rose and dressed.

Rain had fallen throughout the night and tapped on the roof. Hand on doorknob, she hung her head as she clung to the hardware and her memories. Time to find Jette, who might already be back with her grave patient. They would wait if she was in surgery; Evelyn wanted to see her mother as soon as possible.

"Good morning," she said, as she entered the kitchen. A woman about her age stood at the sink with a young child—a boy maybe five years old—clinging to her dress. "Hello. My name is Evelyn Walsh."

"Good morning, Ms. Walsh. I'm Nmaku. This is my son, Okoh."

The housekeeper placed her hand, with forward pressure, on

the back of her son's head, encouraging him to step out from his hiding place in the creases of her frock. A round, dark face slipped from behind the curtain. The sheepish boy looked up and said, "Morning." Released by Evelyn's smile, he pressed his timid grin back into the safety of his mother's dress.

The room rediscovered the stillness she had broken. Evelyn took in the table where Omu's driver waited with Matheo. The men were quiet and appeared glum, seated with their heads sagging from troubled shoulders. Matheo stood to pull out a chair for her. After she sat, he plunked back down onto his seat. Nmaku placed a steaming cup of coffee in front of the puzzled woman.

Now what? Evelyn wondered.

Matheo's introduction was measured. In a dirge's meter, one that priests must practice over and over, he conveyed the news received earlier, while Evelyn showered. Jette had called Holy Name before the plane took off. They were readying to fly back to the hospital from a remote region. There were storms. Her patient was on the edge. She was worried about the transport, but the sick child had little time left. They must come today, or another innocent would, without question, perish.

Once more, Matheo hung his head. The lull was torture for her, and she begged him to continue: "Matheo, what happened?"

Wrenching up, he found her demanding eyes and pushed out words identical to those she had heard before, long ago, at a moment when she was so young that she had not understood.

"Evelyn, there's been an accident."

Standing in the doorway that opened to the wet rooftop of the hospital, the two somber passengers waited to be motioned to the helipad that the Sheldon Fine Foundation had financed years before. The hulking helicopter loomed in the rain on a landing platform designed for humbler aircraft. The chopper was an intimidating military vessel capable of extended journeys at high speed. It stood more than twice the size of the hospital's new medevac, another of the foundation's lifesaving gifts to Holy Name.

Today's flight above the delta would be the second of two pho-tographic-reconnaissance missions: mandated flyovers necessary for planning the complex logistics of the dangerous recovery—not rescue. Jette was presumed lost, along with her pilot, copilot, nurse, and young patient. As the plane descended through the storm, the pilot had radioed their coordinates.

Yesterday, although the downed plane had been easy to spot from the air, the wreckage had been deemed inaccessible by riverboat or chopper. The authorities planned to drop, as close as possible, a detachment of men who, using inflatable rubber dinghies, would weave their way to the site to address the wreckage.

Positive identifications would occur after the site was reached and the bodies retrieved. A man of limited means, Matheo had given Evelyn a magnanimous gift: he had offered to stay behind, identify Jette's body, and accompany her remains back to San Francisco. Sobbing with relief, Evelyn had accepted his generosity, rather than remember her mother as they expected to find her at the morgue. Spared confrontation with Jette's burned and man-gled corpse, she would suffer only the visual memory of today's helicopter flight over the crash site.

Although the overhead rotors had slowed since the landing, a mechanical wind pressed out from the center of the rooftop. Eyes averted, shoulders hunched, Evelyn and Matheo ducked into a trot through the rain to the awaiting helicopter.

Once the cabin doors were closed and sealed, the sound of the thumping blades was somewhat muffled. In the cockpit, be-hind the concave plexiglass windscreen, two uniformed men with matching epaulets sat shoulder to shoulder. The sun's heat penetrated the cloud cover, turning the cramped cabin into a sauna. Sweat ran down the dark-skinned pilots' cheeks and dropped from their jaws onto clipboards as they hustled through their check-down routine. Under bulky headphones, the two passengers strained to listen as the Nigerians voiced each item out loud.

Finished with their preflight regimen, the aviators secured the clipboards. The captain manipulated the controls, and the beast lifted. Hovering above the hospital, the helicopter jerked as if it were tethered at its undercarriage to the rooftop. The aircraft spun and then accelerated, offering slanted views on the city as the blurry hospital disappeared behind them in the downpour.

Evelyn thought that from the air, the delta—a sodden jungle of towering mangrove trees at ground level—took on the appearance of green-brown sludge spilling into the Atlantic. The flight over the wetlands lent views of imperial pipelines, stretched across the muck to siphon crude oil from surface wells. The hollow conduits scarred the amphibious habitat where, for centuries, only water, mangroves, and canoes had carved up the surface.

The percussion from the blades numbed the cabin. When the pilots spoke, she had to concentrate to pick out their messages through the crackling headphones. Their hand signals suggested that they were nearing the crash site. The copilot triggered the outside cameras as if he were firing the craft's guns.

The pilot held them in a hover. He spun the helicopter and dipped it on an angle, pressing Evelyn into her shoulder harness. The copilot, abandoning the camera controls, pointed to the drenched side window. Twisting in his seat, he faced them and roared over his shoulder, "Are you ready?"

Into the din, Evelyn yelled at the cockpit, "What do you see?"

"Only the airplane; except for a section of the right wing, it remains in one piece." In the dismal mash of the delta below, nothing stood out to Evelyn. She shook her head at the copilot, who tapped the captain on the shoulder. He looked through the windscreen, nodded at his copilot, and said into his mic, "I'll hold above wreckage, which lies to the south. Look down, inside the path of the blades."

The captain tilted the helicopter anew. Evelyn clung to the inverted fuselage. Freeing one hand, she squeezed Matheo's arm, before searching through the falling rain for the site. In the gunk, amid cracked and buckled mangrove branches, she spotted a single-engine plane, painted white.

The half-charred hull suggested an engine fire had ravaged the front of the craft. No bodies were outside. Despite triggers to the imagination, nothing repugnant invaded. At their altitude, without visible evidence, reaching a death verdict required conscious calculus.

Mangrove branches were strewn over the fuselage. The chin of the broken plane stuck into the mud, with one propeller buried up to the aircraft's snout. Two exposed blades extended into the open air, promising to lift the plane if the hidden third prop were freed from the muck. She saw no movement except that agitated by the helicopter—tree branches, thrashing above rippling marsh water.

The copilot shouted over his shoulder that it was time to leave. The captain spun the aircraft, leveling it above the delta as he executed the turnabout. Evelyn drew her gaze back inside and found Matheo's eyes. Neither said a word. The monotonous *thump* of the pounding blades granted their silence a practical permission. What could they say that would matter? Jette had not survived that crash. No one had—not the pilots, not the nurse, not her mother's delicate young patient.

She leaned her head against the window and, with a sideways view, watched the world pass by. Nothing but delta sludge. The rotors' beat thumped on in a duet with the storm that drummed the fuselage, as the helicopter settled into an otherwise silent trip back to the rooftop of Holy Name Hospital.

CHAPTER TWENTY-EIGHT

Niger Delta

Warnings came from the control tower, miles away in Warri. When the storm surged, a command came over the radio to put the plane down. Jette understood that it would be foolhardy to press the mission until the system passed. The forced landing on a remote strip angered the captain, but the aircraft was not suited to the task, and the pilot, even less so.

Rain poured down, exploding on the tarmac with ample force to dissuade the adventurous. The captain signed the waiver and staggered back outside. Through blurred glass, Jette watched him stumbling in the rain. She looked from the window into the eyes of the copilot, who had refused to fly. Not the weather; not the craft; not the mission—he had a family, children around the age of her young patient. They needed their father.

He knew the pilot, had flown under him many times. Days like today were the worst. The captain got his courage from the bottle and chewing mind-numbing roots. He believed he could fly through any condition and would have crashed the plane if they had taken off in that weather.

"I have a family," repeated the copilot, who shook his head. He turned to watch with Jette through the window as the drenched pilot fought the hatch of the plane and pulled himself up into the cockpit.

Stubborn like her mother, Jette listened with respect before deciding on her own, as she had been raised. She, too, would not risk the flight with the drunken pilot, but the remaining options were poor: wait for safer weather and another plane to arrive in time, or take the failing boy overland, through the delta, to the closer hospital in Port Harcourt—from there, they could medevac him to Lagos. The child's condition would continue to deteriorate as the rain fell. Soon, he would die.

The copilot radioed his brother, also a pilot, who flew helicopters for Shell Nigeria, making several runs each week to flow stations deep inside the delta. If they could get to the nearest flow station, his brother assured him that he could commandeer the helicopter for a humanitarian mission. Shell had done it before, and the story of the endangered child should be sufficient to ignite their goodwill.

"Can't he fly here?" Jette asked.

"No, Doctor. No time to get the route sanctioned by the authorities. Shell's preapproved for emergency flights from flow stations to hospitals. They could get grounded if they fly without clearance."

"What about a military helicopter?"

"Even if we knew who to contact, I doubt they'd get here in time. We must get the boy to a flow station, in hopes that my brother can take him to Port Harcourt."

From around the back of the rickety hangar came the truck, which the copilot backed to the door that faced the runway. He killed the engine, jumped from the cab, landed with a splash, and sprinted under the awning. He lowered the tailgate, nearing the gurney and the head of the supine patient. Beneath the lintel, the copilot looked at Jette and said, "It's the best we can do. We'll leave the caretaker to his motorcycle. As you requested, after the storm passes, he'll radio for a plane to pick up the nurse."

The boy labored at his breathing as they pushed the gurney forward, sliding it onto the flatbed under a tarp that served as roof and sidewalls. The copilot slammed the tailgate to vertical and ran with hunched shoulders into the downpour to find the driver's door. In a single, long-legged step, Jette followed her patient. She turned to look down at her surgical nurse and said, "I'll see you at Holy Name, Idara."

Standing with her hands on the wet tailgate, the nurse shook her head. She climbed up under the tarp in pursuit of doctor and patient. Idara pulled the flaps together and tied them into position against the wind and rain. In a crouch, she crawled along the slight body to the boy's head and took her position across from Jette. "As you told me, Dr. Walsh, we each must decide for ourselves."

"Thank you, dear," said Jette, who knew Idara was afraid yet sought her courage from neither bottle nor root.

The engine cranked over. The copilot manhandled the gearshift and released the clutch. The truck lurched forward, spewing a cloud of black soot from its exhaust pipe. The smell of damp diesel invaded the covered flatbed and held like an omen above the boy. Idara waved the air to clear his breathing.

Their ride on the smooth runway ended soon after he shifted out of second gear. Downshifting, he applied the brakes. They slid to a stop at the edge of the airfield, where the delta threatened. The clay road ahead was pocked with dancing puddles. Sliding open the foot-long window between the cab and the back of the truck, the copilot shouted to the women over the din of the deluge, "Brace yourselves and the boy."

The tires spun in the mud. After spurts and skids, the driver found tenuous traction. Under the tarp, Idara and Jette each held one hand on the truck's frame and, with the other, gripped the patient's gurney. They rocked as the driver fought to hold the truck steady.

The harrowing journey ate the remainder of the day and bit into the wet night. In the dark, they drove through the downpour until their progress met an abrupt end. Slammed against the cabin wall, Jette reeled back; her grip on the side rail of the gurney saved her from bounding to the tailgate.

The truck stilled. The sound of rushing water muffled that of the rain. She stretched forward to look inside the cab. The driver's hands were frozen on the steering wheel. In a panic, she knocked on the glass. He turned, his fear as obvious as when he had talked about the drunken pilot's infamy in foul weather.

The copilot shook his head. When he turned back to face where the road had been, he dropped his forehead between his hands and kneaded his brow against the steering wheel. Jette looked over his shoulders, her vision guided by the yellow cone from the headlights; she could see that rogue waters had knifed through the dirt road.

The storm attenuated to a soft drizzle. Having breached the riverbanks, an errant tributary cut off their route. Leafed branches waved in passing like the flailing limbs of those certain to drown in the churning rush of muddy water.

The driver reached into the glove box, extracted a flashlight, then turned and frowned at Jette. He stepped down onto the slippery mud and, after wiping his eyes, began scanning their surroundings with the torch. She watched as he held one hand on the fender and walked like a child on ice to the front of the truck, where he paused and faced the rapids. He skated forward in a cautious slither to inspect the drastic bank of the runaway creek. On his return, Jette lost sight of him as he circled the passenger side.

The tarp dripped, missing the boy. She listened as the copilot progressed to the tailgate.

"I can't see anything!" she heard him yell.

Scrambling to where the canvas had been snapped to the steel wall of the cabin, she snuck her finger along the seam and tugged. Through the slit, she glanced outside, following his torch beam as it swept back and forth from the rushing stream to a wall of mangroves, where the artificial light yielded to native gloom.

When the driver's side door slammed shut, he twisted to confer through the window. His soaked shirt clung to dark skin; the beads on his tight hair twinkled. They must wait until dawn to flush out a human from the mangroves.

The spent copilot slept strewn across the bench seat in the cab. Under the soggy tarp, the women took turns napping as the other tended to the struggling child.

Jette was awake. In the early-morning light, she could see the boy from coil to toe. He was long-bodied and slender, reminiscent of Evelyn. His breathing had grown shallower. Across the gurney, at his knees, Idara, asleep in a fetal fold, leaned against the metal frame that supported the canvas sidewall.

An outside rustling alerted Jette. Through the window into the truck's cabin, she saw that the driver had bolted upright and was staring into the windshield. Despite the resting engine, the thumping wipers were at work. The river was visible, as well as the rogue creek, whose waters had flattened and lapped at the breach in the road.

Through the blurry window, a man in a tattered, once-white tank top appeared. Hilts of forged implements stuck out of his wooden toolbox. Skirting the severed road, the stranger stepped along the slippery bank. The weight of the tools pulled his shoulder toward the mud. For balance, his free arm flopped like a broken wing.

"What's he doing out here?" Jette asked the driver.

"The road ran along the river. Look over there—see his boats? When it breached, the water cut off his usual path—our road. His village must be close."

"I can't see the boats; I need to peek out from the side," she said, as she retreated from the window.

With one finger, Jette tugged the seam of the tarp, as she had done in the darkness. Thirty yards away from where the road had been cleaved, she saw a protective cage of roots suckling at the river. Tied inside were two small vessels: a dugout carved from a mangrove trunk and a bruised aluminum flat-bottomed boat with a raised outboard motor.

One by one, he untied the boats and released them from the cage. As each slid out from the safety of the roots, he tied tow-lines from their hulls to the trees. Then he gathered into his arms a bundle of nets and heaved the load from the flatboat to the dugout. He left the canoe and leaned over the aluminum gunwale. His thrashing elbows suggested he was clearing a space on the floor. When he reared up, he spun to retrieve his toolbox.

"A fisherman," the driver said.

Once more, a loose arm winged out for balance. Despite the water at his ankles, the fisherman took confident, barefoot steps through the muck. He reached the lolling flatboat without slip-ping, found the gunwale, then steadied the dent-riddled craft and centered the toolbox on its aluminum floor.

"Doesn't he see our truck?" Jette asked in a loud voice.

She gazed out of the slit as she listened for the copilot's reply. The fisherman turned and glowered, as if he had found her eye peeking through the canvas.

"He does now," the copilot said.

He pulled the door handle and stepped down from the cabin. She watched his tentative steps in the mud as he left the truck. The fisherman appeared leery when approached by the copilot, whom Jette heard call out in English. He told of the sick child and asked the price to commission the flatboat for their remain-ing journey to the flow station.

Grumbling, the man reached into the toolbox. In the air, he brandished a wrench as long as his shinbone. He scowled at the shuffling driver, who, attempting to stop in his tracks, slid to the mud on one knee. Breaking the fall, his hands were gloved in muck. Jette feared for not only the life of the boy.

After cursing in a dialect unknown to her and causing the

copilot no less confusion, the stranger stopped. He twisted to drop the wrench into his toolbox and then, again, faced the fallen driver, who was rising and rubbing his hands together to slough off the mud. The fisherman laughed as he shouted, in English, that he would sell them the dugout. As the flatboat bobbed, he gripped his knees and quoted a painful price—a figure Jette estimated would exceed the full cost to replace his dilapidated metal craft, new outboard motor and all.

He yanked the cord three times; the engine grunted with each pull. After the motor started, he reached across the water, guided the floating canoe alongside, and dipped his hand over the side. Raising a clenched fist through the descending drizzle, he held up an oar. Once more, he laughed out invectives in his native tongue. The joke was clear. The stunned copilot was from the wrong tribe to bargain. If they wanted to reach the flow station, they could buy the dugout or swim.

The rear flap flew open, and Idara crawled over the tailgate. Sliding through the muck in a rage, she screamed at the fisherman in his dialect—her dialect. Within minutes, the copilot had backed the truck to the bank near the metal boat, whose chastened owner stood waiting in lapping water.

The fisherman sulked as they transferred the child onto the flatboat. The men gave each other wide berth. Jette was relieved when the towline was pulled inside and, with a muted metallic *thud*, dropped on the floor in front of the boy's gurney. Roiling the muddy water, the submerged propeller pushed them away from the riverbank where the copilot stood, waving a mud-caked hand at the women as the outboard spewed grimy smoke.

The fisherman, refusing to address the doctor, spoke only to Idara, who translated his cryptic commentary into English. They would reach the flow station within an hour.

The boat picked up speed, and Jette watched the truck disappear as they rounded a bend and puttered into the mangroves.

———◦•◦———

The fisherman held his blank stare at the upcoming turn, one he must have taken a thousand times. Idara was at their patient's head, patting his brow with a washcloth. If the boy did not die en route to the flow station, he must suffer a helicopter flight to Port Harcourt without medical equipment on board. From there, he would have to endure the medevac chopper to Lagos before the hours-long surgery. In passing, Jette's eyes scratched the homogeneous jungle for signs of hope.

Each turn threatened another corridor lined with giant mangrove roots, reaching down, sucking murky water away from an ambiguous shoreline. The fisherman focused straight ahead as he snapped responses to Idara's queries. "Close," he said, whenever she asked about the remaining distance to the flow station; "five minutes" was his recurring estimate of arrival at their destination.

A proud man had been scolded by a woman young enough to be his daughter. He could take them deep into the delta for retribution. Idara grew nervous and whispered to Jette that she regretted her aggressive commands. The nurse whimpered that they would never be found; their fate was now his choice.

A *thud* in the water; Jette shuddered when they smacked into a semi-submerged, floating stump. The boat swirled, and the fisherman fought the current to reset his course. The boy did not move. Jette thought that she had already pushed his frail body near its limits.

By the time the river's width had more than doubled, their dreary voyage had exceeded the fisherman's one-hour boast. As they sailed around the next bend, Jette saw signs of humans' battle with the delta. Set back from the lapping shoreline, the construction broke the monotony of looming mangroves, bleak skies, and turbid water. Trees had been slashed away from a promontory, exposing a cleared site, where she saw a single building, the primitive helipad, and industrial tubing. The hollow strands straddled the marsh and wove between tree trunks, before disappearing into the thicket from which crude oil pulsed to the flow station for consolidation.

At the dock, aluminum tapped wood. The motor idled, then died. The fisherman jumped onto the dock, tied down his boat, and then called out in the direction of the cinder-block barracks that housed the men who maintained the pumps and plumbing.

Jette assumed that her copilot's brother had radioed ahead, when four men exited their domicile in orange jumpsuits and, with anxious expressions, scurried to the dock. The men helped Jette and Idara carry the child inside the crew's quarters, where they would wait for the first helicopter.

Jette's head wrenched at the approaching *thump* of the rotors. The turbulence produced by the craft's descent swept a layer of mud and water to the edges of the helipad. She stayed inside, hands on the boy's gurney, waiting for the blades to slow and a signal from the pilot.

A uniformed arm jutted out of the chopper's window into the drizzle. When the pilot waved them to the aircraft, they rushed out with the gurney, which they would have to abandon after they loaded the patient.

Jette shouted instructions over the din of the rotors and the idling engine. Idara climbed up to clear a seat for the child, who was listless as she took him on board, into her arms.

A menacing sister storm of the weather system over Warri that had grounded their plane arrived in Lagos before their second helicopter: Holy Name's medevac. As they descended, a surge of rain fell sideways, scraping the hospital roof. Despite buffeting crosswinds, the medevac's pilot brought the aircraft to a pinpoint landing in the center of the helipad.

The surgical staff pushed an empty gurney and rushed out

past a rotund young nurse who stood at the rooftop entrance. Under cover of a tarp that the receiving team held over them, Jette and Idara guided the boy's gurney. The wide-eyed nurse kept a redundant grip on the open door, its hook not threatening to escape the clasp. Jette understood that was all the nurse could do. It was not yet her time. If the boy survived surgery, he would be hers.

Above the roar of the rotors, the novice nurse called out to Idara as the gurney passed, "What's my baby's name?"

"Matheo," Idara shouted over her shoulder. "Matheo Aubert."

CHAPTER TWENTY NINE

———◦•◦———

A single seat on a routine flight out of Nigeria had been booked for the next day. Evelyn's itinerary routed her through Frankfurt—the same journey her mother had completed countless times.

For the second day in a row, she entered Holy Name Hospital with Matheo. Their planned homage was to be straightforward: say goodbye to the people who loved the American surgeon who had saved the lives of dozens of African children. Once more, Evelyn must walk past photographs of her mother with the young patients she had rescued.

One hour of tearful hugs later, exhausted by the traveling wake's procession down air-conditioned corridors, she pleaded with Matheo to help her escape. Her Gabonese escort asked for one concession: return tomorrow to bid farewell to the absent Nurse Lolo, who was off-duty today.

"Of course, but just a quick stop on the way to airport, okay?" Evelyn asked, sad that, amid the fretful mourners, the nurse's absence had gone unnoticed.

A rude intervention stopped them at the lobby's exit. The short, bespectacled hospital administrator offered no introduction, much less condolences. Without social ceremony, the balding, middle-aged man launched his imperative: "Follow me." With an index finger, he shoved his glasses up his nose bridge, turned his back, and toe walked down the hallway.

Frozen in place, Evelyn looked to Matheo, who seemed as stymied. The clerk stopped, turned around, and glowered at them. With his eyes bulging at the visitors' delay, in a raised voice that trumped his prior rudeness, he commanded, "You must follow me to my office. There's paperwork to prepare before you can transport the doctor's body to the United States."

Edwin Mbadiwe grew calmer once seated behind his desk. With the opposing pads of two middle fingers, he aligned his nameplate as he proclaimed the impending success of the recovery team. Boasting "high-level contacts" within the military, he debriefed the wide-eyed couple as if they were morticians, not mourners. Without pausing for questions or testing their understanding, Mbadiwe expanded his commentary with the hot air of self-inflation.

"Today, the recovery team was dropped in the delta at dawn, to maximize hours of sunlight. Your mother's body will be here very soon. They're expected to complete their mission within forty-eight hours. The bodies should be here tomorrow, next day at the latest."

The clerk made them suffer through a barrage of indelicate questions. Diluting the surly man's discourtesy with a cleric's practiced decorum, Matheo offered apologies for Evelyn's scheduled departure.

"Mister Mbadiwe, tomorrow, Ms. Walsh returns to the United States. I'll leave a phone number. Please call when the recovery team arrives. I'll come immediately to identify Dr. Walsh's remains."

Mbadiwe's mouth gaped. "I must say, this is most strange," he said. His lower lip, flabby and uncontrolled, hung in the air. Exposed chest-high above the desktop, he fidgeted, augering his elbows into the blotter. After chewing and twisting his plastic pen, he pulled it from his molars, tapped it against his desk blotter, and ranted on about the mission. "Decomposition advances rapidly in the delta; the five bodies must be placed in separate bags and strapped inside the inflatable boats. The recovery team will collect the flight recorder. I confirmed there was a recorder on board. I assume it to be intact, based on the visual sighting of the wreckage."

Evelyn looked around his office. No personal touches. No photographs or even cheap plaques denoting minor accomplishments. She spied a battered lunch pail on the metal credenza behind him and guessed that the administrator spent his days here, alone at his desk, leaving his office only for the toilet or to chase people down in the corridors and browbeat them to complete his paperwork.

She cleared her throat and asked, "When did *you* fly over the crash site?"

Her query had no effect on his discourse. Mbadiwe circumvented requisite respect for the dead, picking at a scab on his forearm until it bled, while he continued the lecture. "Anything of value, lightweight and not too bulky, that the men can transport will be stripped out of the fuselage and transferred to the rubber dinghies in a single pass. I wouldn't ask them to make two trips. Too difficult and dangerous an operation." He dabbed at a drop of blood. After rubbing it dry on the skin of his wrist, he brought the pen back to his mouth for a quick chew. "In a few years, that crumpled plane will be very difficult to spot from the air."

Into an unearned smirk, he drew his lips against his teeth. He seemed pleased with his command of the campaign—a desk jockey's vicarious deployment to the delta. Evelyn wondered if he had ever visited, despite what she assumed was an entire life lived at its edge.

Before letting his lower lip flop back to its natural limpness, he asked, "Any questions about our operation?"

Matheo replied, "No, thank you, Mr. Mbadiwe. Ms. Walsh has requested that I transport her mother's ashes back to San Francisco."

"Not an option," snapped the administrator, intimating insurmountable hurdles to a foreigner's cremation in Nigeria. Mbadiwe spun in his chair to address the credenza. He pulled out a filing drawer, rifled through its hanging folders, stopped, and extracted a blank form.

When he twisted back to the desk, his lower lip hung open. A mouth-breather, Evelyn thought. She chastised herself for judging a person she did not know; maybe he had a history of sinus trouble. Her self-talk proved ineffective. With little to go on, she loathed the man.

He did not look at them; rather, he attacked a stack of paper that had been prepared in advance. Once he had detached the two-inch metal clip, he sorted through the pages until he found his spot. After inserting the new form, which he had marked with a removable tag, he picked up the stack and clipped the pages back together. "Sign the release, Ms. Walsh, and your friend will be allowed to identify the corpse. After a positive ID, he can take your mother's body back to the United States. I've marked the pages for your signature. Three places," he said, as he shoved the paperwork across the desk.

Leaning close to Evelyn's ear, Matheo explained that Nigeria was not the place to press logic, unless she was prepared to exercise a bribe, the efficacy of which could not be predicted. Wise not to alienate the man, Matheo suggested. Mbadiwe might otherwise shut down any movement of her mother's remains.

She scored the required signatures in quick swirls and slid the papers back to the clerk. *Enough*, she thought. Best to get Jette's body out of Nigeria and back to San Francisco, where Evelyn, as the family's sole survivor, would host a dual funeral.

After a brief call to the cardinal's personal secretary, Evelyn's return transportation to the airport was set, including the side trip to Holy Name Hospital. They would run inside, find Lolo, and pull themselves from the wrestler's hold as soon as etiquette allowed. Car and driver would wait in the driveway in front of the lobby.

Omu's private car arrived one hour early, fulfilling a long-established expectation that the senior cleric had set for his own travel. Evelyn entered the kitchen, pulling her wheeled suitcase. The driver sat there, talking to Nmaku and ignoring the visiting priest.

The two men, vying to commandeer her luggage, stood and bumped shoulders. In the male moment that ensued, Matheo deferred, allowing the determined brute to captain the roller bag and lead the procession outside to the automobile.

One more stop; one more sobbing encounter, during which Evelyn would face the most ebullient of her mother's devotees. Yesterday's stopover at the hospital, wherein she had endured the emotional embraces of the staff, who had glowed on about Jette's generosity and surgical feats, had drained her. At Holy Name, Dr. Odette Walsh had been a savior. With each heartfelt testimony, words meant for comfort had collided with memories of Evelyn's vitriol for her oft-absent mother.

The car drew up behind stalled traffic. Evelyn observed children at play in front of a row of storefront shanties. Since their arrival, she had noticed few details of local life, although she typically consumed novel surroundings with an insatiable appetite—another gift by example from her nana. *I'll probably never return*, she thought, growing nauseous.

Cardinal Omu's sedan pulled to a stop outside Holy Name. Matheo stepped out of the car first and extended his hand from the vehicle's right side, above and across the bench seat, to Evelyn. The driver opened the left rear passenger door.

Unable to decide which way to exit, she shook her head side to side. Too much. Everything had become too much. Accepting the shorter route, she took the hand of the driver, who tossed a look of victory over the vehicle's roof.

"Promise me one thing, Matheo," she implored, as the driver sealed himself back inside the air-conditioned cabin. "Promise me we won't go back to that awful man's office."

"No more papers, remember?"

"You were the one who told me that in Africa, 'anything and everything can change overnight.' Promise me."

"His business with us is finished, Evelyn."

Many of the staff whom they had visited yesterday were absent from the building as they walked down the hallway to the nurses' station. When they inquired for Lolo, an unfamiliar young nurse asked their names. With a look of recognition, she picked up the phone and turned a shoulder to them as she waited for the call to go through. Her whispered conversation was brief. Replacing the receiver, she looked up and said, "Mr. Mbadiwe will be right with you."

"You promised, Matheo," Evelyn said.

"Excuse me, miss. Ms. Walsh is on her way to the airport. We met with Mister Mbadiwe yesterday. We came here today to say goodbye to Nurse Lolo."

"Mr. Mbadiwe told me to call him as soon as you arrived."

"He didn't know we were coming," Matheo said.

"I'm doing what he told me to do, sir. Please . . . I'm new here."

"Sorry, miss. I understand. Do you know why he needs to talk to us?"

"No, sir. He said he'll be here in a moment."

"Can you please tell us where to find Nurse Lolo?" Evelyn asked.

"She's downstairs, Ms. Walsh. You can go see her right after Mr. Mbadiwe is finished. I think he's bringing papers for you to sign."

Sparing the novice, Evelyn turned to flash her rolling eyes at

Matheo. The bespectacled gnome she dreaded cleared the corner, toe walking as he made his way down the corridor.

"Mr. Mbadiwe, may I help?" Matheo asked.

"Not you—her," barked the curmudgeon, who flared his eyes at Evelyn. His scowl had relocated his glasses, and he brought up a forefinger to shove them back into position on his nose bridge. "I need you to sign these papers, Ms. Walsh. Then I'll be on my way."

He held out in one hand his pen; the tip of the plastic cap had been gnawed flat. In the other hand, he squeezed a crumpled document of several pages, folded open at the stapled, upper-left corner. The exposed sheet he presented was a signature page with Evelyn's full name typed below a solid line drawn to guide her inscription. He set the papers on the countertop above the head of the nurse, who, avoiding the testy administrator, lowered her attention to her own paperwork.

Evelyn grabbed the pen below gooey teeth marks, signed the page, and slid the papers to Mbadiwe. She handed back the gnarled pen with a two-fingered pinch in the middle of its barrel. He curled an awkward grin that she interpreted as apology for having missed, yesterday, a crucial step in his documentation.

Without comment, he turned around and retreated on tiptoe down the corridor. Once he had disappeared around a corner, Evelyn looked back to the nurses' station and said, "Excuse me, miss. Nurse Lolo? Please."

"As I told you, Ms. Walsh, she's downstairs. She hasn't left the morgue since the recovery team arrived."

The odors in the morgue were of death, not dying. Matheo's nose crinkled when he opened one of the double doors and entered the frigid room. Blindfolded, he would have known the place based upon a familiarity not sought, but rather tolerated, by priests and others who frequented the margins between life's demise and its residue.

Bedside with the dying had become customary long before he had first entered a cold chamber to confront a corpse. Vacant their souls, bodies here were cleansed and sealed for the momentary appeasement of the living. As he approached the two still forms displayed side by side on matching metal tables, Matheo thought that for pilot and copilot, it mattered not whether they had been dead for an iota or an eternity.

Sheeted from skull to ankle, the corpses of the two men lay covered, their faces aimed at the ceiling. Feet and hands protruded. Peeled from bloated extremities, once dark brown skin had been charred to coal. When the priest's gag reflex kicked in, he swallowed his disgust, as trained. Although never before commissioned to identify a body, he had stood by many a grieving relative whose last hopes recognition had dashed.

Tags dangled from the toes of the pilots, skin so compromised that the strings sliced through epidermis. Matheo assumed that the coroner's work on the men was finished; their families must have come and gone. Two of those on board the downed plane had been identified and lay ready for hearses, which might already be en route to Holy Name.

Turning back to view the exit, he looked past the pilots. Beyond those closed doors, along the wall, Evelyn waited on a wooden bench across from the elevator. Minutes earlier, she had slumped down and let her head fall back against the wall with a *thud*. Her eyes had begged him to hurry.

Low-volume sobbing revealed that he was not alone. He decided he would make the identification and excuse himself, tell Nurse Lolo that his companion was headed to the airport—a deceit that Coty Fine might have categorized as merciful white lie.

In one far corner, a girl's body had been pulled into the room from its steel cabinet. Nurse Lolo, emitting a weak moan, stood next to the dead child. Without salutation, Matheo trudged up to the nurse, ensuring that his heels clicked against the tile floor. He wished not to surprise Lolo or announce his approach from across the room with words as cold as the conditioned air.

When he reached them, he lowered an arm around Lolo's shoulder. Quaking under his touch, she clasped her hands together and bobbed over the corpse. Through quivering lips, she drew in a shallow breath and said, "Oh, Father Matheo, my baby! My baby's dead. Look at her."

Lolo was no stranger to the morgue, where she had bidden farewell to many of her babies. He stared down at the child whom she had met in death—to Nurse Lolo, a six-year-old stillborn.

"She was my new baby. Never saw my eyes," Lolo cried, drifting. "My baby never saw my eyes." The girl's body was exposed down to her navel, her feet sticking out of the sheet. Lolo rocked in place, murmuring, "My baby, my baby."

Subdued by her muffled chant, Matheo rubbed her shoulder and kept his eyes upon the dead child, whose skin tone was a rich ebony, darker than either his or Lolo's. Of which tribe? he wondered. Her smooth face spoke clues not only of her heritage, but of the crash. He swiveled his head, toggling his vision between the bodies of the pilots and that of the girl.

The puzzled priest clawed back images of the wreckage they had seen from the helicopter. The white-painted plane had been charred; black soot had smeared the fuselage from nose to midsection. The flames from the explosion had fried the pilots yet spared the sick child's worn-out body. *What of Jette and the nurse?* he wondered, assuming that they, too, had been in the back of the plane with their patient.

The burnished silver doors of the other vaults were shut. He pulled Lolo tighter, hoping that a firm hug might stem her tears long enough for the mourning nurse to point to Jette's cabinet. His touch had the opposite effect; she reared up and began to keen. Her labored heaves strained his sainted patience.

Trapped, with Lolo sobbing into his chest, he looked around the morgue. Confounded by the sheer number of closed lockers, he wondered how to release himself to draw closer to the wall of cabinets, where he might read the handwritten labels affixed to each hatch.

Tucked away in the shadows was a wheeled stool next to another sheeted gurney. Matheo started to cry when he recognized Jette. Abandoning the nurse, he rushed to his friend.

As he stood over the doctor, he was befuddled by her tanned complexion, which was as unaffected by the crash as her patient's. Scattered age spots marked Jette's skin, along with the subtle, expected wrinkling of a woman her age. *Oui*, he would give her daughter a positive identification. Mbadiwe would require more signatures.

The eeriness common among morgues reached out like a desperate leper to touch his clothing as he walked across the cement floor. The pained mantra "my baby, my baby" faded as he neared the doorway.

Eyes closed, Evelyn rested her head against the wall, until the elevator interrupted her solitude. Cables in the shaft were ordered taut, and the snap rattled the hallway, shocking her from her trance.

Staring above the doors, she watched as the indicator lights scrolled down through the floor numbers. The elevator was on the move, descending with what she hoped was not another dead body.

Thud!

The elevator had landed on the floor of its well. She listened, hopeful that the lift would reverse course. Another snap would indicate the empty box had been recalled upward. Instead, the cables' vibration slowed to a hum and she heard clinks.

Swoosh—the doors spread open.

"You forgot to date your signature."

"Can't you date it yourself?"

The pushy clerk approached, holding a folded stack of papers turned to a page with her recent signature, the missing date exposed by an angry, scribbled "X." Mbadiwe offered a chewed-up plastic pen, moist teeth marks glistening under the bank of neon lights. Enjoying his first vertical advantage, he loomed over the taller American. Evelyn refused to stand. She took the papers but waved away the gnawed pen.

The door to the morgue swung open. Startled, Mbadiwe looked up to receive his savior and said, "Oh, good, it's you. You tell her. Tell her she must make the date in her own handwriting. They'll notice the difference. If I do it, I could get in trouble. They don't have anything else to do except check my work."

When Evelyn stood to face them, her legs jellied and she dropped into Matheo's arms. Undaunted, Mbadiwe continued, "It's protocol." He forced an awkward, insincere smile. "Please, Dr. Walsh, tell her."

"Mom?"

Matheo transferred her to her mother's outstretched arms. Jette stroked her head until Evelyn's heaving slowed and her cries turned to a whimper. After a series of cleansing sighs, she cooed as Jette rubbed her back. She was afraid to move, to step away from their embrace and hold Jette by the shoulders so she could look at her again and make sure. Evelyn's eyes were clenched tight as she listened for authentication from her mother's voice.

"Darling, date the damn papers, please, so he'll leave us be. Your nana would say it's the right thing to do, 'under the circumstances.'"

CHAPTER THIRTY

—·—

M atheo awoke and slipped his legs over the edge of the bed. His thoughts were a jumble as he scanned the foreign room —not Coty's home, not a rectory in California or Gabon. He remembered as he gazed outside. The open window looked over the street in front of the house of Cardinal Omu's sister. Laden clouds lent the sky a grim pewter, while humidity's firm press billowed into the bedroom. The air smelled of the approaching storm, which might arrive in a torrential downpour before they drove Evelyn to the airport.

Reaching for the window pull, he noticed that the cardinal's vehicle was already parked outside. On the way downstairs, he knocked on Evelyn's door to suggest they leave earlier than planned.

Matheo entered the kitchen. Stretched out on the floor in a quiet corner, Okoh was on his stomach. The boy was balanced on his elbows, chest raised, knees bent, and feet in the air. The heels of his shoes tapped together to a random beat.

He greeted the child, whose attention remained focused on a wide piece of construction paper. The boy's mother turned from her post at the stove. Matheo took her soft smile as thanks for his failed attempt to draw out her son.

Rain rattled the roof over their heads. The phone on the kitchen wall rang. Nmaku settled Matheo's breakfast plate before him and reached for the receiver. "Yes, I'll tell him," Nmaku said, and then replaced the receiver in its cradle. "He said to tell you to bring the luggage out. He'll open the boot from inside the car. Doesn't want to get his suit wet."

Matheo's head jerked. His surprise must have triggered her to continue.

"I suppose for some men, chivalry's a fair-weather activity."

"You'd do well in America, Nmaku. They enjoy stating the obvious, mixed with a dash of humor."

"When you're ready to make a run to the car, I'll call his mobile. Take the last umbrella. I'll check the entry closet to see if there's one left for Evelyn."

"Thank you, Nmaku; we only need one. I'll come back and escort her to the car."

The dining room door swung open. Evelyn pulled her roller bag into the kitchen, exclaiming, "I've never seen such a storm in San Francisco!"

"Good morning, Evelyn," Nmaku said. "Breakfast?"

"Good morning, Nmaku. Yes, please! I'd better eat before leaving for the airport. Somebody told me that here, 'anything and everything' can change without warning."

Matheo watched the two women exchange looks. When they turned to him in unison, Evelyn asked, "Matheo, is he out there?"

"*Oui.* May I take your suitcase to the car?"

"He's not going to muscle it out of your hands this morning?"

Again, the two women traded glances. Matheo hesitated and then said, "He called Nmaku and told her that he'd open the trunk when I come outside with the luggage."

"Thanks, Matheo. I'm not used to having anyone schlep my bags. Let me grab a quick bite, and I'll run right out."

"One umbrella. I'll load the suitcase and come back to escort you to the car."

The door closed with a muted *thump*; droplets spat onto the kitchen floor. Evelyn took the coffee from Nmaku, who then reached for a plate inside an upper cabinet. As Nmaku stepped back to the stove, Evelyn turned her attention to the quiet corner where the child's legs waved in the air above the floor. "Okoh, I'm sorry—I didn't know you were here. Good morning."

The boy shifted on his elbows and smiled without commenting or looking away from his artwork. His heels clicked.

"May I see?" Evelyn asked, as she accepted the plate and fork from the boy's mother.

Okoh rose into a straight-backed kneel. With a broad grin, he displayed his creation: two stick women with a child, who stood in between them, holding their hands. One woman had no coloring inside her oval face. Wavy strands had been drawn down the length of the clear woman's body. The boy had swirled matted curlicues atop the heads of the other two stick figures and had shaded their circular faces with the flattened tip of his lead pencil.

"It's a picture of the three of us, isn't it, Okoh?"

The child turned his artwork around to study it. Admiring the picture and Evelyn's recognition of its subjects, he did not speak. Nmaku did.

"He's been working on it since we came in this morning. Wanted you to have it for your journey."

"Okoh, thank you! When I get home, I'll hang it in our kitchen, where every day I'll see it and remember my friends in Lagos."

He looked from the drawing to Evelyn, and dread cloaked his face as his muffled groan slipped into the room.

"What did you say, Okoh?" Evelyn asked.

The frantic artist held the paper up and, without words, pleaded with his mother to confirm his error. Nmaku frowned maternal worry and asked him, "Okoh, what's wrong? It's a beautiful drawing. Why are you upset, child?"

Grunts of anger escaped the boy as he pressed the paper flat onto the floor and reached for a rubber eraser.

"Wait!" Evelyn implored in a hushed voice. "I love it! Okoh, are you certain you want to change it?"

The eraser stalled on the paper, one rubber corner pinned at the bottom of a string of curls. Evelyn set her plate on the countertop. Hands on hips, she stood over the drawing.

"My hair? You think my hair is too long?"

Okoh nodded. Through damp eyes, he begged for permission to wipe away his mistake.

"Okoh, your drawing makes me want to grow my hair even longer. When I come back to see you, it might look like your picture."

He cupped the eraser in his hand. Okoh looked to his mother, then craned his neck to study Evelyn, whose white crown must have appeared, from his viewpoint, to brush the ceiling.

"Okoh, if you want to make my hair shorter, it's your choice."

Dropping the eraser to the floor, Okoh stood. His face was beaming again when he presented his gift. Evelyn hugged the boy, who crushed into her as she surrounded him with his masterpiece.

"Let's roll this up very carefully, Okoh; I want it to look this perfect when I hang it in San Francisco."

The outside door swung into the kitchen. Rhythmic drumbeats accompanied the downpour's freshness. Matheo stood outside under the dripping umbrella. Crooking his neck, he motioned that he would wait beneath the nearby awning. The door closed and, once again, sprinkled raindrops onto the floor.

The two women looked at each other. Evelyn laughed, and then said in a whisper meant for Nmaku's ears, "Reminds me of Okoh. Doesn't say what he thinks, either."

"That man doesn't have to say it."

"Say what, Nmaku?" Evelyn asked, as she rolled Okoh's gift into a tube.

"You know." The boy's mother handed her three rubber

bands from a drawer near the refrigerator. With a coy sideways grin, Nmaku continued, "It's so obvious—you must know."

"What in the world are you talking about, Nmaku?"

"I see the way he looks at you."

Huddled together under the umbrella, they scurried to the car. Evelyn hopped over a puddle, causing Matheo to extend the umbrella to keep her dry. Rain fell hard and straight, drenching him. His deference continued until she was inside the vehicle, where she settled on the rear bench seat.

While he backed down into the car, the black nylon shell hovered above the open door. After unlocking the umbrella, he collapsed its ribs, sending rainwater in a rush onto his pants and into one of his shoes. Wet knees swung inside, and he reached for the door handle.

"Matheo, you're soaked!"

A *humph* floated over the front-seat back. In the mirror, she caught the driver's sneer, prompting him to redirect his gaze toward the windshield.

The pounding atop the vehicle's roof had not muffled her words from the driver's ears. When she started to speak in French, Evelyn looked into the rearview mirror and saw Omu's man glower. She leaned forward and sought the man's attention. Not wanting to further vex him, she spoke in calm English. "Excuse me. Please raise the glass. Thank you."

An arm covered by a light gray suit sleeve stretched for the dashboard. He poked an index finger into a button and held it down. As the glass screen rolled up, Evelyn turned to address her escort.

"That's better. You really are soaked."

He smiled and shrugged, while rubbing his arms beneath the hems of his saturated short-sleeved shirt.

"Matheo, I want to tell you something that I hope you already know."

Back when she was arranging their trip, Evelyn had confided to her nana what she planned to tell Matheo. Looking into his eyes, she recalled Coty's encouragement: "Oh, darling, you're in love! Be young. Be curious. Be gentle with our delicate hummingbird."

Nmaku's breakfast flipped in Evelyn's stomach. When she cleared her throat, he drew back, eyes wide. "Matheo, I hope you'll come back to San Francisco."

"If Bishop Myboto approves, I'll be there for Coty's funeral."

"I meant, I hope that you move back home—to your American home. It would be my choice, if it were mine to make." She had not invoked Videsh or his granddaughter. Not the doctors Desai. Not Magdalena. Not Lan. Matheo already knew that they wanted him to return. Lifting his hand, she brought it over her head. A damp ebony arm encircled her. Warm tears bled into his cold, wet shirt.

After wiping her eyes, she lifted his wrist, ducked from under his arm, and straightened her posture. He had not been back to Gabon in years nor leaned for one minute against that wall of his. With a sigh, she slumped into the leather seat as she said, "Sorry— I've been crying a lot lately." When she had last talked to Magdalena, her nanny had begged her to come home and to bring Matheo with her. "Everyone hopes that you'll be back for Nana's service. We need you there, Matheo."

"Bishop Brennan called me last night about Coty's funeral. He said Cardinal Omu had already placed a formal request with Bishop Myboto."

"Call me as soon as you hear. I'll book the flights for you."

He stared out his window and said, "*Merci*, Evelyn." As she watched rainwater stroke the glass, a blurry sign for the airport slipped into view. Evelyn wondered if he would turn to look at her before they arrived.

The driver tapped the turn signal. When the car rolled through the curve, Matheo swiveled toward her. "What about you, Evelyn, when you return to San Francisco?"

"Nana used to kid that she expected a huge party for her wake—lots of Motown. We'll have a bash in her honor; then, I suppose, it's back to business."

"The foundation?"

"Yeah, and a few things on Nana's list: publish that book and finish remodeling. Then I want to have her cottage built. I've been hoping Jette might move in there one of these days."

He flipped his hands over, pinning knuckles to soggy pants. He alternated stroking the calluses of one palm with the fingertips of his other hand. Gauging the marks of his labor, he murmured, "*Oui*, completing the renovations will please Master Joshi."

She grinned as she said, "And once the remodel is done, we mustn't dawdle. Better find pleasure seekers for the new rooms, or we'll have one relentless ghost haunting the place till she's satisfied."

Matheo smiled and then changed the subject, asking, "Have you talked to Neeta? Are you still angry with her?"

"We're fine, Matheo. It's her life. She and Esben worked together and were friends long before the drama started. Who am I to tell her not to see him?"

"Coty smiles, *non*?"

"Well, Nana would insist that I accept Neeta's decision, be her friend, no matter how I feel about Esben."

"Neeta introduced you to him?"

"Yes, months before she introduced him to Nana. As I told you, the foundation's investment saved Zemi."

"Oh. I assumed that you brought the idea to her."

"Why? Nana was like another grandparent to Neeta. She could ask her for anything. Didn't need me."

"So, Coty invested in Zemi before . . ." He paused, looked at his knees, and, with damp hands, squeezed his wet pant legs. Showing no sign of retreat, the deluge amplified, rattling the car's rooftop.

"By the time Neeta talked to Nana, Esben had already asked Karun."

"For money?"

"*Non!* For Neeta's hand."

His mouth gaped open as his head shook side to side. *He's not here*, she thought. Evelyn touched the damp skin of his forearm, and he reared back.

"The diamond ring?"

"Matheo, did you think Esben and I . . ."

Another barrage assaulted the car's roof. Streams of water ran down the windows in narrow channels. An exit sign for the airport appeared in the windshield. The lettering wavered between legible and submerged. The wipers kept quick time.

Omu's sedan plowed into a wall of rain. Through the downpour, the terminal appeared. As they pulled over, the car's tires split puddles. One after another, watery rooster tails arched above the curb and crashed onto the sidewalk.

The glass screen descended into its pocket, and, again, Evelyn found the driver's sullen brown eyes in the rearview mirror.

"There's no awning here, Ms. Walsh. We can wait until the traffic clears—or the rain."

"I'll get your bag and escort you to cover," Matheo said.

"You'll get wet again," she said, before realizing that he was still far from dry.

The door swung out, followed by the umbrella's pointed ferrule, which he aimed skyward on a slant. Matheo popped open the dome and stepped out into the rain.

Evelyn watched as he pressed through the shower's silver needles to reach the back of the vehicle, where, in a rush, he knocked on the trunk. A dry suit sleeve reached for the dashboard and paused. Matheo rapped once more. A smirk met her scrutiny in the rearview mirror, before the lid popped open.

Rather than rolling her exposed suitcase through puddles, Matheo carried it under the umbrella's cover until he reached the awning. When she saw him returning, he slid across the bench seat. The car door swung open, and she took the wet hand he offered. Evelyn hunkered inside the narrow, dry cylinder as they made their way to the airport's entrance.

Three days earlier, all she had wanted was to trudge into the terminal and board a flight for home. That was before the doors of the morgue opened and her resurrected mother had rescued her from Edwin Mbadiwe and before Nmaku had repeated her nana's observation of the man who now stood in front of her, dripping on the floor, his look of wonder locked on her own.

He crossed his arms and slipped his fingers beneath the shirt's short sleeves. Up and down he rubbed. Stopping, he said, "Evelyn, I must go. He might leave without me."

Under the awning, he raised the umbrella, then stepped out into the deluge and ran, splashing. The car's back door spread wide at his tug on its handle. He raised the umbrella higher and, in a quick downward pull, collapsed it. A fat column of rain doused him where he stood, blinking and staring back in her direction. He wiped his eyes with his free hand, while with the other he lifted the folded umbrella and waved it at the terminal.

He can't see me, she realized.

He shrugged, ducked his head, and descended into the backseat. A succession of fresh waves crested over the curb as Omu's car cast off.

She wended her way through the terminal in search of the check-in counter. The female agent smiled, as trained, and picked up the American passport.

How did Matheo look at me? Evelyn wondered as she stood, watching the agent's fire-engine-red fingernails scamper between paper and keyboard. The woman's voice jolted Evelyn back to the present.

"The plane has been delayed, Ms. Walsh—weather."

No surprise—after their amphibious trip to the airport, the delay seemed predictable. She rolled her bag to the assigned gate, where the status of the Frankfurt flight was posted. She knew that soon Jette would be out of surgery. The interlude might afford enough time for another conversation before she boarded. A quick call to whinge about how Neeta's estranged fiancé had sown seeds that sprouted into a gnarled tale in a fertile, innocent mind.

Jette was nearby. If not in person, at least, once more, they could talk in the same time zone; could engage as they had over recent days. Two women talking, listening, supporting—two women who loved each other, needed each other. One had found a mother lost a lifetime ago, while the other had just discovered that hers was gone forever.

CHAPTER THIRTY-ONE

—·—

Eight Months Later

"I've never been more jealous of your long legs!"

"Come on, Neeta. They're going to catch us."

"Those guys aren't trying to run in heels."

"Okay, don't hurt yourself. I'll meet you down there," Evelyn said, not wanting to slip behind the encroaching herd. Lengthening her stride, she accelerated, leaving Neeta to fade to the rear. Three awaiting young adults straightened when Evelyn arrived. In unison, the white-coated trio leaned forward to address the first in a stream of wedding guests pooling around the valet podium.

"Thanks—we're in a hurry," she said, as she held out the ticket wrapped in a twenty-dollar bill. The trio's apparent alpha snatched it. She sprinted in the direction of the parking lot without inspecting the ticket.

Evelyn turned to greet a huffing Neeta, who excused herself as she passed the forming line. Out of breath and without comment, she stooped over her knees and shook her head.

"We did it! First in queue," Evelyn whispered. Waiting for Neeta to rise, she stared out across one of Napa Valley's rolling vineyards and stood silent.

In quick succession, their two car doors slammed shut. The driver grabbed the steering wheel with her left hand and, executing a sharp torso twist, cranked herself to face Neeta. Leaving whispers on the outside, Evelyn said, "That was awkward."

Neeta laughed. She slumped in the passenger seat and said, "As my mom would say, 'indeed.'" Their car rolled away from the valet stand. She tapped her chauffeur's elbow and said, "Evelyn, I can't thank you enough for coming with me."

"I told you, I wouldn't have missed it for the world. It was awkward—and entertaining."

"I'm not feeling entertained right now."

"Let's stick with awkward. We weren't alone, that's for sure. Esben's new girlfriend didn't seem too pleased to be around his ex-fiancée at a wedding."

"She'll get over it. Not sure I will, but . . ." A frantic expression covered Neeta's face. "Hey, is this the only way out of here?"

Esben and the woman had left the large tent and joined the growing line at the valet station. Evelyn said, "Look at me. Act like we're having an excited conversation about her dress."

"The bride's?"

"No, the one Esben's date's wearing!"

Neeta snickered and said, "It looks expensive. I hate her long legs, too."

"You hate my legs? I thought you said you were jealous."

"You know what I meant. Quick, say something else, Evelyn. Please!"

"Okay . . . did you have a nice time, my dear?"

"Lovely, although I don't share your sentiment. I could easily have missed it."

"You enjoyed seeing your old colleagues, right?"

"I did. I'm being a big baby. He's the founder. Whenever a Zemi employee gets married or has a child, Esben has a role to play. I was surprised he stayed at the reception for so long. That's new."

"Think she coaxed him to mix with the people?"

"Doubt it. I didn't see her talk to anyone but him. Clung to his sleeve the entire time."

"Well, maybe it's for the best. You greeted Esben. You met her. You were civil."

Evelyn pressed her foot down on the throttle and the car sprinted into their getaway. Neeta pulled a plastic knob to recline her bucket seat. Evelyn chuckled as it flattened to the limit of its design. With her friend and the auxiliary motor at rest, she said, "And, Neeta, I didn't empty the punch bowl over his head. We're both making progress with your former beau, don't you think?"

An unfamiliar ringtone startled Evelyn. Neeta curled forward, reached for her purse on the floor, and found her phone. "Hey there," she chirped.

Neeta's face relinquished its pout as the man's voice roamed inside the cabin. Evelyn heard his intonations, if few of his words. To offer her friend some semblance of privacy, she tried to keep her eyes on the road, but she could not resist the draw of the fire-ravaged landscape in the distance on the passenger side.

"It was fine. Evelyn put it succinctly: 'awkward and entertaining.' I concurred, although I came down more on the 'awkward' side."

The scorched evidence of the rampage filled the rearview mirror. Evelyn recalled her shock when they had driven to the venue hours earlier. She had not mentioned it to Neeta, who, heads down over her phone at the time, had eschewed conversation to fend off her worries about the impending encounter with Esben.

"Sounds wonderful. That'd be a nice way to end the day. I'll give you a call after I visit with NaaNaa Joshi and leave Evelyn's. Can't wait to see you."

Neeta ended the call and raised her seat back. With a quick glimpse to her right, Evelyn saw that her friend was staring at the photo on her phone's home screen, a shot Coty had taken of the family last year: Parvani, squatting next to her father with her arm around his shoulder, as if she, the healer, could somehow coax the return of his spine to vertical; Karun, standing behind Videsh, with his hands folded and a facial expression that corroborated the story that he had been scolded to release the handles of the old man's wheelchair; the hunched-over master carpenter—holes in his forced grin—looking up, searching sideways for the photographer; and, finally, Neeta, heralding their family's future with her radiance.

Thumbnails clicked the screen as Neeta sought a stored photograph. She leaned over to hold the phone next to the steering wheel.

"Cute, isn't he?" As if Coty Fine had scripted the moment, Neeta did not wait for a response. "Oh, wow, Evelyn, look at where the fire ran over that hill!"

"Yeah. I didn't want to bother you on the way up. You were distracted, thankfully."

They drove in silence for several miles. Once they had gotten past the devastation, Neeta lifted her phone from her lap. She unlocked the screen and once more raised the man's headshot for Evelyn, who stole a peek.

"Neeta, do you think he's hurt that you took me instead?"

"No way! He's intrigued, wants to hear the details." She shoved the phone into her purse. "Evelyn, he's pretty considerate."

"That's new for you, isn't it?"

"Esben wasn't that bad. And, we've only been dating for a little more than a month."

Evelyn let the statement settle as they drove farther away from jarring evidence of the fires. She relaxed as singed countryside gave way to the rural majesty of wine country: unscathed barns; fields of healthy grape vines in vertical rows creeping up their guide wires; trees in full leaf lining the road; and golden blades of grass waving in the breeze.

Traffic thickened as they pressed closer to San Francisco. A slender index finger touched the dashboard, and Motown filled the cabin.

Neeta clawed back the topic of thoughtfulness and broke the

conversation's lull. "Speaking of considerate, Matheo's going to be here soon. NaaNaa Joshi can barely contain himself."

"Yeah, he's been driving everyone around the house crazy, including the contractors—especially Jaime. Sister Lan and Magdalena are really excited about Matheo's return, mostly to see him, but also, in no small part, to have him occupy NaaNaa Joshi."

As they exited the Robin Williams Tunnel, the northern tower of the Golden Gate Bridge greeted them. Snaking with traffic, Evelyn drove down the Waldo Grade. In the distance, San Francisco tempted. She turned off the music, opened the rear windows, and retracted the car's moonroof.

"Ah—time to be with your nana, right?"

"Uh-huh. Motown gets me in the mood."

Since Evelyn's girlhood, the return across the Golden Gate Bridge had been a sacred journey. Coty, despite her disdain for absolutes, had said, time and again, "I always feel Noémie on the bridge whenever I come back to the city. Funny—she's never there on the way over, only when I drive home."

Upon reaching the bridge on such southbound trips, Evelyn would turn off the music and end any conversation, whether on the phone or with a companion in the car. Unless she encountered rain, she would roll down the windows and open the moonroof. Today, the dry wind whistled while the car's tires, rolling across seams in the floor of the bridge, thumped a regular beat.

They left the bridge, ducked into the Presidio, and wended their way through the old military grounds. As was their custom, acquired without debate, Neeta broke the spell.

"Think we'll actually do that girls' weekend in Napa? Mom's excited. Sounds like Jette's up for it."

"She mentioned it the last time we talked, said it was long overdue. They were so close as residents and when we were little."

"Evelyn, they've barely had any downtime over the years to

reconnect as friends. It'll be nice to see them relax together."

"Yeah, if it ever happens."

"Why not? Jette said she'd do it. Sounds like you don't believe she'll follow through."

"Sorry, Neeta. Let me rephrase: it won't happen soon. I guess I'm being pragmatic about our people. For your mom, NaaNaa Joshi's the priority, and Jette's not even planning a trip back to California since I'm going to meet her in Paris in a few days. No matter when she gets home, I doubt Parvani's going to take off on a girls' weekend while—"

She caught herself. Matheo had agreed to come back to help Videsh with the finish work, which the old man had refused to let the contractors touch. Everyone was on edge, although Evelyn, alone, felt the second honed side of the blade: Would Matheo have considered the journey if not for Videsh's condition?

"Evelyn, what were you thinking about when we crossed the bridge? You haven't looked that blissful in a long time."

"Nana's final list. I was wondering how she was feeling as she wrote it the night she died. I want to believe that she was truly happy at the time." Thankful that the subject had been changed, she asked, "How about you, Neeta? Were you pondering the divine Ms. Fine or tossing off your beau woes?"

"Very funny. No, I, too, was driving with Coty. I hadn't thought about her list, but something similar, I suppose."

"What do you mean?"

"How she used to talk about what happens after death—that final voyage across 'Wheel Sea.' That always cracked me up."

"Seems like every time Madeleine joked about 'leaving town,' Nana told her to head to the piers on the way out." Evelyn shook her head and smiled. "She'd say that it was a perquisite only agnostics enjoyed; they got to suspend both disbelief and belief."

"While we were on the bridge, I looked out over the water and wondered if she went on her odyssey," Neeta said.

The car stopped at a traffic light. Her grip tight on the steering wheel, Evelyn turned, again, and asked, "Think she's out there, sailing away?"

"I hope she's still moored to the dock."

"Dock?"

"Your house."

"Why? You want her to haunt the place?"

"No. I like to think she's waiting for NaaNaa Joshi."

The contractors had gone home for the day. Evelyn pulled into the driveway, turned the car off, and climbed out from behind the steering wheel. Looming in her high heels, she stood in the seam between her seat and the open door. She tapped pink-painted fingernails on the rooftop and waited.

Neeta's door opened, and she stepped out in bare feet, dangling her heels in one hand.

Evelyn stared across the roof of the sedan and said, "You made it!"

"I can't put these things back on my poor feet. How do you do it?"

"Lucky, I guess—Nana's genes."

Together, they ambled up the driveway. As they started to climb the back stairs, Neeta noticed the boarded-off opening in the porch railing and asked, "What happened to the ramp Matheo built?"

"I had Jaime take it down a couple of days ago. Your grandfather was not pleased."

"I bet. What was wrong with it?"

"Nothing, other than the slope. NaaNaa Joshi was a little too comfortable driving down it at top speed. Jaime had to catch him last week, just in time; he nearly toppled over when he hit the driveway."

"He has to use the elevator?"

"Or the ramp out front; that one slows him down considerably."

Set to Magdalena's preference, the window over the sink had been cracked open. Voices of a duet sang through the gap, greeting the wedding guests as they ascended. Evelyn did not recognize the tune. The Spanish lyrics suggested that a new telenovela had captured her nanny's fascination.

Neeta stopped on the top step and tugged Evelyn's arm before she could open the porch door. "What's her name, again?"

"Valeria. She's sweet, but she's shy around people who don't speak Spanish."

"I love how Magdalena says she has her own apprentice. And I'm glad I don't have to strain my neck when I look at her. That's three!" Neeta exclaimed, categorizing Valeria among the other shorties in residence: Magdalena and Sister Lan.

The hinges creaked. Four dark brown eyes found Evelyn as she pulled the door open and entered the kitchen. When the singing stopped, Valeria seemed to shrink below Neeta level. Evelyn smiled and waltzed over to the duo. She wrapped her nanny in one arm and, with the other, orchestrated a batonless hand wave.

Evelyn captured the melody but mangled the lyrics while she held her nanny close. Magdalena pressed her head into Evelyn's flat chest, as she had done with Coty for decades. She giggled and said, "You sing like your *abuela*."

"How so?"

"You don't need to know the words. You're just happy to sing, aren't you, *querida*?"

"*Si, si*—like Nana!"

Valeria chortled out the lines, and Evelyn, abandoning her role as conductor, pulled the teenager under her empty arm. Shuffling in choppy steps, Evelyn turned the trio to face Neeta, who was sitting at the kitchen table, her hands massaging a bare foot.

Thud!

The wheelchair crashed into the swinging doors. Videsh missed his chance to clear the entry, and the dining-room doors swung back against his tires. Wrinkled brown hands shoved them apart, and then he reached for his throttle to press the chair into the kitchen. The doors rebounded, crashing into his elbows. "Matheo must fix these doors! I need to add it to the list."

Neeta jumped up to assist her grandfather. He rolled by her without comment; instead, he directed his question to Evelyn.

"Did you talk to my apprentice today?"

"No, NaaNaa Joshi, not today. I talked to him yesterday."

Valeria grabbed a dish towel and hid at the sink. Magdalena lit a ring of flames under the teakettle. She rubbed Videsh's rounded shoulder as she walked to the cupboard, where, on tip-toe, she reached for his favorite mug.

Videsh grumbled, "I called him two hours ago and left a message. He hasn't called back."

"I'm sure he's busy getting ready for his trip," Neeta said, as she coaxed him to the table. She pulled her chair close to his wheel. After taking her seat again, she brought her other ankle to her knee, and began massaging a second tired foot.

"He must call me back."

"Why can't it wait till he gets here, NaaNaa Joshi?"

"Neeta, we won't have time to chitchat. We need to go over the list before he arrives. What if I've missed something else?"

He cringed, shut his eyes, and seemed to beg for breath. When Neeta reached to rub his neck, a brusque backhanded wave dismissed her attention. She shook her head and returned to her self-massage.

Evelyn sat down at the table across from the wheelchair. She worried that the wedding had sapped Neeta of her usual patience with her grandfather. Evelyn spoke in hopes of calming Videsh, as well as giving her friend a breather. "NaaNaa Joshi, when Matheo gets here, you're going to be working hard. You've got to pace yourself, and he'll have to get back up to speed, don't you think?"

Videsh coughed as Magdalena deposited the steaming mug before him. She stood to his side. He coughed again; then came a violent jag, which seemed to last a full minute. The four women kept concerned eyes on the man until his heaving subsided.

Exhausted, he slumped in the wheelchair's lambswool padding. In a deft move, Magdalena drew a wad of facial tissue across the side of his mouth that was aimed at the floor. She wiped the dangling red spittle, rolled the evidence of his decline into the center of a white ball, and shoved it into the pocket of her apron.

Videsh winced. Again, he sought Evelyn's ear. "He's my apprentice. He knows how to work with me. We'll go fast—right away."

Neeta sighed and rubbed her foot. Evelyn sensed that it had fallen on her to protect Videsh from himself. She lowered her head on an angle, as if preparing to inspect the underside of the table. Aligned with Videsh's view of the world, she smiled and said, "Still, NaaNaa Joshi, you don't want to burn out your apprentice. And if *you* don't pace yourself, Parvani will start pestering you."

"No, she won't."

"Oh, you think not, huh?"

Convinced that humor could defuse his anxiety, she laughed at their banter. Evelyn looked at her friend across the table, in hopes that she would join their play. Neeta did not raise her eyes. Instead, she chased a tear down her cheek with an index finger, as Videsh responded, "Parvani promised—no more silly tests."

Evelyn rose early. After showering, she finished packing. Before heading downstairs, she grabbed her phone, dialed her mother, and listened to the tonal babel of the call being routed out of the country.

"Jette. Glad I caught you before I took off."

"Excellent timing, darling—I don't have to scrub for another twenty minutes." Keyboard clicks; Jette must be at her desk, in the closet-size office at Holy Name that Evelyn remembered. "Evelyn, have you seen Father Thom since he was released?"

"Yesterday. I wanted to see him before I left for Paris."

"Hard to believe that he landed in the hospital with pneumonia. How did he look to you?"

"He looked drawn. That said, he seemed very Father Thom, which was a relief; he hasn't acted like that in many months."

"Pneumonia aside, he lost his best friend. It's been tough on him, I know."

"Still coughing a lot, but he'd grin and say something sarcastic, as if he were talking to Nana."

"Like what?"

"I made the mistake of asking him how he felt. He gave me a wry, sideways grin and said, 'Next.'"

Jette's laughter made the journey from Africa. With a sigh, she said, "Sounds like he's much better on both fronts. Good to hear, since I won't see him for a while."

Evelyn had been wondering about another of her nana's priests and changed the subject by asking, "Jette, you flew over to Libreville last weekend. How's Matheo?"

"He looks good. A bit anxious, but good."

"Anxious? About coming back to help Videsh? Or leaving the priesthood?"

"He was really shaken by the news about Videsh. His nature, I suppose—he tends to worry, about people, mostly."

"He doesn't regret leaving the priesthood, does he?"

"No, and he's very happy about nursing. He wants to try surgical; he asked if he could observe me operate and also talk to some of my OR colleagues."

"What about Nurse Lolo? I can imagine how enthusiastic she is about this."

"She's over the moon. Keeps saying, 'My baby, the nurse!'"

"Did he mention studying here? UCSF, maybe?"

"Not to me. Did you discuss it with him?"

"No, Jette. I wanted to, but it felt too desperate. I could almost hear Nana whispering in my ear about free will."

"Well, she might've played the California card herself, but she probably would've suggested that *you* just let it all unfold."

"Is he coming to Paris or straight to San Francisco?"

"I'm not sure. He mentioned that he got your package. Said he was touched. He looked away and started to choke up."

"Everyone here gets to talk to him, but you're the only one who's seen him in person since Nana's funeral. What do you think?"

"I've seen him twice. Two months ago, right after he told Bishop Myboto, he acted lost. Last weekend, he was different. He'd moved into the other boardinghouse, much closer to the clinic. He told me that it was a relief: he no longer had to walk by the rectory to catch the bus."

"Do you think he's okay?"

"Much better. As for Paris, I really can't say."

"If he doesn't regret leaving the priesthood, where's his conflict?"

She heard Jette clear her throat. *Here it comes*, Evelyn thought.

"America. You."

"He said that?"

"No, you asked what I thought."

"Sorry, Jette. I doubt it's got much to do with the United States."

"Don't be so sure, Evelyn. He's committed to the clinic. He feels blessed, compelled to serve."

"He can serve anywhere, right?" Evelyn asked, groping at the dream for which she held little hope.

"It's pretty much in your face here. He has a servant's heart, and I think he feels kinship with those who are helpless, like he was."

"His new calling?"

"That's my guess. To him, it's a calling."

"You can relate, right?" A foolish question, Evelyn realized. Matheo put others before himself. He was in good company with Jette, who, since her daughter could remember, had worried aloud, "Who will save them?"

"He's unusual in many ways, darling."

"Jette, are you trying to make me feel better?"

"How so?"

"Well, if Matheo has a new 'calling,' I won't take it personally if he doesn't come back here to live."

"There's more to it than what's between you two. Doesn't make it less painful, though, right?"

"I get it. I guess no one wants to think they aren't enough." Evelyn hit the mute button and yelled, "I did it again!" Within one minute, she had inserted both feet into her mouth. Had Jette felt the unintended stab? Had she chalked it up to another of her daughter's classic passive-aggressive darts? In person, Jette might have detected a faux pas, rather than an attack. Evelyn regretted the phone call, since, in one day, they would be together in Paris.

"Darling, you talk to him online every day, don't you?"

"Yeah. I depend on him. I like to think he depends on me, too."

"He does. You're his best friend—the best friend he's ever had. He told me that again last weekend."

Evelyn said what her mother already knew. "I love him, Jette. I sometimes can't believe it, but I love him. It'd be tough to see him as only a friend."

"San Francisco's not his world, and he's visited, lived there, so he knows. It's not that he thinks less of you—quite the opposite, I'd guess."

"I'm too good for him? That's nonsense. He's a saint!" The language of victims tasted foul on her tongue. She looked forward to Paris. Who else but your mother cuts you some slack when you're having a pity party?

"Not 'too good,' but different, and with expectations he might fear he could never meet."

"Nana would scold him for absolutes."

"He didn't say it, dear; it's just something you might consider. Be sensitive to his background. He's obviously sensitive about yours."

"Should I be hopeful, or—" Over the phone came the sound of a knock on the door in Lagos, which signaled to Evelyn that her mother was being called to surgery. One more day; then she could ask her in person.

"Okay, Evelyn, five minutes before I've got to scrub. Looks like I'll beat you to Paris. If our planes are both on time, you'll land less than two hours after I get in. I'll stick around de Gaulle, and we can take the train together."

"We'll be there for over a week. You sure you're going to be able to do this, Jette?"

"Today's surgery is my last scheduled for almost two weeks."

One topic would not wait for their face-to-face reunion. "Should I bring Nana's ashes?"

"I don't know what to do, given her late change of mind. Spreading them in her gardens was always the plan. Mother left us 'holding the urn,' as she said."

Shared laughter served as balm. Evelyn reached to her nape and pulled a white, gray-streaked bundle over her left shoulder. The wavy sheaf draped down the front of her peach-colored blouse.

"Is the urn where we put it after her funeral?" Jette asked.

"Still there, sitting in front of the French doors, staring out at the bay. Looks like she's doing yoga or meditating."

"Perfect! That's perfect, Evelyn."

One more day. She could not wait to see her mother. "Jette, I think she was protecting us, by our holding the urn, as you say."

"How so?"

"Spreading her ashes in the gardens could've made it untenable to sell this place. No matter her vision or the family memories, she would've said that it was just an asset."

"She would've said it, but it would've been one of her white lies." Jette let out a long sigh.

Evelyn resisted the urge to fill the lull and waited for her mother to continue.

"Lately, I've been slowing down myself. I'm going to need a place to stay."

"Let's build Nana's cottage, then. That would be the perfect—"

A second brisk knock. The door must have been opened from the hallway. Jette acknowledged someone, agreed to walk together to the OR, and then asked the person to wait in the corridor. "Got to go, Evelyn. Oh, almost forgot: Would you please grab Mother's list? You sent me the scanned copy, but I want to hold the original again. Smell it. Weird, I know, but . . ."

"Not weird to me, and it won't put me over the weight limit."

"All right, Evelyn. I'll see you in a few hours." Jette paused, before asking, "Remember the first time the three of us went to Paris? You were in grammar school."

"Yeah, before I transformed into a selfless teenager."

Jette let the comment rest. "Can't wait to revisit Mother's City of Light with you. Travel safely, darling."

"Okay, Jette. Good luck with your surgery. Hope to see you at the airport, but don't wait around if I'm delayed. I'll meet you at the hotel."

The words had been on the tip of her tongue. Familiar, yet unspoken for years—words necessary for healing; words that must be said to sew up the wound. The surgeon could not wield the needle, nor could any sure-handed intern. Evelyn was ruminating when an irritated knock struck her mother's door in Lagos.

"I've really got to hang up, Evelyn. Love you!"

"Love you, too, Mom."

———•••———

The red lettering on the side of the immaculate white pickup read MALDONADO & SON CONSTRUCTION. A stocky, middle-aged man with a ruddy tan stood before the open toolbox affixed to the left side of the truck. It stretched along the sidewall from behind the driver's seat to the tailgate. The toolbox's twin balanced the truck on the passenger side.

"*Hola*, Hector," Evelyn called out, as she left the front porch and stepped down the stairs to greet her general contractor.

He waved as she approached the truck; then he settled the lid of the toolbox and bolted its padlock. "*Buenos días*, Evelyn. *Cómo estás?*"

"Almost ready. Just a few things left to do before I take off."

"You going to the airport soon?"

"I've got plenty of time. What did you want to show me?"

Hector seemed glum as they walked up the driveway. When they got to the back porch, he pulled the fob from his pocket. A single garage door rolled up, and inside the bay one of Maldonado's crew turned while balancing a floppy ten-foot piece of shoe molding.

Evelyn smiled and said, "*Hola*, Luis!"

"*Hola*, Evelyn. What do you think?" Luis asked, soliciting her appreciation of the shelving that Jaime Maldonado had built yesterday.

"Very impressive, Luis."

Hector removed his cap. With an air of futility, he slapped it against his leg. When he put it back on to cover his baldness, she thought he seemed irritated, not by Luis, but by the job itself. "Evelyn, look at it all! I don't want to bill you, but . . ."

"Hector, you've been very patient. I had no idea that this much material was sitting here. Can you give me an estimate in the next hour? I'll send the progress payment to you while I'm sitting at SFO."

The cap came off again. Scratching his head, he stared at the racks. Without looking from the stockpile, he said, "All of the trim pieces have been delivered. Stacking material isn't progress in our business. We want to finish the job, Evelyn."

"You've done everything we've asked, not to mention on time and on budget."

The baseball cap slid over his tonsure and settled in a ring of graying hair. Shaking his head, he said, "The project should have been done by now. Jaime's really frustrated, says he could knock this out in a couple of weeks."

"I've no doubt whatsoever. Still, finishing the renovations has always been secondary."

"Videsh should understand. My son's also a carpenter. He wants to do the finish work so the place looks like the renderings. It makes Jaime crazy to walk away from it in this state. Me too."

All the exterior windows had been sealed. New shakes had been nailed in place and painted. But indoors, the project seemed to have been abandoned. Missing trim pieces exposed two-by-four frames, six-inch headers, and the snapped-off ends of shims used to set each window and door level and plumb. Drywall had been taped, spackled, and sanded, readied for the painters' rollers. Along the edges of the floors and ceilings, nail heads in the wallboard were hammered flush, not set in dimples to be plastered and sanded. Those borders waited for Matheo to tap into place the molding from Jaime's racks that would provide lasting cover.

"Lately, Videsh has been driving my crew nuts. Jaime was ready to walk off the job a couple of weeks ago, before he heard the news. Made him feel pretty small when he realized that Videsh wasn't going on vacation."

"Vacation?"

"Videsh kept talking about getting everything done because soon he was 'leaving town.' Jaime complained in front of Magdalena, who told him what it meant." Hector tipped his cap up but left it riding on his head. He might be calming down, Evelyn thought. "Jaime wants to help the old man, but Videsh won't let him. Anyway, Evelyn, we'll button things up—for now. You can decide when you get back if you want our help trimming the place out."

"Thanks, Hector. I'll try to catch Jaime, too, before I leave."

"He's on another big job today. Luis will come back tomorrow to clean up a bit, but there's really nothing more for them to do. When do you come home? Couple of weeks?"

"Ten days. In the meantime, I want you to get your full amount, including the labor you bid for the trim work."

"*Gracias*, Evelyn. I won't include the labor for the finish work. Not the way I do business. The painters can come back whenever the trim's done. I'll bill you for that when the paint dries. I won't give you the final invoice till we do a walk-through together."

"You're wonderful, Hector. I still want to have the whole crew back for a party when I get home."

"Not before the trim's painted. We want to take photos—like your *abuela* Coty!"

"Well, that's a great reason to get it done. I promise."

As they stood in the gaping doorway, opposite them, on the back side of the house, Videsh exited the elevator at the driveway. Luis was sliding lengths of shoe molding into the plywood rack that Jaime had constructed in the corner where Matheo had set the parlor carpets on the day of Coty's final bash. Before Videsh wheeled himself inside, he shouted from the driveway, "Luis, you're almost done!" The wheelchair pulled to a stop in front of the racks. "Very organized. Good job, *amigo*."

"Señor Joshi, two more," he said, as he stooped to pick up the penultimate piece of molding.

After racking the final boards, Luis clapped his hands to knock off the dust. He removed his work gloves. Scrunching the leather pair in one hand, he looked to the boss. Hector acknowledged his man with a pat on the back, before telling him to wait in the truck.

As Luis walked down the driveway, Videsh said, "He's a good man, Hector. And your boy Jaime is a careful carpenter. And fast, too! Look at the racks he built for me yesterday. It'll be easy to find what we need when Matheo gets home and we start the finish work." He waited a few seconds, winked, and said, "If I didn't already have an apprentice, I'd try to steal Jaime from you!"

The wheelchair rolled forward and back. Evelyn had not seen Videsh toggle his controller like that in weeks. She stepped closer and tried to make eye contact. He stared at his knees. She thought he might have felt betrayed. "NaaNaa Joshi, I needed to talk to Hector before I left for the airport. I want to get him a progress payment. He shouldn't have to cover the cost of the trim pieces till you and Matheo finish. Everything's been delivered and checked off your list, right?"

His tired eyes brightened as he looked up, but he winced when he found her. He squeezed the wheelchair's armrests as he said, "Yes, yes, it's all here; you should pay him."

Hector faced Evelyn and paused, signaling how his own *abuela* might have schooled him decades earlier: a gentleman never first extends his hand to a lady. Evelyn read his decorum and held out her open hand. She felt years on the calluses of his gentle grip. "*Gracias*, Evelyn. Don't worry about sending the money till you're back. Ten days won't break me."

Videsh raised a wobbling arm and opened halfway his gnarled paw to Hector. He grimaced as he craned his neck to guide their handshake. "Hector, you and Jaime are good men. Evelyn wants to have a big party for your crew. Good job." With a pained attempt at his trademark grin, Videsh sealed the crew's dismissal.

"*Muchas gracias*, Videsh. Here. I won't need this anymore." The garage door remote slipped into the weathered hand of the master carpenter—a hand that had not held a hammer or coping saw in months. Hector brought his left palm atop their embrace and squeezed the fob into a shaky cup of wrinkled flesh.

"NaaNaa Joshi, I'm going up to the gazebo to find Sister Lan. I'll say goodbye now. See you in a few days."

Videsh remained as they left him: bent over, pressed to one side of the wheelchair, his quivering head flopped in a severe crook. When she exited the workshop, he was gazing up at Jaime's racks as if he intended to wait there for his apprentice.

Sister Lan was not on her knees in the garden or sitting in the gazebo, contemplating the bay. Evelyn panicked when she saw the octogenarian standing on the second-highest rung of a ten-foot stepladder, cooing in Vietnamese to her tiny airborne charges. Her green cotton smock flagged in the breeze. A navy-blue sweater cloaked her shoulders and arms.

The ladder did not teeter, although it appeared as if a stiff wind off the bay might topple the entire setup. Lan stretched to reach the hook that Matheo had hung from the eave of the gazebo. The nylon twine had slipped out of the wheel's groove and jammed the miniature pulley. As Lan restrung the device, one bold hummingbird arrived, hovered close, and then bulleted away.

Lan guided herself back to earth. Gripping the frame, she planted her left foot on the next lower rung. Then she brought her right foot down onto that same step, where she steadied herself before descending farther. Evelyn stood at a distance until the nun's two feet were on the ground.

"*Bonjour*, Sister Lan. Will the kids come up here after their rehearsal?"

"*Bonjour*, Evelyn. *Oui*, the children always ask to visit the hummingbirds." Resting her child-size fingers on the side of the ladder, she turned her sunglasses to the bay.

Last year, on the heels of Lan's cataract surgeries, Coty and Matheo had escorted her to the Southeast Asian Community Center so she might commune with others in San Francisco who had emigrated from her native region. The Sheldon Fine Foundation had opened its wallet to the children of the community center. Sister Lan had opened her heart and her new home.

The nun stepped beneath the eave and tugged the line. Rising off the flowerbed, the feeder, refilled with sugar water, floated upward. Lan tied the line to the anchor.

The impatient bird returned and landed. In staccato, it jabbed its syringe-like beak into one of the plastic flowers, stealing gulps as if trespassing. The welcomed thief bobbed and guzzled, its feathers reflecting the sunlight in kaleidoscopic display.

"How did you get that ladder up here?" Evelyn asked in French.

"Luis. He's such a dear young man. I'll miss him and Jaime." Lan glanced from the ladder to the hummingbird feeder. "Soon, Matheo will be here to help with such matters, *oui*?"

"*Oui*, two weeks—a few days after I get back."

Everyone living there knew that Evelyn had invited Matheo to meet them in Paris. As they approached the stairs to the gazebo, Lan repeated the common hope of the household: "He might join you and Jette in Paris, *non*?"

"Sister Lan, have you talked to him recently? Did he say anything about his trip?"

"We talked two days ago. He mentioned returning; he knows it will help calm Videsh."

As they stepped up into the gazebo, Evelyn slowed to match Lan's pace. The nun found her seat. Her toes did not touch the floor. Evelyn sat close and, as she crossed her long legs, said, "*Oui*, he'll be much better once Matheo gets here."

Sister Lan pushed her sunglasses over her forehead and parked them upon her crown of straight white hair. "*Je suis désolée*—Matheo didn't mention Paris."

"Paris is a lark for Jette and me. We haven't been on a vacation together in many years. I think it would make my nana happy to know." Evelyn searched the woman's eyes for corroboration.

"Coty would celebrate your trip; before she died, you and Jette gave your grandmother her most desired gift."

"*Merci beaucoup*, Sister Lan. That makes me happy to hear."

"It's a word that's easy to speak. Are you 'happy,' Evelyn?"

"Getting there. I miss Nana, yet I feel her love more than her absence. Does that make sense?"

"*Oui.* Such love, one feels forever." Weightless fingers touched Evelyn's wrist. Lan quieted, watching the hummingbirds as they darted about. Then the nun turned and narrowed her clear eyes. "Evelyn, I know you're worried that Matheo will help Videsh, then return to Gabon."

"It's his choice."

"Does Neeta think he'll stay here?"

"She's hopeful but doubtful."

"Well, Evelyn, I'm thankful that he's returning to help Videsh. It's all that man has talked about since the day Matheo left."

"*Oui.* It would break his heart if Matheo didn't come back."

"And yours, Evelyn, if he doesn't stay?"

Neither said a word. Evelyn wanted to tell Sister Lan how good a friend he'd been. That she saw why he'd become a priest. Why he'd be a caring nurse. How she'd leaned on him during her toughest hours. Why she thought a permanent move back was unlikely. Different worlds. Different people altogether.

The sunglasses returned to protect Lan's vision. She faced the Golden Gate Bridge and pointed an index finger smaller than Evelyn's pinkie. "People are fragile, Evelyn. Any bridge between them, no matter how strong, must be anchored to delicate beings on each side."

The unmistakable sound of children laughing drew their attention away from the view. Sister Lan pointed to the sidewalk that led uphill to their home. A line of eight backpack-laden children—some tall, some short, all with straight black hair—hiked up the hill behind two women with outsize music books clutched to their chests and handbags strung over their shoulders.

"I'll greet them with you before I get my bags," Evelyn said. "Then I'll slip out the back, so I won't disrupt their rehearsals for the recital."

Sleek fingers roamed the purse in search of her passport as she contemplated which route Matheo would choose. According to Jette, the gift—a mail pouch—had already arrived at the boardinghouse in Libreville. Evelyn wondered why he hadn't mentioned it when they'd last talked. Then she wondered why she hadn't.

Among the pouch's contents were four photographs, including one of a pediatric heart patient reunited, after decades, with his cardiac surgeon. The second was a wide-angle shot Coty had taken, with a timer, of her "family," gathered around the dinner table in celebration of their newest member's successful cataract surgeries. In the third picture, Matheo was dancing with Coty in her yellow dress, her rippling white hair sailing over the head of Neeta and NaaNaa Joshi's wheelchair. The fourth photo was a candid headshot of Evelyn, her eyes searching beyond the edge of the glossy print. Months before sending her granddaughter on a mission to find the nun, Coty had taken Evelyn's picture, framed it, and hung it in the kitchen, where, later, according to Magdalena, Matheo had often stopped and dwelt.

Accompanying the photographs was a personal note clipped to a fully refundable ticket from Libreville to Charles de Gaulle Airport. In her note, she invited him to travel to California with Jette and her, while assuring him that he could skip Paris altogether and fly, as previously planned, from Gabon to San Francisco. A hopeful smile creased her lips, and then she frowned, remembering the phone call with Jette and her mother's sobering words: ". . . not his world."

Evelyn slid her purse inside the carry-on bag and balanced the bundle on top of her wheeled suitcase. She snagged the extended handle and tugged the stacked luggage into the hallway. In the parlor below, the ever-yawning, black-lacquered baby-grand piano exhaled warm up scales. She paused to listen, thought of Matheo playing, then pivoted and turned her back on the music. The first student began the selected piece, which, tickling her ears, chased Evelyn as she pulled the roller bag along the runner to Coty's bedroom door.

The list lay on the surface of the writing desk, where her nana had left it the night she died. Before slipping beneath the covers, Coty had folded the single piece of paper into a triptych, anchoring it with the paperweight Noémie had made in kindergarten: a convex magnifying glass glued onto a felt-backed picture of five-year-old identical twin girls. Evelyn slipped the list into a fresh envelope.

With a *poof*, the suitcase settled into her nana's duvet. After opening the lid, Evelyn removed the gift-wrapped present for Jette: a hardcover first edition of Coty's final photography curation. She placed the envelope on a cushion of packed clothing and pressed the book on top. With her hand on the zipper of the suitcase, she paused and looked over the bed through the French doors. She had time.

Envelope in hand, Evelyn walked to the center of the Persian carpet. She sat down next to the author's urn, folded her legs into lotus, dropped the envelope onto her lap, and stared out across the bay. She rubbed pairs of forefingers and thumbs. Spreading open the mouth of the envelope with care, she teased the list from its paper vault.

She held the single sheet away from her dripping tears—tears of loss mixed with tears of joy. Through the blur, Evelyn savored her nana's optimism and flamboyant script: "My Goals for the Next Ten Years."

The phone's alarm interrupted the pleasant lilt of the children's rehearsal. It was time to order a car, which would arrive within minutes. Her fingertips found the urn. She stroked its top, unwound her crossed legs, and stood.

Four minutes, promised the app. She refolded Coty's list and brought it back to her nose to confirm her first impression. Jette wanted to smell it, but her nana's familiar scent had dissipated.

After discarding the envelope on the writing desk, Evelyn carried the folded list into Coty's walk-in closet. She breezed past the yellow dress, hanging in its clear plastic dry cleaner's bag, and addressed the bureau. Two fingers pinched her target in the second drawer. The top scarf floated up. She unraveled it and laid the silk swath open upon a stack of colorful, fragrant cousins. Then, she spun the perfumed scarf into a cocoon around the list.

Ding!

One minute until her car arrived. The zipper rode along its jagged track, resealing the luggage. Once more, her eyes went to the Persian carpet in front of the French doors. Evelyn looked back and forth from the urn to the closet entry. Before she yanked the suitcase from the duvet, with her elbows locked, she pressed her hands down against the ballistic-nylon top. There was ample space for a last-minute stowaway.

Inside the dressing room, she removed the transparent cover and took Coty's yellow dress from its hanger. She rolled the garment as her world-traveling grandmother had shown her years earlier.

Ding!

At the sound of the second school bell, she knew that her car had arrived. She hurried back into the bedroom and slipped the yellow bundle into her suitcase.

"*Bonjour, madame.*"

"*Bonjour*, Matheo. Ah, the package you want to store here, *non*?"

The cardboard box was sealed with packing tape. His name was printed in bold capital letters on the side in the fat black script of a moving company's marker. He slid the box onto the kitchen counter as he said, "*Oui.* I'll put it in the back room, on the top shelf, as you requested."

"It'll be waiting for you when you return from America. Now, I'll make you some lunch and pack a sack for you to take on the flight."

"*Merci beaucoup, madame.* I'll be back down at half past the hour—time enough to eat before the taxi arrives."

After he ascended the staircase, he entered his bedroom, where Coty's big suitcase, its top zippered open, was perched on the mattress, which he had already stripped of its linens. First, he had scrubbed the soles of his fawn-colored work boots to remove any Gabonese soil. Next, those shoes he had filled with socks, then set the pair inside the cavity, before packing his clothes and the gifts he had purchased for his friends in San Francisco. Atop the contents, he would lay his royal-blue Warriors windbreaker; before checking the luggage, he planned to extract Ralph's gift to bring the jacket aboard the cabin.

His small, spartan room had a bed and two other pieces of furniture: a narrow chest of drawers under the window, and a wooden chair between the wall and the edge of the bed. He often read in that seat with his bare feet propped upon the mattress. Today, he sat on the floor with his back to the wall and his legs stretched out in the skinny corridor between chair and bed. The window was open, the breeze mitigating his sweatiness from the humid weather and his packing.

Master Joshi had embraced every suggestion his returning apprentice had made. Yesterday, during their last phone conversation, Videsh had declared that the list for the house was final.

Matheo thought he himself was now ready to "hit the ground running"—Videsh's expectation for the reunion of Coty's two-man crew. And then he ruminated about his master's fate after their completion of the trim work.

The tickets were in the sleeve of the suitcase, along with his passport. In his hand, he held the remaining flat items, which were destined to ride in the luggage beneath the Warriors jacket. He flipped through the photographs, stopping at the shot of Evelyn. They had talked last night. Soon, he would see her face-to-face for the first time since Coty's funeral. He held up her photo, turning it in the sunlight and noticing that his hand was steady.

The photographs returned to their envelope, which he tossed upon the bare mattress. From a thick fold of papers, he removed another list, which he had paper-clipped to the top page. That list, he had not yet shared with Videsh—or anyone else. With his back to the wall and his elbows propped upon his bent knees, he reviewed each note he had written. Then he set down the list and spread open the blueprints. Once more, he studied each page, challenging himself to look for anything the master carpenter might find lacking when they sat side by side to review the plans.

He worried that once they had completed the finish work inside the house, Videsh might conclude that it would then be time to leave town himself. The apprentice planned to discuss his new list with Evelyn and Jette this week, while the three were together in Paris. After all, Matheo would need their support to retain the enthusiasm of their master carpenter if he were to oversee construction of Coty's garden cottage.

ACKNOWLEDGMENTS

Hilde Wesselink read the original 2015 rough draft of the novel when the working title was *His Imagination About Her Past*. Her feedback stopped me in my tracks. Hilde was effective with her blunt criticism as only a trusted friend could be. Years passed as I reimagined the characters and their experiences. My thanks again to my supportive friend who provided the clear-headed perspective of a reader who knows what works for her and what misses the mark.

Vanessa Hope Schneider is the only person I've met who once worked the slush pile at a major publishing house. We had known each other from a few casual interactions when she granted me a significant gift of time by reading through what I had thought was a revised manuscript then ready to go out into the publishing world for consideration. Vanessa, too, didn't pull her punches. My deep respect for her intellect and industry knowledge led me to grab my red pen and return to the manuscript as well as the earmarked pages of the books on writing in the dusty section of my bookshelf.

Pattie Lawton and her mother Gussie (1929-2013) formed a collective muse inspiring me to imagine a social world far afield from the remote rural family life that I'd experienced as a child. Mother and daughter shared a rare gift for hospitality. Their homes each became haven to many who had been strangers prior to the one sunrise that lit the path to their door. By nightfall, those strangers had been embraced as part of a large, boisterous extended family. I have often observed the pure joy they each displayed with the simple act of inviting people to be among people. The welcome of their open arms not only provided inspiration for writing but for living a fuller human experience, one with more warmth than might have otherwise been felt.

Artist Sally Storch's beautiful painting "Pentimento" graces the interior of this book. The oil painting hangs in my dining room and served as inspiration for the main character's profession of photography. Many hours I sat before this beautiful piece contemplating the possibilities. Heartfelt thanks to Sally as the book could not have been imagined without the art that triggered my own.

ABOUT THE AUTHOR

Michael Rose was raised on a small family dairy farm in Upstate New York. He retired after serving in executive positions for several global multinational enterprises. He has been a non-executive director for three public companies headquartered in the US. He lives and writes in San Francisco.

SELECTED TITLES FROM SPARKPRESS

SparkPress is an independent boutique publisher delivering high-quality, entertaining, and engaging content that enhances readers' lives, with a special focus on female-driven work. www.gosparkpress.com

Dovetails in the Tall Grass: A Novel, Samantha Specks, $16.95, 978-1-68463-093-6. In 1862, thirty-eight Dakota-Sioux men were hanged in the largest mass execution in US history. This is the story of two young women—one settler, one Dakota-Sioux—connected by the fate of the thirty-ninth man.

The Sorting Room: A Novel, Michael Rose, $16.95, 978-1-68463-105-6. A girl coming of age during America's Great Depression, Eunice Ritter was born to uncaring alcoholic parents and destined for a life of low-wage toil—a difficult, lonely existence of scant choices. This epic novel—which spans decades—shows how hard work and the memory of a single friendship gave the indomitable Eunice the perseverance to pursue redemption and forgiveness for the grievous mistakes she made early in her life.

The Takeaway Men: A Novel, Meryl Ain, $16.95, 978-1-68463-047-9. Twin sisters Bronka and JoJo Lubinski are brought to America from Germany by their Polish refugee parents after World War II—but in "idyllic" America, political, cultural, and family turmoil awaits them. As the girls grow older, they eventually begin to ask questions of and demand the truth from their parents.

Seventh Flag: A Novel, Sid Balman, Jr. $16.95, 978-1-68463-014-1. A sweeping work of historical fiction, *Seventh Flag* is a Micheneresque parable that traces the arc of radicalization in modern Western Civilization—reaffirming what it means to be an American in a dangerously divided nation.

The Opposite of Never: A Novel, Kathy Mehuron. $16.95, 978-1-943006-50-2. Devastated by the loss of their spouses, Georgia and Kenny think that the best times of their lives are long over until they find each other; meanwhile Kenny's teenage stepdaughter, Zelda, and Georgia's friend's son, Spencer, fall in love at first sight—only to fall prey to and suffer opiate addiction together.

The Infinite Now: A Novel, Mindy Tarquini. $16.95, 978-1-943006-34-2. In flu-ravaged 1918 Philadelphia, the newly-orphaned daughter of the local fortune teller panics and casts her entire neighborhood into a bubble of stagnant time in order to save the life of the mysterious shoemaker who has taken her in. As the complications of the time bubble multiply, this forward-thinking young woman must find the courage to face an uncertain future, so she can find a way to break the spell.